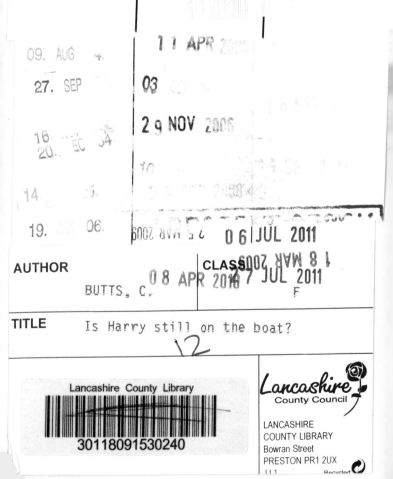

Praise for Colin Butts

Is Harry Still on the Boat?

'Another wickedly funny instalment of Ibiza Club Rep shagging, booze and drugs'   *Loaded*

'If you start reading this be prepared not to sleep until you've finished. Not only is it engrossing, amusing and thoroughly believable, but it also gives more of an insight into what men really think than a dozen *From Venus From Mars* type books . . . You'll be riveted to your deckchair'

Mixmag

'Butts has the spirit of club reps spot on'   *Front*

'If your hols are hotter than *Ibiza Uncovered*, get your hands on this new novel'   *Sun*

Is Harry on the Boat?

'You'll be on the edge of your sun lounger . . . And there's a rather fantastic sting in the tail. Even if you don't manage to hit Ibiza this year, you can pretend you did with this clever and gripping book'   *New Woman*

'A ribald romp through the beaches and hotel rooms of Ibiza – this aggressively non-PC novel mirrors those great, televisual social documents of our time, the "uncovered" programmes'   *Big Issue*

Colin Butts is a novelist, screenwriter, dance-music commentator and record producer who initially founded Tuesday Morning Publishing to publish his first novel, *Is Harry on the Boat?*. After republication by Orion *Is Harry on the Boat?* became a bestseller and went on to be a hugely successful film and TV series for Sky One. Colin Butts lives in Ibiza.

By Colin Butts

Is Harry *Still* on the Boat?
Is Harry on the Boat?

is harry *still* on the boat?

COLIN BUTTS

ORION

An Orion paperback

First published in Great Britain in 2003
by Orion
This paperback edition published in 2003
by Orion Books Ltd,
Orion House, 5 Upper St Martin's Lane,
London WC2H 9EA

A CIP catalogue record for this book is
available from the British Library.

ISBN 0 75284 225 0

Typeset by Deltatype Ltd, Birkenhead, Merseyside

Printed and bound in Great Britain by
Clays Ltd, St Ives plc

Special thanks to Toby Norways

Acknowledgements

My main thank you must go to Toby Norways. Toby is a very talented up-and-coming scriptwriter who helped me develop the synopsis upon which this book was originally based. I trust that it will not be long before he achieves the success he so richly deserves in his own right.

I am also indebted to the following reps/ex reps and Ibiza workers for their anecdotes and advice (apologies if I have forgotten anyone); H&K, Darren Candy, Shaggy, Stevie Sideburns, Tigga, Jamie Burchell, Ilko Muntinger, Craig Beck and Andy Matthews.

Garry Bushell has continued in his support of the unpretentious and I *will* buy you several drinks if ever we meet.

Friends – Steve Lawrence, Dave Thomas, Dean Arden, Mick Crowley and Carl Verges. Also Giles Sawney for the obvious sequel title.

All at Orion, especially Rachel Leyshon for making things swift and painless. Clare Conville and Sam North at Conville and Walsh, for enabling me to pompously drop the phrase 'my agents' into conversation.

The original *Is Harry* was turned into a film by Sky Pictures (still available on DVD and video I believe!) and subsequently a series. Thanks to all involved for making this possible, but especially to Lily Owen for being the one to get the ball rolling by bringing it to her mum Alison's attention at Ruby Films. To director Huds for his belief and persistence, Mark Soldinger for his help in trying to get it to screen in the early days, Daniela Denby-Ashe and Des Coleman for keeping in touch and entering the category headed 'friends' and finally, to Rik Young, not just for a convincing Mario but for an act of bravery that warrants more than inadequate words here.

There is a small continuity point from the first *Is Harry* that I want to briefly mention. The Greg character in the first novel is a Scouser, although he was actually based on a real ex-rep from Littleborough near Rochdale. When Will Mellor played the role in the film in his natural accent, it was so close to the original rep's voice that for me, he actually became Greg. When writing this sequel, I could not get Will Mellor's characterisation out of my head, so apologies for this slight regional change.

Although most who have read the first *Is Harry* (especially those in the travel industry) have commented on how accurate a portrayal of a rep's life it gave, a few holiday reps have approached me moaning that certain incidents would never have happened in 'real life'.

To avoid any more burst blood vessels, I should remind such readers that *Is Harry* Still *on the Boat?* is a work of *fiction*. For example, to make the story read better, I have the club Amnesia opening at the end of June, although it actually opens slightly earlier than this.

There will of course, be a few readers who cannot stop themselves from writing in to highlight these kind of discrepancies. I always welcome such correspondence, so please send it to the following address,

'Bothered'
Ibiza
Balearics
Spain

pre-departure

chapter one

Decisions, decisions.

A line of Charlie?

A pill?

Or spark up a spliff?

'Greg,' yelled Bex from the bathroom, 'have room service brought the drinks up yet?'

Oh yes, almost forgot. There was always the option of getting even more pissed.

It was a difficult choice. Far too difficult to make with two ecstasy tablets, several lines of cocaine and a couple of bottles of champagne already affecting one's faculties.

There was only one sensible course of action.

Greg knocked back the pill with a warm can of Heineken from the mini-bar cum non-functioning fridge. The line of cocaine, neatly chopped on the laminated Slough Holiday Inn information sheet, went up his nose moments later.

'Never mind the drinks, Bex – just get yourself in here.'

A pretty girl with long, straight, highlighted hair and wearing a tiny sequinned dress emerged from the bathroom.

'Wasn't that just the *best* party you've ever been to?'

'Yeah, it was good.' Greg rubbed the remnants of the line of cocaine into his gums. 'You can see why Rich 'n' Famous have got such a good reputation as promoters.'

Bex put her arms round his neck and gave him a lingering kiss. 'Thanks for inviting me, Greg. I've had a wicked night.'

'It's not finished yet.' He gave her bum a gentle squeeze.

'I should hope not.' She kissed him again. 'I'm just going to get my overnight bag from the car.'

'Can't it wait until later?' he said, playfully grabbing her arm and pulling her back to him.

'Not really.'

'Why not?'

'Do you remember that night in Ibiza last summer when you took all of us eager holidaymakers to that big club?'

'Privilege, on the way to Ibiza Town? Of course I do.'

'And do you remember when we were both buzzing, telling me what you'd do to me if I wasn't going out with Rog—' She corrected herself. 'Sorry, The Prick.'

'Not exactly, but if it involved animals, then I promise you, it was just a phase and I'm a changed man.'

'Actually, it was more to do with handcuffs and thigh-length boots.'

A grin spread over Greg's face. 'I . . . think it's coming back to me. But what's that got to do with your bag?'

Bex proffered a sultry look.

'What, you mean . . . you've got . . . in your bag . . . in your car?'

Bex dangled her car keys in front of him, kissed him on the forehead and headed for the door.

Greg called after her, 'I knew we'd have a great night.'

As the door closed, he reflected that this comment wasn't actually true. In fact, Bex had been a last resort. The quarterly parties thrown by promoters Rich 'n' Famous were legendary, with a reputation for attracting gorgeous girls. Greg had met one of the organisers the previous summer, when he had been working as a holiday rep for tour company Young Free & Single, YF&S. The Rich 'n' Famous parties were always on a Sunday and their location kept secret until less than a fortnight before the event. They could be anywhere in the country, but were normally held in a manor house, or elegant (and tolerant) hotel.

When Greg discovered that the March party was being held in a mansion near Egham, he was disappointed. He had been hoping it would be nearer to his native Widnes.

Having spent five consecutive summers in Ibiza, most of the friends he had from his teens had moved on, settled down, or thought the world ended at Manchester or Liverpool. Certainly, he knew none of his local friends would want to make the journey down the M6.

Most of Greg's newer social circle revolved around YF&S, so he tried ringing the reps that lived down south. The start of the new season was imminent, so all had shopping trips to make, friends and family to visit, or partners to placate/finish with.

Greg was determined not to pass up the opportunity to see for himself why the Rich 'n' Famous parties were so renowned, especially as the promoter had given him two free tickets and a room in the nearby Holiday Inn.

For about a nanosecond he contemplated going with a girl – there were several former YF&S clients Greg had slept with in Ibiza and he had tentatively kept in touch. However, where women were concerned, Greg was a man who seldom bothered with revisits. There were of course, exceptions: if he was going through a lean period, if a girl was particularly filthy, or if he was visiting another part of the country and needed somewhere to stay.

(Where the latter was concerned, Greg would go on a boys' night out, then, as a safety net, ring a former conquest who lived in the same town. He would tell her that he wouldn't be round until late because he was going to a wedding/business meeting/visiting relatives first. If he didn't pull, he would lurch round at some unearthly hour and usually very much the worse for wear, make the minimum of small talk, get the besotted girl into bed and be asleep within minutes of ejaculating.)

Taking a former conquest to a party – especially a party as notorious as a Rich 'n' Famous one – was incomprehensible to Greg. It was as foreign to his nature as grazing on a nice dandelion leaf would be to a hungry wolf.

Going alone was not an option either. He would undoubtedly know people there, but he had seen enough clients holidaying alone in Ibiza, desperately trying to engage anyone in conversation so as not to appear a Billy-no-mates saddo, and he did not want to be even vaguely tarred with the same brush.

The solution, when it eventually came, occurred to him during one of the frequent moments Greg had his dick in his hand. Approaching his vinegar stroke, he was accessing his mental wank-bank for a suitable image to produce a satisfactory climax, when Bex entered his thoughts.

Bex Cartwright, eighteen years old, had been a YF&S client towards the end of the previous summer. Although her parents were extremely well off, she was down-to-earth. Her boyfriend, Roger, on the other hand, was a snotty, supercilious arse. It wasn't so much that he was a snob, more that he aspired to be one. A YF&S holiday was anathema to him. The Prick, as Greg had named him, spent the whole time moaning, or trying to find a bar where he could watch the Test match.

Although she hadn't been seeing The Prick long and despite it being clear they were incompatible, Bex was too principled to succumb to even Greg's persistent advances. They flirted and had one particularly great night out clubbing and getting off their faces (The Prick detested clubbing too), but that was as far as it went.

Within a week of Bex getting back home, The Prick was dumped. Greg spoke to her frequently on the phone during the winter, although they never quite managed to meet up as they kept threatening to. The Rich 'n' Famous party therefore presented them with the perfect opportunity to re-acquaint as Bex lived in Windsor, only a few miles from the venue. Greg figured that if she turned out to be a pain in the arse, then it was close enough to Egham for her to go home without being stranded. If his conscience really got the better of him, he even resolved to give her the cab fare home.

As it turned out, any doubts Greg had about not getting on with Bex soon disappeared – she was a full-on party animal. She matched him pill for pill, drink for drink, and line for line. And, without the constraining influence of

The Prick, she not only looked ten times sexier, but acted it too. As such, Greg had absolutely no desire to look anywhere else for his post-party entertainment.

The night seemed to end too soon, but although the after-party beckoned, they were both feeling so horny that they decided to give it a miss.

Greg had been saving a Viagra for a special occasion. On the short cab journey back to the hotel with Bex, he decided to take it. When Bex saw the diamond shaped blue pill, she stopped him. At first, he thought he was going to get a moral or health lecture from her, but instead she asked him to give her half, giggling and wondering if she'd get a 'wide-on'.

All in all, hitherto, it had been a great night.

And looking out of the window, seeing Bex walking back into the hotel with her overnight bag, Greg had a feeling it was about to get better.

chapter two

Adam Hawthorne-Blythe massaged his temples and placed his wire-rimmed glasses on the desk. In his eighteen years as Chairman of YF&S, he had been into the office on a Sunday less than half a dozen times. Never before had he still been there in the early hours of a Monday morning.

He stood up, stretched his back and went over to the boardroom's permanently percolating coffee jug.

'Not for us thanks, H-B,' said Sebastian Hunter.

A year ago, Jane would have bitten Sebastian's head off for answering for both of them, especially at work. Now things had changed. Their relationship was out in the open and everybody at the YF&S HQ knew about it. If they didn't, the fact that the former Jane Ward's surname was now Hunter might have given them a clue.

The worst kept secret in the office became common knowledge at the end of the last summer season as a result of the court action against the former Contracts Director, Felipe Gomez, responsible for a massive fraud against YF&S.

Jane had been largely responsible for his downfall. She also brought about the dismissal of the resort manager for Ibiza, Alison Shand. Alison's scam was on a much smaller scale – lining her own pocket at every opportunity by taking money from bars and excursion owners, and what could be best described as 'creative accounting'. It was accepted that most resort managers earned a little 'bunce' money, but not to that extreme. It was also Alison's brief affair with Felipe that had compromised them both. Alison lost her job and her ill-gotten gains; Felipe lost his liberty. The hundreds of thousands that Felipe stole meant that he would not be seeing a Mediterranean beach on anything other than a prison TV set for a good few years.

With praise heaped upon Jane from all quarters, she finally accepted that she was valued for merit rather than for shagging the Finance Director. She therefore announced her engagement to Sebastian to her unsurprised colleagues at YF&S.

The knot was tied at their spring wedding just three weeks ago, directly after which they enjoyed a two-week holiday in the Caribbean. Sometimes it was great to be in the travel industry.

But sometimes it wasn't.

'Are you absolutely sure about this, Sebastian?' asked Hawthorne-Blythe for the umpteenth time.

'Afraid so. It doesn't matter which way you look at it. And God knows, we've all tried every which way over the last few hours.'

Hawthorne-Blythe stared out of the huge boardroom windows at the deserted Teddington street. The sound of an empty can being kicked along the road got nearer, along with the voice of its kicker, mumbling the words to 'Swing Low Sweet Chariot'. A double-decker bus slowly rumbled round the corner, a few late night travellers sitting with their faces pressed against freshly rubbed clear patches on the fugged windows. Rhombuses of light from street lamps or shop windows reflected an earlier downpour on the pavement.

Hawthorne-Blythe turned and sat back at the boardroom table, placing his coffee on the table's green-tinted glass top. He returned his spectacles to the bridge of his nose and sat thinking for a few seconds, then had to take them off again as the steam from his coffee clouded them over.

'Maybe I should have let the company go public when I had the chance,' he said.

'You know that's stuff and nonsense,' replied Jane in her gentle Glaswegian accent. 'Young Free & Single would just be a small programme by now. One of the big boys would have chewed us up and spat us out. You've always said that we're about more than the bottom line. It's about the holidaymakers, the reps. A balance sheet doesn't always show the real picture or the whole story. We offer cheap holidays and rely on the reps to be good at selling and make up the money on excursion sales. If a bigger company took us over, they wouldn't have understood that. They would have increased the price of the holiday, which would have put off kids from coming.'

Jane paused before she got out of her depth. As Overseas Manager, her speciality was people, not business strategy. Still, you couldn't live with the Financial Director for two years without picking up a few bits and pieces.

'It's not all doom and gloom,' she said hesitantly.

'No, it's not, Jane,' said Hawthorne-Blythe. He looked at Sebastian, wondering if the statement he had just made was correct.

'No it's not *all* doom and gloom,' confirmed Sebastian, 'in so far as we're not about to go out of business . . .' Jane and Hawthorne-Blythe both sat back in their chairs, sharing a visible sigh of relief, '. . . *but*,' continued Sebastian, causing them to sit back up again, 'there's no room for complacency. If we have a bad summer, then that's it.'

This time Hawthorne-Blythe remained composed. Jane didn't.

'But *why*, what's gone wrong?' It stopped just short of a wail.

'It's a number of things,' said Hawthorne-Blythe. It was his company and although he might not have known the exact forecasts in as much detail as his FD, he was well aware of what the causes of a slump would be. 'There was the court case. Although we won it, Felipe didn't have any of the embezzled money to return – God knows where it's gone or how he's hidden it. Our legal fees were astronomical too.'

'Surely he should pay for those – he lost after all?' protested Jane.

'What would he pay with? If the money's not gone, then it's stashed for that rainy day he gets out of prison. And even if he does have it, and even if we track it down, it won't help our current predicament. We just need to be thankful that we caught him and consequently stopped a considerable financial haemorrhage. We've got to take a pragmatic view on what's happened, Jane – it's the only way.'

'Looking to the future rather than the past,' said Sebastian, whose middle name should have been pragmatic. 'I think we need a strategy to make sure that things go right for us this year. We've already put our programme back so that our first clients now arrive mid-June rather than the beginning of May. The clubbing season kicks off then and for the first couple of years we've actually lost money in that first month in Ibiza. Also, I wanted to keep the same prices for our holidays as last year, or maybe put them up in line with inflation. Obviously, we're making more money per bed than last year now that Felipe is no longer taking his cut. As you know, H-B, I prepared some figures—'

'And as *you* know, Sebastian,' interrupted Hawthorne-Blythe, 'I'd rather we passed that saving on to our clients.'

'Yes, well, as we *both* know,' continued Sebastian, 'it's academic now because that weasel Tyrone Lucas is obviously more than aware of what's been going on and the position we're in, so he's dropped the price of a Club Wicked holiday. If we followed my original plan, we'd be almost twenty-five per cent more expensive, which even I'd have to agree is too much.'

'Well, if we do go out of business, at least we'll have given value for money.'

Hawthorne-Blythe allowed himself a short chuckle, but both Sebastian and Jane knew he meant it. Everybody in the industry was aware that YF&S was more than just a business to him – he genuinely got a kick out of seeing youngsters have a good time. Being instrumental in that was more of a motivation to him than the financial bottom line – the main reason he had never allowed YF&S to become a plc.

'It makes it even worse to think that Tyrone Lucas might gain from all this,' sighed Jane.

'Maybe he deserves it,' replied Hawthorne-Blythe, smoothing his grey but still full head of hair, with both hands. 'He jumped on this whole dance music thing way before we did.'

'Not so much jumped. The way he carried on you could have been forgiven for thinking he started the damn thing,' snorted Sebastian. 'I know that he's of the any publicity is good publicity school of thought, but ye Gods, he took it to extremes.'

Hawthorne-Blythe smiled ruefully. 'He did that.'

'I don't think a week went by in those first three years,' continued Sebastian, 'when his slimy face or smug voice couldn't be seen on some obscure cable station, or heard on a radio phone-in at God knows what time. I've never known such a gregarious self-publicist. Compared to Tyrone Lucas, Richard Branson's camera shy. He attracts publicity like his clients attract bright red vest outlines.'

Jane laughed. 'That's very good for,' she looked at her watch, 'one-thirty on a Monday morning.'

Hawthorne-Blythe sighed and sat back in his chair. 'Maybe he had the foresight and I didn't. Don't forget, I must be the best part of twenty years older than him.'

Sebastian leant forward and became serious. 'H-B, there was no way of knowing the dance music thing was going to become so huge. You did the right thing. You researched it carefully and chose to get involved at the right time – the time the clients wanted to. Our infrastructure was too solid to change on a whim. Lucas jumped on a bandwagon and he was lucky. Don't forget, Club Wicked were tiny when they first started. If anything, they were more of a specialist operator.'

'And they've done extremely well,' added Hawthorne-Blythe.

'How can you be so calm about Club Wicked, after all Lucas has done?' Jane was barely able to control the anger in her voice.

'All he's done, Jane,' said Hawthorne-Blythe in his usual calm way, 'is start up a business. There's room for both of us.'

'Yes, but everyone knows he started up the business to get at you after you sacked him all those years ago.'

'I'm sure that wasn't his only reason, besides-'

'And,' interrupted Jane, 'it's also common knowledge how he got the money to start the business. What kind of man rips off pensioners? Disabled pensioners? Lucas Stairlifts went bust and he pocketed tens of thousands of pounds in deposits. And the stairlifts he *did* deliver were sold at ridiculous prices and on punitive contracts. I bet a lot of the poor old dears are still paying for them now, if they haven't already died through worry.'

'That's not entirely fair, Jane. Nobody knows the full story of what happened with Lucas Stairlifts. Look, let's stop all of this nonsense about Lucas. I'd really rather not sink to his level. Let's worry about getting our own ship in order.' He changed the subject. 'What are we going to do about our staffing problems?'

'Well,' said Jane, 'because we've closed the loopholes for fiddling, a lot of the experienced resort managers decided to leave. As you also know, Club Wicked have poached quite a few.'

Hawthorne-Blythe gave her a look and Jane knew it meant that she should not pursue this.

'Getting rid of crooked managers is a good thing,' said Sebastian, just in case Jane had missed Hawthorne-Blythe's stare.

'Of course it is. We need to rebuild things with a strong foundation. We're no longer losing the money from overpaying for accommodation – courtesy of Felipe Gomez – and we should be realising more money from excursions now that the Alison Shands of this world are no longer with us. My main concern is Ibiza. It's become so huge and corporate in the last few years that we can't risk another screw-up.'

'The obvious choice for resort manager was clearly Greg,'

13

said Hawthorne-Blythe. 'Are you sure that there's nothing you can do to convince him to change his mind?'

'Nothing,' replied Jane flatly. 'He's a great rep and after last year, what with him helping to nail Alison and everything, I really thought he'd be up for doing it. I could see it in his eyes though. I knew there was nothing that I could say or do that would make him take the job.'

'I wonder why?' pondered Hawthorne-Blythe.

'He's always hated responsibility. Greg just wants a good time – period. The thing is, he's such a good rep. At the moment, I'd say by far and away the best we've got.'

'And what happened to Heather, the girl who ran Ibiza after Alison's ignominious departure last year?' asked Hawthorne-Blythe.

'Don't you remember, H-B?' smiled Sebastian. 'She's working in that lap-dancing club?' Jane shot him a look. 'Or so I've heard.'

Hawthorne-Blythe sat back in his chair and sighed. 'So it's down to Brad Streeter.'

Jane nodded. 'I'm just a little concerned – we've never given someone Ibiza in only their second season.'

'This year we're going to be doing a lot of things we've never done before, I'm afraid, Jane. Besides, even though Greg doesn't have the title of manager, he gets on famously with Brad, doesn't he? Brad will be able to call on Greg's experience if he needs to.'

Jane nodded. 'I'm sure everything will be all right once the season gets going.'

They all sat in silence for a few moments. Hawthorne-Blythe twiddled a pen between his fingers, staring hard at the sheet of paper in front of him, too hard to be digesting its contents. He loosened his tie and put his hands behind his head. 'Oh, I don't know. Despite everything I said, it does irk me that Lucas is sticking the knife in. Like the proverbial bad penny, he keeps popping up.'

'I only know bits and pieces about him,' confessed Jane. 'It's hard to know what's true and what isn't.'

'Oh, it's no big secret. It's just that normally I'd rather not validate him by talking about what happened.'

Jane and Sebastian said nothing.

Hawthorne-Blythe started doodling on the pad in front of him. 'We'd only been going a few years when he joined as a rep. I guess he was the Brad of his day, the blue-eyed boy – quick-witted, confident, streetwise ... he was a natural leader whom everyone warmed to. Same kind of age too – mid-twenties.'

'He spent five seasons here, didn't he?' asked Jane.

'Five full seasons, then another third of a season before I sacked him.'

'On the fiddle?' said Sebastian.

'It wasn't just that. As you know, most resort managers lined their own pockets back then much more than they can now. It wasn't even the amount he took though, it was the manner in which he took it.'

'What do you mean?'

'It's hard to explain, but there's something particularly unsavoury about Tyrone Lucas. Yes, he's obsessed with making money and being successful, but he also gets genuine pleasure out of seeing those around him fail. And I'm nobody's fool but, I don't mind admitting, he had me hoodwinked. By his fifth summer I trusted him utterly. Without trying to make myself sound regal, he had my ear ... and he knew it.'

'What did he do?'

'Apart from taking me to the cleaners for more than fifty thousand?'

'Jeeez,' whistled Jane.

Hawthorne-Blythe nodded. 'But what hurt more was that on his say-so, I got rid of perfectly good reps, nice people who lost potential careers, just because Lucas liked playing mind games. And God only knows what hell the clients went through on resort in those last few years. I don't think Majorca has ever recovered.'

'He wasn't in Ibiza then?'

'Thankfully not. Back then, Majorca was probably just slightly bigger, in terms of the number of beds.'

'So what happened when you sacked him?'

'That was peculiar too. I thought he would shout, scream, get aggressive. Instead, he just sneered – I can remember the look on his face until this day. It sent shivers down my spine. It wouldn't surprise me if he's got 666 tattooed on his head. In fact,' Hawthorne-Blythe grinned, 'he's losing his hair now, so maybe we'll get to see.'

'What did he say?' asked Sebastian.

'Just that his time would come and one day I'd be a sad old man grovelling to him. He felt too that I was born with a silver spoon in my mouth . . . had this notion that I'd had it easy all of my life. I think that was his real problem. Fucking idiot.'

Jane was a little taken aback. It was rare for Hawthorne-Blythe to swear. He must have noticed the look on her face.

'I don't make a big deal about my background, Jane, but I doubt if it's anything like you imagine. Poor, working-class family, passed what used to be called the eleven plus, got a scholarship to a fancy public school, then next thing I knew I was at Cambridge. With my East End accent,' Hawthorne-Blythe paused, amused to see Jane's jaw drop, 'I stuck out like a sore thumb. One of the tutors at college gave me elocution lessons and by the time I left and joined the RAF for officer training, I was talking like this. Bit of a self-indulgent potted history, I'm afraid.' Hawthorne-Blythe slipped back into his former accent. 'That fahking wankah Tyrone Lucas comes from a poxy middle-class family in bleedin' Ruislip. He ain't got a clue, 'as 'e, luv?'

They all laughed. 'Can I ask you a question, H-B?' Sebastian asked. 'You must have had loads of opportunities to sell this company or turn it into a plc. You'd be set up for life without all of this worry. Why haven't you done it?'

'And do what after exactly? Potter around the garden of my big house tending my geraniums, getting bored and turning into Victor Meldrew? Mind you,' he reflected, 'I'd probably have a gardener, so that's out. Travel? We've been

16

all around the world and back again already. Spend more time with my lady wife? Our marriage has been pretty damn near perfect, so I don't want to ruin things by getting under her feet all day.'

'What about, I don't know, getting involved in something else or starting up another business?' suggested Jane.

'What would be the point? I don't want the hassle of getting a business off the ground at my age. I've been perfectly happy with my life just the way it is. I don't need any more.' His tone became more serious. 'Through being in the RAF and also travelling, Jane, I've seen some terrible things. You begin to realise just how cheap life can be. But you also appreciate how precious it is. And, by the time you get to my age, you are aware of how *short* it is.' He ran his hands over his white grey hair, then his fingers along his moustache. 'If I can help people make the most of this short, precious thing called life, then I've done a good thing. And there's no greater reward than seeing young people have a good time because, believe me, they are the ones best equipped to enjoy it. That, Mrs Hunter, is why I love this company so much and why the hardest thing in the world for me to endure, would be to see it fold.'

They shared a look for a few seconds, a look that said everything to Jane about Hawthorne-Blythe's integrity, compassion and wisdom. He might sometimes come across as a bit of a bumbling old boy, she thought, but there was absolutely nothing wrong with his mind – or his heart.

There was something very special about H-B. There was something very special about YF&S. For the company to go out of business was unthinkable. It simply couldn't happen.

chapter three

Bex opened the door to the hotel room just as Greg was snorting another line.

'Is that my line you've just done?'

'Oops.'

'And have you already taken another pill?'

Greg grinned and shrugged. 'It takes me longer to come up than you.'

She shook her head. 'Drug fiend! I don't believe you sometimes.' She took her bag into the bathroom. 'Well, as they say in all the best films, just going to slip into something different.'

Greg jumped onto the bed and aimed the remote control at the TV to search for the porn channel.

Before the middle of the previous summer, Greg had never even been near ecstasy. Not particularly unusual for a twenty-eight-year-old. Not even for a streetwise twenty-eight-year-old who lived halfway between Liverpool and Manchester.

What many *had* found unusual was that for five years, Greg had avoided the drug despite working as a YF&S rep in the clubbing capital of the world – Ibiza.

During the last season, everything changed. Greg became good friends with first-year rep Brad Streeter. As a result of resort manager Alison Shand's blatant greed and disregard for her staff, the reps pulled together more than in any previous season Greg had worked. He made a point of never getting too close to any of his workmates, but that summer he'd not been able to help it.

Brad and Greg had bonded one drunken night when

Brad was thinking of jacking the job in because of Alison's constant sniping. After the drinking session, they took their clients to a club where Brad suggested taking a pill. As usual, Greg declined, but Brad convinced him that statistically he was more likely to die from a reaction to a tomato pip or peanut. Greg had heard all of the arguments before, but for a reason that he still couldn't fathom, agreed to take a half. The weird thing was that they weren't even going on a special club night, just herding the clients into a West End club called Night Life during a bar crawl.

At first, he didn't think the pill was working. Then, when he started coming up, there were a few moments when he felt a bit unsure, not exactly understanding what was going on. Once he realised that he was not about to be splashed over the tabloids the next day as an ecstasy statistic, he relaxed and enjoyed the experience. An hour later, the Chemical Generation had another new recruit.

For Greg, taking ecstasy had been a revelation. It started with having a shit that gave him a hard-on, and ended with mind-blowing sex with a policewoman from Shrewsbury.

During the rest of the summer, he had taken a pill on a few of the YF&S sponsored club nights, but in the five months since his return to the UK, not a weekend had passed when he hadn't been clubbing or taken a pill. That had included his brother's wedding, where he'd dropped a pill at eleven-thirty – just as his Auntie Elsie had tumbled into a table dancing to 'Come On, Eileen' – and was at Garlands with his arms in the air an hour later.

Although the club scene in Ibiza was already well established when Greg first joined Young Free & Single as a holiday rep, the company tended to shy away from it. Reps were even threatened with dismissal if they so much as went near the sunset strip, a short stretch of beach around the legendary Café del Mar where most of the clubbing pre-parties were held (and quite a few drugs changed hands).

Ibiza was different now and the previous year, Greg sometimes felt as though everybody else was in on a secret that he wasn't.

Until, that was, his first pill.

Greg simply loved enjoying himself. Anything that helped him to ignore the responsibility of everyday life, was welcomed. Greg and ecstasy were, on the face of it, made for each other.

With his new Class A friends a permanent weekend fixture (and sometimes, when a special night out was planned, mid-week) Greg was looking forward to the coming summer more than any before. Although he had managed to (over) indulge his chemically assisted clubbing pursuits on a few occasions towards the end of the previous Ibiza season, it was since his October return to the UK that he had really gone in at the deep end. And he loved it.

This summer, he was intending to hit *all* the major Ibiza clubs, not just the ones he'd had to go to with clients as a rep. In particular, he desperately wanted to go to one of the legendary Sunday daytime sessions at Space. Quite how he was going to manage this between Saturday night flight arrivals and Sunday welcome meetings he had yet to work out. Still, where there was a will there was a way.

And there was most certainly a will.

A couple of weeks ago, it had seemed that Greg's planned summer of narcotic and sexual excess was going to be scuppered. Most reps worked their way up the corporate ladder so that, by their third year, they had their own resort to run. This was to be Greg's sixth season and he knew that YF&S would want him to be resort manager in Ibiza, but he was surprised at the huge amount of pressure that had been applied.

He'd almost buckled. He would be able to visit all of the major clubs as planned and have no on-resort superior to answer to. He knew though, that the super-effective Ibiza grapevine would soon relay any debauched behaviour, news of which would quickly filter back to head office in the UK. Moreover, there were now so many Ibiza magazines that the chances were a photographer would capture his gurning face or hands-in-the-air hysteria and print it for all to see.

Also, having been through four jobs in as many months since returning to the UK, he knew that ecstasy and responsibility were not the most compatible of bedfellows. In fact, even without ecstasy, responsibility was as foreign to Greg as a clear, warm day in Widnes. He wasn't selfish in the sense that he wanted his own way with disregard to the thoughts and feelings of others. It was more that he followed his own path . . . a path normally signposted by whichever way his dick happened to be pointing at the time.

And at this moment in time, his dick was pointing towards the megaclubs of Ibiza.

He eased his conscience in the knowledge that even if he were twatted on pills half the time he was doing the job, he'd still be way in front of most other reps in terms of ability.

This was undoubtedly true, for Greg was a great entertainer and had natural charisma. Part of this was due to the fact that he was very good-looking, but not a pretty boy. Although he was incredibly successful with women, men never seemed to resent him for it. There was no smugness in his success or smarminess in his pulling technique. He was one of them. Greg was a lad's lad, but women adored him. The archetypal incorrigible rogue with a hint of bad boy. A challenge. Almost every girl wanted to believe that she would be the one to change him, and almost every girl knew deep down that she wouldn't be. He never made any promises, so seldom received any recriminations.

He was the perfect holiday fling. What they saw was what they got with Greg – a good time, normally great sex and a huge amount of fun.

Of course, he broke hearts, but they soon mended – usually as soon as they stepped off the plane back home to be greeted by their existing boyfriend – and Greg would enter their thoughts only occasionally. During a tipsy, post holiday reminisce with shocked and giggling girlfriends. Or in the middle of perfunctory sex with a partner where the spark was so lost in the past it could have set off the Big Bang.

But for the most part, Greg would be enjoyed, fondly thought of for a while then forgotten.

And it suited him just fine.

As the most experienced rep at YF&S, he could do the job blindfolded. He knew Ibiza like the back of his hand. Why on earth would he want to be a resort manager? With so few experienced reps left, any new manager would have to cut him a bit of slack. It was definitely not his intention to take liberties; all he wanted was for the occasional missed desk duty to be overlooked, or the odd blind eye turned when he was not running on all cylinders. What he would contribute to a team in terms of experience would more than make up for the odd indiscretion.

No, Greg had convinced himself that someone else could be resort manager. All he wanted this summer was fun.

And that fun was due to start the following Thursday when, as one of the senior reps, he was helping to oversee the new reps' final interview and training at a country hotel near Hereford.

When he took his first pill, Brad had told him he would be unlikely to die as a result, and this indeed proved to be true. What he neglected to tell him was that getting trashed every weekend would make it virtually impossible to hold down a regular nine to five job.

The latest company to tire of his late Mondays and moody Tuesdays was *Motrade*, a motoring publication where Greg worked in the telesales department. Trying to look on the bright side, Greg reasoned that he would have probably had to leave anyway as he was struggling to come up with a valid excuse for taking almost a week off for the reps' training course. He had conveniently omitted to inform *Motrade* during the interview that he was going to Ibiza again for the summer, preferring to tell them he was looking forward to a long and successful career in telesales. Losing a month's work and salary was going to cause him a few financial problems but nothing disastrous.

Waiting for Bex to emerge from the bathroom, Greg slowly stroked himself to an erection watching the porn channel. It was tame compared to the hardcore stuff he'd got used to on the Spanish cable station, Via Digital. After it became clear the on-screen action was not going to get any racier, but with the Viagra having taken a visible effect, Greg started channel-hopping in the hope of finding something more stimulating. Suddenly he stopped and his mouth dropped open.

'Fuck, it's United – I forgot they were playing.'

With no more need for the remote he threw it on the floor, then propped up the pillows and made himself comfortable against the back of the bed. He took a slug from the warm Heineken, re-lit the spliff and sat transfixed, absent-mindedly playing with his rock hard erection.

Bex slipped out of the bathroom. As well as a pair of PVC thigh-length boots, she had put on the full dominatrix garb. Her usually lightly made-up face was transformed with thick mascara and bright red lipstick. She struck a pose with her hands on her hips.

'OK, I'm ready. What do you think?'

Without looking at her he said, 'Fucking great.'

Bex stood there bewildered. A small roar came from the TV as the crowd watching the game expressed their appreciation for a move.

'Ooh yeah,' said Greg, oblivious to Bex and the fact he was stroking his dick. 'You beauty, Beckham . . . you beauty.'

chapter four

'Vasilly Romanov.' He smiled at the receptionist. 'But everyone calls me Vaz.'

The receptionist looked up. She'd seen and heard it all before. It was her third year working at the Bridlehurst Manor Hotel near Hereford, and every April it was the venue for the YF&S final interview-cum-training course.

It amused her that the YF&S trainee reps thought they should behave in a certain way – slightly over-the-top friendly, speaking a little too loudly and enjoying life just that little bit too much.

And, of course, the boys always had to be charming, which normally meant flirtatious.

This one seemed all right. Not cocksure, not trying too hard, good-looking. As he took his sports bag from his shoulder, she noticed he had an exceptionally nice body too.

'I'm here for the YF&S training course interview thing,' continued Vaz.

'I know you are, sir. Everybody here is on the course "thing".'

'Oh, are they? I didn't realise.'

'That's all right, sir.' The receptionist briefly flashed him one of her rare genuine smiles and handed him a key. 'Room one two three, just like dialling the talking clock.'

She smiled again, this time at her own wit. She always smiled when she said it. She always said it.

Vaz resisted replying with a pun of his own, rightly assuming that she'd heard them all before. He headed for the lift. 'Thanks.'

'You're sharing with a Miss Arabella Bowles.'

Vaz stopped in his tracks. 'Did you say *Miss* Arabella Bowles?' The receptionist nodded. 'I'm sharing with a girl? Is that normal?'

She leant froward. 'Just a free word of advice, sir. On a YF&S training course, *nothing* is normal.'

Greg slapped his hands together. 'Oh, Brad. Don't you just love training courses? All of this fresh flesh. Eager to please, eager to learn.' He stood at the top of the stairs, looking down at reception. Wannabe reps were still arriving, or milling around waiting for the course to start. 'There's some fit fanny here this year.'

He hadn't seen Kevin Roundtree sneak up behind him.

'The fact that they're fit, young Gregory, isn't the primary quality we consider when employing them though, is it?'

Greg turned round with a start. 'Oh, hi, Kevin. No, no, of course it isn't.'

'Don't forget page fifty-six of the courier's manual . . . *you can't screw the crew.*'

Head trainer, Kevin Roundtree was renowned for striking fear into new recruits from the very beginning of the training course. He was a big man with unkempt, grey, thinning hair and a moustache, which over the last year had expanded to become an equally unkempt goatee. A few broken capillaries at the end of his nose, an annually expanding waistline, and a tendency to limp through constant attacks of gout, all pointed to a man who enjoyed some of the finer things in life, probably just a little too much. He was a striking and imposing figure, with a voice whose rich range and gentle Welsh lilt could have put him in the same company as Richard Burton and Anthony Hopkins, had he chosen the same career path. But the travel industry had benefited from his talent: Kevin Roundtree was generally regarded as the best trainer there was.

As such, most companies still preferred to contract him in (he had his own consultancy) rather than use in-house trainers. Young Free & Single had used Kevin to oversee their training course for the best part of a decade. Jane Hunter and a group of resort managers or senior reps, including Greg and Brad, made up the six-person training team and selection panel. Despite getting through the interview, reps were told that the training course itself should also be considered as an interview. Some might only be used in high season, and if anyone bombed out in a big way, they wouldn't be offered a job at the end of it.

Kevin shuffled his way between the two of them to survey the nervous or excited attendees below. 'Look at them. That was you last year, Brad. Do you remember what was going through your mind? Shall I tell you? You were thinking, I'd better go and talk to people and be outgoing and friendly. Then you noticed nobody was at the bar drinking alcohol and you thought, Shall I go and get a drink and show that I don't follow the herd? Or will they think that if I can't go for this long without a drink, I must have some kind of problem? Maybe you even thought that the barman was part of the training team, or giving us the nod?'

Brad smiled. 'Pretty much spot on. We weren't told anything about the course apart from to expect the unexpected, so I guess most of us were a bit paranoid and keeping our guard up.'

'And if you weren't, then you would have been off the course straight away.'

'What about training abroad, Kevin?' asked Brad. 'That'd be so good. You could do proper coach training, mock bar crawls . . .'

'It's cheaper to tie it on to the end of the twenty-four hour interview. After we've got rid of the ten per cent that have slipped through the net, the rest of the week's training covers all of those things. Welcome meetings, coach microphone work, administrative procedures . . . I'll admit it's not the same as being in the sun, but when the reps get to resort, they quickly acclimatise, as you both know.'

'Acclimatise to getting pissed is what they do,' said Greg.

Kevin lit a cigarette, then offered one to Brad and Greg who both refused.

'It's all about seeing how people cope when they are at their lowest ebb and their most confused. If they can handle themselves in that kind of situation, then the chances are they'll manage as a rep. Just like you did.' Kevin slapped Brad's shoulder. 'I bet you never thought you'd be one of those doing the training quite so soon though, did you?'

Brad shook his head and laughed. 'No way. After Alison Shand stitched me up in the middle of the season and you came over and sacked me . . . I thought that was me and repping finished. To be here now, helping to train and recruit new reps and getting set to manage Ibiza – it's all a bit much to take in.'

'It's no more than you deserve. You can't know how guilty we all felt at getting rid of you last summer because of that woman.'

'It's a shame there wasn't a way of catching Alison that didn't involve giving me the boot though.'

'I'm sure it's been said before, but there really was no alternative. Our main motivation was the amount of money involved in Felipe's scam. The excursion money that Alison accused you of taking was small beer by comparison. We were all pretty sure at the time that it was Alison behind it, but when she put you in the frame, we had to go along with her. The last thing we wanted was to alert her in any way that we were on to Felipe and the contracting fraud.'

Changing the subject, he turned to Greg. 'I must confess, I breathed a sigh of relief when Jane told me you weren't going to be resort manager, Greg.'

'Oh, cheers, Kev,' replied Greg, feigning hurt.

'Greg, you know as well as I do, that until surgeons find a way of transplanting your brain from your dick back into your head, you won't be able to even say the word responsibility.'

'Re . . . respon . . . response . . . Kev, you're right.'

'In the meantime, you just stick to what you're good at, corrupting our clients and ignoring page fifty-six of the couriers' manual.' Kevin glanced over the balcony, noticing a pretty girl with short dark hair and a superb body. 'There you go, Greg, another potential victim.' He set off down the corridor. 'I'll see you two in about half an hour for the pre-course trainers' meeting.'

'He's human!' said Brad.

'What, old Kev?' Greg laughed. 'He's great.'

'But he was almost encouraging you to shag other reps! What about don't screw the crew?'

'When we're having a drink with Kev later on, and the new reps aren't around, he'll tell you that the rule isn't that you don't screw the crew – it's that you don't get caught.'

Brad shook his head. 'I'd never have thought it. He seemed so by the book when we were doing the training.'

'And he is. That's why he's the best in his profession. He knows the industry inside out – he was a rep himself with Young Free & Single not long after it first started, about the same time as that Lucas geezer, the one who runs Club Wicked. In fact, he did pretty much the same to Tyrone Lucas as you did to Alison. Old Hawthorne-Blythe thought the sun shone out of Tyrone Lucas's arse until Kev Roundtree outsmarted the weasel and Hawthorne-Blythe saw Lucas's true colours. That's why I think he likes you. You probably remind him of all the shit he went through when he was a rep.' Greg paused. 'You do know it was Kevin Roundtree that suggested you as head rep for Ibiza this year, don't you?'

'No way!'

Greg nodded. 'Once you got an endorsement from him, there was never going to be anyone else in the running – that was after I turned it down, of course.'

'I thought he barely knew my name.'

'Well, you'll get to know him over the next few days all right. We'll be supping plenty of ale, and,' Greg looked over the balcony at the girl Kev had pointed out, who was checking in at reception, 'I'll be doing plenty of shagging. Come on mate, let's go and mingle.'

At that moment a soaking wet, very large girl with thick glasses and an extremely loud voice announced that the heavens had just opened and screamed a greeting at another, equally unattractive girl, whom she had obviously met during the interview process.

'Did I say mingle? Better change that to *minger*,' added Greg. 'I hope those two get Corfu.'

chapter five

Vaz knocked on the bedroom door. 'Hello?'

'What is it?'

Vaz pushed the door open. A girl turned to face him, hands on hips. She was wearing a lilac cardigan and her hair was pulled back tightly from her face.

'Yes, well,' she barked, 'what is it you want?'

'I'm sharing a room with you.'

The girl looked him up and down. 'What? No, no, no. You've got it all wrong. I'm sharing with a . . . a,' she rustled through her handbag and pulled out a letter of confirmation, 'here, see – a Vasilly Romanov.'

Vaz smiled and pointed at himself.

'But . . . but I thought Vasilly was a girl's name?'

'Well, I thought Arry was a boy's name,' teased Vaz, having quickly assessed the kind of person Arabella was. It worked.

'It's not Arry, it's Arabella, which is most definitely a girl's name. It even means woman in Arabic.'

'You don't look Arabic.'

'Of course I'm not, you idiot.'

Arabella took a quick inventory of Vaz. Nasty scuffed trainers, a Swatch or something equally cheap on his wrist, a horrid St Christopher round his neck. Not her kind of person at all. She liked her men well-dressed, well-groomed, classically dark and handsome. Definitely not the fair colouring and tousled hair of the mistake in front of her.

'There must have been an error. I wasn't informed it was mixed sex co-habiting. This is ridiculous. I'm going downstairs right away to get to the bottom of it.'

'I wouldn't if I were you,' said Vaz, putting his bag on the empty bed.

'And why is that?'

Vaz threw himself on to the bed and kicked off his trainers.

Ugh, she thought. White socks.

'Well, think about it. A rep has got to deal with unusual situations. Situations we might not be comfortable in or that maybe we've no direct experience of. This could just be part of the test. I reckon for the next five days, we're going to have all sorts of stuff thrown at us.'

'Mmm.' As much as she hated to admit it, he did have a point.

'So, seeing as we're stuck here we might as well get to know each other a bit better. We might even end up working together. Which resort did you put down as your first choice?'

'It wasn't so much my first choice – it was my *only* choice. If I don't get Ibiza then I won't bother working anywhere for Young Free & Single.'

'I don't think that's the kind of attitude they're looking for. Why are you so set on Ibiza?'

'I went there on holiday last year and I don't care what "attitude" they're looking for. Anyway, what are you,' Arabella snapped, 'a bloody policeman?'

'Actually, Arabella,' Vaz sat up on the bed, 'what I am, is a plant.'

Arabella's face froze. 'You're what?'

'I'm one of the trainers. We mingle amongst the new reps to catch them off-guard. Unfortunately, Arabella, I have to inform you you aren't what we're looking for in a YF&S rep, so if you wouldn't mind packing your bags . . .'

Arabella looked as though she was about to burst into tears. Vaz kept a straight face for a few seconds, but that was all he could mange.

'Ha! That got you going, didn't it?'

'What, y-you m-m-mean . . . you're *not* a trainer?'

'Bloody hell – you posh birds are a doddle to sucker.'

Arabella glared at him. 'You . . . *imbecile!* How dare you treat me like that?'

'It was just a joke.'

'The only thing that's a joke in this room is you.'

Vaz smiled, seemingly not in the least offended. 'Ta.'

'I mean, what kind of name is Vasilly?'

'It's Russian.'

'Well, you certainly don't sound as though you come from Russia – unless they've suddenly relocated Bow Bells.'

'I was born and bred near Ilford.'

'Ilford? Isn't that even further than the end of the red tube line? God, I couldn't imagine living there all my life.'

'I haven't lived there all my life. Our family travelled round a lot.'

'Good grief, don't tell me your father was in the forces?'

'No, the circus.'

Arabella looked at him suspiciously. 'Don't think I'm that silly.'

'It's not a wind-up. Here,' he stood on the bed, 'I'll prove it to you.'

Although the room was small, Vaz did a somersault off the bed and a one-armed handstand. He then sprang to his feet and juggled three small candleholders from the bedside table. They were quite awkward and though it was soon clear he was skilled, after nearly half a minute, he lost control and one crashed to the floor. As he snatched at it, his St Christopher chain tangled and broke.

'Bollocks,' he said, picking it up along with the candlesticks.

Arabella considered him. 'So, you're a gypsy?'

'No,' replied Vaz, examining the damaged chain, 'I'm part of a circus family.'

'That's what I said – a gypsy.' Arabella nodded at the chain. 'Isn't St Christopher the patron saint of gypsies?'

'I just told you, we're not gypsies, we're—'

'Well, whatever you are, that chain is tacky. Where did you get it – a Christmas cracker?'

'It's my uncle's.'

'Well, you should give it back to him.' Arabella was enjoying scoring some points.

'I can't.'

'Why not?'

'He's dead.'

'Oh.'

'He died in an accident just over six years ago. I've worn it ever since.'

'I'm sorry,' said Arabella, who was clearly not sorry at all. She couldn't remember the last time she'd seen her own uncle, and assumed that everyone else had a similar lack of attachment to theirs. 'So what happened, did he fall off a trapeze? Get crushed by an elephant?'

Vaz winced. Arabella was obviously a self-centred, obnoxious snob, but had she known how close he was to his uncle, he doubted if even she would have been quite so dismissively callous. Of course, there was always the possibility that Arabella was a plant herself. She certainly didn't conform to what Vaz expected of a typical rep.

'No,' he said, taking a deep breath to calm himself. 'We used to do a fire act – juggling and things like that. There was an accident.'

'What happened?'

'He burned alive. I was fourteen. I hate fire now, almost phobic about it.'

'That's terrible,' said Arabella, sitting on the bed. 'God, I need a cigarette . . . Can you pass me my lighter?'

The same clouds that had burst over the Bridlehurst Manor Hotel in Hereford were now prematurely darkening the Teddington evening sky.

Below the YF&S offices on the High Street, the owner of the franchised travel agent set the alarm, switched off the lights and locked the door. He pulled his collar up and ducked his head against the driving rain, trotting to his car to join the other overworked, over-committed or over-enthusiastic post-rush hour commuters, all struggling to get back to enjoy their precious hour or two of 'quality' family time.

Above the shop, a dissipated lemon glow from a window on the third floor of the YF&S offices showed that there was at least one person in south-west London who was more overworked, over-committed or over-enthusiastic about his job.

Or maybe just more in the shit.

Hawthorne-Blythe was the only person still in the YF&S HQ. An exhausted Sebastian Hunter had gone home an hour earlier, switching all the lights off bar the strip of halogen lamps twinkling in the windowless reception. The rest of the office sat in darkness, except for a finger of light poking from underneath the chairman's door towards a softly humming vending machine in the corridor.

One of Hawthorne-Blythe's little daily objectives was to leave the office no later than seven o'clock. He was already an hour and a half past that deadline. He also liked to get down to Bridlehurst to show his face to the new reps at least once during the final interview and training course. Looking at the sheets of paper spread across his normally tidy desk, he knew this was another objective he was unlikely to achieve.

He had been in meetings all day – all week in fact. The bombshell had been dropped over the weekend. As if things weren't bad enough already.

The call had come from the company lawyer. He had just received information that the ever-expanding Monastery group was moving into leisure. More specifically, the youth travel market.

The Monastery was a club that launched itself on the back of the rave scene. It enjoyed enormous success, but the man behind it had bigger ideas. Charles Moon was hailed by many as the Bill Gates of dance music. He was only in his early thirties, but had already turned The Monastery from a successful nightclub into a hugely profitable and well-known, multi-million pound business. As a result, in recent years he found himself in the upper echelons of the annually published *Times* rich list.

Like Bill Gates, there were as many who considered him a genius as the devil re-incarnate. It seemed as if he was hell-bent on getting The Monastery's gothic, quasi-religious logo everywhere.

The Monastery record label and magazine helped entice corporations eager to align themselves to the youth market. After a few initial sponsorship successes, Charles Moon had been quick to see the potential and swiftly put together a strategic marketing division, a division that within four years had grown to employ over a dozen people. As well as being extremely lucrative, it also had the effect of pushing The Monastery brand ever deeper into the public conscious-ness, particularly to anybody with the slightest interest in youth culture.

Now he had his sights on youth travel, specifically Ibiza. But unlike other tour companies, his eye was on the corporate Euro. Like others in the business world were realising, there was nowhere on earth like Ibiza where so many in the 16–30 bracket were congregated together, eager to soak up dance music culture, seven days a week for nearly five months of the year. The gentle breeze of corporate involvement had already started gusting – Charles Moon wanted The Monastery to be at the eye of the inevitable tornado.

It was logical. The Monastery were at the head of the dance music scene and Ibiza was its centre.

The problem for The Monastery was that it had no experience in travel. While in certain businesses, Charles Moon was happy to buy in expertise, he correctly perceived travel as being too specialist, with too many components to pull together. For this reason, he had decided to buy out and take over an established company, a specialist in travel catering specifically for the 16–30 market.

Hawthorne-Blythe had digested The Monastery's propo-sition and spent the week asking questions, answering queries, looking at implications and cogitating options.

The clear conclusion was that with The Monastery's resources, the company they took over would go from strength to strength, and any remaining competitors would almost certainly go out of business.

The Monastery had expressed an interest in only two companies because in that marketplace, there *were* only two companies.

And the other was Club Wicked.

As calm and even-tempered as Hawthorne-Blythe normally was, he felt agitated. Without hesitation, Tyrone Lucas had let The Monastery know that Club Wicked were interested in the proposition. Hawthorne-Blythe knew he would. For Lucas it had always been about the bottom line.

Hawthorne-Blythe's decision had been more considered. Apart from what was best for the clients, there was a huge emotional attachment to consider: YF&S was his life, his baby. Ultimately, however, Hawthorne-Blythe reconciled the situation in his own mind by accepting that, like a baby, sometimes one has to let go of precious things to allow them to grow.

Looking at The Monastery proposal, that was certainly the plan. The YF&S name (or Club Wicked name) would still stand, but with The Monastery logo plastered across its brochures and merchandise. The chairman of whichever company was chosen would still have control, although Charles Moon would obviously be heavily involved in strategic planning and marketing.

Slowly, Hawthorne-Blythe had come round to seeing the positive aspects of The Monastery proposal. Even in the few conversations he had with Charles Moon during the week, it was clear that this young man was driven like no other he had ever met. Yet despite his quick-fire way of talking and the sense of urgency that seemed to inhabit his every breath, Hawthorne-Blythe sensed in Moon an aspiration towards excellence and quality of service. For this reason, more than any other, Hawthorne-Blythe knew there was only one option.

He picked up the metallic, hi-tech business card in front

of him, with the rarely given out direct line number on it. For a moment, he twiddled it between his fingers, pausing to reflect on the enormity of the call he was about to make.

Slowly, he dialled the number on the card.

'Moon speaking.'

'Hi, Charles, it's Hawthorne-Blythe – H-B.'

'H-B!' It was rare for Charles Moon to be anything but impassive, but the pleasure was audible in his voice. 'I'm so glad you've called. Good news I hope?'

'Mmm, now would that be good news for The Monastery, or for Young Free & Single?'

'Well, if you're coming in to see me tomorrow, I'd like to think it will be for both of us, old boy.' Charles Moon stayed as silent for as long as he could, but uncharacteristically, spoke first. 'So H-B, is this going to be a one horse or a two horse race?'

Hawthorne-Blythe sighed. 'Well, it's interesting you've asked that, because it was more or less exactly what I wanted to ask you.'

'What do you mean?'

'Is this a *fait accompli*, Charles? Are you just going through the motions, trying to learn what you can about the business before buying out Club Wicked? Please be honest with me. I have you marked as a man of principle, like myself. I would like your word.'

'H-B, let me assure you,' Charles Moon's voice took on a tone of extra gravitas, 'no, let me give you *my word*. I am entirely genuine about doing a thorough appraisal of both companies. I will go into more detail at our meeting, but, at the moment, the playing field is entirely even. What makes you think it wouldn't be?'

'Quite simply, Charles, I don't know very much about your business. YF&S are more of a traditional youth market tour operator, whereas Club Wicked are known for clubbing type holidays.'

'Yes, they are, but they have plenty of room for improvement. You say you know nothing about my business but I know nothing about yours either. What I want is expertise in travel. Club Wicked are closer to what we're eventually looking for at this precise moment in time, but YF&S have more experience of the industry. It's swings and round-abouts. There will be all sorts of things that will influence my decision.' Charles paused. 'So, back to my original question. Is it going to be a one or two horse race?'

Hawthorne-Blythe spoke slowly and deliberately. 'I'll take you at your word, Charles. It's a two horse race.'

He heard Charles strangle a 'Yes!' on the other end of the phone. 'Excellent.'

'Just one thing, Charles – does the meeting have to be at such an unearthly hour? I wanted to get up to our reps training course and if we're meeting at just gone midnight, then I'll be too tired to go on Saturday. After making this decision I'm obviously going to be in meetings with directors and senior staff tomorrow, and I'm out with my lady wife all day Sunday.'

'I'm very sorry, H-B. We've a special fashion show at the club tonight so I won't leave here until six tomorrow morning. I'm busy tomorrow evening, then straight after our meeting I'm being taken to the airport. We're launching our new compilation CD in Australia so I'm going to be there for most of the week. I really do need to get this ironed out before I go.'

'OK. You'll have me at a disadvantage though – I'm normally tucked up in bed with a good book and a mug of cocoa by then.'

'I'll get my driver to pick you up about eleven-fifteen. Is that OK?'

'I'll see you tomorrow.'

After he put the phone down, Hawthorne-Blythe sat in the chair for a few moments, a little numb. He loosened his tie, stood up and walked over to the opposite wall of his office. Traditionally, every year since YF&S began, a group photograph was taken at the end of training course of all the resort managers. He went to the top left-hand corner, where the earliest started. A few photos in, he stopped, looking at a grinning Tyrone Lucas in three of the pictures, then only in his mid-twenties.

'Well, Lucas, if it's a fight you want,' he murmured, 'I guess it's a fight you'll get.'

chapter six

Vaz came out of the bathroom in T-shirt and boxer shorts and flopped onto the bed. It had been a long and tiring day.

'There are times when you can't beat a nice hot bath. God, I'm knackered. That was a long day, wasn't it, Arry?'

'Will you stop calling me Arry?'

'I can't believe it's already gone midnight,' replied Vaz, smiling. 'I thought we'd finish about eight, not at gone eleven.' He looked over at Arabella who was rummaging through her bag. 'You're pretty devious, aren't you?'

She stopped for a moment. 'What do you mean?'

'You act differently in front of the trainers. You say all of the right things, act enthusiastically, as though you really care.'

'I wouldn't say that was being devious – just intelligent. As I said before, all I'm bothered about is getting to Ibiza.'

'But what about when you get there? Are you just going to swan around? Suppose I end up working with you? Do you think that would be fair on me and others?'

Arabella turned to face Vaz. 'So what are you saying? Are you going to tittle-tattle on me, tell Kevin that you don't think I'm suitable?'

'No, but I—'

'Because if you did, he'd just laugh at you. They'll probably throw *you* off the course.'

'That's as maybe. Anyway, it's irrelevant. I don't give a monkey's what you do and if we work on resort together then as long as it doesn't affect me, I don't give a toss what you do there either.'

'Good.'

'What I don't understand is *why* you're so desperate to work in Ibiza.'

'None of your business.'

'It is if I work there too.'

'It has got absolutely nothing to do with you.'

Vaz had had enough. 'There's no point talking to you. I'm going to sleep.'

He rolled over and switched off his bedside lamp.

Arabella continued to rummage through her bag and clothes, cursing. Then there was a few minutes' silence, after which Vaz heard a tapping sound. He rolled back over and saw Arabella huddled over the small desk by the window.

'Now what are you doing?'

Arabella looked at him, gave a sardonic smile, then pulled out a small thin silver tube. She bent over the table and snorted the line she had just chopped out.

'Is that speed?'

'Of course it isn't speed, you peasant. It's cocaine.'

'What? Are you mad? We've just been told that we've got to be up at seven in the morning and we're going to have one of the most gruelling days of the course.'

'Well, you shouldn't believe everything you hear, should you?' replied Arabella sniffing, then checking that no stray granules remained on her upper lip.

'What's that supposed to mean?'

Arabella gave him a superior look, then fully clothed, lay on her bed, pulling just the bedspread over her. She pointed the reading light towards her and picked a copy of *Tatler* from the floor.

Vaz shook his head in disbelief. 'You really are a nut-nut. I'm going to sleep.'

He pulled the covers over him and faced the other way.

'Good night, Vasilly,' said Arabella, 'and sweet dreams. . .'

'So, it's the start of desk duty and this young lad comes downstairs. Now, what you've got to remember, is this was one of the hotels that Felipe contracted – probably the worst hotel in Majorca. Um, barman,' Kevin interrupted his story to catch the barman's eye, 'same again all round.'

'Have we got time?' asked Jane. 'It's almost one in the morning.'

'Five minutes isn't going to make any difference – the longer we leave it the better.'

'Maybe he wants to shut the bar,' persisted Jane.

'Nonsense. We might be the only ones in the hotel bar, but we're the only ones in the hotel. Old Mick here doesn't mind what time we stay until, do you, Mick?'

'Not at all, Mr Roundtree, not at all. I'm on duty until four o'clock, and if your previous training courses are anything to go by, I'll be putting in a bit of overtime before it's finished.'

Kevin tapped his nose, then turned to the rest of the group.

'Mick's as good as gold. I always bung him a little extra at the end of the course. Now then, where was I?'

'How *not* to deal with customer complaints,' said Greg.

'Ah yes, so anyway. It was at the beginning of the season. Jason Barnes was still manager and he was overseeing that rep Shagger – probably the closest we've ever got to someone giving Greg here a run for his money when it comes to the fairer sex – on morning desk duty. Now, they'd both been on the Pirate excursion the night before, got horrendously pissed and pulled two old rippers. As I said before, this hotel was awful. The staff were rude, the food was inedible and the place was filthy. So this poor young lad comes down from his room first thing. He goes up to Shagger and Jason and says, "Excuse me, I don't want to cause a fuss but I got up this morning and there was a rat in my bed."'

Greg and Jane shared a look. They'd heard the story several times.

'It was a big blighter too, apparently. Anyway, Shagger looks at him all bleary-eyed and probably still pissed from the night before and says, "You think you've got problems?

He woke up this morning and there was a pig in his bed and when I woke up there was a dog in mine."'

Despite the fact that Brad was the only one who had never heard the story, they all laughed.

'Talking about dogs,' said Greg, have you seen the way that Scottish chap, Hughie's been looking at that fat girl we've got earmarked for Corfu?'

'Greg!' said Jane. 'You're such a sexist bastard at times.'

'No,' contradicted Rita Marchant, a marketing rep turned trainer, whom Greg had slept with four years previously, 'he's a sexist bastard *all* the time.'

'Actually, I'm certain Noreen will make a great rep,' added Kevin authoritatively. 'The man on the street would imagine that we choose Baywatch types when nothing could be further from the truth.'

'Hey, there's always the exception to prove the rule, eh Kev?' said Greg, licking his finger and smoothing down an eyebrow with a big grin. Everyone groaned. 'I tell you what, though, I'm serious about Hughie and Noreen. I'd put money on the fact that he's trying to get off with her.'

'If any of the new recruits are going to shag each other,' said Tom Ortega, the Overseas Controller and the reps' first contact in head office, 'then I reckon it's those two in the proposed Ibiza team.'

'Which ones?' asked Greg.

'Cliff and Claudia,' replied Tom.

'Are they the two you were telling me about, that you thought would be high season reps at best?' asked Brad, who as the new resort manager for Ibiza, had a vested interest.

'Yeah. Claudia doesn't seem that bright and Cliff's acting as though he's already got the job and bought the T-shirt. A tenner says they'll shag each other before Hughie and Noreen.'

'All right then, Tom me old son, you're on.' Greg handed a tenner to Kevin and nodded at Tom to do the same.

'So if you're both wrong, I guess that means I get to keep the money,' said Kevin, stuffing the money in his pocket and rubbing his hands together. He swigged back the remainder of his drink. 'Right then, troops. Let's unleash Armageddon on our poor unsuspecting new recruits, shall we?'

Kevin led the other trainers over to a table, piled high with whistles, klaxons, saucepans with large spoons and a variety of other implements that looked as though they could wake the dead.

'God, I remember when you did this to me last year,' said Brad, rummaging through the table next to Greg. 'I was so knackered that I must have zonked out as soon as my head hit the pillow. When you bastards woke me up an hour later, I didn't know what the fuck was going on.'

'That's the whole point,' said Greg, hanging a whistle round his neck and stuffing a football rattle under his belt. 'Everyone's exhausted and we stress over and over again that the next day's going to be a big one. We shut the bar and virtually order them to get a good night's sleep.'

'But why is the wake-up call so extreme? Obviously, I can see the logic in being kept up and not getting much sleep – it's all part of the job. But why fling doors open, set off fire alarms, scream, shout and all this lot?' asked Brad, gesturing towards the table.

'It disorientates them,' said Kevin, leaning over to grab a walkie-talkie. 'We're looking to see how they react. On a basic level, we can't employ anybody who's moody or aggressive when they wake up. There must have been times on resort when you had to be out of bed and facing clients within minutes?'

Brad nodded. 'You can say that again. I remember times in Ibiza last year when I barely slept for three days but still had to be the smiling face at the airport, the armchair psychologist during desk duty and the accountant after collecting money from a welcome meeting. Looking back on it now, I guess this interview was child's play by comparison.'

'And I bet you didn't get much sleep the night before the

interview either, did you?' asked Kevin. 'Nerves, excitement, the journey to Hereford. It's all part of the plan.'

'I almost feel sorry for them,' said Brad.

'OK, are we all ready?' asked Kevin, holding his walkie-talkie aloft and bringing everyone's attention back to the job in hand. 'Rita and myself will take the Greek recruits on the ground floor west wing. Brad and Tom, you do the Balearics on the first floor here. Greg and Jane can do the wake-up call for the mainland Spain hopefuls on the second floor. Are your walkie-talkies on?' Everyone nodded. 'Any problems? Good. On my signal, do your first door. Speed is of the essence. Nobody has more than five rooms to do. No matter what you find, straight on to the next one. If anything looks suspicious, you can always go back. The fire alarm will be switched on thirty seconds after the first door is opened. All candidates should be awake by then. As soon as all doors are open, I want everybody downstairs. If you look at the sheets you should all have, there are three columns. Next to their names, note the time it takes for each candidate to be dressed and ready to go. In the third column, just a sentence or two about their attitude and demeanour. OK, let's go.'

Arabella could hear the whispering outside. She had switched off the bedside lamp a while earlier, but had been lying in the darkness waiting and listening. The listening had been particularly difficult over Vaz's loud, rumbling snores.

Suddenly it happened.

'Right, you lazy bastards! Come on, get up, out of bed. Everybody up or you'll be going home. We want you downstairs as quickly as possible. You're all going for a little hike!'

The screaming was accompanied by deafening whistles, saucepans banging, horns going off . . . Even though Arabella had been expecting it, it almost made her jump out of her skin. But the best bit was watching Vaz. She could not help but laugh at his total disorientation.

'What the . . . who . . . Jesus . . . fuck me . . .'

'Wakey, wakey, Vasilly,' laughed Arabella.

Vaz rubbed his eyes, still trying to work out where he was. Then, the fire alarm went off.

'Where the . . . oh fuck . . . is there a fire?'

'Yes, yes,' yelled Arabella, seizing the opportunity to exploit Vaz's fear. 'Quick, it's on this floor. No time to get dressed. We've got to go or we'll be *burned alive*. Come on, *hurry!*'

Vaz rushed for the door. Arabella followed, giggling uncontrollably. He sprinted along the corridor and was hurtling down the stairs before Arabella got out of the room.

He was the first in the foyer and was just about to dash out the main doors into the freezing night air, when Kevin Roundtree emerged from the west wing and spotted him.

'Vaz . . . where on earth are you going wearing a T-shirt and boxer shorts?'

'Fire!' yelled Vaz. 'There's a fire!'

'No, there isn't,' replied Kevin, jotting something down on his pad. 'If you'd listened properly, you would have heard us say that you needed to put on some clothes. It's all part of the test. Everyone's going on a little hike, so get back up to your room and get some warm clothes on . . . sharpish!'

Vaz stood disorientated for a moment then noticed Arabella, calmly walking down the stairs. Slowly it dawned on him that she had been winding him up.

'Didn't you hear me?' said Kevin. 'Move it!'

Vaz bounded up the stairs, two at a time, stopping as he passed Arabella.

'You bitch – how did you know about this?'

She shrugged her shoulders. 'Women's intuition?'

Vaz glared at her for a moment, then dashed to his room. Arabella continued walking, a thin smile forming.

'Well done, Arabella,' said Kevin who was standing at the bottom, making another note on his pad.

Rita walked in. 'Jesus, that was quick.'

'Wasn't it?' agreed Kevin approvingly. 'I don't think

we've ever had a girl as the first one dressed and ready to go before. I remember, years ago, when—'

'Kevin! Here a minute.' Greg was leaning over the top of the banister, yelling down.

Kevin briskly walked up the stairs and followed Greg along the corridor to one of the rooms.

Cliff was sitting on the edge of his bed, head in hands. Claudia stood clutching a sheet to herself, covering her nakedness.

'No prizes for guessing what I found,' said Greg.

Kevin shook his head. 'How stupid can you get? Are you both deaf? Didn't you read page fifty-six of the courier's manual? What is it I emphasised time and time again?'

Cliff and Claudia were both guiltily staring at the carpet, too ashamed to speak.

'Well?' persisted Kevin.

'You don't screw the crew,' came the simultaneously feeble reply.

'You don't screw the crew,' Kevin repeatedly slowly. 'Right then,' he sighed, 'pack your things. There's an annexe to the side of the hotel where you can spend the rest of the night. Neither of you drove here, did you?' They shook their heads. 'Good. A driver from the hotel will pick you up at seven-thirty in the morning and take you to the station to get the first train.'

'But—'

Kevin held his hand up, interrupting Cliff's attempt at protest.

'No buts. It's straightforward. You've disobeyed the cardinal rule. It's instant dismissal from the company and that means there's no point in you staying for the rest of the course. Apart from anything else, doing it during the first day, which we make perfectly clear is still an interview day rather than part of the training course, proves that you're both obviously far too stupid to be reps.'

Even Greg winced at this. There was no doubt that as nice as Kevin could be once you got to know him, he could be an unforgiving bastard if crossed. His last comment caused Claudia to burst into tears.

'And you can pack that nonsense up as well, my girl, because it doesn't wash. I want you both out of here within ten minutes. Move it. I've got some reps to train.'

Claudia howled even more loudly as Kevin stormed off. Greg was about to follow him when Cliff spoke.

'There was no need for him to speak to us like that.'

'Yes, there was – every right. You're a pair of fucking idiots.'

Cliff stood up, his mood becoming aggressive. He walked towards Greg, who stood his ground.

'How can you of all people say that?' said Cliff, his voice raising. 'You're *known* for shagging clients – Kevin even joked about it earlier today. *And* I've heard that you've shagged half of the YF&S reps. What happened to don't screw the crew then, eh?'

Greg took a step closer so they were almost nose to nose. He spoke, practically in a whisper.

'Ah, see that's where I'm smart and you're not. The rule *isn't* that you don't screw the crew . . .'

Cliff looked at him confused. 'Yes, it is.'

Greg shook his head. 'No it's not.' He walked into the corridor. 'The rule is that you don't get *caught*.'

The blackness of a bleak, Hereford night faded almost imperceptibly into the grey of a dreary, April morning. A stream of cars swished along the wet country lane at the end of the Bridlehurst Manor Hotel drive, their headlights dipped in resigned gloom as they joined the growing queue of traffic waiting to cross the penultimate set of lights that led to the A road.

Heavy rain rattled against the roof and windows of the hotel's conservatory turned dining-room. The exhausted YF&S trainees sat inside, gratefully attacking a full English breakfast. Although there was a constant rumble of conversation and the odd attempt at a cheery laugh, their relatively subdued tone was unrecognisable compared to the overzealous, excited boisterousness of their arrival.

The trainers all sat on a table, away from the new recruits. 'Wouldn't think it was the same group of people, would you?' laughed Jane Hunter.

'This is the best bit.' Kevin popped a couple of sweeteners in his tea. Greg and Jane shared a smile, given the huge breakfast Kevin had just demolished. 'Can you imagine how they feel at this moment, after,' Kevin checked his watch, 'nearly twenty-two hours of tests? Part of the reason they're all so subdued is that they're dreading to think what we've got in store for them during breakfast. You'll see them visibly sigh with relief when they walk out of here without us doing anything. They're at their most battered right now. In a minute, I'm going to tell them that we're nearly finished. My tone will be friendly, soothing. I'll say words like chat, rather than test. There will be a cadence to my voice that suggests we're coming to an end. I'll deliberately slow down the ... end ... of ... my ... sentences. I'll smile. They'll smile. I'll tell them that the next hour or two is going to be easy. They'll relax ... and that's when we'll whittle out the last wrong 'uns.'

'You love all this, don't you?' said Greg.

'You bet.' Kevin stood up, made a token dab with a serviette at the food caught in his moustache, dropped it on the table, then clapped his hands together. 'Right then, time to get cracking again. Just a quickie before we start though.' He turned to Brad. 'That Mark Ewers lad, what do you think of him?'

'Yeah, pretty good. He started off very strong. Likes to be centre of attention a bit too much and comes across as a bit of a wide boy, but on the whole, I'd say he's got what it takes.'

'Would you have him as part of your team in Ibiza?'

'Yeah, I think so – why?'

'Greg, what about you – would you want to work with him.'

'He seems like a good lad.'

'Mmm.' Kevin paused for a moment, mainly for effect. 'I've seen something in him today that makes me think he wouldn't be suitable.'

Greg looked puzzled. 'What exactly?'

Kevin stood up. 'Why don't you watch the next bit and we'll see if I'm right.'

Kevin had been absolutely correct about how easily all of the interviewees were lulled into a false sense of security. It had been so long since Greg had been a trainee that he had forgotten just how clever Kevin was.

Kevin started off with a quiz. It was set up professionally with buzzers. The interviewees were allowed to organise their own teams of four. This helped Kevin see what alliances had been formed, or what rifts were developing.

Some of the rounds had questions to be answered individually, some as a team. Kevin told Greg and Brad to look out for those who wanted all of the glory and were ultra-competitive, as well as those who lost focus and were happy to let the rest of the team carry them.

Kevin made it such fun that none of the participants perceived the quiz as anything more than a test of general knowledge and a laugh.

After the quiz, Kevin put the interviewees into three groups. In an effort to keep them all relaxed, he said that, as they were just going to have a 'chat', the make-up of the groups was less important than at the start of the interview.

The 'chat' was getting the group to imagine they were financially strapped, hospital governors. They were presented with hypothetical case scenarios of four different people who needed life-saving operations. The problem was that the fictitious hospital could only afford to perform one. By discussion, the group had to decide which of the four should be chosen.

The first candidate was known as George. His case study said that he was in his late forties, had served his country during the Falklands, had just celebrated his silver wedding anniversary and had four children and two grandchildren. For many of the interviewees, he was at first, the obvious choice. If not, they tended to go for Cathy, the single, twenty-two-year-old mother, who lived on a council estate.

The third choice, Norman, was an architect in his late thirties, with a wife and young child – very middle England.

The remaining choice was a medical student with no dependants. He was an Asian immigrant called Ramesh, who had been a British citizen for five years.

Once the groups discussed and looked at things closely, most of the interviewees realised that the main criteria for deciding who should get the operation was who could contribute most to society. As Kevin said to Greg and Brad just before starting, it didn't take a rocket scientist to work out that Ramesh was the candidate who best satisfied this criterion.

Kevin was chairing the group that included Mark Ewers. The discussion had already lasted nearly an hour. They were told before that everyone within the group would have to agree on which candidate they chose for the operation before they were allowed to finish.

Mark Ewers and a girl called Denise were the only two left who did not agree that Ramesh should be given the vote. Denise had just seen the light, so Mark was on his own, but would not budge.

The two other groups had already finished and could be heard outside in the corridor, their initial whispers growing in volume at the excitement and relief of having finished the twenty-four hour interview. Kevin took the noise as an opportunity to have a short break in his own group's discussion.

'OK, let's leave things there for a minute whilst I get the others to quieten down a bit. The three of us will leave you to it for a minute or so and see if that makes any difference.'

They left the room and walked into the foyer, where the other two groups bustled around a table with tea, coffee and biscuits on it.

'Oi, you lot – quieten down,' instructed Kevin. 'We've not finished in there yet. Go and wait in the main training room.' As they left, he beckoned Brad and Greg over to the

51

opposite end of the room. 'Do you see what's going on in there with our friend Mark Ewers?'

'He's not too keen on being part of the group, is he?' replied Brad.

'That's because I bowled him a bit of a googly at the start of the discussion. Remember I said we were looking for how they interacted in their new groups? Mark thinks the most important thing is to show his individuality and leadership. But his not being part of the group isn't the problem. Greg, any ideas?'

'Yeah. I didn't notice it before but he's a twat.'

'Getting warmer,' laughed Kevin, as a grinning Brad shook his head at Greg's bluntness. 'Anything else?'

'Not only is he a twat, but he's a racist twat.'

'Brad, would you go along with that?'

'It's certainly beginning to seem that way.'

Kev smiled. 'Well done – you're absolutely right. I picked up on it earlier in the course. He was very dismissive towards Tamsin, that pretty Asian girl we've got earmarked for Ibiza. That's one of the reasons I put her in a different group – I thought he might be a bit more open in displaying his prejudice.'

'So what do we do?' asked Greg. 'Obviously we're not going to have him as a rep, so what's the point in carrying on with the discussion in there and dragging it out for the rest of the group?'

'None really,' replied Kevin, 'apart from the fact I like things to be cut and dried. Let's go back in. Mark is incredibly tired, probably pretty confused but also no doubt thinks he's sailed through this interview already. Turn the screw and he'll show his true colours. You just watch.'

As they walked back into the room, things had become quite heated. Vaz in particular, was already doing his own bit of screw-turning.

'But you can't want the old bloke to get the op – he's already made his contribution to society.'

'Yeah, he fought in a fucking war. That's more than you have, you . . .' the flustered Mark Ewers noticed Kevin, Greg and Brad walk back in, so modified what he was going to say, '. . . you, you . . . oh, you know what I mean.'

'Look, Mark,' said Arabella, in a superior tone, 'everybody here has agreed that this George fellow has done his bit. But surely the operation should go to someone younger?'

'All right,' said Mark, grabbing the sheet. 'What about . . . Norman, the architect? That's the one you wanted first.'

'Yes, it was, but then we discussed things and I changed my mind. That's the whole point of this exercise, surely?'

'What exactly is your problem with Ramesh, Mark?' asked Vaz, not noticing a little smile form on Kevin's lips at the question.

'I haven't got a problem with him,' replied Mark belligerently.

'So why shouldn't he get the operation?' joined in Scottish Hughie.

'He'll be a doctor himself one day,' added Vaz.

'Yeah, and how will he qualify? He's only been in the country for five minutes and he's already taking advantage of our education system – now he wants a bloody operation too!' Mark laughed and held his arms out, believing he'd made a valid point.

'He's been in the country five years, not five minutes,' corrected Hughie.

'I know that, what I meant was—'

'But Mark,' interrupted Vaz slowly, 'it's *his* education system too, just as it's *his* health service.'

The rest of the group mumbled their agreement. A bewildered Mark looked around them.

'Oh, come on, I don't believe I'm hearing this! He's been over five minutes – sorry, five *years*, and if we're talking about contributions, he's made none. All he's done is take—'

'If you listened,' interrupted Arabella, 'it was about the contribution he was *going* to make.'

'Yeah, so how do we know he'll stay in the UK? He'll probably get his qualification then fuck off back to his own country – that's what they all do.'

Vaz shook his head in disgust. Mark picked up on it.

'What? What's your problem?'

'This *is* his country.'

'What more than it's George's?' Mark tried to validate his argument. 'More than Cathy's? More than Norman's? Do me a favour! At least there's a good chance they'll carry on making a contribution.'

Arabella went to say something, but Kevin had gone to stand behind Mark and put his finger to his lips.

'None of you can seriously think Ramesh is the right candidate, surely,' continued Mark, looking round for support. He hadn't seen Kevin behind him instructing the group to be quiet. Kevin was aware of the power of silence, particularly on someone like Mark.

'This is stupid.' More silence. 'He just can't be the one.' The rest of the group looked at him with expressionless faces. 'Oh, for Christ's sake, what's wrong with you lot?' Finally, exasperated, Mark said it. 'There's no way you can choose him . . . *he's a fucking PAKI!*'

As the group laughed or put their head in their hands, Kevin rested his hand on Mark's shoulder,

'Um, Mark – can I have a quick word with you outside?'

Still shaking his head in disbelief, Mark left the room. A few moments later, Kevin re-entered, the tone having lightened immeasurably.

'Well done, everyone. I knew he'd spit it out eventually. Apart from watching the group dynamic, having a discussion like this when you're all so tired makes it difficult for people like Mark to slip through the net. Fantastic contribution, Vaz and Arabella – great questioning. Needless to say, our friend Mark Ewers will not be waiting in the other room with you all to see whether or not he's passed, but as far as the rest of you are concerned,' he put his hands together, 'you've all succeeded in completing the legendary twenty-four hour interview.'

There was a spontaneous cheer and relieved clapping.

'So now comes the really hard bit.' The clapping subsided, as they wondered what on earth could be left to be thrown at them. Kevin smiled. 'Well, the hard bit for us trainers, at least. We've got to tell you who will, and who won't be making it to resort.' The room fell deathly quiet.

'Thank you all for coming and for those of you who won't be part of the Young Free & Single team, I'd just like to wish you every success for the future. If you could all make your way through to join the others . . . Greg, can you give Jane, Tom and Rita a shout and tell them we're ready.'

A few moments later, Kevin and the other five trainers were alone in the room. Greg slumped in a comfy armchair.

'Thank fuck that's over. I could quite happily go to sleep myself.'

'One last job to do,' said Kevin. 'Tom, any others to be added to the reject list from your group?'

'No, it all went well. I saw a rather bewildered Mark Ewers with his bags packed in reception. Your hunch about him was right, then?'

'On the nose,' smiled Kevin. 'I think we're going to have a good team in Ibiza this year. Vaz and Arabella were both excellent. They'll need good managing though, Brad, but I'm sure Greg here will help keep them in line.' He turned to Jane Hunter. 'How about your group, Jane, anyone crash and burn at the last hurdle?'

'No, everything was fine.'

'Excellent. That means we've still got ten interviewees to break the bad news to. Any volunteers?' There was silence. 'Didn't think there would be.'

'How do we tell them?' asked Rita.

'Obviously we can't split them into two groups,' answered Kevin, 'because the smaller group would immediately know that they hadn't passed. That's why I told them that we do it in groups of ten. We simply bring the first ten in here, and they're the ones who'll be given the bad news. While that's happening, the larger group are told they're staying.' He rubbed his hands together. 'Shall we do it by straws then?' Kevin pulled six cocktail sticks from his pocket and held them in his hand. 'Whoever gets the short broken stick gets the rejects.'

'What about you?' chided Jane.

'There's one in there for me too. I just hope one of you lot pull it before me. Come on then, Jane, ladies first.'

Jane pulled out a stick. It wasn't the broken one. She gave a little squeal of delight. He nodded at Rita. Slowly, she chose a stick and gently pulled it from between Kevin's fingers. It was short. Very short. Her face said it all.

'Oh God, no! It's my first ever time as an interviewer. How can I be the one to tell them they haven't got the job?'

'It's Brad and Greg's first time too.' Kevin laughed. 'You'll be fine. I told you what to say earlier on, remember?'

'No,' replied Rita, already having accepted her fate.

'Yes, you do. The golden rule is getting the bad news out straight away. Don't beat about the bush. Just say, "I'm afraid to say that none of you in this room are going to be offered a position with the company." Bang, job done. Do the damage limitation after that. All the "it was a difficult choice" and "you've all done incredibly well and should be proud of yourselves" stuff. Come on, girl, you'll be fine.'

Rita did not look convinced.

'I'll stay in here with you if you want, Rita,' volunteered Brad. 'You can do the talking; I'll supply the moral support.'

'Very commendable,' nodded Kevin.

'Very fucking stupid,' said Greg.

'Come on then, Jane, Tom, Greg, let's get this over and done with.'

As Greg walked past Brad, he mumbled, 'You twat. I was going to stitch Rita up – now I'm going to have to stitch you up and all.'

'How?'

Greg gave a cheeky little smile and patted him on the back. 'You'll just have to wait and see, won't you?'

As Kevin walked down the corridor, he said, 'What I'll do is string them along a bit to give Rita a chance to let her lot know first. The main group always cheers. If Rita's group hear, then it will make her task even more unpleasant than it already is.'

As the trainers strode into the room, you could have

heard a pin drop. Kevin wasted no time on preambles. He looked down at a list.

'Right, the first ten of you to learn your fate are . . .'

He read the names from the list and they scuttled out, none guessing that they were all about to be told their application was unsuccessful.

They walked into the second training room, where Rita greeted them, trying to appear as relaxed as possible. Brad stood behind her. The candidates all took their seats. Some screwed up their eyes or looked at the floor. A few held hands, while others who feigned indifference couldn't conceal the hope in their eyes.

Rita smiled. She felt nervous, but knew she could do this. Kevin was right; a quick couple of sentences, said in the right way would make it far less painful. She took a deep breath.

'There's no—'

A loud cheer coming from the other room interrupted her. The candidates knew immediately what the cheer meant and looked at her in disbelief. Two girls started crying. A guy stood up and kicked his chair over in disgust. The mood was sour.

Rita gulped. 'Um, well, I guess you all . . . I'm sorry.'

She left the room, close to tears. Brad shuffled out behind her. Kevin, Greg, Tom and Jane were all in the foyer. Rita ran over to Kevin, who held his hands up before she could speak.

'I know, I know. I'm sorry, but it wasn't me.' He pointed at Greg. 'I started my usual long-winded tease, then I started coughing and Greg just came out with it. There was nothing I could do.'

Rita glared at Greg, who grinned. She stormed off.

Kevin was more irritated by the fact that Greg had got one up on him than truly annoyed. 'That, young Gregory, was out of order.' He turned to Brad. 'Do I need to go in there and smooth things over?'

'It wouldn't be a bad idea.'

Kevin looked at his watch. 'OK. Let's all reconvene at six o'clock.'

After Tom and Jane left, Greg was like an excited school kid.

'So come on then, Bradley old son. What happened? I told you I was on a wind up. Sounds as though it worked a dream.'

'More of a nightmare. Rita was nervous but looked as though she'd got herself together. None of them had a clue. When that cheer went up the colour drained from everyone's faces, especially Rita's.'

Greg was laughing. 'Excellent.'

'A few of the girls started crying, that big lad from Newcastle looked as though he was about to kick off.'

'All harmless fun. Doesn't matter how they get told, does it? They ain't got the job and we'll never see them again, so what the fuck?'

Brad shook his head. 'Greg, I've said it before and I *know* I'll say it again. You can be such a bastard.'

Greg smiled and put his arm round Brad's shoulder.

'Cheers, mate.'

chapter seven

Sheets of driving rain poured out of the spring night sky, and swept down the dreary industrialised, East London back street. It was an unremarkable location; a few innocuous looking warehouses, a commercial vehicle body shop, and a long since vacated three-storey sixties office block, now plastered with posters advertising club nights. These posters, and the number of expensive cars that occupied a nearby patch of wasteland turned unofficial car park, were perhaps the only clue to the metamorphosis that the street underwent at weekends.

This unlikely setting was the home and nerve centre of The Monastery. The club itself, which was the starting point for all of the group's other businesses, was still sited within one of the warehouses. The freehold on the property had been purchased from the club's profits, within the first year of its opening. The next door warehouse became available at a good price less than two years later, so Charles Moon bought that too.

Rather than relocate as the business expanded, Moon chose to transform the inside of the warehouses into a designer chic, hi-tech, ultra cool network of offices, accessed via several secret doors within the club and an innocuous and battered red front door. From the street, this was the only feature that broke up the expanse of pollution-stained Victorian brickwork, apart from a large shutter to a loading bay, which became the club's main entrance at the weekend.

There were no windows but a glass roof to the offices gave the impression of a huge atrium. The bright and modern feel was always a complete shock to first-time visitors. They would react as though they had stumbled upon the Batcave, or the hidden hi-tech lair of a secret organisation that would be featured in a twenty-first century remake of *The Avengers*, or Man from *U.N.C.L.E.*

At this moment in time though, the Friday night clubbers waiting to get in probably cared little about any part of the building other than the club itself. They queued in resigned patience, huddling together to squeeze under the short canopy for protection from the rain.

The club was having a good night, but nothing like in its heyday. Of all the business profit centres, the club was the only one that struggled to break even in its own right.

Despite the downturn in custom, the doormen and pickers always managed to keep the queue just long enough to maintain the impression that it was still the place everyone wanted to get into. For those whose image fell on the wrong side of cool, the chances of getting in were still something of a lottery, although in recent years it was true to say they had more chance of holding a winning ticket.

Every so often, VIP's, chancers or blaggers would march to the front to try their luck with the pickers. For the lucky few, over-exaggerated greetings would be exchanged, then they would be given their precious yellow disc to allow free entry, or a bouncer would march the close friends and genuinely important through the security checks and into the club.

The majority trying to gain free entry would gesticulate to the heard-it-all-before head shaking of those doing the door. Some would walk away in disgust; others would join the back of the paying queue. Those who had made a good attempt with a degree of charm would be allowed in without queuing, or sometimes given a red disc, which allowed entry at a reduced charge.

It was while three male media types were playing out this exact scenario that a chauffeur-driven top-of-the-range Jaguar swept to a halt outside the club. A bouncer rushed forward and opened the rear passenger door. Those in the queue craned their necks to see which famous DJ or dance floor diva was about to emerge. They resumed their previous conversations, however, when a grey-haired gentleman in his sixties stepped from the car, wearing a crombie and carrying an umbrella.

Another man followed, in his mid-forties, with greying black hair pulled into a short ponytail. His self-satisfied sneer indicated that he was blissfully unaware that his attire would have suited someone half his age.

'What a crappy night. It's almost summer,' said Tyrone Lucas in his nasal, thinly disguised estuary drawl. 'And look at all these pillocks, standing in the rain just to get into this shit-hole.'

'They're young,' replied Hawthorne-Blythe, courteously sharing his umbrella with Lucas as they walked towards the club's entrance. 'They don't care about waiting when they know they're going to have a good time. Besides, how can you be so contemptuous of club culture when it's supposed to be the whole basis of Club Wicked's holiday programme?'

'Oh, I'm not contemptuous of club culture.' Lucas forced a smile at the pretty girl on the door. 'Just most of those involved in it.'

A bouncer led them along the dark tunnel-like corridor into the club. Hawthorne-Blythe was unprepared for the sight and sound that greeted him as the doors to the main part of the club swung open.

'Good grief,' he yelled, grimacing as the wall of sound struck. Before him, a sea of smiling faces and raised arms bobbed along to the pounding beat. 'Is it always this busy?' he asked the bouncer, having to stand on his toes to reach the stooping man-mountain's ear.

'This is quiet. We've only been doing these hard house nights for a few weeks. The reason it looks so busy is that we've not opened the main room yet.'

Lucas tugged the bouncer's sleeve from the other side. 'Where's the office? Surely we don't have to walk through all this lot.'

'Afraid so. The main door on the street to the offices is locked during club nights. The only entrance is behind the bar.'

'And where's that, exactly?'

The bouncer pointed to the other side of the dance floor. 'Over there.'

He set off, carving his way through the crowd. Hawthorne-Blythe tucked in behind him, happy to see everyone having a good time, but conscious how out of place he looked.

Lucas had no such reservations. His Bond Street shopping spree earlier in the day had left him convinced that clubbers would recognise him as one of their own. He strutted through the crowd with a surly arrogance, clicking his fingers and nodding his head in a 'hep-cat' sixties kind of way.

He interpreted the first few grins aimed towards him as the shared clubbing experience he'd heard so much about. Indeed, he had been to Pacha in Ibiza on several occasions and had enjoyed watching the dance floor from afar, happily isolated in the VIP bar with several bottles of champagne.

Lucas hadn't stepped on to a dance floor for over two decades. Then, it was a place with physical boundaries, with more people watching than participating. Most of those watching would be blokes, perched like vultures on Viagra, waiting for the first strains of Fat Larry's 'Zoom', indicating that the 'slow' records were starting. Then the composition of the dance floor would change. Girls shuffling round shrine-like circles of white handbags would scatter like frightened wildebeest. The alpha males would swoop on their prey, while the less daring would observe, willing them to make prats of themselves, cackling like hyenas every time the alphas were rejected and wallowing in inferiority every time mouths entwined.

The place where Lucas now found himself wasn't so much a dance floor as a space. People just danced where they stood. Lucas had discussed the etiquette of dance culture many times with his Club Wicked reps, particularly in relation to the mating ritual. 'You just stand next to a girl, dance with her, then if she likes you, you'll know – simple as that.' That seemed to be the gist of the advice he'd been given. He'd often thought how much easier the Chemical Generation had it compared to his own.

Now was his chance to find out. Sartorially inspired and on a natural high due to the prospect of entering The Monastery empire at a high level, Lucas spotted a pretty young girl dancing on a small podium a few metres away.

As he walked closer, he started to mimic her moves, until he stood directly in front of her. The girl tried to avoid eye contact, as Lucas got carried away in an exaggerated and barely-in-time parody of her dancing.

The girl had waited for ages to be able to find a spot on the podium, so she was not about to relinquish it just because some embarrassing old bloke had chosen to hit on her. Lucas misinterpreted her stoicism as a come-on. He tugged at her arm so that she had no choice but to bend down and hear what he had to say.

'I've just got to go for a meeting with Charles Moon. He's the owner,' slimed Lucas. 'Do you want to go somewhere a little quieter when I get back?'

The girl looked at him incredulously. 'No thanks.'

This confused Lucas. He had listened to countless stories told by his Lothario reps, where they had simply danced with a girl and ended up getting a shag. Perhaps more physical contact was needed? After all, ecstasy did heighten the senses and the girl had to be on something to be dancing on a podium, he reasoned.

He ran his hands up her legs, over the outline of her hips and onto her exposed midriff. The girl was initially too surprised to react. Encouraged, Lucas let his spindly fingers trace a line over her backside and up her inner thigh.

'Oi, piss off, you fucking nonce case!' yelled the girl, pushing him away, her accent indicating that the cab fare from the East End venue would still see her with change from a fiver.

Lucas was startled. 'What's up?'

'What do you think you're playing at?'

'I thought—'

'You thought what?'

Lucas wasn't used to being spoken to such a way. 'Do you know who I am?'

The girl looked him up and down, then turned to her friend. 'Do you know who he is?'

The friend considered the question for a few moments, then nodded. 'Yeah, yeah. I recognise him.'

Lucas smiled. He was surprised because most of the programmes that he had been interviewed on were daytime or cable. He was hardly a household face, but he had always known there must be something memorable about his appearance.

'Yeah,' continued the girl, 'it's him, innit? It's the ... Raver. The Raver from the Grave!'

The two girls and several friends all started laughing.

Lucas glared at them, flustered by their taunts, then turned on his heel in a fit of pique. As he did so, he accidentally barged into one of their friends and sent a handful of pills flying across the floor.

The small group were aghast and set about retrieving them, Lucas's presence immediately inconsequential. The two girls even jumped down from their precious podium spot to assist in the search.

Lucas spotted three of the pills a couple of paces away.

'Oh look,' he pointed, feigning enthusiasm, 'there they are.'

Before the young lad who Lucas had bumped into could get to them, Lucas stepped forward and stood on the E's, narrowly missing the end of the boy's grasping fingers. Holding the gaze of the two girls, he ground them under his shoe.

'You bastard,' said the dancer.

Lucas gave her a satisfied look. 'Don't worry, there's still a few scattered around. You'll just have to get down on your knees – I'm sure you spend a lot of time on them anyway.'

With that, he strode off to catch up with Hawthorne-Blythe and the bouncer, who had both reached the bar and were now looking back for him. Lucas passed through the happy clubbers with contempt, deliberately barging into them until he reached the sanctuary of the bar.

'Just to let you know,' said Lucas, running his hands over his hair to make sure his ponytail was in place, 'there's a girl by the podium selling drugs.'

'Which one?' asked the bouncer.

'She's wearing white trousers and a small red top.'

The bouncer made to walk over. Lucas grabbed his arm.

'She'll still be there in five minutes. If it's all the same with you, I'd rather you got me out of this hell-hole and into the office.'

Had Charles Moon not been so engrossed in the paperwork on his desk, he would have probably noticed Tyrone Lucas's antics. Every part of the club was visible to him via the bank of monitors on the facing wall.

Tonight though, the meeting that would to all intents and purposes be the beginning of The Monastery's foray into the Ibiza holiday market, took precedence. Making sure that bar staff didn't have their hands in the till or that dealers weren't plying their trade too blatantly had been relegated in Moon's priorities.

He flicked between three flat screen monitors on his vast desk, one containing information on the proposed venture, the other two keeping an eye on the just opened Far East markets.

Charles Moon had spent a few years working for an investment bank and since then he had continued to have more than a passing interest in the financial markets. Even when he was engrossed in another topic, he was still able to make decisions that could win or lose him hundreds of thousands of pounds. Being so intelligent, he had an extremely low boredom threshold and a need to multi-task, which was probably why The Monastery had diversified so much.

Charles Moon's right-hand man was huddled over some paperwork in the room with him. Kevin Kitchener was a style guru, known by everyone as Kit ('Kev' didn't have the same ring to it at St Martin's). As a teenager and while still at Art College, Kit had seen the business potential of the rave scene. Through a mutual friend, he had met Moon and suggested taking raves from fields and warehouses, and putting them into a more traditional environment. Moon recognised in Kit a natural instinct for spotting trends and for understanding what was or wasn't cool. Trusting Kit's judgement totally, Moon had put together a sound but daring business proposal, and got some backing from friends and city contacts. He pulled together every penny he could lay his hands on and thus The Monastery was born.

Although it was undoubtedly Moon's business flair and greater vision that turned what started as a successful club into a worldwide brand, he always ran ideas by Kit. Under Moon's influence, Kit had made the gradual metamorphosis into an astute businessman. Equally, he had not lost his street savvy and several of The Monastery's successful ventures were Kit's brainchildren.

Getting into the Ibiza youth travel market was his latest.

In the corner of the large office was an L-shaped brown sofa. All four men sat down. Moon often preferred to conduct meetings from this, rather than from behind his desk. This was especially the case when he wanted something – he felt removing the physical barrier helped remove psychological and business ones too.

As always, Moon took control of the conversation. Kit sat, listened and observed. After niceties, Moon reiterated The Monastery's plan. He ran through their motivation for entering the youth travel market, together with some forecasts and goals. Finally, he came on to exactly how he was going to make his choice.

'Three weeks. We've discussed things and we feel that should be enough time for Kit, one or two unannounced observers and myself to spend on resort, monitoring things and to make our decision. At the end of those three weeks in June we will get the resort managers of both companies to do a final presentation to us all, after which we shall announce which of you we have chosen to go into business with.' Moon paused, allowing his comment to register.

'Christ, that's a lot earlier than I thought,' exclaimed a surprised Hawthorne-Blythe. 'I thought you planned to wait until the end of the season.'

Moon shook his head. 'I want to get this tied up as quickly as possible. The clubbing season really gets going in July and I want to be up and running by then. We need to know that whoever we choose will be able to adapt with the minimum of fuss.'

'You already know that Club Wicked is . . .' Lucas searched for the right word, '. . . *down* with the whole club thing. We were probably the pioneers, after all.'

'Yes, we're aware of your orientation towards clubbing,' agreed Moon. He noticed a slight expression of defeat sweep across Hawthorne-Blythe's face. 'However, as I said to H-B on the phone, it's not so much about where your respective companies are now, more where you'll be with our input this time next year.'

Hawthorne-Blythe couldn't suppress his disillusionment. 'By the sound of it, where Young Free & Single are going to be is out of business.'

Moon and Kit shared a look. Lucas barely contained a smirk.

'H-B, that's not the case at all,' said Moon. 'I'll readily admit that, on the face of it at least, Club Wicked are more aligned to our way of thinking at the moment. But we'll be looking at professionalism, infrastructure, flexibility, efficiency, profitability, market knowledge and a host of other things. They'll all go into the melting pot when we make up our minds.'

Hawthorne-Blythe nodded. 'OK, Charles, I said I'd take you at your word and I do. However, one thing you haven't discussed is the reps. What happens to the poor blighters who find themselves on the losing side? Many will have given up a lot to work for us,' Hawthorne-Blythe corrected himself, 'or Club Wicked, should they lose.'

Moon stood up. 'My plan is to run both companies for just this season under The Monastery umbrella, from July.'

'What? How on earth can that happen?' protested Hawthorne-Blythe. 'If it is Young Free & Single who lose, then what possible motivation will there be for us to carry on?'

'I'm sorry, H-B, but the losing company will have to stand on their own two feet and obviously, they will then become our rivals. And you are absolutely right, morale will be low and we fully expect the loser to go out of business. It sounds harsh, but . . . well, it goes with the territory. As I indicated, it is more or less a winner takes all situation. I did make that clear, didn't I, H-B?'

'Yes, yes, Charles, you did,' sighed H-B. 'It just sounds particularly final when you say it like that. Anyway, back to my original question – what about the reps?'

'Well, obviously, if the loser keeps going then the reps will have jobs for as long as that company stays in business. If the loser throws in the towel, then our demand will probably increase and we may need some new reps. If there are already trained reps on resort then I daresay we'd use them.'

'But you can't make them any guarantees?'

'Sorry, H-B, no.'

Hawthorne-Blythe sighed. 'It all seems so unfair.'

'It's called progress, dear boy,' said Lucas, raising his eyebrows to Moon and Kit, as though he was already part of their exclusive gang. They ignored the look.

Moon sat on the arm of the sofa, next to Hawthorne-Blythe. 'H-B, I can't claim to enjoy this, but I'm a businessman. I would like to think, however, that I'm an ethical businessman. I will always do primarily what's best for my company, but I also believe in giving the best service possible. All I can promise is that I'll give total commitment to this project and will do nothing to lower the standard of holidays offered – quite the reverse in fact.'

Hawthorne-Blythe gave a small nod and there was a moment of silence. Moon and Kit both stood up.

'Right then, gentleman,' said Moon, slapping his hands together, 'are there any other questions? Good. I'll arrange to get some papers drawn up, ready for when I get back from Australia.'

Lucas swigged back his drink and jumped up smiling. Hawthorne-Blythe rose more leisurely, still with a defeated look about him.

'It's a shame it's come to this,' he sighed. 'Tell me, Charles, how did it all happen? How did Ibiza change so much in such a relatively short period?'

Charles Moon put an arm round Hawthorne-Blythe's shoulder. 'Do you know, the irony is that it was you who probably helped to start this whole acid house, rave culture?'

Tyrone Lucas looked at Moon as though he'd gone mad. 'How on earth can you say that someone like *him* started all of this?'

Moon smiled. 'It's common knowledge that a group of London DJs went on holiday to Ibiza in the late eighties, discovered ecstasy, house music and a new way of clubbing, then brought it back to the UK. What isn't such common knowledge is that I'm pretty certain they originally all went over there on a Young Free & Single holiday.'

Lucas was outraged. 'Never!'

'I think you'll find he's right,' said Kit.

'Great, so it's my fault,' exclaimed Hawthorne-Blythe.

Moon laughed. 'Maybe we're in the presence of the very person who inadvertently kick-started the whole Chemical Generation – now there's a thought.'

'Kick-started it and now the bloody thing looks set to run me over,' said Hawthorne-Blythe wryly. 'Whatever happened to holidays where all people wanted was a beach party, a barbeque and a good old singalong, eh?'

Moon paused at the door. 'Kids don't want to go to a barbeque and hear some old fart playing guitar and singing songs from *Grease*. Ibiza is the new Mecca, clubs are the new temples and DJs the new messiahs.'

'Come back, Gary Davies and DLT, all is forgiven,' said Hawthorne-Blythe.

Moon opened the door, where a bouncer was already waiting to escort Hawthorne-Blythe and Lucas back through the club. 'You must realise that in the long-term this was inevitable. If I hadn't done it, some other superclub would have given it a go.' Moon shook hands with them both. 'Thank you both for fitting your schedule around me. I'll arrange another meeting for the week after next. Obviously, you must say nothing to any of the reps or resort managers. What I propose is that we make an announcement to all of the Ibiza reps when we arrive in June. If you've any questions, contact my secretary and she'll give you a number you can get me on in Australia, or alternatively my email address.'

They left the room. Moon and Kit watched the pair in the monitors for a few moments as they jostled through the crowd.

'Well, Kit, what do you think?'

Kit took two watermelon Bacardi Breezers from a small fridge by the leather sofa, opened them and handed one to Moon.

'H-B's a great old boy. Genuine and he really cares.'

'Maybe that's part of the problem, Kit – he cares too much.'

'I can think of worse problems.'

'What about Tyrone Lucas?'

'He's nobody's fool but he's driven by different motives. You can tell by the way he acts and dresses that there's still quite a big ego in there. He's more the kind of person you get in our game.'

'Yes, he does possess that whole music biz, up himself air. If he was half as smart as he thought he was, he'd be ten times smarter than he actually is. Still, the fact that he fits into our industry so well might be in his favour, perversely enough.'

Kit nodded. 'If you pushed me then I'd say that at this precise moment in time, Club Wicked would get my vote.'

'They'd probably get mine too. I'd rather do business with H-B than Lucas, but maybe H-B is just too entrenched in the past. I guess it will all come down to how the reps perform.'

week one

chapter eight

Vaz steadied himself on Greg's shoulders.

'OK,' said Vaz, 'just hold on tightly to my feet until I say the word, then let go and I'll do the rest.'

'All right, but hurry up. Your fucking feet are hurting where I've sunburnt the top of my back.'

There wasn't a lot of room for Vaz to make his jump on the terrace of the almost refurbished La Luna Café. The terrace itself was quite large but most of it was covered with a bamboo roof. A few of the tables and chairs were still in a pile and because of this there was a small clearing by the steps that led down to the beach. It was here that Vaz was about to perform his stunt, having been pressed into it by the entire YF&S crowd, who had been told about his circus past by Arabella. It was 13 June and the reps had been on resort for a couple of weeks already preparing for the arrival of their first clients. La Luna had been hired out exclusively by YF&S and Club Wicked as an important announcement was to be made, although the reps were more excited about the free bar. Consequently, they all turned up the best part of an hour before the scheduled 3 p.m. start.

The majority of Club Wicked reps were congregated round a table at the opposite end of the terrace. A couple of them turned round to look at Vaz; the rest were feigning disinterest.

'Right then,' said Vaz. 'On three. One, two, three . . .'

Vaz leapt from Greg's shoulders, getting in a somersault and half twist before landing perfectly. There was a ripple of applause and Vaz gave a slightly embarrassed bow. Arabella looked disappointed that he had not fallen flat on his face.

'That was great,' complimented Tamsin, still clapping. 'How long did you say you were in the circus?'

'Pretty much all my life.'

'Can you do any other tricks?'

'You used to juggle with firesticks, didn't you, Vaz?' drawled Arabella, who was filing her nails. Vaz shot her an angry look.

'Did you really, Vaz?' asked Tamsin, her liquid brown eyes looking at him with genuine interest.

Tamsin was still finding it hard to believe she was actually an Ibiza rep. As such, everything she saw, everyone she met, every new experience, were all approached with a sense of wonder and enthusiasm. It was a naïve innocence yet to be sullied by a single iota of cynicism. With the first clients arriving that weekend, it was unlikely to last.

'I haven't done anything with fire for a long time, Tamsin,' replied Vaz, glaring again at Arabella.

Greg slapped Vaz on the back, saving him from further interrogation. 'Mate, that was brilliant. The reps' cabaret needs you. I don't think we've done anything new for years.' He looked round the terrace. 'Where's the other new boy?'

'Scottish Hughie? Last time I saw him was in the bar,' offered Tamsin.

'Sounds like he's got the right idea to me. This meeting's going to start soon so best we get some bevvies down our necks.' Greg still had his arm round Vaz's shoulder. 'Didn't you say you wanted to spin some tunes?'

'Dying to,' said Vaz. 'I haven't had a record in my hands for two weeks – I'm getting withdrawal symptoms. Shouldn't we speak to the owner first though?'

Greg started laughing. 'You've got no worries there. The guy who's just bought this bar used to work with me and Brad as a YF&S rep last year. In fact,' Greg pointed to a muscular black guy with steel-framed glasses, who was struggling to unload some bags from the back of a dirty green Fiat Punto, 'here he is now.' Greg yelled over to him.

'Oi, Mikey, you don't mind if old Vaz here spins a few tunes, do you?'

Mikey had his car keys in his mouth and raised a hand to answer in the affirmative.

'Mikey,' said Vaz nodding. 'Yeah, I've heard of him. He was involved in all that shit that went down with the resort manager last year – Alison, wasn't it?'

'We were all involved, one way or another,' said Greg, taking his arm from Vaz's shoulder and picking up his nearly finished beer.

'Why, what happened?' asked Tamsin.

'It's a long story, but in a nutshell Alison was ripping the company off and didn't give a fuck about any of her reps. Halfway through the season she made it look as though Brad had stolen a load of excursion money, so got him the sack. The company was on to her but couldn't help Brad in case they alerted her. Brad came back to Ibiza and got a job on the beach party and once it all came out he was re-employed. Actually, Brad helped to save the company shit loads of money and that's one of the reasons they've trusted him to be resort manager this year. Anyway, Brad and Mikey were pretty close, so Alison had it in for Mikey too. In fact, she had it in for virtually everyone, apart from this tosser called Mario.'

'Who was he?' asked Sugar Ray, another first year rep, in his slightly effeminate Norfolk brogue.

'He worked for YF&S last year. You would have liked him, Sugar,' teased Greg. 'Ex-male model. Typical Italian Stallion but thick as two short planks. Thought he was God's gift.'

'He was,' sighed Arabella, absent-mindedly thinking aloud before realising all the other reps were looking at her. 'Oh, um, I was a YF&S client here on holiday last summer and Mario was my rep. Obviously, I didn't know what he was *really* like then, but it was the start of the season and he seemed . . . OK to me.'

'So what, was he a bit of all right then, this Mario?' giggled Tamsin.

'He was good-looking if you like that kind of thing but he

was a total knob,' said Greg, before Arabella had a chance to reply.

'How did Mikey end up getting this bar?' asked Vaz.

'He was never that passionate about being a rep – he just drifted into it after he got injured playing American Football – he was one of the top players in the UK. About halfway through the season he fell head over heels with a client, Patricia, and they decided to stay in Ibiza once the season finished. Then during the winter, this bar came up, so they put an offer in.' Greg looked over at Mikey, watching him pick up the toilet roll, but then drop another bag with loaves of bread in it that had been tucked under his chin. 'He looks like a clumsy lummox over there now, but don't let appearances fool you. Mikey susses people out quicker than anyone I know.'

'Is it normal to have a joint party with Club Wicked at the start of every season?' asked Tamsin.

'Fuck no. I mean, we generally know the Club Wicked reps, say hello to them when we're out and all that, but there's always been a bit of rivalry between us and it's not always friendly.'

'So why are we all here?'

'I haven't got a clue. This is the first time we've ever had a meeting like this. We normally keep ourselves to ourselves. Maybe it's to try and make the working environment a bit friendlier.'

Greg finished off his drink then looked over to the table where the Club Wicked reps were sat in their trendy all-black uniforms. One, a girl with spiky blonde hair stood up and walked into the bar, glancing at Greg and smiling. Her Club Wicked T-shirt had been cut in a small V at the front, an action that probably had more to do with necessity than fashion.

'And I tell you what,' he murmured, 'if they've all got tits like her then I'm all for us getting even friendlier. Come on, let's go inside and get a few more drinks in before this meeting starts.'

'It's a bit bloody quiet,' moaned Lucas.

'I thought it would be a nice place to have lunch before the meeting,' replied Hawthorne-Blythe. 'It's more or less on the way and I thought you might like to sample a more tranquil part of the island.'

Lucas snorted and returned to sending a text from his mobile.

'I think it's very nice,' said Charles Moon, pulling his Oliver People sunglasses over his eyes from his forehead. He slid down in his chair and tilted his head towards the sun.

Kit emerged from a small antique shop, which was part of the bar they were sitting outside. 'There's some great stuff in there,' he said, squinting as his eyes adjusted to the bright sunlight. 'What's this place called again?'

'The bar is called Casi Todo,' answered Hawthorne-Blythe, 'but the village is Santa Getrudes.'

'Santa Getrudes,' said Kit. 'I'll have to remember that. What a crazy place – bar, antique shop and auction house all in one. I'll probably come back and have some stuff shipped over to the UK.'

'Antiques?' said Hawthorne-Blythe, a little surprised. 'I must say, Kit that I always imagined you living in one of these modern loft-type places, or perhaps somewhere minimalist, with some well chosen modern art and classic retro furniture.' He pointed to Kit's expensive looking camera on the table. 'I would have expected your place to be stacked with hi-tech gear and loads of gadgets.'

'Not me, H-B,' replied Kit sitting down. 'I haven't got a bloody clue how to operate that camera. We bought it on the way out here. In fact, we were going to get you and Lucas to give it to the reps to take some pictures. When we do the brochure we want it to look like a clubbing magazine, you know, photos taken in clubs on the dance floor and all that. The reps will be in the thick of it so we were hoping they would be able to get some action shots. As for the City loft, I'm sorry to disappoint you but it's a three-storey Victorian house in Islington, crammed with antiques.' He reached over to the half full wine bottle. 'Top you up?'

Hawthorne-Blythe nodded. Kit poured some red wine into all of their glasses and they briefly toasted each other.

The bar was situated at one end of the short road. At the other end was a square, which doubled up as both a parking area and a forecourt for the old village church. The church had a bell tower and in a vaguely accurate manner, the bell would gently rock from side to side to announce the hour. Not that time was a concern to the majority of those enjoying the glorious June afternoon, as they sat along the half a dozen or so bars that made up the small main village road.

As well as a few tourists, a bohemian menagerie of locals and European ex-pats languished at the tables, drinking or skinning up. Many had dogs, which for the most part would be calmly sat between the stools or under their owners' legs. Occasionally, one would give a little bark, to indicate their boredom or perhaps to let their owners know that they had not become passively stoned (although half of them probably had). Once one dog made its presence known, a short canine chorus would ensue, quickly followed by a rebuke in German, Dutch, French, English or Spanish.

Kit looked at his watch. 'Guess we should be putting the wax on the tracks in a minute, guys and get going.' H-B nodded but Lucas was still engrossed in sending a text message. 'I can never be bothered with sending texts,' said Kit. 'I'd rather just ring.'

Lucas pressed the send button and looked up. 'Ringing costs a fortune. I'm trying to get in touch with an English mobile. Far better if I get them to call me.'

'Oh come on, Tyrone,' said Hawthorne-Blythe, 'you're not exactly in the poor house, are you?'

'Look after the pennies and the pounds will look after themselves. It's one of the golden rules of business,' replied Lucas, giving a 'doesn't-he-know-anything?' look to Kit.

Kit ignored it and caught the eye of the waitress. 'The bill, please.'

Charles Moon stood up. 'Don't worry, I'll get this. I'm just going to the loo then we'll jump in one of those taxis in the square up there and head for La Luna Café to announce to our troops what's going on.'

He disappeared into the bar. Lucas returned to his texting, cursing at his phone to bloody well ring. Hawthorne-Blythe and Kit finished off the last drop of wine.

'So, do you like Santa Getrudes, Kit?'

'Love it, H-B. Give me the real Ibiza any day.'

'You would have liked it even more a few years ago. I don't suppose one could really call this the real Ibiza any more – it's far too trendy. When I first came here with my wife back in the early eighties, there wasn't even a tarmac road here – just a dirt track. There's a Wild West excursion up the road that's been here donkey's years. The entertainers used to be dressed as cowboys and they'd come down after the show and tether their horses outside the bar. It was almost like the Wild West. Now of course—'

'For Chrissakes!' yelled Lucas. *'Hello?'* He got up and walked out of earshot. 'About bloody time, where have you been? What do you mean friends? I didn't think you had any friends. All right, all right. Where are you now? So what time will you get there? Are you sure? Good. No, we're just leaving. Some shit-hole called Santa something or other. Just make sure you're there. If you arrive before us, sit in the car for a while. I want you to make an entrance.' Lucas smiled. 'See you soon.'

Lucas got back to the table just as the others were standing to leave.

'You seem a little chirpier,' remarked Kit.

'Yes,' said Lucas slapping his hands together, 'I'm on top of the world. Shall we get this show on the road then?'

With that, he bounded off, leading the way to the taxi rank with a spring in his step. Hawthorne-Blythe watched him, feeling slightly uneasy. He knew through experience that when Tyrone Lucas was happy it meant only one thing.

Trouble.

Back at La Luna Café, Vaz finished executing another perfect mix. He was so happy, lost in his own little world he hadn't seen Mikey watching him. As he was delving into his record bag, Mikey tapped him on the shoulder.

'You been DJing long?'

Vaz stopped going through his records and stood up. 'Hi. You're Mikey, aren't you? I've heard a lot about you. My name's Vaz.'

Mikey looked at Vaz's name tag. 'Yeah, I know. That's the thing with badges, always a bit of a give-away.'

Vaz looked down at his badge and back up at Mikey's deadpan face. Had he got off on the wrong foot? 'Sorry . . . yeah, of course . . . if you don't like . . .'

Mikey's face broke into a smile. 'I think your DJing's wicked, better than any rep I've ever heard actually. A lot of reps think they can DJ but all they can do is just about mix a couple of records together. You've got a real feel, a real flair for it.'

'Cheers,' said Vaz, relaxing.

Mikey looked round and offered Vaz a spliff. 'Do you want to toke on this? It's all right, none of the big bosses are around.'

Vaz looked uneasy. 'Is this some kind of test? I mean, I know you're good friends with Brad and all that, but he is my boss.'

Mikey laughed. 'I was as paranoid as you when I first started working for Young Free & Single last year. No, it's not a test and as for Brad, well, he smokes nearly as much of this stuff as I do. Still, if it makes you feel any better, duck down behind the DJ stand and do it.'

Vaz crouched down and quickly inhaled a couple of lungfuls of smoke, before passing the spliff back to Mikey.

Mikey spent a few more moments looking at Vaz. 'You've

got a different attitude to the other reps, not running round like a headless chicken. You've got a different agenda.'

'What do you mean?' asked Vaz. Mikey was close to Brad and was well respected by everyone. The last thing he wanted was for Mikey to think he was in some way not up to the job.

Mikey smiled and rested his hand on Vaz's shoulder. 'Relax, man. What I'm saying is that I'd put money on you having the same kind of attitude to the job as I had when I did it. You're not brainwashed by all the bullshit. Of course, what nobody knew about me was that the reason I was able to take a step back from the job and see it for what it was, was that I always planned to try and get a bar out here.'

'And now you've done it,' said Vaz, looking round. 'It's a nice place – should do well.'

'Cheers.' Mikey paused for a moment. 'You'll do it too, Vaz.'

'Do what? I don't want a bar – far too much like hard work.'

Mikey ignored him and continued. 'You're a laid-back individual with a bit of spirit and you're not sucked in by all of the ra-ra-ra stuff they chuck at you. Like I said, you're not brainwashed.'

Vaz bent down to go through his record bag, not sure where this was leading. 'We're only working as holiday reps. It's not like we're in MI5 or the SAS, is it?' He laughed, keen to lighten the conversation.

Mikey stubbed out the joint in an ashtray. 'What I'm saying to you, Vaz, is being a rep is just a job. It's easy to get swept up in it all if you start believing your own press. Never forget that the only reason you're so popular most of the time is because you're in charge of a load of people with money in their pocket to spend in bars and clubs.'

'I guess you're right.' He cued up the record. 'Mikey, don't take this the wrong way, but why are you telling me this?'

'When I came over here last year all I wanted was get my own little bar – the repping was just a means to that end.

But the job can fuck with your head and I almost lost sight of that. I could have so easily jacked everything in and gone home.' Mikey grinned and tapped his nose. 'Don't worry, I won't tell anyone. Just remember that when it's time and you need help, I'm in a position to offer it.'

Vaz pushed a headphone to his ear and started mixing the record. 'Mikey, I know you mean well, but I've no intention of getting a bar out here.'

Mikey walked away smiling. Vaz almost screwed the mix. He'd only been doing the job five minutes – had he really made his hidden agenda that obvious?

'You are *so* naughty.'

Mel let Greg sprinkle some more cocaine onto a perfectly manicured fingernail, then tossed her head back as she sniffed.

The breasts stretching the material of the Club Wicked T-shirt had proved too much for Greg and, rival or not, he had followed her into the bar. Quickly realising that Mel wasn't the sharpest eyeliner pencil in the case, he had challenged her to an inter-company drinking contest to knock back three vodka lime chupitos in succession. Unless the plant in the corner of the bar had a high alcohol tolerance, it was likely to be dead soon, as that was where Greg's drinks ended up when he threw them over his shoulder.

With Mel's defences weakened, he had persuaded her – if saying, 'Do you fancy a sniff' could be defined as persuading – to do a line out the back of the bar. Now on to her third, Greg was beginning to realise her resistance to cocaine was far higher than her resistance to alcohol. He'd suggested another drink but was dismayed when Mel said, 'It's weird, when I take Charlie I don't want alcohol. All I want is a coke. Coke wiv me coke!'

Even though it was clear this was a 'joke' Mel had told countless times before, she didn't seem to find it any less amusing. Not only did she have a piercingly loud cackle but also emitted small piggy-sounding snorts.

The cocaine had made her more talkative. When Greg first started a conversation with her, she hadn't said much, preferring to give flirty looks and cute smiles. Greg had found this very sexy and assumed her quietness to be an enigmatic quality that suggested perception and intellect.

However, as soon as she opened her mouth and the slow Bexleyheath drawl lumbered out, it became clear that it was more to do with having nothing to say.

In the brief time they had been talking, Mel had warmed to a couple of themes. She claimed to read a lot and have a spiritual side. When questioned, these two claims were restricted to having read *The Celestine Prophecy*. Well, half of it. She'd told Greg that one of the main reasons she had wanted to work in Ibiza was that it was 'a right spiritual place, innit?'

Never a man to let conversation stand in the way of a fine pair of breasts, Greg had nodded at the right places and kept the cocaine and conversation flowing, checking his watch as three o'clock and the start of the meeting got ever closer. There wasn't really enough time for a proper shag, so he'd decided to go for the slippery tit-wank, reasoning that it shouldn't take too long and that he could have a proper go another time.

However, Mel had moved on to another topic, which she had warmed to even more – Tyrone Lucas. One area where Mel clearly did have a reasonable degree of perception was men.

'Yeah, slimy git that Lucas. I knew as soon as 'is beady little eyes were running up and down me body that 'e fought 'e was going to shag me. Finks 'e's still in wiv a chance . . . as if! I reckon that's the only reason 'e gave me the bleedin' job in the first place. Come on then, mate, knock anuvver line out.'

'Yeah, look, let's go in that storeroom in case anyone sees us. It's getting a bit close to three o'clock and one of the big cheeses might catch us and we don't want that, do we?'

'I know what you want!' Mel started cackling again. 'I ain't saying no never, cos you're all right, but you ain't going to shag me in no broom cupboard, if that's what you're finking.'

'Don't be silly,' replied Greg, disappointed, but buoyed up by the fact that she seemed to be giving the green light to a future liaison. 'I wouldn't insult you by trying to shag you in there – I don't do quickies.'

'Oooh, ark at you.'

'I wouldn't mind a slippery tit-wank though.'

'Oi!' Mel started cackling and snorting again. She grabbed hold of Greg's hand. 'Come on then, we'll do a quick line, 'ave this meeting then we'll see what 'appens.'

As they approached the door to the small storeroom, they could hear a banging noise from inside. Above the door was a glass panel, so Greg pulled over some crates to stand on and see what was going on. As he did so, Mel searched the main road outside the bar.

'Shit, we'll 'ave to leave this line to anuvver time. Old silly bollock Lucas's outside wiv free uvver geezers.'

Greg stopped moving the crates and looked towards the road, where the four men were getting out of a taxi.

'One of the others is our chairman, Adam Hawthorne-Blythe. Looks like this meeting is about to start.'

'Do you know what it's all about then? No one ain't told us nuffink.'

'I've got about as much idea as you,' replied Greg, shrugging.

'We don't even know who our resort manager is. We've just been told it's a surprise.'

'Well, if you like surprises, I might come up with one for you a bit later.'

Mel giggled. 'We'll see.' She kissed Greg softly on the lips, letting a breast brush against his forearm. As she skipped off back to the bar, Greg grabbed hold of his crotch and let out a little moan.

Still curious to know about the noise in the storeroom, he climbed on top of the crates. The sight he was greeted with almost made him fall straight back off. Scottish Hughie had not been around for over half an hour – now he knew why.

Bent over a worktop, with her uniform pulled over her waist, was a Spanish woman Greg had seen cleaning the bar. The reason he remembered her was that Hughie had been talking to her and making her laugh, something he found difficult to understand as Hughie spoke hardly any Spanish and, he assumed, the cleaner no English.

It was only a few moments before Hughie looked up and noticed Greg. Greg was impressed that it didn't put him off his stroke. He was less impressed with the cleaner, who was barely five foot, weighed at least fourteen stone and was probably out of the age range that would have enabled her to come on a YF&S holiday.

Greg pointed to his watch and managed to convey to Hughie that the meeting was about to start. He got down, pulled the crates away and went to wait for Hughie at the end of the corridor.

A few minutes later, a beaming Hughie emerged, a little dishevelled, but otherwise reasonably presentable. Greg just looked at him, shaking his head.

'Not bad going, eh?' said Hughie, picking up a tea towel from another pile of crates and wiping it over his face.

'How about quality rather than quantity?'

'Ah, now by quantity, do you mean the number or the size of the girls?'

'Both.'

'Well, I think that's where you and I differ, young Gregory. You see, this wee laddie has always had a bit of a penchant for the more ample woman. Not only that, but also for the kind of woman who probably would be more likely to grace the pages of an over-forties edition of *Readers' Wives*, than page three of one of yer Sassenach tabloids.'

'Fuck off, you're winding me up.'

'No, I kid you not. I do it not out of charity, but out of pure lust. This caber of mine would rather be tossed by the dumpy, calloused fingers of a seasoned sow, than those of a finely manicured minx.'

'For fuck's sake, Hughie, you're not at drama school any more.'

Hughie returned to his less theatrical brogue. 'I like old fat birds.'

It took a few moments for the comment to sink in. 'You what?'

Hughie shrugged. 'Don't ask me why. I'm sure a psychologist would have a field day, but I'd never go and see one because I'm happy as I am. I can't help myself. There's just something about fat women that I love. I'm not even interested in their faces, just that lovely, rolling, squidgy—'

'Yeah, all right!'

'And of course, the advantage is that the type of woman I am drawn to isn't used to getting the attention I pour on her, which makes the whole seduction process somewhat easier. That's also the reason why I'm going to win The Competition.'

'You what?' Greg was momentarily taken aback. 'How do you know about The Competition?'

'Are you joking? *Everyone* knows about The Competition. One point for a wank, two points for blow job, three points for a shag, four points if it goes up the balloon knot, eight points for a threesome and bonus points at the discretion of the Shag Master General, which over here is, of course, you.' Hughie recited the rules like verb tables.

'The *what*?'

'The Shag Master General. Someone came up with that one on the training course.'

'What do you mean?'

'Greg mate, you're a *legend*. All of the other resorts do The Competition now. Everyone knows that you've won it in Ibiza each year that you've been here. That's why this summer, every resort is calling The Golden Dick, The Greg.'

'Hang on. So what you're telling me is that every resort is doing The Competition, with the same rules, and at the end of it, they've all gone to the trouble to buy a big rubber dick from a sex shop, spray it gold and have it mounted?'

'That's right!' nodded Hughie enthusiastically.

'And that this Golden Dick is now known as The Greg?'

'Great, eh?'

'Mmm.' Greg dwelled on this new piece of information for a moment. 'I'm not sure if I like the idea of being known as a dick.'

'Are you joking? It's an honour, mate. Everyone knows who you are.'

When Greg had first started repping, he had assumed that any girl who wanted to be with him once they knew of his reputation, wanted to because they thought they were going to be the one to change him. However, by implication, this pre-supposed that they wanted a long-term relationship, which more often than not, was not the case.

Three seasons earlier Greg had learned an important lesson. He became good friends with two props who worked in the heart of the West End called Toby and Ace. They were good-looking lads with bundles of chat, so consequently shagged themselves senseless. Ace went through one hundred and five girls in that season, including six in one night, a San Antonio record.

A few of Greg's fellow reps were jealous of their success, so when they had to take their clients into the West End following an excursion, they would get on the coach microphone and warn the girls about Toby and Ace, telling them exactly what they were like.

After a few weeks, Ace pulled Greg to one side. 'Listen Greg, we just wanted to thank you. I don't know if it was your idea, but girls who are on holiday with Young Free & Single keep asking us if we're the two guys the reps have warned us about, the ones who do all the shagging. I tell you what, we've had more luck since the reps started doing that than we've ever had before. They just can't get enough of us. We've had threesomes, foursomes, swapsies, the fucking lot. It's great!'

Greg wasn't interested in the psychology or the social dynamics of why this was – he was just happy to have an additional weapon in his lady-killing arsenal. For the most part, the more he told the female holidaymakers that he was a total male slut, the more they wanted to find out for themselves.

So, if he was becoming known as the Shag Master General, experience told him he was in for some fun.

He pushed open the door to the main bar area looking for Mel. Before he could spot her, Brad came rushing over and grabbed his arm.

'Greg, quick mate, come over here.'

'What's up ?'

Brad dragged Greg through the small crowd towards the door. As Greg got closer, an athletically built Club Wicked rep with short dark hair who had his back to them was just finishing talking to Mikey. Mikey looked quite serious, but shook the rep's hand and nodded, before walking out of the bar onto the terrace.

Greg felt there was something familiar about the rep, confirmed as soon as he turned towards them.

Greg couldn't believe his eyes.

'Mario! What the fuck are you doing here?'

Sarcastically, Mario looked at his badge and read it monosyllabically. 'Ma-ri-o. Club Wic-ked.' He looked at Greg and Brad with a satisfied smirk. 'I got a phone call from Tyrone Lucas. He told me about ... oh no, they haven't made the announcement yet, have they?'

'What do you mean?' asked Brad.

'Oh, don't you know? I thought you were resort manager this year.' Mario laughed. 'You'll find out in a minute with all of the other reps.'

'I can't believe you've got the audacity to show your face after last year,' said Greg. 'I doubt if Mikey's too pleased.'

'Mikey and I have come to an understanding.'

'What's that, you understand that if you step out of line, he'll flatten you?'

Greg and Brad laughed. For a moment Mario appeared to lose his cool, then composed himself as he realised he was playing into their hands. 'Mikey now knows that it wouldn't be a very good idea to threaten me. Let's just say that things have changed a little since last year.'

90

'Don't tell me you've been watching those old Teenage Mutant Ninja Turtle films,' said Brad. He made a few karate chop motions. 'Been learning a few moves, have you?'

Mario smiled. 'Things are about to change more than you realise and neither of you have got a fucking clue.'

'Let's assume nothing,' said Brad. 'Maybe Mario's the surprise resort manager they've been talking about.'

Mario's smile grew broader as he looked over their shoulders to the entrance door. 'Good old Brad, smart as ever. Of course, you're absolutely right. I'm not the new manager.' He gestured at the door. '*She* is.'

Greg and Brad turned. The bright sunlight initially made it impossible to tell anything about the person, other than the shape was female, standing with one hand on her hip, blowing a plume of smoke into the air.

As she stepped into the room and became more visible, the smiles instantly fell from Greg and Brad's faces.

Mario put his arm around her shoulder.

'I believe you know our new resort manager . . . Alison Shand?'

chapter nine

The reps spilled out of the bar and split into their respective groups, the Club Wicked reps filing onto a waiting coach. The mood in both camps was of shock and surprise. The former shrillness of pre-season excitement had been replaced by the worried murmur of uncertainty, as pairs or trios of reps broke off to discuss the implications of the announcement made by Charles Moon during the just finished meeting.

Brad and Mikey were standing away from everyone else on the terrace. Mario and Alison sauntered over looking very pleased with themselves.

'Just like old times, eh Brad?' Alison chided. 'Mind you, I don't suppose you know much about old times, seeing as you've never even completed a full season. I must say, I was more than a little surprised when I found out they'd made you manager. I understand that most of the good reps – sorry, I mean *experienced* reps – have joined Club Wicked. Apparently quite a few of them left when they heard how badly I'd been treated.'

'That's bullshit, Alison, and you know it. Only a few have joined Club Wicked. Most left because all of the fiddling that used to go on has been stopped, and the reason it's been stopped is because you were so greedy last year that it all came out into the open. So, I very much doubt if any of them give a toss about you. If anything I would guess that most of them would like to have seen you end up in jail with your partner in crime . . . how is Felipe, by the way? What about his wife, do you see much of her?'

Alison didn't even flinch. 'Felipe? He's a loser, always

was, always will be. I didn't care about him last year and I care even less about him now. The only thing I do care about is making sure that Club Wicked win this little battle so you lot can all collect your P45s.'

'Battle? I thought Charles Moon said that we should just do our jobs as normal. That we should even help each other if needs be. I take it you won't be following his advice then?'

Alison moved closer. 'Make no mistake, Bradley Streeter. This is a battle all right and this time it's a battle I'm going to win. Oh yes, you might well have been the blue-eyed boy last year and you may have a badge on that says you're a resort manager, but I've had the best part of seven years at this job.'

'Yeah, but where we differ is that you think you've got a monopoly on being right. That's why you were such a crap manager last year – you don't know how to get the most out of your *team*. And I've got Greg.'

'Greg? Ha! If you're relying on him, then Club Wicked have got nothing to worry about.' She pointed at Greg who was round the back of the Club Wicked coach, clearly flirting with Mel. 'He only cares about one thing. Why do you think he's never been made a manager? Mention the word responsibility to him and he'll run a mile. Believe me, I'm *glad* you've got Greg working with you – it'll make our winning even easier.'

She turned her attention to Mikey.

'You're very quiet. Bit of a change from last year, isn't it? We couldn't shut you up then. What's up, cat got your tongue? Or is it more a case of the bank having you by the bollocks? That's right, Mikey, I've done my research. You've had to borrow up to the hilt to get this bar. All of your figures to stay in business are based on Club Wicked and Young Free & Single coming in here.' Mikey's look of unease confirmed that Alison had scored a direct hit. 'I was going to tell Tyrone Lucas not to use this bar, but I thought, no, why be bloody-minded? Apart from that of course, it's nice to have a bit of security, an insurance policy so you don't go sticking your nose in again, or feel inclined to have another "go" at Mario.'

'If I was going to have another go at Mario then I would have done it ages ago.' The hint of a smile played across Mikey's lips. 'How about you, Alison – have you had another go at Mario.'

Mario looked uncomfortable. Alison was unamused. Brad burst out laughing.

'Yeah, that's one thing I don't understand, Alison. How come you two are such good friends again? I thought old Mario here would be the last person you'd want to see after he secretly filmed the two of you at it last year.'

Mario stepped forward. 'If you hadn't nicked the tape and showed it to a room full of people, nobody would have known.'

'Oh Mario, I'm hurt that you thought I did that on purpose,' replied Brad. 'It was a genuine mistake. I just put the wrong video into the machine. Admittedly, it was a shame that a couple of hundred clients, Alison's parents and her boyfriend were in the bar expecting to see the beach party video when it came on. And I suppose it was an even bigger shame that it was the bit when she was on all fours begging you to shag her up the derrière. I just can't have been thinking straight. Maybe it was caused by her framing me and getting me the sack, while she was on the fiddle – must have made me a little absent-minded.' Brad and Mikey shared a smile.

'You'll be laughing on the other side of your faces after The Monastery's decision in three weeks' time,' snapped Alison. 'Once we've won and I'm in charge then I'll be in complete control of whether or not this bar succeeds. Just remember that. Also,' she pointed over to the coach, where a massive Club Wicked rep was standing, 'I've got an added bit of security. That six foot five and eighteen stone of Neanderthal over there is Stig, my deputy resort manger. He'd do anything for me.'

'Yeah, apart from cut his hair and have a wash, by the look of him,' said Mikey.

'I'll tell him you said that if you like.' Alison smirked. 'Right then boys, as much as I've enjoyed renewing our acquaintance, I've got a resort to run and a superclub to impress. If you get stuck on anything, Brad, well . . . Come on, Mario, let's go.'

Brad and Mikey watched them walk away.

'Lost none of her charm, has she, Brad?'

'I still can't believe the pair of them are here. And that Stig looks more like he should be in a WWF ring than guiding a coach. Still, the bigger they come and all that. I'd still put my money on you on a one to one.'

'It wouldn't be a very wise bet. Alison's right. I am up to my neck in it and I have based my whole business plan on Young Free & Single and Club Wicked using the bar. My hands are completely tied. This is a total nightmare.'

'It's only a nightmare if Club Wicked win, and we're going to make sure they don't, aren't we?' said Brad, trying to reassure.

They both looked over to the coach where Greg was still talking to Mel.

'I hate to say it, Brad, but you're going to need Greg this year, probably even more so now. Can you really see him changing?'

Brad shook his head. 'I honestly don't know. When he wants to be, Greg's the best rep I've ever seen. It's just that it's not often he wants to be.'

'The signs aren't too good, are they?'

Greg waved at Mel as the coach pulled away, then turned round and punched the air, mouthing, 'Yes!'

'Alison could be right,' muttered Brad. 'Greg might become a liability rather than an asset. He didn't really want to get involved when I found out she was fiddling last year, and that was before he got into clubbing and necking pills. If anything, he'll probably be even less concerned this year.' Brad sighed. 'From what I've heard of Tyrone Lucas, getting Alison and Mario back is the typical kind of stroke he'd pull. You could tell by the look on Adam Hawthorne-Blythe's face that he was as shocked as us to see them. I'd love to be a fly on the wall in the meeting they're all having now.'

Adam Hawthorne-Blythe sat at the table on the decked terrace of San Antonio's Club Nautic. It was one of the few sanctuaries from the everyday madness of the Ibiza summer, practically a tourist-free zone.

Tyrone Lucas was pacing up and down outside the club with his phone pressed to his ear. Every so often he would look over. Hawthorne-Blythe guessed that he was probably gloating to Alison.

Charles Moon and Kit were deep in discussion at the bar. Hawthorne-Blythe looked away from them towards the jetties leading out from the yacht club. None of the boats moored were particularly spectacular, certainly not compared to the ones he had previously seen in the harbour at Ibiza Town. Although he had been out on plenty of yachts and many of his close friends owned their own, it was a hobby Hawthorne-Blythe had never been tempted to pursue. He felt it a covetous pastime.

The other thing that had put him off was that several of his yacht owning friends were wannabe playboys and used their nautical appendages to assist their nocturnal activities. Hawthorne-Blythe thought it sad to see men in their fifties trawling the Med to catch girls less than half of their age. He had been with them on occasions and witnessed their 'successes'. They would take the girls out for a day, anchor close to a trendy beach or a secluded cove and be poised ever eager and ready to swoop when suntan oil application looked imminent.

In the evening they would strut into a club with their trophies, then march through to a waiting VIP table. The girls would eagerly drink their champagne and spend an obligatory thirty minutes or so with them, laughing at their jokes (or laughing off their advances), before heading for the safety of the dance floor, only returning when they needed to re-charge their glasses. With each visit, the girls would feel the obligation to indulge their hosts diminished, so by the third or fourth glass they would just help themselves, smile sweetly, then head back to the dance floor. Usually, once out of sight they would meet a young beau and so re-double their visits back to the table to keep him supplied in free champagne too, until they eventually disappeared without so much as a goodbye.

Hawthorne-Blythe looked at Tyrone Lucas, now walking along one of the jetties in search of a better reception. Now there was a man who would be well-suited to having his own yacht.

Beyond Lucas, a dirty blanket of cloud had moved in and was sagging over the east of the harbour. The formerly clear blue sea had turned a greyish green and the building wind was causing the row of boats to rock against each other. It matched Hawthorne-Blythe's mood entirely.

Charles Moon and Kit came back to the table.

'Well?' asked Hawthorne-Blythe.

'To be honest, H-B,' replied Charles Moon, 'there isn't really very much we can do. Club Wicked is still his company after all.'

Lucas had finished his call and joined the group at the table. 'Haven't missed anything, have I?'

'Yes,' replied Hawthorne-Blythe curtly. 'What you've missed is the spirit of this exercise.' He turned to Charles Moon. 'Or has he? You said that we should carry on as normal, for our reps to even help each other if needs be. Would you define employing someone like Alison as such? Is this a free-for-all, no-holds barred competition? Because if it is, Charles, that's not the way I operate and I'll have no part of it.'

Lucas smiled.

'Of course it isn't, H-B,' replied Charles Moon. He turned to Lucas. 'Would you care to explain yourself?'

Lucas lit a small cigar, sat back in his chair and puffed on it a couple of times in a self-important way, his relaxed demeanour suggesting that it was a question he was more than prepared for.

'Just so I know what all the fuss is about, presumably you

are talking about my appointment of Alison Shand as resort manager?'

'No!' yelled Hawthorne-Blythe. 'We want you to explain why you had prawn cocktail for your starter . . . Ye Gods, man, *of course* this is about Alison!'

Lucas raised his eyebrows. 'I take it you don't approve?' The hint of provocation was more than enough for Hawthorne-Blythe, who looked as though he was about to burst a blood vessel.

'I think H-B is upset that you didn't tell him first,' said Kit, trying to act as peacemaker.

'I see,' said Lucas smoothly. 'Well, to tell the truth, right up until the last minute, I wasn't actually sure she was going to accept the position. She was naturally concerned that there would be some hostility from her former employer and I must say, judging from his reaction, it would seem with good reason.'

'Good reason?' exclaimed Hawthorne-Blythe, unable to control himself. 'Let me give you the "good reason", shall I? Alison Shand single-handedly ruined this resort last year. All of the reps hated her. She was taking backhanders from bars, clubs and God only knows where else. We knew what she was up to but could do nothing, because she was also involved in one of the biggest frauds in the history of the travel industry, being perpetrated by our then Contracts Director, Felipe Gomez. Which, incidentally, cost my company several hundred thousand pounds, probably more. As soon as we had the evidence on Felipe, we fired her.'

'Yes, well, of course I know all about Felipe Gomez,' replied Lucas. 'What he did was a terrible thing and he's quite rightly in prison, where he belongs.' He leant forward and tapped some ash into the ashtray. 'But correct me if I'm wrong, didn't Alison give evidence *against* him in court, and wasn't her testimony one of the main contributing factors that led to his conviction?'

'Yes but—'

'So if anything there is an argument,' interrupted Lucas, 'that it was Alison who was treated unfairly.'

Hawthorne-Blythe couldn't believe his ears. 'What?'

'My understanding is that Alison was the victim. If my facts are right, there was no evidence proving that she was on the fiddle, or in any way involved in Felipe's scam.'

'Not presented at court no – that was part of the deal to get her to testify. But we found all of her paperwork and a substantial amount of money, both proving what she was up to.'

'So why wasn't it shown at court?'

'As I've already told you, compared to the amount Felipe was syphoning off it was peanuts and we dealt with it internally, after we sacked her.'

'Ah, but you didn't sack her, did you?'

'We certainly did.'

Lucas reached into his small briefcase. 'I'm sorry to disagree, H-B, but I've got a copy of her letter of resignation right here.'

Hawthorne-Blythe looked at it briefly. 'That's a technicality. She was asked to leave and we allowed her to resign as one of the conditions of her giving evidence against Felipe. The main reason that she gave evidence of course, is that we agreed not to bring charges against her. There was no way Felipe could be allowed to get away with his crime and although we had a superb case against him, with Alison's testimony it was rock solid. We felt it to be a good trade-off.'

'Well, again, I'm sorry to disagree but that's not what she says. Alison claims that she resigned after being humiliated by Brad, who showed a private video of her in an intimate moment, to a bar full of holidaymakers.'

'But that's preposterous,' blustered Hawthorne-Blythe.

'Is she lying about the video then?'

'No, but she'd already been—'

'Because what Alison claims is that she was victimised by her reps, in particular, Brad – who incidentally, was himself sacked for fiddling.'

'She framed him!' This was proving too much for Hawthorne-Blythe.

'Again,' replied Lucas, barely containing a smirk, 'where's the evidence?' He turned to Charles Moon and Kit. 'The reason I've employed Alison, gentlemen, is quite simply that she's good at her job and was badly . . .' he pretended to search for the word, '. . . *managed* during her time at Young Free & Single. Alison is forward thinking, part of the new breed, just like me. Not only am I going to show you that we're the better company, but also that we've got the best reps, because I know how to choose the kind of reps the kids of today want.'

'Oh my word,' sighed Hawthorne-Blythe, throwing his napkin on the table in disgust. 'I don't believe I'm hearing this. Alison is selfish, narrow-minded and a thoroughly nasty piece of work. Speak to any of the reps from last year.'

'What about Mario then?' asked Lucas. 'He's come back. Why don't we ask him?'

'From what I was told, the only reason she liked Mario was because he's a good-looking young man and she singled him out for favouritism, which concluded in them sleeping together, I might add.'

'Well, if we're going to talk about favouritism, let's look at Brad.'

'What do you mean?'

'I don't know what kind of hold he's got over your company, but first he gets sacked, then re-instated. He behaves disgracefully towards poor Alison and now – after less than a season as a rep – he's made manager in the biggest resort there is. Now call me a suspicious old Tyrone, but something doesn't smell right to me.'

Lucas stubbed out his cigar and sat back in his chair triumphantly.

Hawthorne-Blythe turned to Charles Moon. 'I'm not sure how much more of this drivel I can listen to, Charles. I'm very close to withdrawing from this whole thing and to hell with the consequences. Why am I considering your take-over? Because our financial position has deteriorated, mainly due to the huge amount embezzled last year by Felipe Gomez and to a lessor extent, Alison Shand. And now the latter is, to a degree, helping to determine the future of my company.'

'Ironic, isn't it?' grinned Lucas.

'OK, that's enough, Lucas,' said Kit.

'I'm sorry, but what do you expect? If Alison was that bad, do you honestly think I'd employ her, with everything that's at stake? My argument is that Young Free & Single couldn't get the best out of Alison and for whatever reason, had it in for her. I just want the opportunity to prove that with our more *contemporary* style, she'll flourish.'

Charles Moon and Kit looked at each other.

'Excuse us for just a moment,' said Charles. They stood up and walked to the other end of the decking where they had a whispered conversation.

Lucas looked at Hawthorne-Blythe and grinned again.

'You lying, conniving, scheming bastard,' said Hawthorne-Blythe.

'Do you remember when you sacked me, Adam, sorry, I mean *H-B*? Do you remember me telling you that one day you'd come grovelling to me? Well, get ready to grovel, because that day's just round the corner, old man.'

But instead of blowing a gasket, as Lucas had expected, Hawthorne-Blythe began to laugh. He sat back in his chair.

'Tyrone Lucas, you really are a man consumed with bitterness, aren't you? I am so pleased that you made that last comment. In so doing, you have just played your hand and I now realise that irrespective of whatever cards I may or may not be holding, I still win.'

Lucas looked confused.

'You know full well that it would hurt me terribly to lose Young Free & Single, yet life goes on so even if that sorry day ever came, I would simply find happiness elsewhere. Whereas you, my friend, will never be happy. Even if Club Wicked succeed and get taken over by The Monastery, then it won't be long before you find something or someone else to hate.' He sat back calmly. 'Do you remember, after your first summer with us, we had a party to celebrate moving into the new offices at Teddington?'

Lucas shrugged.

'You were our star rep back then. Do you recall how happy you were when your father dropped into the party on his way into London?' Now Lucas looked uneasy. 'How pleased you were when I told him what a great future you had? You were glowing with pride.'

'This has got nothing to do with The Monastery proposal,' said Lucas.

Hawthorne-Blythe sat forward and lowered his voice. 'When you first started working for me I'm sure you recall those little tête-à-têtes we used to have. In those days I always used to make a point of asking my reps about their parents and their upbringing. I found it helped me to understand their motivation and potential. It was at the reunion after your first season, when you were morosely drunk, on gin I believe. Oh yes, I remember it like it was yesterday, how angry you became when you told me what a domineering father you had, how no matter what you did he would always make some kind of negative or derogatory comment, how you were never good enough. That's why I made a point of pulling him to one side to tell him that you were so highly regarded by us when he turned up at the party. But he even did it on that night, didn't he? Something belittling about you being a holiday rep, wasn't it?'

Lucas looked flustered. 'I can't remember. It was a long time ago. He was a silly old sod then and he's an even sillier old sod now. I have nothing more to do with him. Anyway, even if you are right, it hasn't done me any harm, has it? Look at me now.'

'I am, Tyrone, I am. And what I see is that same little boy still angry with his father, except for the moment it is me fulfilling that role, that focus of your hatred. I doubt if it's only me of course. If you do win, then I am equally sure that Charles Moon shall become that person. It has been eating away at you all of these years. You gave me no choice but to sack you, yet in your own way you felt you were not good enough.'

'Psycho-babble,' spat Lucas.

'No, Tyrone my boy,' replied Hawthorne-Blythe, deliberately paternal, 'it's true. And do you know – you are turning into exactly the same kind of person.'

Hawthorne-Blythe had no idea if this was actually true or not, but he liked the sound of it and had a hunch it would get a reaction. He was right.

'*I'll never be like him!*' Lucas screamed, sounding like a petulant child.

Charles Moon and Kit stopped talking and walked back over.

'Everything all right?' asked Charles.

'Fine,' smiled Hawthorne-Blythe.

'Lucas?'

Tyrone Lucas rubbed his temples and sat upright. 'Yes, no problem. No problem at all.'

'Good,' said Charles. He looked at Lucas again. 'Are you sure you're all right?'

'Yes, yes. What have you decided?'

Charles turned to Hawthorne-Blythe. 'Look, H-B, we've discussed things and I'm afraid that it is entirely up to Lucas who he employs as his resort manager. We take on board everything you've said but a) the situation happened before our involvement and b) as Lucas says, there isn't any evidence to back up what you're saying. Please don't think I'm calling you a liar – either of you – but if you put yourself in my position then you can see my dilemma.'

'Not to worry, Charles,' replied Hawthorne-Blythe, a half smile on his lips. 'I probably over-reacted. Tyrone and I have sorted it out, haven't we, Tyrone?'

Lucas nodded. Charles was taken aback.

'Oh . . . right then . . . yes . . . that's good. Marvellous.' He clapped his hands together. 'OK, well I know the first clients arrive at the weekend but on the Monday directly after their arrival both of your companies only have bar nights, in other words there are no excursions, so the clients are pretty much free to do what they want. Also, seeing as it's the opening night of Manumission at Privilege I'm sure most of them will want to go up there. What we have therefore arranged is for all of the girls from your two companies to have a night out together at one venue and all of the boys at another. Just a way of breaking down the barriers so that this whole thing doesn't get too competitive.'

'We thought it a good idea to keep the sexes apart,' added Kit, 'because there were some barriers we felt best left *un*broken, if you get my drift.'

'So,' continued Charles, 'we tossed a coin and H-B, you've got the pleasure of the girls' company. We'll let the groups vote as to where they want to go.'

'Actually,' added Kit, 'why don't we let one of the groups use the new Monastery camera and they can take some shots and work out how the bloody thing operates? We might get some good shots for our first brochure.'

'Good idea,' agreed Charles. 'Who wants to take it?'

Hawthorne-Blythe was magnanimous. 'Why not let Tyrone have the honour?'

Lucas shot him a look.

Kit handed him the camera. 'There you go, Lucas. We'll see you both tomorrow then.'

They all shook hands. Charles and Kit left and Lucas grabbed Hawthorne-Blythe's arm.

'I hope you meant what you said about finding happiness elsewhere when Young Free & Single go out of business because believe me, out of business is *exactly* where you're going.'

chapter ten

Arabella popped open the top button of his trousers, slowly slid down the zip, and rubbed his hard-on through his pants.

Lying on the back seat in the darkness of the empty coach, he looked up at her sitting astride him and smiled cockily.

'What you waiting for?'

Biting her lip in anticipation, Arabella let her fingertips gently glide along the outside of his Calvin Kleins until they rested on his waistband, then eased her fingers under the elastic. She yanked them down and gasped as he sprung free.

'Oh God, I've missed this.'

She leaned forward and kissed him, running her tongue along the outside of his lips. He cupped her breasts then urgently undid the first three buttons of her YF&S airport uniform shirt. This allowed him to slip it over her shoulders, hooking his thumbs under her bra-straps and pulling them down as he did so.

He moved one hand to her crown and pushed, while at the same time scurrying to get into a more upright position, his feet slipping on the cloth seat, so that his attempt to cajole her into performing oral sex on him was made with all the grace of a hermit crab.

'Go on, Arabella, suck it.'

Arabella grabbed his wrist and took his hand from the top of her head. 'No . . . no.' She was panting. 'God, I've waited so long for this. Feel how wet I am.'

She guided the hand she was still holding between her

legs and on to her soaking cotton panties. He raised his eyebrows, then slid a finger inside her. She gasped, but pulled away.

'Oh baby, that's not what I want.'

She kissed him again then lowered herself onto his twitching erection.

'Oooh . . . *Mario!*'

Mario managed to force the look of ecstasy she was waiting for. 'Oh God, Arabella, you're so, so . . . sexy.'

Mario wasn't sure if he had made it sound convincingly enthusiastic enough for her to believe him, though her level of infatuation was such that he was fairly certain it didn't matter.

'Make love to me, Mario, make love to me like never before.'

Mario had forgotten quite how irritating Arabella could be – he certainly never really enjoyed *having sex* with her. She'd always tried to turn it into so much more than the 'just-another-shag' that it actually was.

Arabella had been a single-share holidaymaker with Young Free & Single the previous summer and he had slept with her on three occasions. The first was simply to get the points for The Competition. On the second he was so drunk that he couldn't remember a thing, and that included waking up in the middle of the night and pissing in her suitcase in the inebriated belief that Samsonite had gone into the water closet business. The third and final time was when he had unsuccessfully tried to persuade her to have a threesome with another client he had been sleeping with that week (unbeknown to Arabella, of course), once he realised how besotted Arabella had become with him.

Admittedly she was not as sad or mad as most of the single-shares Mario had met during the season. In fact, he actually believed the reason she had given for coming away on her own, namely to use up her holiday entitlement at work. He was not so sure that she was telling the truth however, when she claimed she didn't understand what a single-share was when she booked the holiday, somebody who opts to share a room with a total stranger.

Although she was reasonably attractive, he found her a total turn-off. The correctly pronounced clichés during the act were a particular deflater. Somehow 'Oh yes, make love to me, big boy' and 'This is simply the most exquisite experience' never quite did it for him.

Worse was how she behaved after. Mario was very much in the dump-me-muck-and-turf-'em-out camp, whereas Arabella belonged to the doey-eyed-let's-have-a-cuddle-and-plan-the-rest-of-the-day-together school of thought. Their post-coital agendas could not have been more diametrically opposed.

Mario's sigh of relief as she went through passport control at the end of her holiday was almost as loud as Arabella's sobs. Despite having her phone number pressed into his palm he seriously doubted he would ever take her up on her offer of a visit to her home in Ealing.

She had rang and left messages for him once he was in the UK (even though he had never given her his number) but he always ignored her calls or fobbed her off on the rare occasions she got through. In the end he lied and told her that he was going to open a bar in Ibiza so wouldn't be contactable during the summer, just to stop her from pestering him.

Within a week, she rang to excitedly tell him she had applied for a job as a rep with YF&S (as well as several other tour companies) so they could be together in Ibiza. At that time, Mario had no intention of setting foot outside of the UK, and he had given her all of the inside information he could to get her through the interviews and hopefully as far away from him in the UK as possible.

A couple of months later she rang him with the 'great news' that she had got the job with YF&S in Ibiza. Not long after that, Alison had also called him. Alison had just been offered the job by Tyrone Lucas as Club Wicked resort manager. Alison had found out about Arabella's appointment through a contact and remembered how Arabella doted over Mario. To have someone working for YF&S whose real allegiance would be to one of her own reps was too good an opportunity to miss, so she offered Mario the chance to work for Club Wicked. Mario accepted without hesitation, eager to get his own back on his tormentors from the previous summer.

The one proviso Alison made was that he rekindle his relationship with Arabella. The substantial 'sweetener' from Lucas had helped to persuade him.

Now though, having to listen to Arabella moaning 'I'm your princess' and 'Baby, we were made for each other' that sweetener didn't seem nearly enough. Apart from her Sloaney drone, the other thing annoying him was that where she had pulled her panties to one side, the elastic was chafing the side of his dick. He was worried he would end up with a graze.

He put his hands on her hips to stop her.

'Arabella, get off.'

'Though the night was made for loving and the day returns too soon . . .' Arabella was lost in a poem.

'Arabella, your fucking knickers!'

'. . . Yet we'll go no more a-roving by the light of the moon.'

'Fuck the moon – get off, you're going to scar me.' He pushed her away roughly.

'What's the matter? Why did you stop, baby?'

'Because the elastic from your panties keeps rubbing against my knob.'

'I know just the thing for that. Here, let me kiss it better . . . just how you like it.'

Mario had a penchant for having girls gently bite his length. Unfortunately, Arabella had made a point of remembering everything about Mario. She closed her teeth around him just a little too hard and on the exact spot her panties had been rubbing.

'Ow!' yelled Mario. 'You dozy cow – fuck off.' He pushed her away again, this time far harder than before. She tumbled to the floor. Mario pulled his trousers up and glared at her. 'You're a bloody nightmare.'

There were a few seconds of silence as she looked at him bewildered. Then her face crumpled and she burst into tears.

Mario curbed his natural desire to laugh and go. Alison had made it abundantly clear that Arabella was their ace in the sleeve. Mario knew that at some point being nice to Arabella would prove too much for him, but he hadn't expected it to happen quite so quickly. Like it or not, he was going to have to bite the bullet and be conciliatory. He held his arms out.

'Come on, baby, I'm sorry. I didn't mean it. It hurt and I knee-jerked.'

Arabella wiped her tears and moved towards him, putting her arms round his neck.

'I've been *so* looking forward to us being together again,' she snivelled. 'I just wanted it to be perfect.'

Mario considered for a moment exactly what level of perfection Arabella hoped to achieve having a quickie on the back seat of a coach outside the airport on their first arrivals night.

He patted the back of her head. 'There, there. I did too. Look, let's leave this for now and wait until we can do it properly, yeah?' Arabella nodded and Mario breathed a sigh of relief. 'Good girl. Maybe we can meet after this night out on Monday.'

Arabella's face brightened up. 'Really? Oh that would be divine! Why have they split up the sexes though?'

'I guess they want to encourage us all to mix.'

'We're all going to Raison D'Etre in Ibiza Town. I think the plan is to have a meal then there's a DJ or something playing afterwards. Where are all of you boys going?'

'Um, to a lap-dancing club.'

'What?'

'Pathetic, isn't it? I was totally outvoted. Once Greg and Hughie came up with the idea they steamrollered everyone else into it.'

Arabella looked less than impressed.

'I suppose we'd better get back and welcome the first clients of the summer.'

They walked to the front of the coach.

'I bet you're glad you haven't been chosen as the rep who gets the guy from The Monastery on the coach with you to see how you do, aren't you?' asked Mario, changing the subject again before Arabella sank into deeper dotage. 'Doing your first airport transfer is nerve-racking enough without that pressure.'

'God yes! Brad's on my coach. He told me that he'd take over if I started getting it wrong. Sugar Ray actually volunteered to have the guy from The Monastery with him.'

'Sugar Ray? He's the little poof, isn't he?'

'Mario! Sugar Ray's lovely and yes, he is gay. He's also great on the microphone so I'm sure he'll do well. I met Kit – he's the guy from The Monastery – and he seems really nice. I feel more sorry for your rep though because she's got Charles Moon on her coach and he's the head honcho, isn't he?'

'Yeah.' Mario was keener to gather information than divulge it. 'So who's going to oversee Sugar Ray at the airport after you and Brad have left.'

'Greg supposedly.'

'What do you mean supposedly.'

Arabella stopped at the front of the coach. She lowered her voice. 'I'm not meant to say anything so you'd better not tell anyone. Greg is meeting up with that tarty looking rep who works for you – Mel, I think her name is.'

'But Mel isn't even due to come to the airport.'

'Exactly. Greg had a word with Sugar Ray earlier and asked him if he would be all right on his own, in case he was late getting to the airport. Sugar Ray's really confident so he said it wouldn't be a problem.'

Mario digested the information. 'Interesting.'

'So, which flight are you doing?' asked Arabella.

'Gatwick,' replied Mario, 'due in just before one in the

morning. You'd better get your skates on. Brad will be here and your lot will be coming through any minute.'

She looked at her watch. 'Shit. I didn't realise what the time was.'

As she passed the front passenger seat she picked up a clipboard.

'Oh look, the rep has left her arrivals list on the coach. I wonder which company it is?'

'The name should be at the top,' replied Mario, only half-interested.

'Never Too Old Holidays. Isn't that the tour company for over fifty-fives?'

'Yeah. Who is the rep?'

'Let's see. Manchester, twenty-three thirty-five . . . ah, here it is . . . Gill. Do you think the reps are over fifty-five too?'

Mario ignored the question knowing only too well that Gill wouldn't be over fifty-five for the best part of another thirty-five years, having slept with her the previous Friday.

'Shall I take it to the arrivals hall and give it to her?' asked Arabella.

Mario had an idea. 'No, no don't do that. We don't want her knowing we've been on her coach, do we? It's all right, I know the manager of Never Too Old, I'll say I found it on the floor.'

'OK. I'll see you tomorrow then.'

She insisted on giving him a lingering kiss before she left.

He watched her walk into the airport, then as soon as she was out of sight he ran round to another door beyond the arrivals lounge, which led to a small café area where most of the reps congregated while waiting for their flights. Mario scanned the café, which was packed full of just arrived holidaymakers taking up an unnecessary amount of space with their over-burdened luggage trolleys, locals and ex-pats anxiously looking at arrivals boards as they waited for friends and loved ones, and holiday reps trying to appear as nonchalant and disinterested as possible.

Sitting on her own reading a newspaper was Gill.

'Hi.'

She looked up and her face broke into a smile when she saw it was Mario.

'Hi, Mario. How are you?'

'Yeah, fine, fine.'

'I really enjoyed Friday night.'

'Me too.' He looked up at the arrivals board. Good. There was no expected arrival time for the twenty-three thirty-five from Manchester. 'I've just found out my bloody flight's been delayed by nearly two hours.'

'Oh what a bummer. Which flight are you doing?'

'The Manchester one, due in just after eleven-thirty.'

'Oh you're joking! That's the one my lot are on too.' She turned to the board. 'It doesn't say it's delayed.'

'No. I only just found out myself through a contact I made last year.'

'Shit.'

'I tell you what, why don't we get away from the airport for an hour? There's a little bar just up the road.'

'Mmm. I don't know. It's only my second ever airport transfer. There's no one else from my company here.'

'Well, there you go. Nobody to tell you off. Come on. I had such a wicked time the other night. I'd hate for it to just be a one-off.'

'So would I.'

'I'd also hate you to think it was just the points – sorry, I mean just the sex. It would be nice to go for a drink and have a chat somewhere away from all of this.'

'Maybe . . . I've only got forty arrivals, so I suppose . . .'

'Sorted,' said Mario, making her mind up for her. 'Right, I've just got to see one of the reps and I'll be straight back.'

Mario briskly walked down to the departures lounge, where Stig was talking to Alison.

'Call me a genius,' said Mario, handing the Never Too Old arrivals list to Alison and smiling broadly.

'What's this?' asked Alison.

'This is the first nail in YF&S's coffin, that's what it is.' They looked at him baffled. 'The Never Too Old rep that this arrivals sheet belongs to doesn't know it's missing. I've just told her the flight's delayed by an hour and a half and persuaded her to leave the airport to come for a drink with me. So that means that when her clients come through she won't be there.'

'Um, Mario, it's *YF&S* we're meant to be stitching up, not Never Too Old.'

Mario grinned. 'I know. But as Baldrick used to say, I have a cunning plan.'

'Come on then, let's hear it.'

'Right. Sugar Ray's YF&S flight is due in about twenty minutes after the Manchester Never Too Old one. Assuming everything is on time, which it seems to be, we get old Stig here to tell Sugar Ray that The Monastery have just sprung a test on us and instead of greeting our YF&S clients, he has to greet the Never Too Old ones. It's not going to look good on them with Sugar Ray sitting in a coach with a load of geriatrics while the arrivals hall is full of his lost clients.'

'What about Brad, won't he be able to sort things out?'

'No, because he'll have already left with Arabella and the earlier arrivals.'

'Well, they aren't going to leave Sugar Ray on his own, surely?'

'Greg's meant to be coming to the airport. But a little bird just told me that he's up to his old tricks. He's taken out Mel and he told Sugar Ray he might be late . . .'

'Which knowing Greg means he'll *definitely* be late,' finished Alison.

'Exactomundo.'

'This "little bird" – she wasn't about five eight and frightfully posh, was she?'

Mario just smiled.

Stig was scratching his head. 'I'm a bit lost.'

Alison took his cheek between her thumb and forefinger and gave it a little squeeze. 'That's OK, my man-mountain-munchkin. We don't expect you to weigh eighteen stone and be able to think too. Your talents lie elsewhere. We'll tell you exactly what you've got to do, step-by-step.'

'You'll have to keep Kit talking, Alison. If it all goes according to plan, then Sugar should be on the coach just as his clients start coming through.' Mario turned to Stig. 'Stig, once Sugar Ray has got all the Never Too Old clients on the coach your job is to persuade him to get out of the arrivals hall as soon as possible. As soon as he's gone, wave down to Alison and she can bring Kit up. Hopefully by that time it will be total chaos with loads of YF&S clients wandering around like lost sheep with no rep. Try to wind them up about Sugar Ray as well, you know the fact he's a poof and all that. Seeing as it's the Glasgow flight, tell them he hates Jocks too. That'll make it a fun week for him.'

'As long as Greg doesn't turn up,' added Alison.

'He won't. If he gets here halfway through we'll just deny all knowledge. Brilliant or what?'

'But what will Gill the Never Too Old rep say when she discovers you've stitched her up?' asked Stig, still scratching his head. 'And what will Sugar Ray do when he finds out I've lied?'

Mario and Alison both looked at him as though he didn't know that two and two makes four, which he probably didn't.

'Well, I'm sure you're big enough and ugly enough to take care of a little queen like Sugar,' mocked Alison. 'Deny everything.'

'And I don't give a toss about Gill,' added Mario. 'I'll just say I got my facts wrong. I'll tell her that one of our other reps looked after my arrivals so I'm doing a later one. If she doesn't believe me . . . tough. It's her loss.'

Stig gave a gappy grin.' So we're not even going to pretend it's a clean fight?'

'The only people we keep the pretence up for,' continued Alison, 'are the observers from The Monastery. If YF&S keep moaning about the things we've supposedly done, The Monastery will think that they're just a bunch of whinge bags. Got it?'

'Loud and clear.'

Stig marched off.

'Are you shagging him?' asked Mario.

Alison lit a cigarette and lied. 'God no. By the way, The Monastery have given me a camera so that our reps can take some clubbing pictures. I thought that seeing as you're going to a lap-dancing club, you could try and get a few pictures of the YF&S reps in compromising positions. There's bound to be a bit of Charlie knocking around and you know how paranoid The Monastery are about the whole drugs thing.'

Mario shook his head. 'Fucking hell, this really is a dirty fight. Total filth.'

'Honey, that's my middle name.' She checked nobody was looking and gave his crotch a playful squeeze. 'But you already know that . . . don't you?'

chapter eleven

'Doris and Bert.'

'No,' said Sugar Ray, 'I meant your surnames.'

'Oh I beg your pardon, dear. Mr and Mrs Tanner.'

Sugar Ray looked down the list. 'Here you are.' He put a tick by their names. 'If you would like to make your way through the doors over there you're on coach M21.'

Sugar Ray had one final look at his sheet. All present and correct. He walked over to Stig.

'Everyone arrived?' asked Stig.

'Yep. Wasn't as bad as I thought it would be. Have you seen Kit from The Monastery? He's meant to be on my coach.'

'Yeah, he was talking to Alison. He'll probably be here in a minute. If I were you, I'd go though and see the clients are all OK out there.'

'Yeah, you're probably right. I hope The Monastery don't pull any other surprises on us like this one. Are you sure that someone's coming up to check through the YF&S clients I was supposed to be meeting? Their plane landed ten minutes ago.'

'Yeah, I think I saw Greg in departures,' lied Stig.

'Oh good. Thanks for your help by the way. I must admit I was a bit worried, what with all of this stuff I've been hearing about Alison and Mario last year. I thought there might be a little animosity between the two companies.'

'Listen, we're all in the same boat. I know you'd do the same for me.'

'Yeah, for sure. Anyway, catch up with you at the lap-dancing club on Monday night.'

'I wouldn't have thought that was your scene.'

'Ooh, you'd be surprised,' replied Sugar Ray camping it up. 'I'm sure the shoes will be fantastic. See you later, sweetie.'

Sugar Ray deliberately minced out of the airport. Stig screwed his face up in disgust, then waved down the other end of the terminal to Alison, to let her know everything was going according to plan.

Sugar Ray's coach was furthest from the exit. He was dreading this. Ever since he had volunteered to be the YF&S first year rep that The Monastery observed for microphone skills and technique, he had been psyching himself up for a boisterous load of 18–30s, not a downbeat troop of pensioners.

As he got closer, it appeared as though things were going to be even worse than he had imagined. A group of about a dozen clearly disgruntled elderly people were standing a few metres from the coach, and the raised voices from within sounded as though those on board were getting out of control.

'Hi,' said Sugar Ray as breezily as possible to the small group off the coach. 'Everything all right?'

Before any of them had a chance to answer, the coach driver stepped from his vehicle.

'Los viejos son mas locos que los jovenes.'

Sugar Ray didn't have a clue what this meant, but guessed it wasn't good. With considerable trepidation, he walked up the four small steps.

Most of the Never Too Old clients still on the coach had opened the YF&S welcome pack, which was always left on the seat by the company for their young arrivals. Packets of condoms were being dangled in the air and one old boy was trying to blow it up with his nose over his head, to the clapping of those in adjacent seats. The free disposable cameras were nearly all out and being used, with a few of the women cackling away and hoisting up their skirts, happily having snaphots taken of their underwear.

A burly pensioner from the group who had got off the coach appeared in the doorway.

'Bloody disgrace this. Not what we expected at all. There were nowt about this in't brochure. And this lot are old enough to know better.'

'If you get back on the coach I can explain,' said Sugar Ray.

'No chance,' replied the burly pensioner.

'Please,' implored Sugar Ray. 'It's my first ever night at the airport and my boss is coming in a minute.' The burly pensioner stood firm. 'Please,' repeated Sugar Ray.

'Come on, you miserable old sod,' joined in Mr Tanner, who was sitting at the front of the coach waving a brochure, 'give the lad a chance. What are you going to do otherwise – stay there all night?'

Muttering under his breath the man led the others back on to the coach, to some barracking and cat-calling.

'You wouldn't believe that some of these people had come away to enjoy themselves, would you?' said Mr Tanner to Sugar Ray, loud enough for those getting back on the coach to hear.

'It's not their fault,' replied Sugar Ray diplomatically.

'I wanted to ask you,' said Mr Tanner lowering his voice, 'I was looking at all these clubs in the brochure. Do they still do that sex show thing? I saw it on the TV last year.'

'Bert!' said Mrs Tanner.

Before Sugar Ray could answer, a woman a few rows back called, 'Excuse me, dear.' Sugar Ray moved down the aisle to her. 'Some of these excursions look fantastic. I must admit, we weren't expecting anything like this, were we, Alec? This looks like so much fun. How do we sign up to go on them?'

'Um, just give me a minute,' replied Sugar. 'I need to restore some order first.' Confidently, he picked up the microphone. 'Hello, everyone!' A few people looked up but a lot were still laughing. 'Sorry if this wasn't quite what some of you were expecting. I'll explain all on the way to your hotel. We're waiting for one more person and then we'll be off.' Sugar Ray could tell that the majority of those on the coach were in good sprits and he needed to get them all on the same wavelength before Kit arrived. A sing-song? Sugar Ray racked his brain for an old-time favourite.

'*We're all going on a summer holiday, no more working for a week or two . . .*'

Greg jumped from the cab outside the airport and quickly paid the driver. He looked at his watch.

'Shit.'

He knew he was late and hurtled into the terminal. Sugar Ray was definitely going to get a big drink for this one. Mel had proven to be far better than even Greg had imagined. As well as the great sex (and not forgetting the four points) Mel had confided that the only reason she had joined Club Wicked was as a safety net in case she failed her audition as a lap dancer in Ibiza Town's Labiarinth Strip Club.

Earlier that day she got the call to say the dancing job was hers, so after the Monday night bonding session and piss-up, she was planning to hand in her notice to Alison. Greg was sure that a Club Wicked rep leaving that early had to be good news for YF&S's Monastery chances.

But the spring in Greg's step as he skipped through the automatic doors that led to the arrivals hall soon disappeared. It was pandemonium.

Kit was the first to see him. 'Greg! There you are. Where on earth have you been?'

'The bloody taxi had a blow out between San Augustin and San Jose,' he lied. 'My fault – I should have come up on the coach, but I had a bit of running round to do. What's happened?'

Alison stepped forward. 'We've just found out that your rep Sugar Ray has taken it upon himself to do the arrivals for Never Too Old – he's just put them on the YF&S coach.'

'Why on earth would he do that?'

'Beats me.'

'Where's the Never Too Old rep?'

'No one's seen her,' replied Stig.

'Luckily Stig was here to check your clients in. The first few have already come through,' said Kit.

'So where's Sugar Ray now?' asked Greg.

'He must be on the coach,' said Kit. 'We were all about to go and find him.'

'I'll get one of *my* reps to look after this lot,' offered Alison, with her most charming smile.

'Come on then,' said Greg. He set off with Kit.

Alison hung behind with Stig as they walked towards the coach park. 'Now remember what I said, Stig. When Sugar Ray says it was you who told him he had to look after the Never Too Old arrivals, deny it. In fact, say you were with me in the café – I'll back you up.'

The airport doors swept open and they were into the warm Ibiza night.

'I can't wait to see him sitting there, all nervous with loads of coffin dodgers nagging him,' chuckled Stig.

'What's that noise?' asked Alison as they got closer to coach M21.

'Sounds like singing.'

Kit, Greg and Sugar Ray were already deep in conversation next to the coach as Alison and Stig approached. Everyone on board was boisterously singing 'Roll Out The Barrel' and were in great spirits. Alison and Stig looked at each other bemused.

'. . . and that's the truth,' protested Sugar Ray. 'Look, here's Stig now – just ask him.'

Kit turned to Stig. 'Sugar Ray claims that you told him this was some kind of test we instigated. He said you told him to check through the Never Too Old clients.'

Alison didn't wait for Stig to answer – she knew that she was by far the more accomplished liar.

'What? That's preposterous. Stig has been with me all of the time. It's his first airport transfer tonight and I was going through what to say on the coach with him. Besides, a beginner rep on his first night is hardly going to be in a position to tell another what to do. It's ludicrous.'

Greg eyed her suspiciously.

'But it's true,' protested Sugar Ray. 'Stig told me he'd seen Greg in departures and that Greg was going to look after my flight for me.'

'Well, we know that's a lie,' retorted Alison, trying to disguise the triumph in her voice. 'We all saw Greg turn up a few minutes ago.'

Kit looked pensive. 'I'm really not too sure what to do about this. I must say, it doesn't look—'

'Oooh there you are, Sugar Ray.' Mrs Tanner stepped from the coach. 'Sorry to interrupt.' She turned to Kit. 'Are you his boss?'

'Er, no, not really, I—'

'Well, I've got to tell you that he's the most delightful young man I've met in many a day,' she gushed, not really listening to Kit's reply. 'We've all been having a marvellous time – well, apart from a few old fogies. And the holiday's not even started. Now then, Sugar . . .'

She pulled him to one side. As she did so, a grey-haired lady in a blue rep's uniform came striding up to join the mêlée.

'Now what?' mumbled Greg.

'I'm Yvonne, resort manager for Never Too Old. Would somebody please tell me what on earth is going on and why all of my clients are on this Young Free & Single coach?'

'There was a mix-up,' said Alison, keen to break bad news. 'We still haven't yet quite worked out why, but that Young Free & Single rep over there decided to check all your clients in.'

'But where's my rep, Gill?'

'Nobody's seen her,' replied Alison.

Yvonne took stock of the situation for a moment. 'Well, it's probably just as well for us he did in that case.'

'Yes, for you it may be, but not for his company Young Free & Single and most certainly not for ours. My rep here had to pick up the pieces.' Alison twisted the knife and Stig stood proud.

'Um, excuse me, Yvonne, is it?' Sugar Ray handed her a wad of money. 'I've collected this for you. I'm sorry if I've inconvenienced you but I swear it wasn't my fault. There were a few clients that weren't too happy to start with but we had a bit of a sing-song and they seem all right now. I also told them about some of the excursions on the island. Quite a lot of them wanted to come along so Mrs Tanner over there helped me write down the names and take the money.'

Yvonne looked at the list. Then she started to laugh.

'What's so funny?' asked Kit.

'If for whatever reason you decide to get rid of this young man, send him to me – I'll probably have a vacancy after tonight.'

Everybody looked puzzled. Kit asked the question.

'What's happened?'

'I'll tell you,' laughed Yvonne, flicking through the money. 'In twenty minutes he's sold more excursions than all of my reps used to do in a month last year. It's absolutely incredible.' She turned to Sugar Ray. 'God only knows what motivated you to check in my clients, but after I've sacked Gill, I'd love you to work for us. You're something special.'

Greg seized the opportunity. 'There you go, Kit. One in a million is our Sugar Ray. Sorry, Yvonne, but Sugar Ray's not going anywhere, are you, mate?' He turned to Kit. 'Everybody's been messed around enough for one night, Kit. Let's get this lot onto their right coach and I'll bring the YF&S clients through. It was probably just a mix-up but you've got to admit, Sugar Ray's shown that he can think on his feet and is more than up to the job.'

'I'll give you that,' replied Kit.

Alison went to interrupt. 'But—'

'So give us ten minutes, Kit,' continued Greg, not allowing Alison to get a word in, 'and I'll be back with a coach load of happy punters before you can say superstar. Come on, Sugar Ray.'

As the Young Free & Single coach pulled away, Greg finished talking to Kit at the back of the coach and came back to sit next to Sugar Ray on the front seat.

'Have I fucked up or is everything OK?' asked Sugar Ray.

'I think it's OK. I'm glad it was Kit and not Charles Moon though. Kit seems the more laid-back of the two. So tell me, what really happened at the airport?'

'Exactly as I said. That horrible Stig told me that The Monastery had set us some kind of initiative test. I didn't even consider he was lying – I guess it was because I was so nervous.'

'Well, that's understandable.'

'You do believe me, don't you?'

'Oh, I believe you all right. It sounds like typical Alison to me. As usual, she's not going to be playing by the Queensbury rules. I'm sure this'll just be the start of it. Only problem is we can't keep going to Kit or Charles all the time because they'll soon get the hump and she knows it. We'll just have to keep our guard up. Don't worry, Sugar Ray, you've not blotted your copy-book as far as I'm concerned. Apart from that I owe you one for letting me get to the airport late. Right then. All the controls are set for when you get on the microphone. The clients were a bit stroppy but now they're on the coach that'll soon change. We're lucky that it's more or less fifty-fifty boys and girls . . . always puts 'em in a good mood. Just be yourself. In fact, camp it up a bit if you want. The girls will love it and the boys won't feel threatened by you. I reckon you'll have some trouble with that group on the back seat though. They're pissed and seem like thick bigots, so you can be sure they'll chuck some abuse at you. Let it ride or take the piss a bit at first if you want. If they keep it up, then say what you want. By then, the rest of the coach should be on your side.'

'I can be rude as I like with Kit on the coach?'

'Yeah, sure. Nothing you say is going to shock him.'

By the time they got on to the main Ibiza to San Antonio road Sugar Ray had them eating out of the palm of his hand. His camp mannerisms naturally won people over, a giggle seemed to be perpetually trying to force itself out of his larynx. Most of all, he could laugh at himself and it was simply hard not to like him.

Not that it stopped the guys at the back from trying, just as Greg had predicted.

The first heckles naturally referred to his sexuality and Sugar Ray dealt with them brilliantly. All but one. This particular individual was wearing a kilt, Scottish football shirt and a tartan hat with orange tufts sticking out of it, beloved of Scottish football and rugby fans.

It had got to the stage where the whole coach wanted the drunken heckler to shut up, even Kit. All he was doing was shouting increasingly vulgar, humourless abuse. 'Right then, everyone,' said Sugar Ray suddenly. 'As fascinating as our friend's last comment was, I thought you might be interested in something of biological interest, especially as it's to do with naughty bits.'

'Yeah, bet you'd like to sook mah naughty bits, you fookin poof cunt!'

'I'd have to find them first, sweetie. So as I was saying, I read the other day that the average female vagina can accommodate seven and three-quarter inches.'

'How would you know?' shouted a rather large girl, giggling and egged on by her friends.

'Well, of course, I wouldn't know from personal experience, would I, petal? It just says the average. I'm sure in your case it's much more. In fact, if you're ever thinking about having a coil fitted you'd probably be better off going to Carpetright and get them to measure you up for a carpet instead.'

Everyone started laughing, even the girl. Sugar Ray glanced over at Kit, who was sitting back with a grin of anticipation.

'Now this survey also said that the average male member is actually only five and three-quarter inches.'

There were predictable male protests. 'Yes, I'm sure there are some of you who are bigger than that – I'll be seeing you by the pool.'

The heckler slurred, 'You fookin gay wanker.'

'But back to my biology lesson. If the average vagina can take seven and three-quarter inches and the average willy is only five and three-quarters, then that means the average spare space per vagina is two inches. Now I've had a quick count and there are thirty-four girls on board.'

Greg looked confused.

'So,' said Sugar Ray, winking at him, 'to put it another way, that means that there are sixty-eight inches of useless twat on board this coach. If you're wondering where exactly that five foot eight of useless twat is, ladies and gentlemen, then perhaps you'd all like to look to the back seat of the coach and you'll see that it's wearing a kilt, football shirt and has orange hair.'

The whole coach started laughing, cheering and clapping, none more so than Kit. The heckler was beaten. Sugar Ray sat down.

'Was that all right, Greg?'

'Perfect. Yvonne was right – you are a natural.'

'Thanks. And Greg . . .'

'What?'

'Cheers for all your help.'

'Don't mention it, Sugar Ray . . . that's what I'm here for.'

Almost immediately, Greg was reminded that this last comment was not strictly true. They were driving past two of the biggest clubs on the island, Amnesia and Privilege. Greg looked out of the window longingly, impatient for the clubbing season to get properly under way.

Now *that* was what he was really here for . . .

chapter twelve

Alison, Mario and Stig sat at a table outside the Bon Tiempo apartments, watching the sun set. A surprisingly high number of Club Wicked clients were already milling around the bar in full on clubbing gear, ready for the 16 June opening Monday night of Manumission at Privilege, even though the club didn't get going properly for another six or seven hours.

The other Club Wicked reps were also dressed up and ready for the night out that The Monastery had organised – male reps to the Labiarinth Strip Club, the girls to the upmarket Raison D'Etre restaurant. The venues were close to each other in Ibiza Town and coaches were to pick up the reps from both companies.

Alison handed The Monastery camera to Mario. 'Are you sure Arabella is going to meet you?'

'Absolutely.'

'When's the wedding?' said Stig.

'As it happens, I *will* be the groom at a wedding in the not too distant future but you can rest assured that Arabella won't be within miles of it.'

'Oh really? So you've got a proper bird then?'

'If you define proper as an absolute babe from California, who currently lives in a mansion in Hampstead, thinks I'm the best thing since sliced bread, and whose dad is a film producer who reckons I've got what it takes to go all the way in Hollywood after we get married in the States in eighteen months, then yes, I have got a proper girlfriend.' Mario sat back in his chair.

'Oh right.' Stig nodded and fiddled with a beer mat. 'What's her name?'

'Coral.'

'What, like the bookmakers?'

'No you fucking moron, like the Great Barrier Reef.'

'Huh?'

'What happened to that Never Too Old rep?' asked Alison, changing the subject. 'Gill, wasn't it?'

'She got the sack, I think,' replied Mario.

'And has anyone said anything to either of you about what happened at the airport?'

'Only Greg and Brad,' said Mario. 'They said they knew what we were up to.'

'Sugar Ray told me he was really hurt by what I'd done,' added Stig.

'What did you say?' asked Alison.

'I just told him that if he didn't fuck off I'd hurt him properly.'

'Excellent,' replied Alison, clapping her hands together. 'But Charles Moon or Kit haven't asked about it?' They both shook their heads. A waiter put a toasted cheese sandwich in front of Mario. 'Make sure you get some good pictures tonight,' she said to Mario. 'Are you absolutely certain you know how to use that camera?'

'Yeah, seems straightforward enough.'

'Good.' She held her hand under the table and passed Mario something. 'Here, take this.'

'What is it?'

'It's a gram – of ketamine. Tell Greg it's Charlie and he'll be hoovering it up his nose like there's no tomorrow. First of all, try and get a picture of him taking it, then make sure you get a few afterwards when he's totally fucked.'

'*That* is evil.'

Alison noticed Trev, the co-owner of the Bon Tiempo apartments, coming over. 'Sshh, not another word.'

'What do you mean not another word?' whispered Mario into her ear, 'It's only Trev. You *are* still shagging him, aren't you?'

Alison kicked Mario under the table, worried that Stig would hear.

For a number of years, the Bon Tiempo apartments, which were at the back of San Antonio not far from the recently built Coastline Bar, had been contracted to Young Free & Single. During the winter however, Tyrone Lucas had made Trev a financial offer he could not refuse, so they were now the flagship apartments for Club Wicked. YF&S were now housed in the Hotel Arena. Just to seal the deal, Alison made Trev another offer he could not refuse not long after she arrived on resort. Since then, Trev had become one of Alison's more regular bedfellows. While he had no illusions about the relationship, he absolutely loved sleeping with her – it seemed there wasn't a thing she wasn't prepared to do.

Trev was in his late forties and was obviously an attractive man in his younger days. Even now, despite too many days spent under the Mediterranean sun and too many nights spent lying drunk under tables in Mediterranean bars, he had a certain roguish charm. The twinkle in his eye was still beguiling enough to earn him female admirers less than half his age, and his sense of humour was laddish enough to allow him popularity with most of the young male reps, workers and holidaymakers. Lean and tanned, he had accepted his advancing years and shorn his receding hairline. Though there was no preening vanity about him, it was clear he looked after himself – the winter visits to the gym, the games of squash and being constantly surrounded by young people ensured he looked a good decade younger than he actually was.

He had a gruff London accent that he often accentuated to play up to the pre-conception most had of him as an ex-pat who had chosen Spain as an alternative to residing at Her Majesty's Pleasure. Nothing could have been further from the truth. Trev had been a law-abiding London taxi driver who had been doing the job long enough to remember the good old days and had no desire to join the growing queues on taxi ranks at London mainline stations.

'My, my, we're all looking a bit glammed up tonight, ladies,' said Trev, as he sat down with Alison, Mario and Stig.

Trev had long since realised that Mario took himself far too seriously. When it came to piss-taking, Trev was the adept matador with a very red flag to Mario's extremely stupid bull.

'You look almost pretty enough to be going out with the girls, Mario.'

For once, Mario didn't bite. Trev turned his attentions to Alison.

'And how's the Queen of the Bon Tiempo?'

'Same as always, Trev, overworked, underpaid and running late.'

'Coach still not here?'

'Delayed . . . as usual.'

They fell into silence for a few moments. A brown and white mongrel that Trev had practically adopted as the apartments' dog came sniffing up to the table. The only living creature Trev enjoyed tormenting more than Mario was that dog. The difference was that the dog seemed to like it. Trev playfully attacked the dog then started rubbing its balls.

'Trevor!' exclaimed Alison. 'What on earth are you doing to that poor dog?'

'What?' he replied. 'He loves having his balls tickled, don't you, boy? He used to belong to the Las Huertas Hotel over the road, but he must prefer it here because he never goes back.'

'I'm not surprised with you tickling his balls all the time,' said Mario.

'Why?' Trev leant over to Mario and waved the hand he'd been tickling the dog's balls with under Mario's nose. 'Would tickling your balls make you stay?'

'Fuck off.'

Mario curled his lip, parried Trev's hand and looked away. As he did so, Trev nudged Alison and winked, then very quickly wiped the same hand over Mario's toastie. When Mario took a bite from it, they all burst out laughing.

'Right, as much fun as this is, I've a resort to run. See you all later.' Alison got up.

Trev followed her out. 'What are you up to later?'

'I don't think this meal thing is going to finish until late. It depends on what time the reps want to come back into San An.'

'If you like, I could come and pick you up. Come back to mine, you know . . .'

'Thanks, Trev, but I've got a busy day tomorrow. I'm up early.'

'Oh, that's a shame. I've some wicked new Charlie in too.' He grinned at her. 'Apart from anything else, I thought we could try rubbing it into those parts other Charlie doesn't reach. It might even help me with my temporary problem.'

Trev's problem was a pronounced attack of premature ejaculation. It only ever happened with Alison. There was just something about her that made him feel as though he had lead implants in his testicles. As soon as they were alone together he had a dull ache and a tightening in his loins that he just had to be rid of. Without doubt, he considered her to be the horniest, naughtiest woman he had ever slept with.

'Mmm.' Alison quite liked the idea of some high-quality cocaine, but she knew she would probably need to have her wits about her the next day. 'Let's wait and see how I feel later.'

They were interrupted by shouting and cheering from a group of a dozen or so clients standing near the road. An angry middle-aged Spanish man was barging his way through the group. As it parted, they saw that the cause of the commotion was a very drunk female client lying on the roof of a parked car. Pumping away on top of her, punching his arm in the air and yelling, 'C'mon,' was Del, one of a group of six lads from Reading.

Mario joined them at the door. 'Go on, Del my son!' He

turned to Alison and Trev. 'I told them at the welcome meeting that I was running a competition to see who could have a shag in the strangest place. Old Greg ran one last year. Right fucking laugh it was.' He started to make his way over to the cavorting couple. 'I better go and check the old wop who owns the car doesn't get the hump. You should join in The Competition, Trev. You must have done it in some strange places.'

As Mario made his way over to the car, Alison playfully turned to Trev. 'Yeah, I bet you've done it a few strange places – where's the strangest?'

A smile slowly spread across Trev's face. 'Mmm, let me see . . . where would it be?' Exaggeratedly, he clicked his fingers. 'Ah yes, I know. I would say that the strangest place I've ever had sex has got to be,' he leaned over and whispered in Alison's ear, 'up your bum.'

chapter thirteen

The Labiarinth Strip Club would have had a normal, quiet, early season night had it not been for the arrival of the YF&S and Club Wicked group.

It was a small club – even at its busiest there were only fifteen dancers operating at any one time. Tonight there had been half that figure and by midnight, there were just five dancers left to entertain the boisterous reps.

Greg was in his element. As soon as Charles Moon left he had taken a pill, not something he would normally have done on top of a couple of bottles of wine. One of the first girls he got to dance for him was a sexy American called Rio, petite, perfectly formed with a deep all-over tan and long jet-black hair. After the dance he got talking to her and soon discovered that her enthusiasm for clubbing and all things narcotic almost surpassed his own. She had dropped several hints about how she would love a pill, which Greg initially ignored – he had only brought three with him and he fully intended necking them all himself. However, when Rio whispered into his ear that stripping and taking ecstasy made her incredibly horny, Greg had the little white tablet out of his pocket and into her mouth before she could say G-string.

The thought of going on a pervey pill-munching session with Rio dangled before Greg like a nipple tassle. However, such a session was going to prove difficult with the principal element absent. He needed more pills.

Greg always got his drugs from his old friend Ace, the womanising West End prop. Due to his job, Ace never normally delivered – if someone wanted ecstasy or cocaine they would meet him at the bar where he worked and he would go to his secret stash hidden in the staff room. The deal would then be made either in there or in the darkness of the bar. But tonight Ace wasn't working, so was able to drive into Ibiza Town to sort Greg out. When he was told there were lap dancers involved, he was even happier to make the twenty-minute journey.

Ace was every bit Greg's equal when it came to charming the fairer sex. Within fifteen minutes of arriving two dancers called Bambi and Sky were eating out of his hand (and sniffing out of his wrap).

With plenty of narcotics doing the rounds and Lucas flashing a wad of cash, the up-for-it manager and remaining dancers were happy to lock the doors and make the party a little more private. A few of the reps left prior to the lock-in. The first to go had been Brad, who had a meeting with the owner of a West End bar called the Drunken Lizard.

Hughie left with him, partly because he was upset that there were no fat dancers at Labiarinth, but mainly because he wanted to make some progress with Roz, the Drunken Lizard's fourteen-stone female bouncer whom he had met earlier in the week. Sugar Ray also left not long after, tired of Stig's incessant taunts about his sexuality.

Whenever Rio wasn't being paid for a dance she came over and sat with Greg. Once the doors were locked, the drug taking became less discreet, with lines being chopped on tables or snorted out of glass, bullet-shaped phials.

As the pills kicked in, Greg and Rio started talking dirty to each other. After a while, they went and sat in a dark corner where she did a 'special' dance for him. Rio normally strictly adhered to the no physical contact policy, but with Greg she was more than happy to bend these rules. After a minute or so of her well-practised routine, she let her full, firm breasts glide along the outside of his trousers then up along the outside of his face. Greg looked her in the eye, opened his mouth, then just gently breathed over her nipples, letting his lips lightly brush against them. It took

Rio by surprise and she shuddered as her nipples went instantly hard.

She quickly straddled him and for a few moments wriggled about on his erection, an erection that the zip on his jeans was barely managing to contain. Back in control, she continued to tease him, occasionally touching him and whispering into his ear what she planned to do to him later. Greg would have quite happily done the deed there and then in front of everybody. Rio instinctively knew this, so to prolong his agony, gave him a little squeeze then went over to dance for Lucas. Over Lucas's shoulder, she simulated oral sex with a beer bottle. Greg could only groan.

Mario was getting similar treatment from Bambi, whom he had managed to pry away from Ace. He was so engrossed in her dancing and so full of himself larging it with a glass of brandy and a massive cigar, that he had completely forgotten to take any pictures or to get out the wrap of ketamine. It was only when Bambi asked him if he had any Charlie that he remembered Alison's instructions.

As soon as Bambi finished dancing for him, Mario got up and walked over to Greg.

'All right, mate, mind if I join you?'

'Yeah, I do.'

'Oh, come on, Greg, there's no need to be like that. It was Brad and Mikey I always had the problem with, not you.'

'What about Sugar Ray? You stitched him up too, didn't you?'

'That had nothing to do with me.'

'Whatever.'

'It's true. I'm like you, mate, I just want to go clubbing and shag loads of birds. I'm not into all of this political bollocks.'

'It didn't seem that way at the joint meeting the other day.'

'That was just because Brad was there. Seriously, Greg, I haven't got a problem with you at all. Here . . .' Mario reached into his pocket. 'I've got some Charlie. Have a line if you want.'

Greg eyed Mario uncertainly. Mario held it out.

'Be a bit more discreet, you knob,' said Greg, pushing Mario's hand down, then taking the wrap.

'What's up? Everyone's doing it out in the open.'

'And everyone's just about run out of gear. If they see this it'll be gone in one go. Come on, let's go into the bogs and do a line then.'

Greg's benevolent attitude towards Mario was undoubtedly helped by efficacy of the ecstasy now fully surging round his bloodstream.

'Don't you want to do it here?' He wouldn't get the clubbing picture he was after. A photo in some random toilet wasn't the same.

'No. Come on, let's go.'

'Oh, er, no. I've just done one. You take it. I trust you.' Even if he didn't get a picture of him taking the gear, there would be plenty of opportunity to capture its effect later.

Greg shrugged his shoulders and went to the Gents. As he walked in, Ace was at the sink washing his hands.

'Fucking sound this place, I'm glad I came along. What do you reckon on those pills I got for you?'

'Yeah, tops,' replied Greg. 'Do you fancy a line?'

'Just a very small one.'

Ace made a fist and Greg put a pinch of white powder on the back of Ace's hand.

'Are you sure that's enough?' asked Greg.

'Yeah. I only want a tiny bit. If I do too much it fucks up the E's.'

Ace raised his hand to his nose and sniffed. Almost immediately he blew the contents out of his nose on to the floor.

'Fucking hell, Greg you cunt, what are you trying to do to me?'

Greg looked at him surprised. 'What do you mean?'

'That's not Charlie, it's fucking ketamine.'

'*You what?*'

'Ketamine, Special K. Fucking animal tranquillizer. What you playing at?'

'I didn't realise. Mario . . .' Greg's voice trailed off. 'The slippery fucker.'

'What, are you telling me that Mario gave you that wrap?' Greg nodded. 'And he told you it was Charlie?'

'Yep. Loved up on E's or not, I'm going to go in there and rip his fucking head off.'

'Hold on,' said Ace, grabbing Greg's arm, 'there must be a reason he's trying to stitch you up.'

'Maybe he's after Rio.'

'Yeah, maybe. He's already prised that Bambi away from me. Listen, I've got an idea. Why not play him at his own game?'

'What do you mean?'

'Don't let him know that you know it's ketamine. When we go back we'll stop at the bar and buy three shots, then we'll put some ketamine in the one for Mario – let's spike the fucker. If we get something like Jaegermeisters, he won't taste a thing, especially as we'll down them in one.'

'I've never done ketamine before. What'll it do to him?'

'Oh trust me, he'll be messy . . . *very* messy.'

At Raison D'Etre with the girls, Hawthorne-Blythe wasn't having a good time either. Kit had left directly after the meal and Hawthorne-Blythe was beginning to wish he had left with him.

Although he loved being around people enjoying themselves and maybe even being a little outrageous, he loathed being cornered by self-indulgent, opinionated, unintelligent, boorish drunks. When the drunk in question was female, constantly blowing smoke into his face and partly responsible for embezzling his business out of several hundred thousand pounds, he had to call upon all his reserves of restraint to maintain his usual standard of courtesy and impeccable manners.

Alison was extremely pissed. Even before the meal was finished her voice could be heard above all others, as she hogged the spotlight or bragged about her so-called achievements. After the meal when the DJ started playing,

Alison was the first on the floor, flirting with the waiters, cackling in a loud voice and dancing exaggeratedly.

When she tired of that, she sat herself next to Hawthorne-Blythe and started a one-way conversation. Every time he escaped, she cornered him. Never a rude man, Hawthorne-Blythe had got to the stage where he could stand listening to her no longer. He was contemplating leaving the venue to get away, but for a temporary respite, settled for yet another visit to the Gents.

When he re-entered the main room, Alison was at the DJ stand trying to take over. The DJ was clearly annoyed, particularly when her shoving caused the needle to slide across the record that was playing.

Hawthorne-Blythe shook his head and went to the bar, which was the point in the room farthest away from the DJ. The first year YF&S rep Tamsin was just being served. Hawthorne-Blythe added to her order, not an unreasonable thing to do as he was picking up most of the bill.

'And get me a large brandy please, barman.' He turned to Tamsin. 'Are you having a good night?'

'Great, fantastic.'

'And what about repping, what do you think of it so far?'

'Yeah, fab, triff, love it,' gushed Tamsin.

Tamsin's enthusiastic response had nothing to do with the fact that Hawthorne-Blythe was her boss, because in the world of Tamsin, everything was fab, triff, great and fantastic.

'I haven't seen Arabella for a while,' said Hawthorne-Blythe. 'Where is she?'

'Oh, she left about twenty minutes ago.'

They stood at the bar, both watching Alison, who had now found the microphone and was trying to switch it on. The DJ was attempting to mix a tune with one hand and restrain Alison with the other.

'She's mad, isn't she?'

'Mad,' repeated Hawthorne-Blythe. 'Perhaps not the first adjective I'd use to describe her.' The barman handed Hawthorne-Blythe his drink. 'Thank you. I'm just going to sit over there, Tamsin. I'm afraid my legs aren't what they used to be.'

'Yeah, cool, triff.'

Hawthorne-Blythe sat down with his back to the DJ and sipped his brandy. He decided that once he finished his drink he'd leave. He had been sitting there for barely a minute when Alison stumbled over.

'H-B, you old devil,' she slurred, 'fu'in' DJ's ushless, in't he? Only thing he can mix is his drinks an' only thing he can scratch is his nuts. Ha!' She pulled up a chair, burped and sat down. 'Now lishen, H-B. I dunno if I've already told you this, but we're alike you an' me. We're both good with people; we're both used to gettin' what we want, am I right?'

'Yes, you have already told me this.'

'Eggs-hackly. Oops!' Alison covered her mouth as she hiccuped. 'You see, H-B, even in the unlikely event that YF&S win this thing and get taken over by The Monastery and Club Wicked go out of business, I don't care. An' you know why?'

'Yes, you've explained several times.'

'I'll tell you then, shall I?' said Alison ignoring his reply. 'It's because I've got my own biz back home. Sunglasses. Drivin' up and down fu'in' country, sellin' sunglasses. Like an agent only better – and richer.' Alison laughed and belched again. 'All the top stores stock 'em. I've got my own car at home. Fu'in' gorgeous it is. Sports car. Here, I've got a pixshure of it in me purse.'

As she rummaged around in her purse she knocked a glass of vodka and cranberry off the table and all over Mel's little yellow dress.

'Oi, you clumsy . . .' Mel jumped up.

Alison was oblivious. She thrusted a photograph at Hawthorne-Blythe.

'Here, fu'in' lovely motor, in't it?'

'You've shown it to me several times, Alison.'

'Now, I know you an' me haven't always seen eye to eye,

H-B, what wiv old silly bollocks Felipe an' all that. But what I did last year, it was jus' bizniz.'

'No, Alison, it was fraud, and you are extremely fortunate that you are not now in prison rather than sat here making a nuisance of yourself. Now if you'll excuse—'

Before Hawthorne-Blythe had a chance to finish his sentence, Mel grabbed hold of Alison's shoulder and swung her round.

'Are you going to apologise for what you've just done to my dress, or what?'

Alison looked Mel up and down. 'What y'on about?'

'You just knocked a drink all over me.'

Alison focused on the stain. 'I did that?'

'Yes, you did.'

Alison giggled. 'Oops.' She reached into her purse and pulled out a ten Euro note. She handed it to Mel. 'Go on. Get yourself a new one – that should cover it.'

She punched Hawthorne-Blythe's arm. He was about as amused as Mel.

'Alison, I think you're drunk. It might be best if you apologise to Mel and get a cab home.'

'Apologise? Moi? I'm her fu'in' man-ger. I don't have to apologise. If she don't like it, what's she going to do?'

As Alison finished her sentence, Mel threw a glass of white wine in her face. Alison was too shocked to react. A few of the other reps now looked over.

'That's what I'm going to do, you stupid tart!' screamed Mel. 'And I tell you what else I'm going to do too. I'm going to start working at the Labiarinth later in the week, so you can poke your stupid job.'

As the wine dribbled down Alison's chin, she flew at Mel and grabbed hold of her hair. They tumbled over a table sending its contents flying and two waiters had to break them up before they did each other any serious damage.

'You fucking bitch,' screamed Alison as she tried to wriggle free of a waiter's grasp, 'you're fired.'

'I've already resigned, you dried-up old hag.' Mel straight-ened herself and stormed out.

'I think it might be a good idea if I ordered the coach,' said Hawthorne-Blythe. 'It's a shame you didn't carry on selling sunglasses, Alison. You are nothing but trouble and stupid at that.'

Alison picked up the picture of her car and held it under Hawthorne-Blythe's nose. 'If I am stupid then I don't know what that makes you, because it was your money that paid for this car. And here I am, large as life and twice as beautiful, about to fuck you up again.'

Alison swigged back the remnants of her drink, swept up her bag and left.

For a fleeting second, Hawthorne-Blythe agreed with her. He was stupid, allowing himself to get into such a mess.

And the way things were going, it was probably only going to get worse.

Mario started to feel very strange within twenty minutes of knocking back a Jaegermeister with Greg and Ace. His limbs didn't seem to be attached to the right parts of his body, his vision became very narrow, almost tunnel like, and there seemed to be a constant dull hum in his ears.

He was aware of what was going on but it was almost as though he was observing himself with a bizarre kind of detachment in exaggerated 3D. He tried to move a couple of times, but the floor had taken on a kind of wavey liquid form and any attempt to stand up required a firm grasp on an inanimate object to steady himself. He started sweating profusely.

There was also something niggling him, a recollection that he had some sort of task to perform. A few times it would flash into his memory but before he had a chance to act upon it, it would be gone. On one occasion though, it stayed in his head long enough for him to remember – it was something to do with the camera. Quite what it was he was supposed to do with the camera he couldn't quite recall, but he reached into his pocket and got it out. He took a picture of nothing in particular. Taking photographs in the club was prohibited and Rio quickly snatched the camera from him.

The next thing he remembered was being on stage naked.

To Greg, Ace and the others watching, Mario went downhill very quickly after knocking back the spiked Jaegermeister. Lucas had already left so, luckily for Mario, his subsequent antics were missed by his superior.

His initial trance-like state was replaced with one of total euphoria as he jumped up onto a table and started dancing, taking his shirt off. Greg and Ace persuaded the girls and the manager to let get him on stage. He didn't need much encouraging and he was soon starkers, his abundant tackle attracting a few nods of approval from both sexes.

Greg also persuaded Rio to let him use Mario's camera for a permanent reminder of his Labiarinth debut.

But the cigar was Ace's idea. He whispered to Greg, 'Let's nip into the bogs with Mario's cigar.' Greg looked confused. 'And bring the camera and a tray.'

In the Gents, Ace's plan became clear as he started to undo his trousers and open the cubicle door. 'Give us the camera and that tray.'

'No,' said Greg, 'please don't tell me you're about to do what I think you are. That's just too disgusting . . . you can't!'

Ace grinned. 'Meet you back in the bar.'

'He's going to go green when he sees the pictures.'

A few minutes later, Ace walked back into the club with the most evil of grins and the cigar held at arm's length.

'Where's the tray?' asked Greg.

'It had my shit all over it – I threw it out the window.'

'Yuk.'

Mario was strutting round in the altogether, clearly proud of what he had been blessed with and clearly through the worst stage of the ketamine experience.

Ace went over and patted him on the back.

'Nice one, Mario.' He pointed to the cigar that he'd placed back in the ashtray. 'D'you want a light?'

Mario puffed on the cigar, at first pulling a face as though it had a strange taste, but quickly dismissing it as he slipped his boxer shorts back on. Greg thought he would be sick.

Seconds later the manager came up to Mario.

'Oi, Dreamboy, there's some girl at the door for you.'

Still puffing on the cigar, he walked to the club entrance. He was feeling slightly better. When Arabella saw him only wearing boxer shorts she was horrified.

'Mario! What have you been doing? Where's all of your clothes?'

'Just been having a laugh, babe. Come 'ere.'

He grabbed hold of her and started kissing her. She pulled away.

'God, you smell and taste awful, what have you been doing?'

'Nothing, babe, it must just be the cigar. I'm feeling really randy. Let's do it here, now, in this alleyway.'

He went to grab her again but she moved away.

'I thought you said you wanted to do things properly? If a coach isn't good enough then I'm certainly not going to do it here. I'm more used to four-posters than footpaths.'

'Come on, babe,' implored Mario making one last attempt. 'You know that caviar tastes good no matter where you have it.'

She responded to his kiss but stopped him as he shoved his hand up her skirt.

'Please don't, Mario. Let's leave, go back to your place and do this properly.'

Mario reluctantly gave up. 'OK. I just need to get my clothes.'

He gave her another kiss and went back into the club. Sitting by his clothes was Bambi.

'Hello, big boy,' she said, in her barely discernible Danish accent. 'What are you doing later?'

'I've got to go. Things to sort out.'

'That's a shame. Do you want to meet up sometime? Maybe just me, you and Sky?'

Mario gulped and under his breath cursed Arabella for

being there. He knew, though, that if he blew Arabella out tonight then any chance of using her to stitch up YF&S would be gone. Bambi and Sky would have to wait.

'Yeah, that'll be great.' He pulled his shirt on. 'Give me your number.'

Bambi already had a card in her hand. 'Make sure you call.'

'Yeah, I will.'

He went to leave but she stopped him. 'Haven't you forgotten something?' She handed him the camera. 'Rio told me to give this back to you.'

Mario slapped his forehead. 'I forgot all about it. I can't even remember if I took any pictures.' Looking over his shoulder to check Arabella wasn't in the club, he gave her a long kiss. Bambi wrinkled her nose. 'I'll give you a call.'

Outside, Arabella had already flagged down a taxi. As they got in she noticed the camera.

'What's that for?'

'The Monastery camera. They want some clubbing shots.'

'Take any good photos tonight?'

'I don't know, babe. Anything in here's probably shit . . .'

chapter fourteen

'Love!'

Greg spluttered out his beer, covering Vaz and the others sitting around him on the beach in a fine alcoholic spray.

'Yeah, love,' repeated Vaz. 'Cupid's arrow right up the Jacksy. It'd be perfect.'

Greg started laughing. 'Please tell me you're joking.'

'All I'm saying is that it must be great to be out here in Ibiza and to fall in love with somebody. I mean look at this place. It's beautiful. It's romantic.'

'Yeah, he's right,' giggled Tamsin. 'This island is gorge, amazing, triff . . . total paradise. What's the name of it again?'

'Espalmador,' said Hughie, juggling a football in the air on the edge of the group.

It was Wednesday, 18 June, two days after the reps' night out and the first YF&S cruise of the season to the tiny island of Espalmador, a thirty-minute ferry ride from Ibiza Town. It was a lazy day and given the excessive intake of alcohol on the Monday night, that was no bad thing, even with the day and a half they'd since had to recover. Most of the clients simply wanted to sunbathe and although the reps started up the odd game of beach volleyball, the only two things that were organised for the day were lunch and a trip to the nearby mudbath.

'I mean,' continued Vaz, 'could you imagine being here with someone that you were truly mad about? It's absolutely idyllic.'

'Vaz, trust me on this one. If ever you get those little

butterflies in your stomach, it just means that you've eaten some dodgy chicken.'

'Oh come on, mate, you're not seriously telling me that you've never fallen head over heels for a girl in all the time you've been a rep?'

'Vaz, I'll tell you seriously or I'll put on a fez and wear a little red nose and tell you very *un*seriously if it makes you feel better . . . no, I have not.'

'I don't believe you,' said Tamsin. 'There must have been someone.'

'No,' replied Greg, with a moment's hesitation so slight that only the most highly trained of non-verbal communicators would have picked up on it. 'No one.'

'So, what you're saying,' said Tamsin, 'is that all you're interested in is shagging about?'

'No, not just shagging about.' The football that Hughie had been juggling fell near Greg, so he picked it up and bounced it on his head. 'I'm also interested in how United get on when they're playing, although that's not often during the summer.'

Tamsin wasn't sure if he was being serious. In truth, though he would never have admitted it, neither was Greg.

'Aren't you worried that your willy's just going to, I don't know,' Tamsin screwed up her face, 'drop off?'

'I can assure you that there's nothing wrong with the organ between my legs.'

'I'm sure there isn't,' said Vaz, 'it's the one between your ears that we're worried about.'

All the reps laughed, including Greg, who stopped heading the football and threw it at Vaz.

'On me head, son,' yelled Hughie.

'So do you think you'll ever settle down?' asked Tamsin.

Greg flopped back on to the sand. 'I don't know, darling.' He looked over at a family further along the beach, where two little boys were playing football with their father. His tone became less flippant. 'I mean, I always imagined myself doing what that bloke over there is, y'know, being the dad playing footie with his kids. But now? Even if I met someone tomorrow – which is fucking unlikely – it'd probably be another few years before kids arrived.' He drew a shape in the sand. It was the first time any of the new reps had seen him even close to being rueful. 'By the time they were teenagers, I'd be too old to be running round kicking a football – kicking the bucket more like.'

'Or kicking yourself for being such a knob when you were younger,' joined in Hughie.

Greg looked at him. 'I thought you were on my side.'

'Yeah, I am. I just thought it sounded good.'

Everyone chuckled.

'I suppose I've got a really biased view because of my parents,' said Tamsin. 'I'm the first generation in our family who hasn't had to have an arranged marriage. The whole idea of falling in love and meeting a soulmate, it just seems so . . . so triff.'

'Maybe your parents had the right idea,' said Greg, to everyone's obvious surprise. 'That whole love stuff is over-rated. I had this conversation with Brad last year, on this very beach, funnily enough. He was going on about wanting the butterflies, the fireworks and all that crap. I told him that once all that's gone, all that's left is what you've got in common and then shared experiences. Maybe having someone older who can see how compatible a partner might be isn't such a bad idea after all.'

'Yeah,' replied Tamsin, 'you wouldn't be saying that if your dad was trying to palm you off with an old minger in exchange for half a dozen cows.'

'Why are you so cynical, Greg?' asked Vaz.

'Because I see the same thing happen year after year. Take Brad for example. Last summer Brad was convinced that a particular woman was The One. Carmen, her name was. Now to an old cynic like me it was obvious that they didn't have that much in common but Ibiza worked its magic on them and that was it.'

'What happened?' asked Tamsin.

'Usual story. After a few months back in the UK they split up.'

'Fucking hell,' sighed Vaz, 'I hope I don't become as cynical as you.'

'You will, mate. The only thing that'll keep you sane is The Competition – which once again, I'm leading, by the way.'

'Only because you won't give me any bonus points for shagging fat birds,' protested Hughie.

'Yeah, but that's because you enjoy it. For most normal blokes it'd be a chore and they'd deserve the extra points.'

'Don't you find you get bored with it all though?' continued Vaz. 'And don't you feel bad about the way girls get used?'

'What? Fucking hell, I can tell it's your first year. It's more often a case of them using us! They come over here, then go back to their jobs and more often or not, boyfriends too. Yeah, we'll sleep with thirty, forty, maybe fifty girls in a summer. But if you think about it, we're not having sex any more than Mr Average – it just happens to be with different people.'

All the reps started laughing.

'It's true. Trust me, these are probably going to be among the best days of your lives. You'll still be talking about them in ten, twenty years' time. My advice is to make hay while the sun shines, and in case you hadn't noticed, it's over thirty degrees.'

'Well, each to his own,' said Vaz. 'I'm not planning to be a monk while I'm here, but if the right girl comes along then that's it. I'll sweep her off her feet and make her feel like a princess.'

'Ah,' said Tamsin, stroking his leg, 'that's so sweet.'

Greg and Hughie stuck their fingers down their throats.

Arabella stopped reading her copy of *Tatler* for an instant. The 'princess' remark stung. Mario had not made the slightest romantic overture towards her since he had arrived in Ibiza and probably couldn't even spell the word princess, let alone treat her like one. She returned to her magazine.

'See,' said Tamsin, playfully snuggling up to Vaz, 'not all

men turn into total bastards as soon as they put on a rep's badge.'

'Tamsin, girl,' declared Greg authoritatively, 'if you work on the basic premise that all men are bastards and if we work on the basic premise that all women are mad, then relationships would be a lot easier. Forget all that Venus and Mars bollocks.'

'Except for male reps,' she retorted, 'they're bastards *and* mad.'

They were distracted by giggling from a group of lads a few metres away. Sugar Ray was walking away from the group and towards the reps, shaking his head.

'What are they up to now?' asked Hughie.

Sugar Ray sat down. 'They're fucking nutters. Didn't you say they were out here in your hotel last summer, Greg?'

'Yeah. See the bloke in the wheelchair?'

'What, you mean Crip?'

Tamsin was appalled. 'Sugar Ray! You're the last person I would have thought to come out with a comment like that.'

Sugar Ray smiled. 'That's what *he* calls himself. I think his real name is Chris, but all his mates call him Crip and apparently it was his idea. He's a wicked guy.'

'He had a really bad motorbike accident a few years ago,' said Greg. 'It left him without the use of his legs. Last year he got huge compensation so he paid for all of his mates to come on holiday on the condition that they treat him exactly the same as before his accident.'

'He's done the same this year,' added Sugar Ray. 'I hate to admit it, but I've always felt uncomfortable round people in wheelchairs and that. I suppose it's because I can't imagine what it would be like to be in their position, but still kind of knowing that there but for the grace of God go I.'

'How's Crip's mate Dean getting on with that fit-looking Scouser?' asked Greg.

'Is Dean the one who's the absolute dreamboat, with dark hair and come-to-bed eyes?' sighed Sugar Ray.

'Yeah that's him. Fancy him, do you, Sugar Ray?'

'I'm only flesh and blood, Greg,' said Sugar Ray camply. 'He's a babe.'

'I don't suppose you fancy trying to persuade him to turn, do you? I was getting on great with that Scouser until he came along.'

'Sorry, Greg. I'll admit I'm partial to turning the odd straight guy, but he's most definitely one hundred per cent hetero. You'll have to rely on your own natural charm.'

'Yeah, that's what I'm afraid of.' Greg jumped up and clapped his hands. 'Right, come on then, let's get this lot to the mudbath.' He turned to Arabella. 'And that includes you, madam.'

Arabella looked horrified. 'I take it you are joking. There is absolutely no way that I'm going into a mudbath.'

'Oh yes you are.' He turned to the other reps. 'Leave me and her ladyship for a sec and round up all the clients.'

He snatched the copy of *Tatler* from her and dropped it on the sand.

'Hey, what do you think-'

'Shut up, Arabella. We've only been doing the job a few days but I can already tell that you're not interested. God knows how you got through the interviews and frankly, I haven't got a clue why on earth you wanted to work as a rep. What I do know is that if you don't pull your finger out, you'll be on the next flight home.'

A calm smile formed on Arabella's rosebud lips. 'Oh, I don't think you will get rid of me, Greg.'

Greg was taken aback. 'And why's that?'

'Because it wouldn't look good if a rep leaves in the first week. You must have heard how badly The Monastery viewed Mel's departure on Monday night. I think Hawthorne-Blythe would be most upset with you if you got rid of me. I get on so well with him too – we've got the same kind of background.'

'You don't know how wrong you are about that,' replied Greg, who was one of the few people who knew about Hawthorne-Blythe's working-class roots.

Arabella picked up her *Tatler*, dusted the sand off and laid back on her sunlounger.

Greg thought for a moment. Arabella did have a very good point about it not reflecting well on YF&S if she left. Equally though, it would look bad if she carried on doing the job and behaved in the way that she was. Greg's mind was made up.

He snatched the magazine from her again.

'First of all, you're wrong about not being prepared to sack you – I am. I don't want to because all those things you said were right, but I'm pretty sure that there's a reason you want to stay here, although I haven't worked out what it is. So, like it or not, you're going in that mudbath.'

Before Arabella had a chance to protest, Greg had picked up a klaxon and let it off to get everyone's attention.

'I've got a bottle of champagne for the first one of you to get Arabella and throw her into the mudbath . . .'

Arabella didn't stand a chance. Within seconds, Crip's gang had her thrown headfirst into the foul-smelling pit.

She emerged, coughing and spluttering like Swamp Thing.

'*Bastards!*'

chapter fifteen

As Lucas walked towards Koppas Café, a bar at the bottom of the main San An drag that overlooked the harbour, Alison could tell he wasn't happy. She thought it would be easier if she dealt with him on her own.

'Mario, make yourself scarce. Lucas has just had a meeting with The Monastery and H-B and it doesn't look as though it went well.'

'Where should I go?'

'Walk round with your shirt off like everyone else, or go and watch *Only Fools and Horses* somewhere.'

Obediently, Mario got up.

'Better still, nip into the photo place and get the pictures from Monday night, then come back. He looks in a bad mood and I might need to get away.'

'OK.'

'And Mario . . .'

'What?'

'Don't open them. I don't want you taking any out of you making a prat of yourself. Understand?'

Mario trundled off, nodding at Lucas and being roundly ignored.

'That went fucking well,' spat Lucas, taking a chair from another table without asking.

'What happened?' asked Alison sheepishly, knowing that it was largely her fault that Monday night had gone so badly.

'Thankfully, stupidly, H-B being H-B was far too much of a gentleman to go into the gory details of your drunken behaviour, but he made it abundantly clear that he was less

151

than impressed and said that, in his opinion, you were a liability.'

'Shit. What did you say?'

'Oh, I just reverted to the usual, saying that his opinion was irrelevant because you worked for me. I tried to maintain that it was meant to be a night where everyone let their hair down. I told them that the whole ethos of Club Wicked is to cut loose and have a good time. I tried to turn it round but they didn't totally buy it. Maybe he was right and you *are* a liability. What on earth were you thinking of getting so pissed?'

'Oh, Lucas, I'm sorry. It must have been those bloody chupitos they kept bringing over – I forgot how strong they were. What did they say about Mel leaving?'

'I did a bit of research. Luckily I got on well with the owner of Labiarinth – not surprising really given the amount of money I spent in there the other night. He dug into things a little for me and found out that Mel had applied for the job *before* she came out here with us. It looks like she was planning to work there all along.'

'Crafty fucking bitch.'

'Thankfully that made it seem as though it wasn't bad management on your part – I even implied that you had a suspicion she was up to something and that you'd been putting pressure on her, which was why she snapped.'

'Lucas, you're so clever,' she giggled, resting her hand on his thigh.

'It still didn't reflect too well on us as a company though – it makes our selection procedure look suspect.'

Under different circumstances, Alison would have remarked that employing someone on the basis of her cup size was suspect, but given her own recent shortcomings, she decided to keep it to herself.

'I gave the manager an incentive to look for another girl. He told Mel he'd changed his mind about the job and apparently she's leaving this afternoon.' He looked at his watch. 'In fact, she should have already left.'

'Good riddance.' Alison stirred her coffee. 'So how did the meeting finish?'

'All in all, I would say that I did a reasonably good damage limitation exercise, given what really happened, but don't you ever let me down like that again.'

'I won't . . . I'm sorry.' Inwardly, Alison breathed a sigh of relief, knowing that the outcome could have been far worse. 'Anything else?'

'Yeah. The Monastery want us to do a joint party this Sunday in Eden. They're calling it a DJ Face-Off.'

'A what?'

'A DJ Face-Off. It's meant to be a joint party where YF&S get one of their reps to DJ and we get one of ours to as well. It's meant to be a good-natured competition. They've got a couple of promoters and DJs coming down to decide who's best – there's talk of giving the winner a spot at one of the clubs later in the season. A few of our reps are pretty good, aren't they?'

Alison looked a little worried. 'Yeah, two or three of them can play a bit – Smiffy is probably the best. I doubt if he's anywhere near as good as Vaz though – everyone says he's brilliant.'

Lucas threw his arms out. 'Fucking great. Here we are meant to be the clubber's holiday company and YF&S have got the best DJ.' They sat and looked at each other for a moment. 'I guess we'll have to find some way of stitching him up. Can't we just break his arm or something?' suggested Lucas, matter-of-factly.

'He looks quite a wiry little sod. Anyway, that sort of thing might be a little too obvious.' Alison had taken the suggestion seriously because she knew Lucas well enough to realise that he was serious. 'Leave it with me, I'll think of something.'

'The Monastery have also got a singer coming over – Jocelyn Brown, I think they said. A rep from each company has to get on stage with her and sing. Who do you suggest?'

'Stig.'

'What, the big hairy one?'

'Believe it or not, he's got a great voice. He sounds like that bloke out of The Commitments.'

'Are you sure you mean he sounds like him and not just *looks* like him.'

'Relax. He's our boy.'

'Who will YF&S use.'

'From what I've heard probably Sugar Ray.'

'He's the little queer one, isn't he?'

'Yeah. Utterly camp and totally scared of Stig.'

'Good. Let's also get the reps to really gee up the clients. On the night, get them to chant Stig's name and boo the queer. Let's get a bit of real competition going.'

Alison ordered them both a drink just as Mario turned up.

'And I'll have a beer,' he said, joining them at the table.

Lucas looked at a couple of girls walking by. Alison took the opportunity to give Mario a little nod to let him know everything was all right. She took the photo pack from him. 'Shall we have a look at these pictures?'

'Are these the ones from Monday night?' asked Lucas. 'Didn't you say that there weren't any good ones, Mario? And what happened to giving Greg that ketamine? The state you were in it looked more like he gave it to you.'

'Actually, I think that's what happened,' replied Mario sheepishly. 'Fuck knows how, but I think they spiked my drink.'

'Great!' said Lucas, snatching the pictures from Alison. 'Between the two of you, I think I can safely say Monday night was a complete fuck-up.'

He started sifting through the photos, quickly and with no particular interest. He was almost up to the last one when he stopped and screwed his face up. 'Oh my God! Yuk! Who took this?'

'What?' replied Alison and Mario simultaneously.

'This.'

Lucas showed them a picture of a cigar, stuck into a pile of shit on a beer tray. Alison looked at it as baffled as Lucas.

A wave of realisation swept over Mario's face at about the

same time the grip of nausea took hold of his stomach. The reason the cigar tasted funny after his striptease became suddenly apparent.

'Oh fuck!'

Mario retched over the back of the chair, just missing the waiter's foot.

It was unlikely he would ever smoke another cigar again.

After they left Espalmador, Arabella sulked all through the champagne diving until Greg warned her that if she didn't join in he would be giving out more champagne to whoever could get her into the sea topless.

Most of the champagne was being retrieved by Crip and his crew. Crip couldn't actually dive into the sea, so relied on his friends to throw him in and then haul him out. The pretty Scouse girl that Crip's mate Dean seemed to be making progress with was at the other end of the boat. Crip had just been hauled out of the water, so Greg went up to him and whispered in his ear. Crip burst out laughing and nodded. Greg made his way to the other end of the boat and sat next to the Scouse girl.

'Not diving for champagne, Janine?'

'I don't really like going underwater.'

'Is this the first time you've been to Ibiza?'

'It's my first time abroad.'

'Really! So what do you think?'

'Yeah sound, I've really enjoyed myself. I suppose the only downer is that I'm missing my pets.'

'What have you got?'

'Three dogs, a cat, two hamsters and a rabbit.'

'Bloody hell!'

'Have you got any pets?'

'Yeah,' lied Greg. 'That's the worst thing about doing this job. Six months away from Magnum. I can't wait to get back to see him. He's an Alsatian.'

'Ooh, I love Alsatians.'

They sat in silence for a moment, watching as Dean picked Crip up, ready to throw him in again.

'Terrible really, isn't it?'

'What is?' asked Janine.

'The way Dean bullies Crip.'

Janine looked surprised. 'Does he?'

'Yeah, haven't you seen him throwing Crip into the water?'

'But I thought he wanted him to.'

On cue, Crip started screaming and yelling. 'No Dean, you bastard. No more. Please don't throw me back in the water. A joke's a joke. Come on, mate, be fair, pleeeaaaase!'

Splosh. Crip landed in the water. Dean, unaware that Greg had asked Crip to act as though he didn't want to go into the sea, had naturally assumed that Crip was just messing about. It didn't look quite so innocent to Janine.

'What a shit! Dean seemed so nice when I was talking to him earlier.'

'Oh, I'm sure he's all right. He just doesn't know when to stop, I guess. You see it a lot with groups of lads – there's always one who gets picked on. I suppose Crip's an easy target.'

Janine's opinion of Dean was clearly fast changing. Greg had a flash of inspiration.

'Apparently Dean's got quite a good job at home. Did he tell you what he does?'

'No, he didn't actually. We were just talking about clubbing and that.'

'He told me works with animals.'

'Does he? Well, he can't be all bad then.'

'Exactly.' Greg paused for a moment. 'I can't remember exactly what he does or who it was he said he works for. Something-or-other Laboratories, I think.'

Janine's expression changed.

'I wasn't really listening, to tell the truth. I know that whoever it is he works for has contracts with some large cosmetics companies.'

She stood up. 'I'm going to give him a piece of my mind.'

'Don't do that,' said Greg, grabbing her arm. 'I've probably got it all wrong. I'm sure he's not the one who actually kills them or puts stuff into their eyes or whatever it is they do. Besides, he told me in confidence and I'd feel bad if he knew I'd said anything. Please, Janine, just keep it to yourself.'

'All right,' said Janine sitting back down. 'How do people do jobs like that?'

'Beats me. I guess it's just a power thing. It's probably the reason he bullies Crip too. I'm sure he's not all bad though. Anyway, let's change the subject. Where are you going tonight?'

'I was supposed to be meeting up with Dean and that lot. I don't think I'll bother now.'

'Well, if you fancy it, there's a wicked Mexican round the back of San An that I haven't been to yet. We're all meeting up in the Drunken Lizard later, so maybe we could go there after.'

'That sounds great.'

'Cool. Well, I'd better tell the captain to head back to Ibiza. I'll see you later.'

With a smile on his face, Greg walked over to the other end of the boat and made sure everyone was out of the water so that they could set off. He winked at Crip and gave him two bottles of champagne.

'All go according to plan?' asked Crip.

'Swimmingly.' Greg smiled. 'She loves animals, which is just as well because tonight I'm planning to give her a beasting she won't forget . . .'

chapter sixteen

That night Greg left the Drunken Lizard to get some cocaine from Ace. Crip's little crew wanted half a dozen grams and Greg knew that Ace would give him half a gram for himself for putting the business his way. In the end, disappointingly, Janine had been too tired to come out after the cruise, so Greg decided to trawl the West End to see if he could find any other potential points.

As he walked towards Ace's place of work, two pretty girls walked past him. Greg gave them an appreciative look, then noticed they had large patches of hair missing from the back of their heads. What was that all about? he wondered. Some new trend?

Ace worked hard, trying to attract punters into the bar, and as Greg approached his corner, he wasn't surprised to see Ace and another prop snogging two drunken holiday-makers. As he got closer, the hair loss mystery suddenly became clear. The props were running their hands over the back of the girls' heads, and as they did so, clumps of hair were tumbling to the ground. The girls staggered off, seemingly unaware of their enforced alopecia. Other props started clapping.

'What are you doing?' asked Greg.

'We've been having a competition for the last week,' said Ace. 'We've all got these battery operated hair clippers.' He opened his hand to show him. 'Every time we kiss a girl we lob a bit of her hair off.'

'I wondered what was going on. I've just seen two girls with clumps of hair missing. How many have you done?'

'Between us I'd say well over a couple of hundred. Put it

this way – after the first night we had to bring the re-chargers in.'

'Who's winning?'

'He is,' replied Ace, pointing to his fellow prop, 'but only because I had those few days off when I wasn't working. Thanks for the invite to the Labiarinth the other night, by the way, it was wicked. Do you know if Mario saw the picture?'

'I'd guess so. I doubt if he'll be smoking any cigars for a while.'

Ace laughed. 'He is a complete tosser, isn't he?'

'One hundred per cent.'

'Do you want this nose then? Six, wasn't it?'

'Yeah.'

They made their way through the noisy bar to the sanctuary of the staff room.

'I heard you were fed up with propping, Ace. Couldn't you make a living knocking out gear?'

Ace shook his head. 'I sell the odd bit of Charlie and a few pills to you and some of the crew, but I don't want to turn into a full-time dealer. Another couple of weeks and I reckon I'll probably go home. I've been propping for too long and it's not the same crack without Toby working with me.'

'The place won't be the same without you.'

'Cheers. Still, it'll leave more girls free for you. Any young fillies lined up for tonight?'

'I was meant to be taking some fit little Scouser for a meal at the Mexican but she's blown me out.'

'So what are you going to do instead?'

'Most of our lot are in the Drunken Lizard so I'm nipping up there. I quite fancy that barmaid.'

'What, you mean Imogen? She's a babe. She loves GHB as well. My mate shagged her on it last year.'

'Really? I don't suppose you've got any GHB knocking about, have you?'

'As it happens, I think you might be in luck.' Ace

159

rummaged around in a box. 'Here we go.' He pulled out a small clear plastic bottle.

'Wicked. How much do you want for it?'

'You're all right. Call it your commission on the nosebag.'

'Nice one. I'll catch up with you tomorrow.'

Greg made his way back to the Drunken Lizard with the six grams and the GHB. There were not many clients at the Drunken Lizard, so Greg had time to concentrate all his attentions on Imogen.

Hughie was also focused on seduction, though the object of his desire was a good deal more substantial – Roz the bouncer. His ardour had increased logarithmically when Roz had demonstrated one of her party pieces, namely removing her three false front teeth then rinsing them in unsuspecting holidaymakers' beer before putting then back in her mouth.

Despite Hughie's enthusiasm and conviction that due to being unaccustomed to the attention, larger women more readily succumbed to his flattery-based seduction techniques, Roz was not falling for it. Greg was within hearing distance when Roz rejected Hughie, so broke off from the progress he was making with Imogen and went over to goad him.

'What's up, Hughie, losing your charm?'

Hughie was too flabbergasted by the rejection to deny it. 'I can't believe she's not interested,' he said. 'I mean, she can hardly have men falling at her feet, can she?'

'No idea,' said Greg, 'although I'm sure there are other weirdos like you around.'

'You're the weird one. How can you not fancy her?'

Greg shook his head. 'I tell you what. To give you an added incentive to get her to fall for your charms, if you crack her, I'll give you three bonus points.'

'Right – now I'm definitely going to have to shag her.'

'If you do though, you need to show me some kind of memento.'

Hughie slowly nodded. 'All right then. As long as you do the same with the next girl you get on the scoreboard with.'

Greg looked at Imogen and smiled. 'Shouldn't be a problem.'

Two hours later, the GHB bottle almost empty, Greg staggered out of the bar with a giggling Imogen. Hughie was standing outside and watched them head towards the beach. Roz had popped in the bar to get a drink and returned to the door at more or less the same time as Greg and Imogen disappeared from view.

'You still here?'

'Of course I am,' answered Hughie.

'Shouldn't you be in there trying to score some points with your clients?' Roz was well acquainted with the shagging competition between the reps.

'You've got me all wrong, hen,' he protested. 'I'm not saying that I'm celibate or even necessarily a one-woman man, but I'm not into silly girls like those in there. I prefer women.'

'Yeah, of course you do,' snorted Roz derisively. 'Like me you mean?'

'Yes, now you come to mention it, exactly like you. You've got character, Roz and that's an extremely sexy trait.'

This was too much for Roz. 'So go on then, how many bonus points has Greg put on offer if you shag me?'

For a moment, Hughie was flummoxed that Roz had been both so direct and so accurate. His face almost gave the game away.

'Don't be silly. I'm here because I fancy you.'

'Oh fuck off, you idiot – do you think I was born yesterday? I've been doing this job long enough to spot a bullshitter when I see one. All of you reps are the same. Half of you are worse than the clients. There's only one rep I've met in the last few years who's even halfway genuine and that's your boss, Brad. Now if *he* wanted to meet me in the little dark room out the back of the bar that you seem so keen to get me in to, I might say yes.'

Though stung by her comments, Hughie had a sudden

brainwave. 'Actually, loathe though I am to admit it, Brad has got a bit of a crush on you.'

'Piss off.'

'I'm serious. He's always saying that he thinks you'd be a wicked shag.'

'Well, he'd be right about that.'

Hughie looked at Roz and realised that he was beginning to go off her. He liked big women, but not masculine ones. Still, there were three bonus points up for grabs if he did the deed and if his plan worked, he might just get them.

'So what, you'd be happy to shag Brad then? Nothing more, just a shag. You don't want to go out with him or anything like that?'

'I've got a boyfriend – Jed, the Maori bloke who worked on the door with me last year. He gets here in three weeks. If I shagged Brad it'd have to be a one-off.'

She sipped her drink. The thought of having a clandestine night of passion with Brad excited her. A barmaid friend had slept with Brad a few times the previous summer and had given him a glowing report. Roz had not had any carnal activity for nearly five months. The more she thought about it the more she warmed to the idea of Brad being the perfect person to unleash her growing frustration.

'So, shall I play cupid then?' asked Hughie.

Roz eyed him suspiciously. 'What's in it for you?'

'Ideally I'd like you to change your mind about shagging me. If you don't, then let's just say you owe me one. Maybe you could let me use that back room of yours one night, if I meet a girl who doesn't reject me like you have.'

They shared a look for a moment then both smiled.

'All right. How are you going to do it?'

'I'll tell him to meet you here tomorrow night in the back room. Leave the other door that leads in from the street unlocked. Give me your mobile number so I can give it to him in case he can't make it for any reason.'

Roz still wasn't convinced that Hughie was being genuine, but he wasn't suggesting that she meet Brad anywhere that they could be seen together or that she would suffer the indignation of being stood up, so she decided to go for it.

'What the hell.'

As she was giving Hughie her phone number, Ace came trotting up the road.

'Have either of you two seen Greg?'

'I saw him heading off with Imogen a few minutes ago,' replied Hughie as Roz went back into the bar. 'Why, what's up?'

'I gave him some GHB earlier on and I've just found out that it was double strength so I wanted to warn him.' He shrugged and laughed. 'Oh well, I guess he'll find out for himself.'

'I'll be seeing Greg in the morning – shall I tell him?' asked Hughie.

'Knowing Greg,' replied Ace, 'it'll be far too late by then.'

Greg had tried to let Imogen have most of the GHB . . . he'd *really* tried.

Unfortunately, he simply loved the buzz it gave him. The secret was knowing exactly how much to take. If he got it right, then it would be every bit as good as a pill with the added benefit of making him feel incredibly horny. But just a little too much and that was it – comatose for several hours.

His first experience of GHB had been the previous summer, before he had even joined the Chemical Generation. A YF&S client had overdosed on it but prior to passing out though, she and Greg had had the most amazing sex.

Since then, he had overdone it himself on several occasions, each time culminating with him passing out into a deep sleep with very little warning. If he took GHB, Greg now told whoever he was with not to ring for an ambulance. It was scary to watch and Greg was not surprised that the drug attracted such bad publicity.

These days, Greg was always over the moon when he discovered a girl who liked GHB. He had read about it being used as a date rape drug and wondered just how sick the men who used it in that way must be. In his experience, a girl buzzing on GHB was as in charge of her faculties as a girl who'd had a few drinks or taken a pill. It was only when they took too much and passed out that they were vulnerable and Greg didn't go there.

Imogen was anything but unconscious. Greg had intended giving her more GHB but she seemed horny enough without it, so he had necked most of it himself. Imogen was unable to take Greg up to her flat because her parents and younger brother had come over for a week to stay with her. The previous summer, her father had seen a documentary about life in Ibiza and was especially horrified at two girls who claimed to have slept with almost a dozen men during their holiday. Despite Imogen's assurances that it was a set-up and that workers had a different outlook to tourists, he'd wanted to check for himself that his daughter was giving that kind of activity a wide berth.

Set a little way back from Imogen's apartment block was a communal pool. It was surrounded by fauna and in virtual darkness. Imogen had taken a small amount of GHB, just enough for her to find the idea of some outdoor, slightly risky sex exciting.

They stopped next to the outdoor shower. Greg took her face in his hands, parted his lips and let them brush against hers. Imogen swung Greg round so his back was against the whitewashed wall of the pump house and urgently kissed him, moaning as she rubbed herself against the erection that he'd had to walk with for the previous few minutes.

Her fingernails raked his shoulders, then dug into his scalp. Still kissing, they maneouvred round so Imogen was now against the wall. She fumbled to undo Greg's jeans as he lifted her dress. When she had Greg in her hand, she stood on one leg and rubbed him against her panties. They disentangled so she could remove them, then quickly resumed their former position. This time she rubbed him against her moist nakedness, just feeling the very end of him inside her.

Slowly, Greg pushed his hips forward. Imogen was not

able to contain a low moan. Greg did this a couple of more times, then to her surprise, withdrew and stepped back.

'What's ... wrong?' she gasped, trying to catch her breath.

'Do you like being teased?'

It was not the most genuine of questions. A more truthful one would have been, 'Do you mind if I stop for a few minutes because if I don't there's a good chance that another two thrusts and I'll shoot all over your leg.'

Aware that a good mention in dispatches could lead to further opportunities with friends, or friends of friends, Greg always made a point of concealing any sexual shortcomings (or in this case, very shortcomings) from partners.

Moreover, he had perfected a few tricks to make his performance remain in any girl's top five shags. (For all his experience, he still had not grasped that most women didn't make lists like men.)

His speciality was the fake orgasm, which he sometimes employed to give the impression of having an unbelievable recovery rate. His build up to climax would not have been out of place in *When Harry Met Sally*. As the 'moment' arrived he would yell, 'Oh shit, I'm coming.' He would make all of the requisite grunts and groans, tense, then apologise for ejaculating too quickly (which usually wasn't too quickly at all, but by saying it was, girls would wonder how long he normally lasted). After lying next to them breathless for a few minutes, he would stare at his still erect member with apparent surprise and say, 'God, I can't believe it hasn't gone down. You must be really turning me on.' This comment always went down particularly well.

Now though, his imminent orgasm was anything but fake.

Some washing line cord lay nearby, so Greg went over to pick it up. As he bent down he started to feel strange and light-headed. It was a familiar feeling. He tried to shake it off and unsteadily made his way back to Imogen.

'Are you all right?' she asked.

The wooziness came in waves and Greg straightened up a little. He nodded and helped her slip out of her dress. He took her hands and tied them above her head, on to the shower pipe.

He grinned. 'All trussed up. Now then, what shall I do with you? I know . . .'

He reached for the shower lever.

'Don't you dare,' she hissed.

Playfully, he turned it on for a fraction of a second. Imogen let out a short squeal as the tiny amount of the cold water came into contact with her warm skin. Before she could say anything, Greg kissed her then ran his tongue down the crevasse between her breasts, where the short spurt of water had cascaded. Then he broke off a branch from a nearby palm tree and ran its spindly leaves over her naked body. Imogen's breathing shortened. Lightly, he whipped her breasts with it, then did the same all over her, harder with each strike.

But another wave of nausea swept over Greg, this one much stronger than the first. He tried to ignore it and traced his fingertips down her flat stomach. His tongue followed and he knelt in front of her. She parted her legs slightly and Greg ran his tongue up her inner thigh. He flattened his tongue and expertly ran it along her outer lips, allowing the tip to pause as he got to the top. Another overwhelming feeling of claustrophobia and dizziness. He knew that this was it. He stood up and staggered backwards.

'Greg . . . oh shit.'

He knew he was in trouble and about to pass out, but he still had a soppy grin on his face. His legs had gone to jelly and for one horrible moment, Imogen saw him toppling towards the pool. Tied up and unable to move, she could see a potential nightmare unfolding.

'Greg, the pool . . . look out!'

Greg had almost drifted into unconsciousness but straightened himself out just in time. Still grinning, he lumbered towards her.

'I think I've done too much GHB . . .'

'Quick, untie me before you pass out.'

Greg's last thought before hurtling into unconsciousness was that he needed her panties to show Hughie, in order to claim the points. His brain now scrambled, it was the only thought left in his head.

'Your panties. I need your panties. Must show Hughie to get the points. Got to give me your pant—'

As Greg tumbled to the floor he vainly reached out to stop himself from falling. The only thing within reach was the shower lever. He crashed into the bushes and a GHB coma – and sent a torrent of freezing cold water on to the naked and bondaged Imogen.

If there had been a more embarrassing incident in her life, Imogen could not think of it.

In fact, other than a mishap compilation video she had once seen in Koppas Bar, where an elephant backs on to a zookeeper and the zookeeper's head disappears up the elephant's backside for a few moments after which he staggers back vomiting like no man has vomited before, Imogen doubted if anything worse had ever happened to anyone, anywhere.

Imogen had not vomited, but she did feel as sick as the proverbial parrot.

Why did it have to be her father who had heard her shrieks and been the first of half a dozen men to come running out of the apartment block?

It was clear that neither her father nor the growing number of assembled onlookers believed her mumbled story of going for a midnight shower and getting entangled in some rope. Her father had not pursued with any further questions, no doubt scared of finding out what really had happened. Also of course, he was less than thrilled to have the others who had come out to see what the screams were, gawping and giggling at his naked daughter, tied to a shower head and soaking wet at three in the morning.

The only thing Imogen could salvage from the situation

was the fact that Greg had fallen so far into the bushes nobody had seen him.

What she was far less happy about was his final comment. Passing out on her was bad. Passing out on her after tying her to an outdoor shower was unforgivable. But passing out after tying her to an outdoor shower, then saying that he needed her panties to prove to another rep that he had shagged her ... well, that meant only one thing – revenge.

When her father and would-be Samaritans left her to gather her clothes, Imogen crept into the bush. Greg was in a deep sleep, quietly snoring. If she hadn't known better, she could have sworn that he had passed out with the trace of a smile on his face.

'If it's my panties you want,' she said quietly, 'it's my panties you'll get.'

She removed all of his clothes, walked a few hundred yards to the edge of the small rock face on which the apartments were built, and launched them into the sea. When she went back, she took her lipstick out of her pocket and wrote on her panties, placing them under Greg's nose.

'C how U like it – bastard!'

chapter seventeen

Vaz stood outside La Luna Café, waiting for Mikey to turn up. He had two record bags with him and couldn't wait to get behind the decks again. Thursday, a glorious June morning and Vaz was in an equally fabulous mood.

The job was proving to be a lot of fun. It was harder than he had ever imagined and every day there seemed to be something else to remember, or another lesson to learn. The added pressure of the proposed takeover by The Monastery was not helping matters either. The only other cause of stress was Arabella, who was proving to be a total pain. Most of the time Vaz was able to ignore or laugh at her comments and attitude, but it was still a mystery to him why she wanted the job in the first place. It certainly wasn't to follow a career with Young Free & Single.

At least that was one thing they had in common.

Five minutes after their scheduled ten in the morning rendezvous, Mikey ambled round the corner arm in arm with his girlfriend Patricia. It was so obvious that they were madly in love. Vaz felt a pang of jealousy. They seemed not to have a care in the world, just happy to be in each other's company despite all of the pressure that the commitment of taking the bar on must have been causing them. Brad had explained to him that if Club Wicked were the company chosen by The Monastery, then there was every chance that Alison would do everything she could to put the La Luna Café out of business.

There was something about Mikey that made Vaz feel uncomfortable. Nothing sinister, just a feeling that Mikey was always one step ahead of him. The comment Mikey had made to him at the joint meeting about knowing what Vaz was up to had been particularly unsettling. Vaz wanted to confide in someone, but given Mikey's history and closeness to Brad, he didn't feel he would be the ideal person to choose.

Yet conversely, there was something about Mikey that made him *want* to open up. He seemed to possess a quiet wisdom and Vaz also felt that they were similar people. Neither had been taken in by the holiday rep hype and neither of them had embraced The Competition. Like himself, Vaz could see that Mikey was a bit of an old-fashioned romantic.

Mikey slipped his arm from Patricia's and took a large bunch of keys from his pocket. 'Sorry we're late,' he said to Vaz with a relaxed smile. 'Have you met Patricia before?'

'Not officially.'

Patricia smiled and they kissed each other on both cheeks. He noticed how naturally pretty she was. There was not a trace of make-up on her face and her long red hair was pulled back in a pony-tail. Her skin was unblemished and evenly tanned, which helped make her clear green eyes sparkle.

'So this was Brad's idea, was it?' said Mikey, unlocking the door to his bar.

'Well, partly his and partly mine. He said that with this DJ Face-Off coming up I should get in some practice and I asked him to see if it would be all right to do it down here.'

'Any particular reason?' asked Mikey, opening the door and leading them into the dark room, which still smelled of stale beer and cigarette smoke.

'The set-up and the acoustics are good. It's a wicked view when the shutters are back and I suppose it made sense because you and Brad are good mates.'

Mikey smiled. 'I'd better open the shutters then.'

'I'm going to put the kettle on,' said Patricia. 'Would you like a cuppa, Vaz?'

'Yeah, thanks.'

'OK, you know where the decks are,' said Mikey, letting

sunlight flood into the bar. 'I'll switch the power on and leave you to it. We've got a room out the back that we've got to sort out for storage. If you need anything, give us a shout.'

Vaz nodded. 'Cheers.'

He switched on the decks, took out his first record and within minutes, could have been anywhere in the world.

Greg could have also been anywhere in the world when he came to that morning. He knew he wasn't in bed, but also knew that he was quite comfortable, so without really being sure of his exact location, had happily gone back to sleep. Three hours later, he woke up properly and took a confused inventory of his surroundings. As he lay there, he slowly started piecing together the events of the previous night. The one thing that was obvious was that somehow he had taken too much GHB. He could remember everything up until getting back to the apartment block, but after that it was a blank.

He didn't see Imogen's panties until he stood up. That was a good sign, he thought. At least he'd got his three points and had a memento to show Hughie.

It also took him a few moments to realise that he was naked. Again, at first he took this to be a good sign. He surmised that he'd passed out after doing the deed and that Imogen had been unable to wake him.

He still felt quite randy. He would have loved to have seen Imogen to start the day with a bang, but apart from not knowing which apartment she was in, he also remembered her telling him that her parents were over.

One of the blanks in his memory was what he'd done with his clothes. As he searched for them, he picked up Imogen's panties. It was then that he saw the writing on them. This was not such a good sign. Greg racked his brain to try and recall what he had done to upset her, but it was no good.

What did slowly dawn on him was that whatever he had

done was almost certainly connected to the disappearance of his own clothes.

He looked round to see if there was anything he could find to cover his dignity, but the only option seemed to be Imogen's panties. He tried them on but couldn't get them past the top of his knees. There was no way he could go back to the hotel in case any of the The Monastery crew were there. The closest place to get to would be La Luna Café, but he wasn't sure if Mikey or Patricia would be there this early in the morning. Luckily, he was round the back of San An so most of his walk could be made through relatively quiet streets.

Although the panties didn't fit, he kept them to prove to Hughie he'd got the points. He was going to have to do the walk covering his privates with his hands and pray that no police were passing.

As he stepped out onto the road, he picked a flowerpot from the top of the wall and walked with it in front of him, as much for having somewhere to put his hands as anything else. Despite his devil-may-care attitude, Greg did experience a few twangs of embarrassment as he got closer to San An and more and more passers-by, motorists and people on balconies stared at him in disbelief.

Not far from one of the main gift shop streets, he turned a corner and to his horror walked straight into a gathering of about fifty tourists waiting to board an excursion coach. It was too late to dash back round the corner as he would have liked. Instead, he held the flowerpot out with a grin on his face.

'Hi there, folks – no kids amongst you, are there? Good. I'm doing a sponsored nude walk to raise money for local charities. Chuck any loose change you've got in the pot, please.'

To his surprise there was no animosity and the giggling tourists, most of whom were middle-aged, happily obliged.

From then on, Greg carried on using the same excuse with everybody he came into contact with. It wasn't long before the pot started to fill quite nicely.

Maybe taking the long way round via the centre of San An wasn't such a bad idea after all, he thought.

Vaz was so lost in his music that he didn't notice that Mikey had been watching him for nearly ten minutes. In the end, Mikey tapped him on the shoulder. Vaz removed his headphones and turned the music down.

'There you go, mate,' said Mikey, 'cup of tea for you.'

'Thanks.' Vaz stopped the record.

'Don't stop playing on my account. I was enjoying it.'

'Nice of you to say so. To tell the truth I could do with getting out in the sun for ten minutes.'

They walked out of the bar onto the terrace and sat at one of the tables. San Antonio had come to life, with small groups of holidaymakers clutching their towels and beach bags. Many were making their way to the ferries, waiting to take them to the island's beautiful beaches, others to the nearby beach of Calo des Moro.

'Are you feeling confident about this DJ Face-Off on Sunday?' asked Mikey.

'Yeah, I'm really looking forward to it.'

'There's going to be a few promoters there. Couple of well-known DJs too I understand.'

Vaz wasn't certain, but he was almost sure he detected a glint in Mikey's eye.

'Really?' Vaz tried not to sound too excited.

'Yeah. If there was a good, unknown DJ there, it could be just the start he needed.'

'You could be right,' replied Vaz, as disinterestedly as possible.

Mikey sipped his tea. 'Is it just you and the Club Wicked rep who are playing?'

'Yeah, a guy called Smiffy.'

Suddenly Mikey put his tea down and sighed. 'Vaz, it doesn't matter.'

'What?'

'It doesn't matter that your main reason for getting a job

173

with YF&S was so that you could come out to Ibiza and try to make it as a DJ.'

So there it was. He did know. But Vaz still wasn't quite ready to confess all.

'What makes you say that? I love working for Young Free & Single. I'm totally committed to the job.'

Mikey laughed. 'I'm not about to go running to Brad – not that he'd care. Brad's not been brainwashed by it all either, it's just that working for them suits him at the moment, like it suits you and like it worked for me. Do you honestly think that they expect you to be a rep for the rest of your life? Most reps do well if they get through a season. If someone manages to do the job for more than three summers then I'm afraid that in my opinion they've got a serious personality problem. You've got be one sad, insecure motherfucker to do it for any longer.'

'Greg doesn't strike me as insecure.'

'Greg is probably the exception that breaks the rule. He's a one-off. Even so, there are still issues that he's trying to deal with that make him keep coming back year after year, even if insecurity isn't one of them.'

'Like what?'

'Like . . .' Mikey paused, putting his cup to his lips. 'Like I'm no more about to go into conversations I've had with Greg, than I would conversations we have together.'

'Fair enough.'

'What I *am* saying is that some reps are bigger than the badge and use it as a means to an end. Others become *dependent* on the badge, especially the guys. I call them badge boys. Back home they're nothing – shit jobs, can't meet any girls. They live for the summer so they can large it as centre of attention for another six months.

'Before I'd got the job as a rep, I'd decided that I wanted to open a bar in Spain – I wasn't even sure where. All I knew was that I'd had enough of the UK. I figured that by working as a rep I'd get to know a lot of the right people while having a secure job. Straight away, I sussed out that a lot of bar owners and the main movers and shakers look at reps as a necessary evil: Big egos, but lots of clients and thankfully, normally only around for a summer or two. That's why I made a point of winding my neck in and not larging it too much when I worked here. What I hadn't counted on was the job being so full-on. Sometimes I lost sight of my original plan. A few times I wasn't far away from getting the next flight home. It's easy to lose sight of the dream.'

'So how come you're sitting here now then?'

'Probably because I met Patricia. It meant I had someone I could trust to talk to. Someone who's not tangled up in the same web as you.'

'And is that why we're having this little chat?'

'The point I'm making is don't lose sight of what it is you came here for.'

They sat in silence for a few moments. Then did a simultaneous double-take as a naked man walked up the road carrying a flowerpot.

'Greg!'

chapter eighteen

It wasn't often that Trev was up early enough to sample a Bon Tiempo breakfast. Today there was a reason.

The hotel mongrel came trotting round the corner, just as Trev was finishing his *al fresco* food. When the dog saw Trev, it barked and, wagging its tail, came over to him. Trev took the last piece of bacon from his plate and dangled it for the dog to grab. After about a minute of this, two girls wearing bikini tops and sarongs emerged from the apartment's bar and sat at one of the nearby white plastic tables. Trev was distracted by them and took his eye off the bacon. Recognising the opportunity, the dog jumped a little higher and successfully snapped the bacon, as well as the top of Trev's fingers.

'Ow, you little sod.'

Trev had a mock fight with the dog, clenching his fists then playfully tapping the dog's snout, while the dog tried to bite Trev's hands. Eventually Trev rolled the dog onto its back and tickled its tummy. Each time he stopped, the dog gave a little yap. They both tired of this at about the same time, so Trev rounded things off by getting the dog to chase its own tail.

Trev felt a certain empathy with the dog's unsuccessful yet persistent pursuit. He had been pursuing Alison to spend another night together for nearly a week, yet the harder he tried to persuade her, the less interested she seemed.

Trev wondered if Alison had been put off due to a couple of poor performances on his part. It wasn't so much that Alison hadn't enjoyed the sex – Trev was experienced enough to know what buttons to press and Alison was certainly vocal in her appreciation. However, he found her so sexy that the actual love-making part of the act hadn't really lasted quite as long as he would have liked. In fact, he doubted that eighteen seconds would have been to anyone's liking. Alison teasing him by getting out a stopwatch hadn't exactly helped.

Tonight Alison had promised him that after her reps all left for their fancy dress club night, she was going to come up to his room. Trev had immediately jumped into his car and zoomed over to the sex shop near the port in Ibiza Town. Among the goodies he bought was what he hoped to be his salvation – a delay spray called 'Retardo'.

The reason for Trev's early start was that Alison had told him she was being picked up by The Monastery's Kit at just gone ten, to be taken to a meeting. Trev wanted to intercept her leaving to confirm that their proposed night of passion was still on.

He was so engrossed in tormenting the dog that he missed Kit's arrival at the Bon Tiempo and had it not been for the unmistakably strong waft of Alison's perfume, would have missed her too. She hadn't been expecting to see Trev up so early and had walked straight past him. He called after her.

'Oh, hi, Trev.' She let Kit carry on to the car. 'Sorry, I'm in a bit of a hurry. We've got this meeting and I need to pop into Mikey's bar on the way. What's up? Not going to blow me out tonight, are you?'

Trev breathed a sigh of relief. 'No, no. Everything is fine. More than fine. I'll be down here when you see the coach off. I've got a few nice surprises lined up.'

'Ooh good,' she giggled. 'I like surprises.'

Even Alison couldn't have anticipated the surprise she received just a few minutes later. As she pulled up to La Luna Café with Kit, a naked and obviously worse for wear Greg was walking up the steps carrying a flowerpot full of money. With Kit in the car, she couldn't have scripted it better.

Greg, on the other hand, couldn't have felt worse. The carried over buzz from the GHB was now well and truly replaced by a splitting headache. A night lying unconscious in the bushes had left him battered and bruised, and the adrenaline that had forced itself into his system to enable him to start his naked trek had long gone.

More though, he knew that he had badly screwed up. Alison witnessing his nude arrival was bad enough, but for Kit to be in the car too . . .

Alison had milked every second. Kit said nothing. Greg had used up all of his bravado and energy making the walk so had not been able to defend himself. Instead he scurried to the back room where a suitcase of his old belongings had been stored during the winter.

Before Mikey bought it, La Luna Café had been a fairly quiet and not very well-promoted beachfront venue. It was Mikey who first started frequenting it as a way of escaping the pressures of repping the previous summer. The fact that it was one of the few venues where reps paid for their drinks was more than outweighed by the fact that no clients ever visited it. By August, all of the other reps were using it as a sanctuary too.

Also that August, Greg hit on the idea of making a small race car track for The Competition. Each rep was allocated a model car and every time they scored points, the car moved up the track. The track was placed on top of an unused second bar and it became a weekly session where the reps cut loose from the clients and were awarded their points. On the last day before the reps started to go home, Greg, who had trounced the opposition, was presented with The Golden Dick.

At the end of every summer he'd been working, Greg left certain belongings and summer clothes in the Bon Tiempo apartments ready for the following year. There had been some uncertainty at the end of the previous season as to whether YF&S would be contracting the apartments again and Greg had asked Mikey, who was staying through the winter, to look after them for him.

Greg found an old pair of YF&S tracksuit bottoms in the case and put them on. In melancholy mood, he went through some of his belongings. Apart from clothes, there were personal mementos – love letters from ex-clients, photos and old YF&S uniforms.

Greg looked at a group photo from two summers earlier. It seemed hard to think that he had changed so much. He knew that a lot of that change had occurred since he had first taken ecstasy.

Yet he didn't feel totally out of control. Although that first pill was definitely the catalyst for taking more cocaine and trying drugs like GHB, he had absolutely no intention of trying harder drugs like crack or heroin, any more than he would have started drinking methylated spirits after his first beer. Nor did Greg feel addicted to the drugs. What he was addicted to was the scene.

Yet as he looked through his things, he could not help but feel a certain disquiet. Greg was a social animal and great with people. But he also realised that to have been a rep for as long as he had was not 'normal'. Although he hid it, Greg was capable of the odd reflective moment and if ever one was due, then having to walk naked through San Antonio with a pair of girl's panties after passing out mid-shag was reason enough.

Mikey smoothed things over with Kit, telling him that he'd bet Greg he wouldn't run to the end of the road and back naked. Kit accepted this explanation and seemed to have more important things to worry about. Alison, however, kept asking questions: 'Where are his clothes then? Why does he look so rough? Why is he carrying a pair of girls' panties and a flowerpot full of money?'

Mikey managed to swerve most of Alison's interrogation. But at the end of it he was certain that if Club Wicked won The Monastery deal Alison would not use his bar, and it would spell the end for his business.

He didn't blame Greg for this – the chances were always

going to be that Alison would find an excuse not to use La Luna Café.

As he walked into the storeroom, he saw Greg going through his old things. Mikey stood back from the door and watched him for a while. Greg seemed to be dwelling over one particular letter and photo.

'A penny for them?'

'Huh?' Greg was miles away. He quickly put the letter and photo down. 'Sorry about all that. I shagged that barmaid from the Drunken Lizard last night and I took too much GHB. Fuck knows what happened but I woke up in a bush and she'd hidden all my clothes. She left me these,' he held the panties aloft, 'complete with message, so I obviously did something to upset her. I came here because it was the closest place. Just my luck for Alison to turn up with Kit. What did she say?'

'She was just shit-stirring. Kit didn't seem too bothered. I told him it was a silly bet.'

'Cheers, Mikey.'

Mikey sat on the edge of a box. 'Reminiscing?'

'Just going through old stuff.'

Mikey nodded at the letter and photo. 'Anyone special?'

Greg picked them up. 'Her? No, not really. Well, not any more. I met her in my first week as a rep. Years ago. I guess I was a bit green. Dawn.'

'I'm surprised you can remember her name.'

Greg said nothing.

'Did you carry on seeing her when you got back?'

Greg shook his head. 'No. Like I said, I was green.' Rather more quietly, he added, 'Actually, I was mad about her. I couldn't believe I'd only been here for a few days and I'd already met the girl of my dreams. That's what Ibiza does when you've never been abroad before.'

'Does it?' Mikey raised an eyebrow.

'It has to be. I've had . . . lots of girls since. None of them have ever done the same to me so that proves it must have been the place.'

'Or that maybe it was her.'

'No offence, mate, but just because you went all Mills and Boon in your first year, it doesn't mean that everyone else has to.'

Mikey laughed. 'Yeah, I guess I was lucky. So what happened?'

'Usual story.'

'Would this be the "usual story" you warn all the reps about?'

'Yeah. We sent each other letters, spoke on the phone every few days. She was from down south. A month or two went by and she was due to come back out in late August then, bang. Out of the blue she sends me a Dear John saying she's back with her old boyfriend. I tried calling and writing but she wouldn't take my calls and never wrote back. In the end I just thought, fuck her.'

'And turned into the old cynic that we all know and love.'

'Realist, you mean.'

'Greg, not all girls are like her. I've heard your spiel to the other reps a hundred times, but every year at least one of us ends up meeting someone that we carry on seeing.'

'There might be the odd exception.' Greg stood up and walked over to the old Competition race track. 'I reckon I might set this back up in my room.'

'Going for The Golden Dick again this year?'

'In the lead as ever.' For once it sounded slightly hollow. He picked up the toy E-Type, which had been his car on the race track the previous summer. He sat on the edge of a table twirling it between his fingers. 'You know, I don't think I even respect women. I mean, don't get me wrong, I'm not a misogynist.'

'Greg, where did you get that word from?'

'Oh, some student last year when I farted on her leg then held her under the covers.'

'That would explain it.'

'For a few weeks I thought it meant someone who blows off in bed.'

Mikey laughed. 'If it did, then I'd be one too.'

'Seriously though, I adore women,' continued Greg. 'I just find it hard to respect them. I never used to be like that, Mikey. This job's done that to me. I mean, Jesus, you've seen them. Remember that girl last year who was on her hen week? She shagged Ace on the Thursday night – without a fucking condom – flew home on the Friday and got married on the Saturday. And Brad got propositoned by a monster who was on her honeymoon and eight months pregnant.'

'Yeah, I remember her.'

'And what about all the girls who come away saying they've got a boyfriend at home, then an hour later they're shagging one of us?'

'Well, if you don't at least try to find a girl you've got respect for, ultimately you'll end up not respecting yourself.'

'But Mikey, I'm not bothered about respecting myself.' Greg recovered his composure, tucked the race track under his arm and put the toy cars into a plastic bag. 'I'm bothered about *enjoying* myself.'

chapter nineteen

'Is it a bird? Is it a plane?'

'No.' Ace palmed Trev a gram of Charlie. 'It's just a tosser in a bad Superman outfit.'

Nevertheless, Trev and Ace watched Mario drawing admiring glances from the appreciative girl Club Wicked clients gathering in the Bon Tiempo bar for the Fancy Dress bar crawl.

'What do they see in him?' asked Trev.

'Fuck knows. I just wish I had some sodding kryptonite.' They both chuckled. 'You haven't bought any nose from me for a while, Trev. What's the special occasion?'

He looked over to Alison who was at the kerbside, leaning into Lucas's car. 'Her ladyship.'

'What, you're still knobbing old Alison?'

Trev nodded. 'I can't help it. She's filthy. After this lot have buggered off we're going up to my apartment for a night of debauchery.'

'Nice one. Want to buy some Viagra?'

'Have you got any?' Ace nodded. 'How much?'

'Fifteen Euros, or seeing as it's you I'll do two for twenty.'

Trev was determined to give Alison the seeing to of her life. Two Viagras and some Retardo delay spray – he couldn't go wrong. He passed Ace the money, took the Viagras, then promptly popped them both into his mouth and swigged them back with some lager. Ace looked at him flabbergasted.

'You can't do both at once! They're the hundred milli-gram ones.'

Trev shrugged. 'I've done 'em loads of times before.'

Ace laughed. 'I hope you don't OD. If you snuff it, they won't be able to shut the coffin lid for a week.' He patted Trev on the back. 'Have a good night.'

'I intend to.'

When Alison finished talking to Lucas she gave Trev a little wave then went over to Mario who was lapping up the attention his outfit was causing. She pulled him to one side.

'Have you asked her yet?'

'I'm going to meet her later.'

'Do you think she'll do it?'

'Of course she will. Arabella worships me and she hates Vaz.'

'Just make sure Arabella knows what to do.'

'Remind me again. She's got to find out what Vaz's opening record is then scratch it.'

'Yeah, but not all the way to the outside edge. If she does that then he'll hear the record jump when he cues it up.'

'OK. And then she's got to put the records I give her into the sleeves of the ones in his record box.'

'Correct. I'll be getting them later. Hopefully Vaz'll leave his record box in the room at the back of the club.'

'Why can't Stig do it?'

'Because YF&S and Club Wicked have got separate rooms. Most of the time nobody will be in them, but just in case someone comes in it won't look so suspicious.'

'What records are you going to swap?'

'Just shitty old albums or cheesey twelve-inchers with white labels on.'

'Won't Vaz know that they're the wrong records when he sees them or listens to them through the headphones?'

'He'll be in such a flap he won't even notice.'

The large bulge in Mario's red pants started to vibrate, causing a group of girls nearby to start giggling. Fixing them with a seductive stare, he slowly pulled out his mobile.

'Talk of the devil,' he said looking at the screen, 'it's Arabella.'

'I'll leave you to it. Get this lot on the coach.' Trev had

made his way over to her. She gave him a cheeky smile then turned back to Mario. 'Good luck with Arabella. I'm going to sort out a premature arrival.'

Some hours later, things had not gone terribly well for Trev.

He had taken Alison out for a few drinks to get her in the mood. But before any alcohol had passed either of their lips, Alison received a call from Lucas. He was having a meeting with the The Monastery people and one of their major investors and his wife. There was a possibility that Alison might have to join them all a little later and he gave strict instructions that she was to be on her best behaviour.

When they got back to Trev's apartment, the majority of the meal that he had painstakingly prepared ended up in a dish outside his door for the hotel mongrel. He had forgotten about Alison's seafood allergy.

Due to Lucas's instructions and her drunken antics on the company bonding night the previous Monday, Alison decided not to risk drinking *any* alcohol. Trev had been looking forward to getting bang on the booze and Charlie, but didn't want to do it on his own, so things were not as relaxed as he had hoped.

Despite not drinking, Alison had no such qualms about cocaine and had got through almost the whole gram with Trev only having taken two lines. Although he knew that Viagra was supposed to merely assist the mechanics and maintenance of the erection process and not increase libido, all Trev had to do was look at Alison and he got a massive hard-on.

Alison pushed a microwaved lasagne around her plate, watching Trev eat. His near permanent erection had not gone unnoticed. Alison gestured towards it.

'If I'd known the pasta was *that* good I would have had some.'

She slipped under the table and undid his belt. 'Trev, I don't remember it being this big! What *did* you put in that pasta?'

Trev hadn't told Alison about the Viagras – far better for her to think he was *au naturel*.

She took him in her mouth and slowly slid down his shaft. Trev let out a long groan and sat back in his chair.

'No, don't stop eating,' she whispered. 'Just imagine we're in a restaurant and nobody can see what I'm doing to you under the tablecloth.' She let her tongue glide across his glans. 'Would that turn you on?' She gripped him hard at the base then let her head go back and forth a few times. 'Mmm,' she sighed, dribbling saliva down his length, 'you'd love that, wouldn't you, Trev?'

What Trev would have really loved was to not feel as if his balls were about to explode and whizz out the window. He pulled back.

'What's up?' she asked, rubbing the back of her hand across her mouth like a navvy wiping egg from his chin in a transport café.

'Al, you turn me on so much. I've never known anyone like you before. I so badly want to fuck your brains out but all I've got to do is look at you and I want to come.' He reached behind him and picked a white plastic bag from the floor. 'I said I had a surprise for you.'

'What is it?'

'It's a delay spray.'

'How does it work? What does it do?'

'The bloke in the shop said I just spray it on the end of my dick, wait a minute or so and bingo – problem solved.'

'How can a man of your age have premature ejaculation?' asked Alison, rather unkindly. 'I thought it only happened to teenagers.'

'It can happen at any age . . . especially when there's someone as horny as you around,' he added gallantly.

He slid his chair back from the table and leaned forward to kiss her, slipping his hand between her legs. 'And how many teenagers do you know who can do this to you?'

Alison moaned as he slipped two fingers inside her, slowly circling then urgently tugging as she bucked against his palm. Within less than thirty seconds her short screams crescendoed until with a howl, she released a torrent over his hand.

'Oh God,' she gasped, 'how *do* you do that?'

Nobody had ever made her come as much or as effortlessly as Trev. The love-making was secondary and he certainly didn't really do it for her in the looks department. But each time she decided not to bother with him any more, she'd have a little flush and remember *those* orgasms.

She got off the floor and went over to the sofa, picking up the delay spray. 'Retardo,' she read out.

'It means delay,' he said.

She looked at him, his erection poking out of his trousers and his shirt askew, his face flushed, rivulets of sweat pouring from his near-bald head.

'Are you sure? Someone always said to me that if ever you see a word in Spanish that you don't understand, just take the 'O' off the end. Are you sure this isn't a spray for, you know, retards.' She started giggling.

'Ha, ha. Very funny.' Feeling a little more confident and in control he walked over to her. 'You'll be laughing on the other side of your face when you're begging me to stop in three hours.'

'Mmm. Promises, promises. Give it here then and I'll spray some on. Take your trousers off first.'

Trev obeyed and with a surprising degree of coyness for Alison, she sprayed it on to the end of his penis.

'There you go, all done,' she said, with the cheery detatchment of a washing-machine engineer. 'Now what?'

Trev went back to his chair. 'I guess we just wait for a bit.'

They sat in silence for a few moments, Alison finding it difficult not to look at Trev's erection, Trev drumming his fingers on the table. Alison started smiling, then whistling.

'Don't take the piss.'

'Well you must admit, it's not exactly textbook passion. I mean, what are we supposed to do while we're waiting for it to take effect?'

'Talk? What was it you were saying earlier about stitching up Vaz?'

'We've got a thing called a DJ Face-Off on Sunday night at Eden. Smiffy – one of our reps – is DJing for us and Vaz is DJing for YF&S. Vaz is meant to be brilliant. The whole point of the next three weeks is to prove to The Monastery that Club Wicked are more suited to their way of thinking than YF&S. It's hardly going to go in our favour if the YF&S DJ is ten times better than ours.'

'So what are you doing about it?'

'Stacking the odds in our favour. The Sloaney YF&S rep is obsessed with Mario, so he's going to get her to fuck up Vaz's opening record and switch most of the others in his box for shitty old ones.'

'Nasty.'

'I'd rather call it clever.'

'So I guess that means it was your idea then?'

Alison smiled, then knelt between his legs. 'Oh, I'm full of good ideas, Trev. Do you reckon this is ready for me yet?'

She took him in her mouth and to Trev's delight and astonishment, he couldn't feel a thing. This was it. At long last he was going to do all the things to Alison he'd blistered his hands thinking about.

He let her carry on a little longer then gently put a hand on either side of her head to stop her. He kissed her softly on the lips.

'Come on,' he whispered. 'Let's go to the bedroom.'

As they were walking through, Alison's mobile rang.

'Leave it,' he urged.

'I can't, it's Lucas.'

'Oh nooo!'

The conversation was short.

'I'm sorry, Trev,' said Alison, flipping her phone shut. 'They need me to go over to the restaurant. I'll try to come back.'

'What do you mean "try"? I've had two fucking—' Trev almost let slip about the Viagras. 'I've had two fucking lines of Charlie. You can't leave me.'

Alison looked at him puzzled. 'You've done more than two lines before without any problem.'

Trev noticed she was pulling a few strange shapes with her lips. For a moment he thought she was mouthing to someone, but as they were on the fifth floor and no other apartments were overlooking them he dismissed it and focused on his own feeling of woe.

'When do you think you'll be back?'

'I honestly can't say,' she replied still making shapes with her mouth. Was it some kind of facial exercise? Or a special thing she did after giving head?

Alison was still dressing herself as she dashed out of the door.

A defeated Trev flopped into an armchair, his erection showing no sign at all of subsiding. He wished he had insisted on a quickie. Surely a couple of minutes wouldn't have made any difference? All he wanted was to feel himself inside her without worrying that the pressure valve in his little semen factory was going to hit the red at any second.

Bloody Retardo. Would it last? He picked up the delay spray and read the bottle. The instructions were in English and Spanish. At the bottom of the English side it read:

'*WARNING. Retardo acts like a local anaesthetic and can cause lack of feeling for up to two hours.*'

Mario managed to slip away from his clients just after eleven. The bar crawl was well under way and Arabella had told him that YF&S were also planning to move on to the Drunken Lizard – Mario didn't particularly want to see Brad or Greg. As irritating as Arabella was, he fancied some good hard sex. Plus he wanted to christen the Superman outfit for an extra point.

When Mario had been working for YF&S the previous summer, Greg had not initially allowed him to join The Competition. As a result, Mario copied the rules and started it amongst the reps of Club Wicked, with himself as the Chairman (or the Shag Master General as Greg had since been named). Mario loved being able to award himself points but now it seemed all of the Club Wicked reps were running their own shagging competition without him.

As he did not need to go to his apartment to change, he went straight to Arabella's room still wearing the outfit. The other reason for going there was that unlike the Bon Tiempo, there was a secluded back entrance that he could sneak in and out of.

When he arrived he explained what he wanted her to do to Vaz's records at the DJ Face-Off. Arabella loved the idea. She was particularly annoyed that she'd had to cover Vaz's desk duty whilst he was down at La Luna Café practising. Arabella also had an idea how to distract Vaz long enough to mess up his records. A group of girls calling themselves the Hartlepool Honeys had come away for a YF&S fortnight with the specific intent of getting the one virgin amongst them 'broken in', as they called it. The girl in question was keen and without much egging on, had gone along with her friends' choice of Vaz as the man to do the deed. Arabella was going to ensure that the Hartlepool Honeys cornered Vaz and told him about their plan in Eden just before the Face-Off, thus allowing her time to get into the room allocated to YF&S, where his record box would be.

Arabella adored making love to Mario while he was wearing his Superman costume, although even she thought he looked faintly ridiculous with his blue tights round his knees. It allowed her to make soppy comments about speeding bullets and locomotives.

For Arabella, the experience was simply beautiful. She couldn't believe that she had such an exquisitely gorgeous boyfriend.

Mario couldn't believe that he had such an exquisitely compliant and besotted stooge to do all of his dirty work.

Sa Capella was a restaurant in a converted church on the road out towards Santa Innes. Despite its proximity to San Antonio, its clientele was distinctly upmarket consisting of wealthier locals and British music and media types. The table that Charles Moon was sitting at the head of was at the far end of the restaurant, where the pulpit would have once stood. Part of the kitchen was visible to customers and the waiters scurried between huge candelabra in baggy white shirts and trousers with a red sash, similar to the traditional costume worn by those participating in the Pamplona bull run. Twenty years earlier, they would have been the height of New Romantic fashion.

Arthur Bairns was the guest of honour. Charles Moon had known Arthur for as long as he could remember and he was the closest thing to a mentor Charles had. A successful banker, he had been a source of invaluable advice at the beginning. When The Monastery needed money for its ambitious expansion programme, Arthur had come up with the majority of the required finance. Other than Charles and Kit, he was The Monastery's largest shareholder. Whereas Kit had a feel for trends, Arthur had an intuition for making money. Charles secretly hung on to his every word.

Arthur was only in Ibiza for the one night, mooring his private yacht on his way to Palma in Majorca. He had expressed an interest in meeting the respective resort managers of YF&S and Club Wicked – the 'troops' as he called them. Thus Brad and Alison were both summoned to join Arthur and his wife Kristina, Charles, Kit, Hawthorne-Blythe and Lucas for post-meal liquors.

Charles was far less keen on Arthur's wife. Kristina was fifteen years Arthur's junior and her perpetually made-up face had a permanent sneer. The only time it lit up was when discussing Arthur's latest acquisitions or bragging about gifts he'd given her. The most current of these was a stunning white Chanel dress. She showed no reticence in declaring the cost over twelve thousand pounds.

When she spoke Charles often searched Arthur's face for the smallest sign of intolerance at his spouse's bombastic offerings and snobbish tone, but he never found even the smallest hint – quite simply, Arthur worshipped her. And if Arthur worshipped her, Charles knew that the very least he could do was to be friendly.

Brad got to Sa Capella a good twenty minutes before Alison. He had successfully managed to charm everyone around the table but had wisely not overstayed his welcome, politely making his excuses and leaving to meet Greg at the Drunken Lizard.

Alison arrived just after Brad left. As soon as she joined them, she felt uncomfortable. She could never understand why small groups made her feel so edgy when she was perfectly happy to get on the microphone in front of tens or even hundreds of baying holidaymakers.

The cocaine she'd taken and the fact that she was sitting next to the VIP's wife did nothing to help, but even without those added pressures the location of the table was particularly intimate and the other guests extremely important.

Once the introductions were over and Arthur had asked her a few questions about her job, Alison got sucked into a conversation with Kristina. Their only real shared interest was other people's money and as it was a pursuit that neither readily admitted to in public, the conversation remained fairly stilted. Kristina seemed happy to just talk about her new white dress and how it showed off the suntan she had acquired during the Mediterranean cruise on their own yacht.

Alison nibbled at the cheese and biscuits placed before her without any real enthusiasm. The cocaine had suppressed her appetite plus everything she put in her mouth seemed to have a funny taste, including the obviously expensive red wine.

At the other end of the table, Hawthorne-Blythe and Arthur were discussing British hooliganism abroad. Both were well-educated, successful men of similar age. As such, the discussion was lively and well-balanced and though Arthur was far wealthier and was to a certain degree helping to decide Hawthorne-Blythe's future, no sycophancy was expected nor given.

'. . . But you see them over here all of the time, H-B,' said Arthur, pressing on with a point he had just made. 'Rutting in the streets like rabbits, wearing football shirts and singing "Here We Go".'

'Many would argue it to be a rite-of-passage.'

'Nonsense. Most of these youngsters are from the poorer regions of the UK. They are not very well-educated. They have no discipline. Not their fault, of course,' added Arthur, not wanting to appear too politically incorrect, 'the bloody system's let them down.'

'Still, doesn't give them the right to behave like savages,' added Lucas, who had been on the periphery of the discussion.

'Nonsense,' laughed Hawthorne-Blythe, who was thoroughly enjoying the lively debate. 'It's got bugger all to do with class or education. Look at the Cambridge Ball, or spend a Saturday night at any university campus and you'll see much the same thing going on. You can't condemn them because they're wearing football shirts rather than tuxedos. And as for it being to do with discipline, try having a night out in Aldershot.'

'I remember discussing all of this when I did an interview on Talk Radio,' said Lucas, still trying to add to the conversation. 'I was explaining how and why I believe that Club Wicked seem to avoid the hooligan element. Our clients are clearly a different breed to the lager lout.'

'What was the discussion about?' asked Arthur. He felt a little conscious about omitting Lucas from the discussion but Lucas seemed to have had little to contribute other than trying to turn everything into a positive comment about Club Wicked.

'Oh, something to do with Brits abroad. I used to do so many—'

'And that's another thing,' interrupted Hawthorne-Blythe, warming to his theme. 'Why is it only us Brits who get a reputation for this type of thing? I've been the guest of certain Scandinavian tour operators and I can assure you that as soon as their little darlings are in an environment where the licensing laws are nowhere near as Draconian or pernicious as their own, all hell breaks loose. Then of course, there's American fraternity life, which you could hardly define as sedate.'

'True,' agreed Arthur, 'but you must admit, H-B, that there is something unique about Brits in other countries. It's probably got something to do with not truly coming to term with the fact that maps of the world are no longer predominantly red.'

'I think what it is, Arthur, is that we're so bloody awful at cricket, rugby, football, tennis and everything else, that we have to prove we're best at something. A shame that it's being sick in the streets and fighting.'

Arthur laughed loudly and raised his brandy glass, chinking it with Hawthorne-Blythe's.

'I think it's awful when you see brawls out here,' said Lucas, feeling left out. He recalled Charles had earlier mentioned how much Arthur hated violence. 'I remember Alison telling me about some of her YF&S clients last year, setting about locals, fighting amongst themselves. No need for it at all as far as I'm concerned.'

Arthur had long since tired of Lucas's attempts to curry favour, but nevertheless felt it right to be courteous towards him.

'Yes, I must admit that wanton violence sickens me too. I remember a young broker who used to work for me, regularly coming in with black eyes or a bloodied nose. I could never understand it. He was earning a six-figure salary with more than enough pressure to use up any excess energies. Instead of relaxing at the weekends though, he was travelling the country supposedly following his football team but using it as an excuse to become involved in fights. Eventually I had to sack him. Battered faces do not impress clients in any business.'

Back at the other end of the table, Alison's ears had taken a battering, as Kristina babbled on about her dress, her new car and all of the superb restaurants she had visited around the world. She also went on at length about how she and Arthur detested bad table manners, adored fine wine, could get a table at The Ivy whenever they wanted . . . it was a constant drone of me, me, me.

Alison was torn between throttling her and asking her if she would like a student.

She was relieved when Charles Moon suggested that it was time to wrap things up. He ordered the bill and made sure that everyone had a drink. Alison hadn't really bothered with her glass of red wine, partly because she did not want to risk getting drunk and embarrass herself, but mainly because her lips still felt strange. During the previous twenty minutes it had dawned on her that it must have been something to do with the delay spray on Trev's dick and the blow job she had given him.

'Before we leave,' announced Charles, 'I would like to propose a toast. Nothing grand, just a thank you to Arthur for his advice and guidance over the years. He is a man of wit, intelligence – and sophistication.'

'I do hope that I'm not going to be the toast,' joked Arthur.

'That was my intention,' laughed Charles. 'But if you're not keen let's just toast the last quality – *sophistication*.'

'Sophistication,' everyone replied.

Alison put the glass to her lips and to her horror, the red wine dribbled down her chin.

'My lipth have gone numb,' she spluttered, spraying what red wine remained in her mouth all over Kristina's white dress.

Kristina screamed. Lucas held his head in his hands. Charles and Arthur looked appalled.

Trevor and his sodding surprises.

chapter twenty

Hughie's heart was racing with fear and excitement.

The plan was risky and audacious. If he got caught he dreaded to think what Roz would do to him. Maybe that was part of the turn-on.

Hughie had a strange feeling, however, that his plan was destined for success. It had started out as an impulsive dare to himself, but each piece had fallen into place unbelievably well.

The original scam – to arrange for Roz to meet Brad in the dark room out the back of the bar but for Hughie to pretend to be Brad – had not been particularly well thought out. At best it was half-baked, at worst, ludicrous. Over the course of twenty-four hours though, it had gathered momentum.

During the day Hughie had gone down to the Drunken Lizard. It was quiet and there was only one barman and Hughie slipped unnoticed into the back room. He replaced the light bulb with one that didn't work, because if he did follow things through then he would need it to be dark so Roz couldn't see him.

Later in the day came more good fortune when Brad left his phone on the table in the reception of the Hotel Arena. Impulsively, Hughie grabbed it and rang Roz, doing a fairly poor but nevertheless, adequate impression of Brad's voice. He knew Roz already had Brad's number in her phone and this meant that his name would have come up on her screen. Even at that stage, Hughie still didn't seriously think he would see the plan through. What if Brad turned up? What if she rang Brad back for any reason? Suppose Brad found out? Would he see the funny side, or sack him, or hit him, or sack him *and* hit him?

Then, a few hours earlier, he'd heard Brad telling Greg that he would probably have to attend an important meeting some time close to eleven and that his phone would be switched off. Hughie had arranged for Roz to meet 'Brad' in the back room at eleven. It was a sign and from that point on, the plan started to become a definite reality.

The only flaw – and quite a major one – was what to do afterwards? He wouldn't be able to leave without Roz knowing it was him rather than Brad. Even if he could, it wouldn't take her long to find out she'd been tricked. Hughie was still banking on his theory about large women, that Roz should be grateful for any shag she got. It wasn't as if Roz was a sensitive shrinking violet either – she gave as good as she got and it didn't seem to bother her too much that she'd be cheating on her Maori boyfriend. Of course, Hughie knew that he was trying to justify his actions to himself – but he was doing a bloody good job of it.

The loose plan was therefore to start off pretending to be Brad but then reveal his true identity. Roz would give his arm a friendly punch and say, 'Heavens, you cad, Hughie,' then engulf him in a passionate embrace amongst her voluminous muscle and flesh.

Or something like that.

One factor he had not banked on was Club Wicked being at the bar too. Things soon got rowdy and there was the distinct possibility that Roz would be too busy to sneak into the back room for fifteen minutes. Luckily, there was a man-mountain who seemed to be helping to keep things in check.

Hughie had told Greg of his plan. Greg thought it bonkers and had therefore given it his wholehearted support, even promising another two bonus points if Hughie pulled it off.

Greg originally came into the bar to placate Imogen or at the very least, to fill in the blanks from the previous night.

He also had an hour or so to kill until he was due to meet Rio later on. However, Imogen wasn't working, and it wasn't long before another girl caught his eye.

The object of his attentions had a disinterested detachment from everything and everyone around her, which initially included Greg. Enigmatism alone was not a trait Greg was particularly drawn to. However, when combined with high cheekbones, full lips, long legs and big tits, it was an altogether different matter.

'You're either a reporter, an undercover policewoman or you work for Club Wicked in the UK,' said Greg. He had successfully pulled other girls who were horrified by the YF&S type of holiday, so he already had an idea of her mind-set.

'I beg your pardon?' replied the girl.

'Sorry, I'm Greg.' He held out his hand, deciding that a handshake would be better appreciated than a kiss on both cheeks. 'This obviously isn't your kind of thing, is it?'

'You can say that again.'

'I was wondering what you were doing here – it's not exactly the kind of bar I'd imagine you choosing to go to. Fancy a drink?'

'Vodka Red Bull, thanks. I'm Sandy.' She looked at Greg properly for the first time. 'I got talked into coming here by my rep – I'm here with Club Wicked. God knows why. I'm going to kill my boss when I get home.'

'Why, what do you do?' asked Greg, as he pointed at their drinks to order the same again.

'I work for a DJ agency – we look after a lot of the top boys. They needed me to come over here at the last minute and all that was available was a Club Wicked package.' Greg started laughing. Sandy joined in. 'I know, not really me, is it? That bloody Italian rep persuaded me to come here tonight. He even tried to get me to wear fancy dress.'

'What, you mean you're not?' teased Greg.

She gave him a playful slap. 'Cheeky.'

'Only kidding. You look lovely – more than lovely.' He handed her her drink.

Sandy knew she had a flirty charmer on her hands. She thought he looked a little older than most of the other reps and he definitely had something about him. She started to enjoy herself.

'I take it you've been here before then?' continued Greg.

'You could say that. First time this year though. One of our DJ's is playing at Space on Sunday.'

'Really? That's great. I'm going there on Sunday too.'

'I didn't think reps went to those kind of clubs. I thought you only did the in-house stuff and Manumission on Mondays?'

'To be honest, the only reason I'm doing this job is so I can go clubbing. I get cut quite a bit of slack so they don't mind too much if I miss the odd morning. What time are you going to Space?'

'About four in the afternoon.'

'Pretty much the same time as me. Were you going on your own?'

'Yeah. I'll know some people in there though.'

'If you want we can go together.'

'Have you got a car?'

'It's in the garage,' lied Greg. He was thinking on his feet, though not particularly well, given that the Sunday of the Space opening coincided with an eleven o'clock welcome meeting, then the massively important DJ Face-Off in the evening. Still, there was an eight-hour gap. As long as he kept off the pills . . .

'I was going to get a cab,' he continued, 'you can jump in with me if you like.'

Sandy thought for a moment, then smiled. 'OK. Take my mobile number.'

Greg punched her number into his phone. Instinctively he knew that making a move on her before Space would be wrong and likely to lead to failure (not to mention the fact that he had already arranged to meet up with Rio the lap dancer later.) Without a doubt she was different from most girls Greg met in Ibiza – as much as anything else Sandy seemed to have respect for herself in abundance. His recent conversation with Mikey floated in the back of his mind.

In addition, it was clear she had been involved in the club scene for a number of years and was now, from what she said, right in the thick of it. She had a weary sophistication, a 'been there-done-that-got-the-T-shirt-but-only-if-it's-got-the-right-label' attitude whereas Greg was still a relatively new convert to clubbing. He was ever so slightly intimidated by her.

It was clear that Sandy was going to be a tough nut to crack, but it simply served to make her all the more appealing. She was going to be a challenge and Greg was going to enjoy the hunt.

She stood up to leave and he walked her to the door. He was just giving her a peck on the cheek when he saw Imogen striding up to the bar. He had a feeling the next few minutes were not going to be all that pleasant, so ushered Sandy away before she witnessed anything that would ruin his credibility.

As far as Imogen was concerned, seeing Greg kissing another girl removed any doubts she had about him being a one hundred per cent bastard. She stormed over and within a couple of minutes, she had reminded Greg of what had happened during his 'missing hours'. He was not entirely surprised that Imogen was so annoyed.

When Imogen saw the faint smile on Greg's face, she exploded. Greg was glad that Sandy had long gone.

Then, the man-mountain who had been helping Roz sort out the troublemakers came over to see what the shouting was all about. This didn't surprise Greg. Girls could sometimes be even more vicious than guys and having a bouncer around to calm things down always helped.

'Everything all right?' The booming voice matched the massive frame.

'Yeah, no problem, mate,' replied Greg, 'just a misunderstanding.'

The man-mountain glared at Greg. 'I wasn't asking you, pipsqueak.'

'No, it's all right,' said Greg pointing at his badge, 'I'm a rep.'

'I don't care if you're King Juan fucking Carlos. I was talking to her.' He turned to Imogen. 'Everything OK, sis?'

Imogen nodded. 'Yeah, no probs. Greg, have you met my *little* brother Lars?'

Greg offered his hand. 'No. Um, hi, Lars.'

The man-mountain took Greg's hand in a bone-crushing shake.

'Lars has decided to stay out here and try to find some work for the summer.'

'Yeah. Thought I'd keep an eye on my big sister. Make sure nobody takes the piss out of her.' He turned to Imogen. 'He's not the sort of bloke to take the piss out you, is he, sis?'

Greg gulped.

'I don't think so,' replied Imogen sweetly. 'You'd never do that, would you, Greg?'

'No, no of course not.' Greg doubted that he had ever shaken his head quite so vigorously.

Lars paused for a moment, then when Imogen nodded, he left. Imogen put her arm through Greg's and walked him through the bar.

'So shall we say that what happened by the pool was a misunderstanding? Shall we just blame the GHB, call it one of those things you put down to experience and move on?'

As far as Greg was concerned she could call it a misunderstanding, a mistake, Eric, Reginald or anything she bloody well wanted as long as the 'moving on' bit could be enforced ASAP.

'Yeah, of course.' He was relieved. Easier than he'd thought.

'So when are we going out again?'

'Hang on—'

Imogen's face froze. 'You're not telling me that was it, are you? That you really did use me the other night? Lars . . .'

'No, no, wait,' said Greg. 'No, of course I didn't mean that. But . . . I thought you said you were working every night now the summer's under way?'

'I get two nights off a week and start late every Thursday. I'm off again on Monday. Where shall we go?'

'I can't do Monday.' Imogen glared at him. 'I can't,' insisted Greg, 'honestly. I've got a job and I can't just drop things.'

'But you do still want to see me again, don't you?'

'Of course.'

What I actually want, he thought, is to get this bunny-boiler carted off by the men in white coats.

She kissed him on the cheek. 'See you later.'

As Greg stood there, recovering, Hughie bounded up.

'Did she ask for her panties back? You look like you've seen a ghost.'

'I doubt if there are too many ghosts the size of that fucker,' he said, pointing towards Lars. 'That's Imogen's brother.'

'Oh shit. Oh well, if it makes you feel any better, I'm probably about to get my wee head kicked in too.'

'You're not seriously going through with it?' said Greg.

'I'm just about to go round the back and into the special room with freshly fitted duff light bulb, put there by yours truly.'

'You're serious, aren't you?'

'Wish me luck.'

'Don't forget I'll need some proof,' Greg called out after him.

Once inside the room, Hughie was quite nervous, but still having little giggling fits as he thought of what he was about to do. He'd had quite a few drinks and without that Dutch courage, doubted he would have seen his plan through.

Bang on time, the door opened. As the light from the hallway filled the room, Hughie moved into the darkest corner.

'Brad, Brad are you here?'

'Yeah,' said Hughie, trying to disguise his voice, 'over here. Shut the door.'

Roz shut the door and flicked down the light switch.

'Shit, the bulb's gone.'

'Don't worry, come here.'

There was a tiny amount of light coming through a grill, but still not enough to stop Roz from banging her thigh against a table and knocking over a chair.

'I haven't got long,' she said. 'I wasn't sure you'd be able to turn up. It's funny, Brad, I always had a feeling you fancied me.'

As soon as she was close enough, Hughie walked behind her and put his arms around her waist – well, almost. He didn't have to move his hands far before he was cupping her full breasts.

Roz moaned. 'Do you like big ones, Brad? They don't come much bigger.' She reached behind and felt that Hughie was already hard. 'Looks like I'm turning you on. Come on, put it inside me, Brad.'

Hughie didn't need any further encouragment. She pulled her leggings down but before she could get them off completely, he entered her from behind. He started easing in and out. He wondered if now would be the time to reveal his true identity. But there was something else he wanted her to do first.

He pulled out and offered himself to her for a blow job. Roz took him in her mouth but after a few moments, Hughie stopped her.

'Roz, can you do something for me?'

'What?'

'Your gums.'

'What?'

'Your gums. Can you take your teeth out?' Hughie's attempt at Brad's accent almost cracked. 'It'd really turn me on.'

As if it was the kind of thing she was asked every day, Roz took her teeth out and placed them on the table. She gave head and Hughie lost his hands between her fleshy thighs. It didn't take long for Hughie to shudder to a climax and a few moments after, Roz had her own orgasm, causing her to slump on to a hard wooden chair panting.

As she sat there trying to get her breath back, Hughie did his trousers up. He'd intended to tell her that he wasn't Brad during the act. Telling her now though, didn't seem such a good idea. In fact, now that he'd ejaculated, for the first time he saw just how foolish the whole plan was.

There was only one thing to do – a runner. Run now, worry later. As he edged towards the door he rested his hand on the table, right next to Roz's false teeth. He slipped them into his hand and sprinted for the door.

'Brad, where are you going? Brad?' Roz pulled her leggings up and reached for her teeth on the table. 'You bastard! Come back here with my teeth.'

Giggling manically, Hughie hurtled out of the door. As he turned the corner, he saw Greg standing outside the front entrance. He ran towards him, almost colliding with a cab that had just pulled up, and chucked him the teeth.

'There's your proof. My bonus points I believe and I reckon I should get an extra one for a gum job. See you later.'

Hughie sprinted back to the Hotel Arena.

Brad stepped out of the cab. He paid the driver and walked over to Greg. 'Was that Hughie?'

'Yeah, don't even ask. How was the meeting?'

'Yeah, went well. How are we doing in here?'

'Not bad. Stig and a couple of Club Wicked reps turned up with some of their clients but it seems all right. I think Stig's been giving Sugar Ray a bit of stick though.'

'We'll have to keep an eye on that. Mind you – I wouldn't fancy having a ruck with him. He's a lump.' Brad noticed the teeth. 'What are those?'

Greg passed them to him. Before he had a chance to explain, Roz came flying around the corner. She saw Brad holding the teeth.

'I thought you were different . . . *bastard!*'

Brad wasn't expecting the right hook. As he stumbled to the floor, he fell awkwardly on his arm and yelped.

Roz didn't wait to see the outcome of her punch. She jumped into her car and sped off.

'What the fuck did she do that for?' asked Brad, lying on the floor with a hand clasped to his eye, which was already beginning to swell.

'God knows,' lied Greg. Not his problem.

Brad went to get up, but as soon as he put weight on to his right arm, it buckled and he screamed in pain.

One of the Hartlepool Honeys appeared and bent down next to Brad.

'Looks like it's broken.' She stood up. 'I'm a nurse,' she added.

'Are you sure it's broken?' asked Greg. (He liked nurses.) 'Should we call an ambulance?'

'It's an arm, not a ruptured spleen or a broken leg,' replied Brad, grimacing. 'I've probably just bruised it. I'll walk down to Galeno Medical Centre, it's only down the road. I'll get Tamsin to come with me and you can look after this lot. We're due to leave here in an hour.'

Responsibility. Just what Greg didn't need – especially with Rio due to turn up at any minute and even more especially because he had taken half a pill just a short while earlier to boost his sagging energy levels.

After some organisation, Brad and Tasmin set off down the road.

The nurse looked after him shaking her head. 'That arm is definitely broken. It's just numb. He's going to be screaming in agony in five minutes.' She turned back to the bar. 'I'm going to get a drink. Do you want one?'

'No, I'm fine thanks,' replied Greg

He looked into the bar. There weren't too many clients. The problem was, with Brad, Hughie and Tamsin all gone, there weren't too many reps left either. He knew that the golden rule when sharing a bar or club with clients from another tour company was for the reps to lead the way in having a good time. The theory behind this was that the clients from the other company would think that the company they had come away with were boring by comparison and book with YF&S the next year.

Then he spotted Sugar Ray. 'How's tricks?'

'That Stig from Club Wicked is really getting on my nerves.'

'Why?'

'All the usual backs to the wall crap. I mean, as if? I'm gay not blind.' Sugar Ray looked over at Stig, who made a limped-wrist gesture back at him. 'What an oaf.'

'Unfortunately he's a fucking big oaf, otherwise I'd have a word with him for you.'

'Fuck him. He's not worth bothering about. Big body, tiny mind.' Sugar Ray changed the subject. 'What's the plan?'

'Actually that's why I've come to find you. Can you do me a favour?'

'Sure, what?'

'Brad looks like he might have just broken his arm.'

'What? How?'

'I'll tell you another time. The thing is, I've got an important meeting so I can't hang around. Hughie's had to leave too and Tamsin's gone with Brad to the medical centre, so I want you and Vaz to look after this lot. The only thing is it means there'll be just you two and over twice as many Club Wicked reps, so you'll have to work twice as hard.'

'You mean four times as hard. Vaz is leaving in a minute. Brad said he could go early as he's got to be up in the morning to practise his DJing for Sunday at La Luna Café.'

'Shit,' said Greg.

Greg knew it was wrong to leave Sugar Ray alone to look after all of the clients, especially with four Club Wicked reps around. However, Greg also knew that since Monday he and Rio had sent each other so many filthy texts that he fully expected to see a headline saying that the share price of mobile service provider Movistar had gone through the roof. Greg knew a good shag when he saw one and was convinced that Rio was going to be sensational.

'All right, here's what we'll do. I'll go and get this meeting over ASAP, but if I'm not back in half an hour, you take them down to Night Life and I should be on the door as you arrive.'

It wasn't pleasant lying to Sugar Ray but Greg reasoned that it would have been even less pleasant going home alone when he could be having fantastic sex with Rio.

Sugar Ray agreed. Greg went in the bar and told Imogen that he had to go back to the Hotel Arena because of what had just happened to Brad. He downed a quick chupito with her, then walked to the parking area near the large sculpted egg on the roundabout at the junction of the San Antonio to Ibiza and San Antonio to San Jose roads.

As he got closer to the parking area where he was due to meet Rio, he had a pang of conscience. Leaving Sugar Ray on his own was not the right thing to do, but in an attempt to justify his actions he told himself that had he wanted responsibility, then he would have taken the manager's job. Besides, this was all Hughie's fault, trying to get the two bonus points from Roz.

Two bonus points that he'd egged him on to go for . . .

For his Competition . . .

Oops. His fault. Indirectly.

This momentary introspective soon disappeared when he saw Rio leaning against her Renault 5, wearing a short leather mini skirt and crop top.

'Hey, honey,' she said, tossing back her mane of hair.

She gave Greg a long full-on kiss that made Greg tingle and completely forget about Sugar Ray.

'I've got some wicked pills,' she said. 'I dropped one about ten minutes ago. Do you want one?'

'I've just done a half. Let's do some more when we get to yours.'

'Sure. But I thought you had to be up for work tomorrow?'

Greg opened the passenger door.

'Work?' he said. 'What's that?'

chapter twenty-one

It had been an extremely long, depressing day, most of it spent in hospital having his arm set. Brad had rang Hawthorne-Blythe at nine in the morning.

Hawthorne-Blythe immediately went to the hospital and despite Brad's protests, insisted that he get his arm fixed in the UK. The Spanish doctors had explained that it was quite a bad break and would require a second operation. In Hawthorne-Blythe's opinion, this meant that Brad would be out of action anyway, so it would be far better for Brad to have treatment at home. Brad was to stay in Ibiza as long as possible but they both realised that he would almost certainly have to return to the UK before the The Monastery assessment was finished. That meant that a replacement would be needed and the more they discussed it, the more inevitable the conclusion that there was only one person for the job. Greg.

Hawthorne-Blythe suggested calling Greg into the office but Brad thought it would be better if he had a chat with him first. After all, Greg had turned down the position when it was offered to him so why should he change his mind now? There was always the possibility that Greg would say yes now that he was actually on resort.

They also decided that it would be prudent to recruit another new rep. Brad told Hawthorne-Blythe about Ace, who was thinking of going home. All of the reps and bar owners knew and liked Ace, and Brad thought that he had a lot of the required qualities. If it didn't work out, then they could find someone from the UK but given the special circumstances, Brad argued that they needed somebody who could hit the ground running to get them through the next weeks. Brad said that he would show Ace the ropes prior to going back to the UK, if he accepted.

As a contingency to Greg, Hawthorne-Blythe was going to line up Mitch Clarke, the resort manager in Majorca. Mitch had only been doing the job a year longer than Brad and knew little about Ibiza, or anybody on the island. But without Greg, they both knew that Club Wicked would wipe the floor with them.

And after almost two decades as youth market leaders, Young Free & Single would be no more.

Ace crawled out of Garden of Eden at ten-thirty in the morning. He was battered. He was also bored.

Four years of propping in the West End had taken it out of him. He'd had enough. Six hours a night of standing outside a bar trying to get passers-by to come in, with the French co-owner Gilbert constantly buzzing round outside, on their backs if they slackened off for a minute.

Ace had worked out how to play Gilbert though. For a start, Gilbert knew that as props go, they didn't get much better than Ace and finding a prop who lasted a season, let alone four, took some doing. Male tourists never really seemed to take offence to Ace and if they did, he could look after himself. Girls adored him and Gilbert knew only too well that getting girls into the bar was the key to The G-Spot Bar's success.

Girls also happened to be Gilbert's weak spot. He got lucky maybe twice a season, when an English girl was so drunk she didn't know or care that a slimy, pot-bellied, fifty-year-old Frenchman was pawing her.

Pulling for Ace was the easiest thing in the world. Over the years he had worked with props who were far better looking and came out with more original lines. But Ace understood that girls expected props to be cheeky. If he saw a girl he liked, he'd simply say, 'I really fancy you.' (The girl would giggle.) 'I'm serious, I really do fancy you. Come in the bar and I'll get you a drink.'

Usually that was all that was needed, apart from returning with the odd wisecrack and implying that she was coming home with him that night. It wasn't so much what he said, more the way that he said it. Confident, assumptive, not at all bothered by the prospect of rejection. Full of life and a carefree attitude that screamed, 'Girls, I'm going to give you a good time!'

Often they would sit there waiting for him all night, sometimes even after their friends left and went somewhere else. Other times he would get them into the staff room and do it there and then. Occasionally, they would come back at four o'clock as he finished work. It was not uncommon for five or six girls to be hovering around The G-Spot Bar at that time in the morning.

Gilbert marvelled at Ace's prowess and lived his sex life vicariously through him. As such, if ever Ace needed to get away from work for half an hour all he would have to do was come back and tell Gilbert in graphic detail about the girl he'd just shagged and Gilbert wouldn't mind that Ace had disappeared. More often than not, Ace would have simply popped round some of the bars to catch up with his friends and then select a story from his considerable arsenal of conquests to tell Gilbert.

Tonight though, Ace had not bothered with any of the girls he'd chatted up. He had left work and decided to get bang on it. He'd taken two and a half pills and got pissed in Eden, then in the adjoining after-hours bar, Garden of Eden. About an hour earlier, his fellow prop and flatmate Nigel had sneaked off with a Welsh girl they'd both been chatting up. Ace wasn't bothered. It just irritated him the way Nigel went about things. It probably wasn't even Nigel's fault. Ace was simply getting irritated by virtually everything. He needed a change and, loathe though he was to admit it, going home to Liverpool was becoming more appealing by the day.

When Ace returned to their apartment, the bedroom door was closed and it was obvious what Nigel was up to. They shared the room but inevitably one of them pulled so the rule was that the first one in got the bedroom, the second the sofa.

Ace laid on the sofa and stuck on a porno. He started having a wank, not in the least bit bothered that the porno was on quite loud or that Nigel or the girl would come out and catch him mid-stroke.

As Ace got closer to climax, his ecstasy-addled brain threw an idea at him. Still wanking, he walked across the room and stopped by the bedroom door. Just as he was about to come he flung the door open.

Nigel was thrusting away behind the Welsh girl, who was bent over a chest of drawers. At first there was a look of total bewilderment and confusion on Nigel's face. Ace was giggling and wanking like a maniac.

As Ace stepped towards him, Nigel realised what he was trying to do.

'Fuck off, you dirty bastard!'

He withdrew from Welsh girl then grabbed her shoulders to use her as a shield. Ace was about to come and was trying to side-step the girl to get to Nigel like an American football forward trying to dodge a linebacker to get to the quarterback.

As he grunted and aimed at Nigel, Nigel swung the girl in front of him, so that Ace ended up shooting all over the Welsh girl's ribcage.

'Ha . . . *missed!*' taunted Nigel.

'Bollocks.' Ace slapped his thigh and walked out of the bedroom.

Things just weren't the same . . .

Sugar Ray pulled up outside the Hotel Arena and opened the passenger door for a very tired Brad, who had his arm in plaster and an eye that was now bruised and almost totally closed.

Hawthorne-Blythe had rung the hotel to get one of the reps to hire a car from Moto Luis, the car company they recommended to clients, then to come and pick Brad up from the hospital at C'an Misses. Most of the other reps were going for a football match so Sugar Ray had volunteered to make the journey.

Sugar Ray told Brad he didn't have a clue why Roz had hit him (true) and said that Greg was on desk duty (false).

They made a detour via Ace's apartment who reacted positively when Brad put the idea of joining YF&S as a rep to him, which surprised Brad but pleased him nonetheless. They arranged to meet later that evening to discuss it.

As they walked towards the hotel, Charles Moon and Arthur Bairns were just coming out of the main door.

'Great,' muttered Brad, 'that's all I need, those two seeing the resort manager looking like he's been in a brawl.'

'Brad,' Charles called. 'What on earth has happened to you? Alison told me earlier that you got into a fight outside one of the bars last night.'

Brad noticed the disapproving look from Arthur.

'Well, as she wasn't there, I'm surprised she can comment,' replied Brad, snapping more than he would normally have done.

'Apparently her reps told her. I haven't heard the full story – what did happen?'

'I wish I knew.'

'Who hit you?' asked Arthur.

'The girl who works there.'

'A girl did *that*.' Arthur seemed more than a little surprised.

'This was no ordinary girl,' intervened Sugar Ray, seeing that Brad was far from at his best. 'She's a bouncer there . . . huge.'

'Why did she hit you?' asked Charles.

'That's what I intend to find out. I'd literally just stepped out of the cab after meeting you at the restaurant and she hit me for no apparent reason. I wasn't expecting it and fell awkwardly on my arm. It's broken.'

'Oh dear. So what happens now?'

'It looks like I'll have to go back to the UK at some point in the next few weeks for another op. H-B said he was going to call you to arrange a meeting and have a chat about things.'

'Yes, Kit just rang to tell me. That's where we're going now.'

'Well, if you'll excuse me, I've got to sort a few things out,' said Brad.

'Yes, of course. Well I do hope everything works out all right for you. Oh, and by the way,' said Charles, 'there were four or five clients in there asking me if I knew where they could find a rep.'

'Thanks,' said Brad. 'Enjoy the rest of your cruise,' he added, nodding to Arthur.

As soon as they were gone, he turned to Sugar Ray.

'Where's Greg? He's meant to be on desk duty. It's five in the afternoon. Hasn't he been around all day? Is he at the football match?'

'I haven't seen him,' replied Sugar Ray truthfully.

'He'd better not still be in bed. Can you deal with the clients while I go up to his room?'

Greg's room key was hanging up at the reception. This normally meant he wasn't in, which proved to be the case. As he looked out of the window, he saw Greg getting out of Rio's car. He walked out to the street where Greg was kissing Rio goodbye.

'Greg!'

Greg turned round. When he saw Brad he looked a little sheepish. Rio roared off.

'All right, mate,' he said, as innocently as possible. 'How's your arm?'

'Never mind my arm – what are you playing at?'

'What, Rio? A bit nutty but fit as fuck – what a shag!'

'But you're meant to be working. You were supposed to be on desk duty.'

'Come on, Brad. It's not often a girl like that comes along. Cut us some slack. I guessed that somebody else would cover desk for me.'

'Well, you guessed wrong. All the other reps are at a football match and Sugar Ray came to pick me up at the hospital. We got back here to a queue of clients. And to make things worse, Charles Moon was here with a major investor.'

'Oh.'

'Oh,' Brad repeated.

'Still it could have been worse.'

'Yeah . . . how?'

'Rio could have been a crap shag. Mate, she was filthy,' continued Greg, trying to return Brad to the laddish camaraderie they had shared the previous summer. 'I can honestly say that she was one of—'

'For fuck's sake! Is that all you think about? Don't you realise what's at stake here? In two weeks' time, Young Free & Single might cease to exist. Can you honestly see Alison employing any of our reps? Do you think she'll employ *you*?'

'Fuck her. If she doesn't, I'll just get a job with another company or work in a bar somewhere.'

'Oh, well, as long as you're all right that's fine. What about everyone else? Can't you see that you've got a responsibility to them?'

'Come off it, Brad. Just missing one poxy desk duty isn't going to put us out of business. All right, I'm a bit out of order but you know I'll come good when it matters.'

'I'm not so sure. I wish I'd never persuaded you to take that half a pill last year. Maybe you'd be doing my job and making something of yourself.'

'And that's what you're doing, is it?' Greg's tone changed. 'Is managing a few reps making something of yourself? There are no loopholes left to make real money so if it's not money then what's *your* motivation. Ego? Power?'

Brad considered his response. 'No. It's loyalty. To those who are relying on me to help them keep their jobs, because the person they wanted to manage Ibiza is shit scared of responsibility and only cares about himself and his dick. Yeah, you are a brilliant rep when you want to be and yes, you can do the job blindfolded. But when did you last challenge yourself, Greg? When did you last step out of your comfort zone and do something different?'

'Last year when you gave me that pill,' Greg replied instantly. 'Everything changed. I finally get Ibiza. It's like a whole new world.'

Brad shook his head. 'Nothing's changed, mate. It's still about Greg having a good time. Instead of getting pissed like you have every other year, you're taking Class A's, that's all. And even if you hadn't started taking pills you would have come back, because what else are you going to do, Greg?'

'What do you mean by that?'

'Exactly what I said. You've had your head buried in Balearic sand for most of your adult life. How much longer can you carry on being a rep?'

'Maybe I'm happy as I am.'

'Perhaps. But will you be happy in five years' time? Will you still be happy trying to win The Golden Dick?'

'Fucking hell. Is this the same Brad I knew last year? Where's all this shit coming from?'

'I'm resort manager because you didn't want to do it. I take that responsibility seriously because people are relying on me.'

'Yeah and you chose to do it, just as I chose to carry on repping. It doesn't mean that you're right and I'm wrong.'

'Well, I guess it doesn't matter who's right or wrong,' replied Brad, 'because I'm going back to the UK soon.'

'You're what?'

'I've got to have another operation on my arm.'

'Shit, I'm sorry.'

'It's not your fault.'

'When are you going? Who's going to be the new resort manager?' asked Greg, not wanting to dwell on the fact that indirectly, Brad's broken arm probably *was* his fault.

Brad took a deep breath and stared over Greg's shoulder for a few seconds, then looked him in the eye.

'You.'

'What?'

'You're the only man for the job. You've been repping longer than anyone else, you know Ibiza and you know how to deal with Alison.'

'But I don't want the job. I made that clear.'

'Things have changed. This takeover will spell the end for YF&S if Club Wicked win. But you could turn it round. You've got a chance to do something worthwhile, something that you won't get any Competition points for but something that could affect the lives of loads of people around you.'

'But I don't want that responsibility.'

'Please, just think about it, Greg. Hopefully I won't have to go back for my second operation until after this assessment is finished, but in case I do, we need to know that you're ready to step in.'

'But I'll be crap at it. It's not me.'

'It is you but you can't see it. You're a natural leader, people respect you, they want to be your friend, they listen to you. If you put your mind to it you could be so good. You've got great communication skills. You've just got no focus. It could be the best thing you ever did, trust me. Please, just mull it over.'

Greg liked Brad a lot. He felt bad about what had happened to Brad's arm and there was some truth in what he'd said. So, for now, he went for the easy option.

'I'll think about it.'

As soon as Brad left though, Greg was thinking about only one thing . . .

The cooler than cool Sandy and Space the next day.

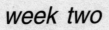

week two

chapter twenty-two

Mario stood on the stairs at Eden, in a slightly elevated position so he could see if anybody approached the small room behind the downstairs bar, which had been allocated to YF&S.

The club had only been open for an hour but it was already very busy. It was Sunday, 22 June, the night of Judge Jules's Judgement Sunday. Jules was good friends with Charles Moon, having mixed several compilation CDs for The Monastery. He had agreed to do Charles a favour and allow the DJ Face-Off to be staged in the smaller funky room, annexed from the main part of the club. He had also agreed to listen to both the DJs and have a chat to them afterwards, then give Charles his verdict.

Vaz had left his records in the YF&S room and was in the annexed part of the club, dancing with the other reps and getting to know the new clients who had arrived the previous night. Mario had turned up at Eden before everyone else and hidden the bag of records that Arabella was to switch, in the YF&S room.

Mario had Arabella's number programmed into his mobile and was ready to press dial if any of the other YF&S reps turned up. It wasn't going to be simply a case of switching one set of records for the other: Each of the records had to be taken out of their individual sleeves and replaced with the crap ones that the Club Wicked DJ Smiffy had painstakingly stuck white labels on.

There was little chance that any of the YF&S reps would need to go into the room. As a joint night with The Monastery VIPs in attendance, they were all under strict instructions from their respective managers to be seen having the time of their lives.

Mario had not counted on Ace, the new YF&S rep. Within six hours of agreeing to do the job, Ace was in a YF&S uniform, at the airport and welcoming clients. As Brad had suspected, he took to the job like a duck to water, even happily doing the microphone on the way back from the airport although Brad was with him and offered to do it.

Now Mario spotted Ace heading for the YF&S room, leading a young girl by the hand. Rather than ring Arabella and stop her in mid-switch, Mario dashed over to stop him.

'All right, Ace? Where are you going?'

'I hear they've got a bingo night starting over the road in Es Paradis, so I'm taking this lovely young lady over there.'

'What bingo?' Mario realised he was being wound up. 'Oh right.'

'Assuming you've nothing else of mind-blowing importance to say, would you mind stepping out of my way?'

Mario blocked Ace's path. 'I think I just saw Hawthorne-Blythe go in there. Why don't you use our room?'

Ace eyed him suspiciously. 'This better not be some kind of stitch-up.'

'No, it's not – I swear. Fuck it, go in there, let Hawthorne-Blythe catch you if that's what you want.' Mario walked away, hoping his bluff would work, his finger poised on the send button to warn Arabella if it didn't.

'OK,' replied Ace finally. 'You're sure your room's empty?'

'Totally. No one will be in there for ages.'

Ace nodded, then set off through the crowd and up the stairs to the room allocated to Club Wicked.

Mario breathed a sigh of relief and resumed his post.

Five minutes later, Arabella emerged from the YF&S room and walked over to Mario.

'All done?' he asked.

'Yes. Mario, I feel a bit bad.'

'You were all for it when I suggested it.'

'I know, but listening to Vaz talking earlier – it means so much to him.'

'Good, all the better.' Mario looked around and shared a brief smile with a sexy new arrival he'd been talking to. Arabella spotted the exchange.

'Who's she?'

'Who?'

'That girl you just smiled at.'

'She's a client. Fucking hell, Arabella. I've got to be nice to girl clients too.'

'Yes, but there's being nice and there's being nice.'

'Don't be so silly. Listen, I've got to get back over there and do my job – we can't let anyone see us talking for too long.'

'I hate all of this secrecy. I could happily leave YF&S and work somewhere else, then we could let everyone know about us.'

Mario looked horrified. 'You can't do that! Alison would throw a fit, even if you weren't working for YF&S. Anyway, what would you do? I can't exactly see you working in a bar, or as a prop.'

Arabella had to concede that he did have a point.

'Are you still going to cook me dinner tomorrow night like you promised?'

'Yeah. It'll have to be early though. I've got a meeting with Alison later.'

'What, so I can't stay the night again?'

'Sorry, babe.'

'Sometimes I think all you're interested in is sex.'

Mario was tempted to disagree with her. When it came to Arabella, he wasn't even interested in that. He couldn't keep up the pretence of fancying her much longer. He was going to have to speak to Alison.

Brad was upstairs in the VIP with Hawthorne-Blythe, Charles Moon, Lucas and Alison. Alison knew that Greg had yet to turn up to the DJ Face-Off that had started over an hour earlier – her rep, Smiffy was in mid-set – and she was intent on making maximum capital out of it.

'So where's Greg?' she asked in a voice loud enough for Charles Moon to hear.

'He's had to pop round to one of the bars,' lied Brad.

'Why's that?' asked Alison. 'Has another one of your reps got into a fight with a bouncer?'

Brad and Hawthorne-Blythe moved away from the main group.

'This isn't looking too promising, Brad.'

'I know. I haven't got a clue where he is. After I spoke to him yesterday I was sure some of it sank in.'

'I spoke to Mitch today in Majorca. I told him that Greg would probably take over and I could hear the relief in his voice. I'm afraid that I don't think Mitch is the right man for Ibiza.'

'Let's hope that I don't have to go back for my operation until this madness is all finished.'

Brad and Hawthorne-Blythe both leaned against the balcony and looked down at the swelling crowd.

'Did you get to the bottom of why the bouncer hit you?' asked Hawthorne-Blythe.

'No. I went to the bar earlier and apparently she's left the island. It's a mystery.'

'Rather like Greg's whereabouts. Shall we go downstairs and see how this DJ Face-Off is coming along? I believe Club Wicked's DJ is playing now.'

'Fag boy! Come on, why aren't you doing one of your little gay dances to our DJ?' Stig turned to a group of Club Wicked clients with whom he'd been drinking heavily. 'Backs against the wall, lads.'

Sugar Ray tried to ignore him, but Stig slapped him on the back, spilling the red wine Sugar Ray was holding all over his white trousers.

'You prick. You've ruined my trousers.'

'Oooh, you've ruined my trousers,' mimicked Stig. 'Here

lads, have you met Suuugaaaar!' Stig blew him a kiss. 'Sugar *Gay*!'

Sugar Ray 'accidentally' spilt the rest of his red wine over Stig. 'Oops, clumsy me. Still, it probably won't make any difference to that shirt, what with all of the food you've got down the front of it. How *do* you miss a mouth so big?'

Stig grabbed Sugar Ray's slender neck with his massive hands and roughly pushed him into a dark corner of the room. 'Listen to me, you little fucking poof. I could break your scrawny neck if I wanted so do yourself a favour and keep out of my way.'

'Let him go.'

It was Vaz.

Stig looked even angrier. 'What are you going to do about it?'

'It's all right,' said Sugar Ray, before Vaz could answer, 'I'm OK.'

Vaz held Stig's gaze. 'Why don't you pick on someone your own size?'

Stig looked around the room and started laughing. 'Because there is no one my own size.'

Stig made his way towards the DJ booth and small temporary stage that had been erected, where the singer Jocelyn Brown was just getting ready. Smiffy was coming to the end of his set and the singers were due on before Vaz.

'Thanks for that, Vaz. He's such a tosser.'

'Yeah, I know. Typical bully – probably wasn't potty trained.'

Sugar Ray laughed. 'I was standing near Judge Jules earlier on. He was talking to one of the promoters about Smiffy.'

'What were they saying?'

'Jules asked the promoter what he thought of Smiffy's DJing and the promoter said that Smiffy can mix but that was about it.'

'I hate to slag off the opposition but he's right. There's a lot more to DJing than just being able to mix records. All Smiffy was doing was sticking on one banging trance tune after the other – and this is meant to be the *funky* room.'

'It's a shame really because two of the other promoters that were here decided to leave after seeing him.'

'Fucking great!' spat Vaz.

'It doesn't matter that much, does it?'

Vaz remembered that only Mikey knew of his ambition. 'No, I guess not.'

'You all set to play?'

'Yeah, just need to get my records. What about you, are you all set to sing?'

'Kind of. I need to go and change these trousers first – do you want me to grab your records for you?'

'Yeah, cheers.' He noticed Arabella sitting alone at the bar. 'I'll go and cheer up her ladyship over there.'

Arabella's hair was normally pulled back severely from her face into a tight gelled pony-tail. Tonight, for the first time, she had simply let it down. It had a natural wave to it and seemed blonder than usual. Combined with her newly acquired suntan, it made her features seem softer and more vulnerable.

Had Vaz been able to read her mind, he would have known that she felt vulnerable too. As blinded as she was by her obsession with Mario, she was nobody's fool and though she still was not prepared to admit it to herself, she could sense that their romance was not going the way she had hoped.

Vaz had always had a natural interest in people and Arabella actually amused him. He had certainly never met anyone like her before and was still puzzled why she'd wanted to become a rep. One thing he had observed was that she was besotted with Mario. He had noticed the way they interacted, subtle nuances that nobody else saw, because nobody else was looking. He was equally sure that Mario had little interest in her.

Even though he and Arabella seemed complete opposites, Vaz felt a bond. He didn't fancy her, but they were working together, had been through the training together and he felt as though he should look out for her, even if she did yell at him and try to make him look stupid at every opportunity. Once Vaz convinced himself that it was all bravado, he was able to take Arabella's attitude with a pinch of salt.

As usual, Arabella was showing no interest in proceedings around her. Vaz was on a natural high because of his imminent DJ spot so decided to break the ice.

'Having a good time, Arry?' He was still unable to stop himself from teasing her occasionally.

'What do you want?'

'Thanks. I'll have a JD and coke if you're buying.' She ignored him. 'Sugar Ray and Stig are about to get up and do their thing with Jocelyn Brown in a minute. It should be a laugh.' He attracted the barmaid's attention. 'Do you want a drink, Arabella?'

Arabella was surprised at both the politeness of Vaz's question and the fact he used her full name. 'Thank you. I'll have a dry white wine.'

Vaz ordered the drinks and they clinked glasses.

'Cheers.'

'Arabella, you don't seem too happy tonight.'

Normally, Arabella would have told Vaz to mind his own business. However, she was feeling sorry for herself. Mario had been her total focus since arriving in Ibiza so she had not exactly gone out of her way to make friends. Consequently now, when she needed someone to talk to, there was nobody . . . apart from Vaz. As much as she would have liked to discuss the turmoil going on inside her head, she wasn't able to.

'Oh, just tired, I guess.'

'Anything I can do to help?'

'No, not really. Thanks for asking.'

For the first time Arabella considered why she disliked him so intensely. The more she thought about it, there was no actual reason, other than the fact that he made fun of her. They stood together for a while not talking. Vaz downed his drink.

'I'd better be off. If you need a chat though, don't forget a problem shared is a problem halved.'

'Not all of the time.' It was Greg. 'When confessing to infidelity, a problem shared is a problem doubled in my experience. But I guess that wouldn't apply to you, Arabella?' Greg was obviously buzzing, drunk or most probably both. 'I mean, you hardly ever talk to anyone, let alone shag them.'

'Leave it out, Greg,' said Vaz.

'Oh, and since when did you start sticking up for her? It's about time someone gave her a few home truths.'

'Not now, Greg. You're pissed.'

'So what if it means I'm being honest?' He turned back to Arabella. 'You have got to be the most stuck-up, pretentious cow that's ever worked for YF&S. I've shagged some fucking mingers in my time, but I'd rather put a cheese-grater over my knees and crawl round in vinegar than put my old chap . . .'

Before Greg could finish, Arabella had run off in tears.

'Nice one, Greg.'

'And when did you start giving a fuck about her?'

'I think something's troubling her,' said Vaz.

'Yeah. Well, ditto.'

'What's that?'

'I've just spent the afternoon and evening in Space with that girl Sandy I was telling you about. Mate, what a club and what a girl! We had a wicked time. She knows everyone. We had some brilliant pills and I was dying to fuck her but she wouldn't come home with me – I tried everything. She's proper.'

'Because she knows everyone and wouldn't come home with you?'

'Not just that. She's just different to any girl I've ever met. All the DJs know her, the way she moves – everything. I'm going to take her for a meal tomorrow night.' Greg noticed some activity on the stage. 'Looks like Jocelyn Brown's about to start.'

Sugar Ray came over with Vaz's records. 'Hi, Greg. Brad was looking for you earlier.' He handed Vaz his records.

'You'd better take those – it looks like I'm about to do my singing stint.'

'I'll go look for Brad,' said Greg.

Arabella was standing near the entrance to the other room. She could see Mario dancing closely with the client he'd smiled at.

'Don't pay any attention to Greg,' said Vaz.

'I don't,' she replied, regaining some of her composure.

At the DJ stand, Kit from The Monastery switched on the microphone. 'OK everyone. Once again, let's hear your appreciation for Club Wicked's Smiffy!'

There was a polite round of applause with the Club Wicked reps all shouting and whistling at the tops of their voices, trying to get the crowd to join in.

'Thank you,' continued Kit. 'Right we've pulled out all the stops for you tonight. Ladies and gentlemen, The Monastery is proud to present one of the greatest divas of all time, please give it up for the one and only, Joceyln *Brown*!'

The opening chords of 'Somebody Else's Guy' started.

'How y'all doing, Ibiza?' yelled Jocelyn. 'Tonight I've got a couple of very special guests on stage with me who you might recognise. Tell me, *do we have anyone here tonight from Club Wicked*?' There was a cheer. 'I can't hear you, I said, do we have anyone here from Club Wicked?'

This time a much bigger cheer went up.

'OK, on my left, from Club Wicked, we have the one and only Stig.'

The cheer continued and Stig punched the air. Jocelyn sang a couple of vocal ad libs as the song sat in a groove.

'And do we have anyone here from Young Free and Single?' Again there was a cheer. 'Aw, c'mon guys, you can do better than that. One more time – do we have anyone here from Young, Free, and *Siiinngle*?' The crowd went mad. 'And tell me, do you want to hear Sugar Ray sing for you tonight?'

Most of the crowd started yelling, though the small group of lads at the front started chanting obscenities.

'What a bunch of wankers,' said Vaz. 'Stig's put them up to that. How can he be so fucking nasty?'

Arabella looked at Vaz's record bag and for the first time, asked the same question of herself, but quickly pushed the thought to the back of her mind. 'I've got to go.' She stood up and made her way through the crowd and past Mario. Vaz picked up his records and headed for the DJ stand.

Jocelyn Brown got into her stride and the crowd were soon all dancing and having a good time. After a couple of choruses she handed the microphone to Stig. Everyone was surprised at how good his voice was. Although nowhere near as good as Alison had claimed, it had a gravelly quality and was, at least, in tune. As he finished, he gave a salute and the crowd cheered.

Sugar Ray took the microphone and, although it was immediately clear that his voice was nowhere near as good, he began to prance around Stig as he sang the verse.

He ran his fingers along Stig's cheek. Stig angrily brushed Sugar Ray's hand away and Sugar Ray waved his index finger at him, like a dominatrix scolding her slave. All of the Club Wicked clients that Stig had put up to jeering Sugar Ray started laughing instead. This made Sugar Ray camp it up even more. He turned to the audience and gestured to Stig in a limp-wristed way, singing the song title at him.

Stig was furious but in front of the crowd, could do nothing. Sugar Ray was really getting into his stride. He bent down in front of Stig patting his own bottom invitingly, singing the song title in an outrageously camp way.

Stig aimed a kick at Sugar Ray's backside. With perfect timing, Sugar Ray jumped out of the way and Stig fell over, just as the song came to an end.

Even Jocelyn Brown was in tears of laughter and gave Sugar Ray a big kiss, to thunderous applause. Stig stormed off stage.

Once the fuss had died down, Kit got on to the

microphone again and introduced Vaz. There was a big cheer from the YF&S clients.

The uplifting brass stabs and choppy guitar of 'All Funk'd Up' filled the room. Within seconds, the place was going off, and Vaz was bouncing up and down in the DJ booth, clearly loving it.

At the back of the room, Charles Moon turned to Judge Jules. 'Now that's more like it.'

'It's amazing how a crowd picks up on if a DJ's enjoying himself and really loves the music he's playing,' remarked Jules.

'If he keeps playing records like this and can mix,' said Charles, 'then I think we've got ourselves a winner.'

Lucas and Alison were standing nearby.

'Did you hear that?' hissed Lucas. 'Fucking great! Are you sure Arabella's done the switch?'

'Mario assures me it's all in hand,' she replied.

'After that little performance it had better be.' A minute or so later the crowd were all still dancing and Vaz was jumping up and down beaming. 'Alison, I thought she was meant to have scratched the record!'

'She told Mario she had.'

'Well, it doesn't sound like it.'

Moments later it happened. A couple of little jumps then a total skid-out. Lucas and Alison barely contained their glee as the crowd started jeering.

Vaz dived behind the decks to his record bag.

Brad was over to him in a flash. 'Quick, Vaz, get another record on.'

'I'm trying, but I don't understand.'

'Don't understand what?'

'I don't recognise half of these records. Some of them are in the right sleeves and have got titles written in felt pen on white labels that I know, but they're not mine.'

'Vaz, you've got to stick something on . . . anything!'

Had Brad known what exactly the record was going to be, he would have happily withdrawn his last comment. The crowd fell into a disbelieving silence then howls of derision as the chorus of 'I Should Be So Lucky' boomed out of the speakers. After the initial shock and now in a complete panic, Vaz threw the record from the turntable and snatched another one from his bag.

' . . . and it's Hi-Ho, silver lining . . .'

Lucas doubled up and slapped his thigh.

Vaz stood there helpless, watching his dream disappear. All around mocking and laughing faces pointed at him. Judge Jules, Charles Moon and the other VIPs were shaking their heads in disbelief.

Vaz was sure that there could not have been anyone in the whole of Ibiza who felt worse than he did at that moment.

Actually, perhaps just one . . .

chapter twenty-three

The following evening, Arabella sat on the sofa in Mario's apartment twiddling her hair, looking and feeling thoroughly depressed.

Mario was in the kitchen chopping chillis and green peppers unaware of her mood. Had he known, it was still unlikely that he would have been too bothered. But when he came into the room, he knew something was up. Wrongly and narcissistically, he assumed that he was the cause.

'You haven't got the hump about that girl last night, have you?'

In fact, Arabella was thinking about how upset Vaz had been. It surprised her that she felt more than a little guilty. The only good thing about experiencing this alien emotion was that it had taken her mind off Mario's synchronised disappearing act from Eden. One minute he and the new buxom client had been in the club, albeit a fair distance apart, the next they were both nowhere to be seen. Not long after he had left, she had called his mobile.

'Why did your mobile ring then go to voice mail?' she asked, when Mario came into the room to top up his own wine glass. 'It was like you deliberately switched it off. It went to voice mail every time after that.'

'I've already told you,' he replied, 'I was having a bite to eat with a group of lads in a little bar and before I could answer the phone the battery went flat.'

'What group of lads?'

'You know, the ones from up north.'

'You haven't mentioned them before. Whereabouts up north?'

'Manchester . . . Liverpool . . . They all sound the same to me.'

'Which bar were you in?'

'The . . . er . . . hang on a minute! What is this? Look, I've told you the truth, if you don't believe me, then fine.'

Arabella felt a sharp pain, fearing he was about to say the words she dreaded. The thought of Ibiza without Mario, of life without Mario . . .

'No, I do believe you, it's just me being silly, I suppose.'

She wasn't to know that Mario had brought the client back to his apartment and gained his points on the very sofa upon which Arabella was sitting.

'I'll finish the food,' he said, changing the subject.

'Did you manage to find out why Roz hit Brad the other night?' she called into the kitchen, getting up to change the CD.

'I heard that she shagged someone. Maybe Brad was going to tell her boyfriend or something. All I know is she's left Ibiza. I think she was going to get the sack anyway after that, but she's gone to Tenerife to persuade her boyfriend to stay over there in case he found out she'd messed around. You know what the Ibiza grapevine is like. The brother of Imogen the barmaid – Lars – has taken her job.'

'I still don't see why she would whack Brad like that though. You don't think he slept with her, do you?'

'No,' Mario started laughing, 'but it would be bloody funny if he did.' He walked back into the room. 'All done.'

Arabella had put on a slow CD.

'Ah, nice romantic music,' said Mario. He patted the seat. 'Come and sit next to me.'

Arabella skipped over and curled up next to him. He stroked her hair in an affectionate way.

'You did well last night. It worked like a dream, didn't it? Vaz was totally humiliated. And you should have seen Charles Moon's face, it was a picture.'

'Hmm.'

'I bet you were pleased.'

'Uh-huh.'

'Vaz is a wanker, in't he? No wonder you hate him.'

'He's not as bad as I first thought.'

Mario grunted.'Well, I know that he can't stand you.'

'How?'

'Oh, I heard him talking to Greg last night.'

Arabella sat up. 'When?'

'I think it was when he stopped DJing, just after Hi-Ho Silver Lining.' Mario laughed.

'What did he say?'

'I can't remember exactly.' This bit was at least true, as Mario had heard nothing of the sort. 'Just the usual about you being a stuck-up bitch and all that.'

Mario didn't know what a direct hit he had scored.

Arabella would never forget what Greg had said to her. She was also surprisingly hurt that Vaz had repeated it.

'Actually,' continued Mario, 'I was wondering if you wouldn't mind helping me again?'

'How?'

'Well . . .' Mario turned towards her and started stroking her inner thigh, '. . . I've heard that there's probably going to be another joint club night. Now we don't want to risk Vaz getting behind the decks again – even though they probably wouldn't let him – because he is actually bloody good.'

'So what do you plan?'

'I haven't decided yet. But you'll help, won't you?'

He ran his hand up her thigh.

'I don't know, Mario . . .' she replied hesitantly, 'what is it . . . oh . . .'

She let out a little gasp as he slipped a finger inside her. She opened her legs and pulled Mario towards her to kiss him. Mario continued his probing.

Suddenly, Arabella let out a scream and leapt from the sofa clutching her privates.

'Ooowww! Ouch! Ouch! What's that? What have you done?'

Mario looked shocked. 'Nothing, what's wrong?'

'Your fingers . . . what have you put on your fingers? It's burning!'

Still puzzled, Mario held his hand up in front of his face and examined his digits, while Arabella sprinted for the bathroom, jumped into the bath, turned the cold tap on and aimed the shower head between her legs.

'Oh shit,' said Mario as it dawned on him. He started laughing, then yelled out to her, 'I've just realised, I didn't wash my hands after chopping up the chillis and peppers.'

'You idiot!' she screamed back.

'Sorry,' he replied, 'it won't happen again.'

And that was the absolute truth. Very soon she would have served her purpose and he wouldn't have to put his fingers or any other part of his anatomy near her ever again.

Ace was undoubtedly going to give Greg some serious competition.

Greg knew that he should have been out clubbing with clients – there were at least a couple of definite three-pointers showing out – but he was determined to crack Sandy.

The day together at Space had made him fancy her even more. He was in truth, a little in awe of her, or more probably, still in awe of the club scene, where he was a new recruit and she seemed to be so comfortable and well-known.

To get into Space, Greg had tried his 'I'm a rep' ploy, which normally guaranteed him free entry to anywhere on the island. At Space, however, it fell on disinterested ears. Sandy saved the day when she spotted a DJ she knew just inside the club. He came over, had a word with the door staff and whisked them through.

Greg had made a point of not getting too trashed, not so much because he had to go to the DJ Face-Off later, but he didn't want to turn into a gurning wreck and appear uncool. Cool was clearly very important to Sandy.

Which was why Greg was wondering if bringing her to the Mexican restaurant in San Antonio was such a good idea.

The restaurant deserved its excellent reputation. The décor was lavish, large and sumptuous with no expense spared. The staff were attentive and the food was great. Greg couldn't help feeling though, that Sandy was used to better.

Greg had wanted to order his favourite nachos with melted cheese as a starter. He chose jalepenos instead because it was simply impossible to eat nachos in a cool way, without stringy tendrils of cheese dangling between mouth and plate. Similarly, he had chosen chilli con carne instead of his preferred chicken fajitas, because he normally put lashings of sour cream and guacamole on his tortillas, which inevitably dripped ungraciously out of the end.

They had just finished their starter and the evening had been going well. Sandy thought Greg was cute, though not at all the type of guy she normally went for. He had nothing like the sophistication (nor the bank balance or career prospects) of her normal romantic interests. (Her current boyfriend was a wealthy club promoter who didn't pay her the attention she thought she deserved. There were also abundant rumours that fidelity was not exactly his prime virtue. It had not been her specific intention to get back at him by sleeping with someone else in Ibiza, but if the opportunity arose, then well, what the eye doesn't see . . .)

She found Greg entertaining and he was clearly comfortable around women. He was a biggish fish in the Ibiza pond and had a definite sex appeal. There were the odd occasions when she found him slightly embarrassing in a socially liable kind of way but not enough to put her off him. Sandy had pretty much decided that as she was going home the next day, it would do no harm to have some fun on her last night and Greg certainly seemed to be more than willing to oblige.

The restaurant was busy, a combination of local families,

couples and groups of British holidaymakers clearly the worse for wear from too much Tequila and Corona. All of the chairs had brightly-coloured sombreros strung over their back and more than two-thirds of the restaurant's patrons were wearing them and taking pictures of each other.

Sandy was unimpressed. 'God, how humiliating. Why would you want to have your picture taken wearing one of those things?'

'Pathetic, isn't it?' replied Greg, reminding himself to make sure that the thirty or forty pictures he had of him wearing a sombrero, taken with clients in the very same restaurant, were hidden away if Sandy came back to his apartment.

'So where are we going after this?' asked Sandy, running her finger round the rim of her Margarita glass.

'Well, I don't know about you but I'm pretty much clubbed out. I thought that maybe we could go back to my place, do a few lines, have a bottle of wine . . . y'know, a nice way to end your stay.'

'Oh,' replied Sandy. She leaned forward, her mouth curving into a small smile and fixed Greg with a seductive gaze. 'So there's no chance of any sex then?'

Greg gulped, uncharacteristically thrown for an instant. He quickly regained his composure, feeling confident on the more familiar territory of sexual predator.

'Sex,' he repeated slowly. 'I suppose it all depends on your definition of the word. Now if you mean what most blokes mean then probably not.' Greg too, leaned forward. He took hold of her hand and lowered his voice. 'If by sex though, you mean having someone who's going to . . .' He froze mid-sentence.

'What's the matter?'

Greg tucked his head into his shoulders and stared at the floor.

'Greg?'

He withdrew his hand from hers as though it were

radioactive. He had spotted Imogen coming into the restaurant with her gigantic brother Lars.

'Come on, Greg,' she went to take his hand again, 'what were you about to say to me?'

Greg grabbed the bright red sombrero from the back of his chair and pulled it over his head, then changed seats so that he had his back to Imogen and her brother.

'What are you doing, Greg? Take that silly hat off – you're embarrassing me.'

'No, they're great. Go on, put yours on too.' He took a green sombrero and placed it on her head. 'It looks fantastic. You've got to get into the spirit, haven't you? Another drink?'

Sandy snatched the sombrero from her head and slammed it on the floor.

'Get this thing off me – it'll ruin my hair. Take yours off too – you look ridiculous.'

He covertly turned round and saw that Imogen and Lars were being seated downstairs but in a position where he could still be seen. There was no way he could risk taking off the sombrero.

'I like it.' He tried to make light of the situation. 'If you don't think the colour suits me I could always change it.'

'People are looking at us.'

'Don't be silly.'

'If you don't take that hat off, I warn you, I'm going home.'

'Oh, come on, Sandy, it's only a stupid hat.'

'I know it's a stupid hat, that's why I want you to take it off.'

Greg was torn. He desperately wanted to go home with Sandy. In truth, for the first time in many years he would have even liked to take things further and keep in touch with her after she had gone. She was the sort of girl he could see himself going out with. But if Imogen saw him with another woman, on the very night when he said he couldn't go out with her because he was busy, then Lars would probably take great pleasure in sticking the sombrero in a place where it would be largely redundant – that is, a location where the sun didn't shine.

Even if Sandy did stay, Imogen and Lars would probably still be there long after they had finished eating, so there was no way that he would be able to leave the restaurant with Sandy, without being seen. He was defeated – Sandy was not going on the score sheet.

'I can't.'

Sandy glared at him. For a horrible moment he thought she was going to start shouting, which was the absolute worst scenario. No Sandy *and* a beating.

Thankfully she didn't say a word. She just stood up, grabbed her bag and walked out of the restaurant. As she did so the waiter turned up with the two main courses.

Greg sat there in his red sombrero, utterly dejected. 'I suppose it's too late to change this to chicken fajitas?' he said.

chapter twenty-four

Alison and Lucas sat in the cool bar, looking out at the beautiful cove of Cala Moli. An isolated flotilla of stringy clouds drifted across the otherwise perfectly clear blue sky, which turned the millpond Mediterranean a deep and shimmering blue. Framed by ragged cliffs, the cove had inspired many an artist.

Of course, what might have been more difficult to capture on canvas were three hundred screaming young holidaymakers throwing themselves into a series of outrageous beach party games.

The Monastery had insisted on yet another joint excursion, which meant that the reps were being even more exuberant than usual, all trying to outdo each other, aware that their every move was being monitored by two consultants flown in by The Monastery. Once the games finished, the observers left. It was clear that the pressure being felt by the management was filtering down to the reps, who all looked visibly relieved once the observers had gone.

Alison and Lucas stayed for coffee in the small beach bar. It was the first time that they had been alone since the incident with the delay spray. Alison was not sure how the faux pas had gone down. Had it done any real harm to Club Wicked's chances of gaining The Monastery prize?

'Have you any idea as to how we're doing?' asked Alison.

Lucas shook his head. 'What's the date?'

'Um, Tuesday,' Alison counted backwards on her fingers, 'the twenty-fourth.'

'Great. We've only got just over a week left. The

Monastery announcement's next Friday at the final combined party on the fourth of July.'

'We're not doing too bad though, are we?' she asked tentatively.

Lucas knew Alison well enough to realise what she was getting at. 'Not as well as we would be were it not for your uncanny knack of managing to even the balance every time we stitch up YF&S.'

'I said I was sorry. I've no idea what happened.'

Lucas sighed. 'Let's hope there are no more cock-ups today. At next Friday's party the last thing I want is Vaz DJing. We managed to make him look stupid last time but I can't see us being able to do it again.'

'So, how many pills are you having planted on him?'

'Fifty.'

'Suppose he gets arrested?'

Lucas drew an imaginary circle round his face. 'Bothered?'

'I'm serious. What would you do if he ends up in prison over here? Would you help him?'

'Of course I would.' Lucas grinned. 'I'd teach him how to say, Would you mind picking up that bar of soap for me, in Spanish.'

'You're a real bastard.' Alison didn't sound all that bothered either.

'Vaz will be all right. The Monastery won't want any whiff of scandal. They'll just insist that he gets sacked and it will be another nail in the YF&S coffin.' Lucas lit a small cigar. 'Is Arabella all set?'

'Mario's primed her. He's going to give her the pills after the beach party games are finished.'

'Will she do it?'

'From what Mario says, she'll do whatever he asks . . .'

Greg was relaxing on the sunlounger he had carefully positioned away from the clients and in the shade. He was glad that all of the beach party games had finished and that most of the clients were now happy to simply sunbathe.

Beach parties were normally the more enjoyable trips. But Greg wasn't having a particularly good time, largely because of The Monastery's insistence on it being yet another joint excursion between YF&S and Club Wicked, and the reps were expected to make even more of an effort than usual. Brad had been called away to yet another meeting with Hawthorne-Blythe, so Greg was the most senior member of YF&S staff in attendance.

The other main factor that added to Greg's desire to be somewhere else, preferably alone in bed, was the insatiable Rio.

After the disastrous Mexican with Sandy on Monday night, Imogen and Lars had taken forever to finish their meal so Greg was stuck alone in the restaurant for almost two hours, drinking tequila and wearing a sombrero. When he left, he was quite drunk and with his resolve suitably weakened, agreed to see Rio when she called.

That was three nights ago and it had become clear that despite Rio's apparent brash confidence and liberal attitude towards sex, she was actually extremely insecure and more than anything else, wanted a steady boyfriend. In Greg, she was convinced she had found her soulmate.

Greg couldn't believe that, within the space of a week, he had slept with yet another head case. Rio used sex as reassurance. It was her ultimate weapon, her way of keeping control. However, Greg was far too experienced for it to have the same effect on him as most of Rio's previous partners. Thus the less interested he appeared, the more clingy and demanding Rio became. It had just dawned on him that Rio was a nightmare. He'd also been feeling increasingly guilty that he wasn't pulling his weight with YF&S. Thankfully, Brad had not yet received the call to return to the UK for his operation so Greg's offer to think about taking the resort manager's job had not been pushed. It was just as well because Greg had been beating himself up about it more than he thought he would. He also knew that no matter how highly he was valued, if he went on the missing list again and carried on in the way he was, then

Hawthorne-Blythe or Brad would be as likely to send him home as to persuade him to take over as resort manager.

It was not that Greg had no interest in the outcome of the assessment: this was his sixth summer working for YF&S and as such, he felt a reasonable degree of loyalty to the company and in particular to Hawthorne-Blythe and to Brad. Moreover, Greg disliked Alison and Mario intensely, and from what he had heard and seen of Tyrone Lucas, he wasn't about to be added to Greg's Christmas card list either.

For Greg, the dilemma was simply that all winter he had been looking forward to having a carefree, clubbing season. Everything had seemed so straightforward before The Monastery got involved. The summer was meant to be a cruise – no pressure, doing the job with his eyes closed, special allowances made in return for his experience and knowledge. Now it had gone completely Pete Tong.

The advantages of the resort manager's position were negated by The Monastery's involvement. Their additional scrutiny meant that the resort managers carried even more responsibility and were being watched very closely. It also meant an increased workload, earlier starts, later finishes . . . in short, the total antithesis of what Greg had planned.

Yet Greg had not lost his instinctive sense of right and wrong. He wanted to come good for YF&S, Hawthorne-Blythe and Brad, but he had a different agenda. The solution, as he saw it, was finding a way of marrying the two, of finding a happy balance. Today though, with the Rio sex and drugs marathon taking its toll and Greg feeling decidedly unsteady on his feet, finding his physical sense of balance was proving hard enough. Solitude, shade and sleep were the only three S's that currently interested him.

At least Sandy had called him from the UK earlier in the day. He had somehow managed to talk his way out of the sombrero incident by saying that he was trying to hide from a dealer he owed money to and that he hadn't wanted Sandy to think he was short of money, seeing as she moved in such rich circles. As he'd hoped, Sandy had found this endearing. She was coming back over for the opening of Amnesia on the Thursday of the following week, the night before The Monastery's final party and announcement, and she had promised Greg a night he wouldn't forget.

As he'd been with Rio since Monday, he hadn't really got to know the new arrivals. Crip and his crew were still around, now into the second week of their holiday. Looking down the beach, Greg could see that they were up to no good but he had neither the energy nor motivation to go and see what they were doing. Vaz and Arabella walked by and he waved, then flopped back on his sunbed.

Vaz and Arabella strolled past the Hartlepool Honeys who started cat-calling and whistling at Vaz.

'Phwoar, look at those muscles!' yelled one.

Vaz took it in good humour and struck a comical muscle-man pose for them. Arabella couldn't understand what the girls saw in Vaz, but as she stood waiting for him to finish play-acting she had to admit that his now tanned body did have bumps in all of the right places.

'So did you deflower Lou-Lou then?' asked Arabella as Vaz skipped away from the admiring glances.

'No, of course not.'

'She seemed awfully keen.'

'Yeah, I know. Her friends all egged her on and sent her round to my room the other night.'

'What happened?'

'Nothing. I told her that her first time should be special and that just doing it because her friends were teasing her wasn't the right reason.'

'Very commendable.'

'Ta. I don't know what came over me.'

'Well, I'm sure she'll thank you when she gets home with her virtue still intact.'

'You must be joking!' laughed Vaz. 'About an hour after she left my room Ace and Hughie ended up spit-roasting her.'

'What?'

'Yeah. She came out of Ace's room and all of her friends

gave her a huge cheer. She slept with Dean the next day and Crip last night.'

'She had sex with the guy in the wheelchair!'

'I don't know if he was actually in the wheelchair at the time,' teased Vaz, 'but Crip is fully functioning in that department by all accounts.'

Vaz and Arabella sat down on the sand. Arabella appeared to be deep in thought, which didn't go unnoticed by Vaz. They had been forced to spend quite a lot of time together during the previous few days. It had become even clearer to Vaz that Arabella had a blind spot where Mario was concerned. It was also patently obvious that Mario was treating her with absolute contempt. Vaz had no intention of getting involved and Arabella was undoubtedly her own worst enemy. However, working so closely together, her mood affected Vaz, particularly if she was down, as she now appeared to be.

Unfortunately, since the Sunday night DJ Face-Off fiasco, Vaz had needed to call upon all of his resources not to sink into depression or to catch the first plane back to the UK himself. He felt as though he had failed at the one thing he most wanted to succeed at and in front of those who could play the biggest part in helping him to achieve his DJ dream.

Despite Vaz's humiliation and dented pride, the following day Mikey had managed to convince him that what had happened would prove to be inconsequential and that the promoters who were there weren't that influential anyway and wouldn't really have been looking for DJ talent amongst tour company reps.

More importantly, Mikey helped Vaz to get things in perspective. Working as a YF&S rep was never going to give Vaz the exposure or credibility he needed to make it as a DJ in Ibiza. All it could do was open doors and give Vaz a better idea of how the island worked.

While Mikey's pep-talk undoubtedly stopped Vaz from leaving Ibiza, he was still down about what happened. It was obvious that someone had gone to a lot of trouble to make him look stupid. What could he have possibly done for anybody to hate him so much?

Arabella too was thinking about the DJ Face-Off. She had come to realise just how important DJing was to Vaz. Although she didn't care whether YF&S won or lost, she was beginning to hate herself for switching his records.

And she was certain that no matter how much she loved Mario, she could not go through with what he had asked her to do earlier that morning. Switching records felt like a practical joke, albeit cruel. Planting drugs was completely different.

She looked over to Mario, strutting around in front of his clients on the other side of the beach. She couldn't help herself; he was so totally gorgeous. She would do almost anything for him, but this . . . He wasn't going to like it but she knew that she was going to have to say no.

'What do you mean, she won't do it?' asked a clearly agitated Alison. 'I thought she'd do anything you told her.'

Mario ran his fingers through his thick, wavy black hair. 'That's what I thought, but she's flatly refused.'

'Great,' said Lucas, opening a sugar sachet and pouring it into his coffee. 'So now what? I've told Charles Moon that I've had a tip off that a rep is dealing. I even suggested it was one of ours, to give it more credibility. He's on his way down with Kit and they're going to search everyone's bags.'

'Shit,' exclaimed Alison, 'I hope that doesn't include mine. The pills are in my bag right now.'

'In that case, there's only one thing for it.' Lucas's phone rang. 'You'll have to plant them. Excuse me. Hello?'

Immediately, the colour drained from his face. He got up from the table.

Alison turned to Mario. 'Which one is Vaz's bag?'

All of the reps' bags were on a pile near the bar. 'Arabella says it's an old record bag that he keeps his beach stuff in.'

Alison picked her briefcase from the floor and put it on her lap. She opened it, carefully making sure that nobody was watching them.

'Here,' she passed Mario a bag of pills, 'find out which one's Vaz's and put these in it.'

'Why me?' replied a horrified Mario.

Alison pressed the bag into Mario's hand. 'Because you were the one who said Arabella would do whatever you told her. Go on, I'll keep watch.'

Before Mario could argue she had stood up and made her way to the door. Mario wanted to be rid of the pills as quickly as possible, so scurried over, found the bag eventually and slipped the pills down the side, then dashed back to the table.

Smiling, Alison walked back and sat next to him.

'Are you sure you put it in the right one?'

'Positive. You're out of order doing that to me.'

She patted his leg. 'There, there. You must be losing your charm in Arabella's eyes, lover-boy.'

'I'm telling you, after today she can go fuck herself. I don't care what you say, I've had enough of pretending I fancy that dozy stuck-up bitch.'

'That's fine by me. She's served her purpose. Actually,' Alison lit a cigarette, 'with any luck, when she realises that you're not the man of her dreams, she'll leave as well.' She drew on her Marlboro Light. 'Now that could be a real bonus, Vaz getting the sack and Arabella leaving. What with Brad having a broken arm, the way things are going, the only YF&S rep left will be Greg.'

'And from what I hear, he's about as interested in repping as you are in being celibate.'

'Exactly.' Alison sat back in her chair. 'We can't lose . . .'

Lucas had moved away from Alison and Mario as soon as he realised who the call was from.

'Hello, Riordan, how are you?' he gushed. 'I've been meaning to call you for a few days but I'm out in Ibiza on business and it's been a bit hectic.'

'And would the reason you have been meaning to call me be to say that you were about to pay off some of the money you've been owing Mr Reynolds for far longer than originally agreed, Mr Lucas?' asked Riordan in his Irish lilt. It chilled Lucas that someone with such a pleasant sounding voice could be such a brutal debt collector.

'That's what I'm doing in Ibiza. I told Mr Reynolds that I'm expecting my company to be bought out within the next month and we're out here finalising everything now. As soon as the money comes through I'll pay up immediately of course.'

'Ah, that'll be grand. So I'll be telling Mr Reynolds that he can expect his money within a month, can I, Mr Lucas?'

'Without a doubt, Riordan, without a doubt.'

'Good man. And Mr Lucas – be sure to stay away from casinos and the gee-gees while you're over there. We don't want you losing any more of that hard-earned money of yours when it should be finding its way to Mr Reynolds, do we?'

'Of course, of course. Rest assured, those days are behind me now. Apart from anything else, what have I got left to gamble with?'

There was a pause. 'Only your life, Mr Lucas . . .'

The line went dead. Lucas flipped shut the phone and wiped sweat from his brow. Nobody knew that he had been siphoning off funds from Club Wicked for a number of years to support his rather severe gambling habit. It hadn't been so bad up until about eighteen months ago, when a run of bad luck coincided with a downturn in profitability at Club Wicked. His financial director was easy to bully. Consequently Lucas had steamrollered through some disastrous ideas, which had put Club Wicked in the red and this year they were looking at a considerable operating loss and over the precipice of insolvency.

Without The Monastery takeover, Club Wicked would not last the summer.

More worrying was the personal debt to Mick Reynolds, who ran a high-roller card school, a small private casino and acted as a credit phone bookmaker.

When Lucas hit his losing streak he had gambled ever more rashly and for increasingly higher stakes, throwing good money after bad in the belief that his luck had to change. It didn't. Having exhausted his liquid assets he was put on to Mick Reynolds who happily let Lucas put up his house and other goods and chattels as collateral. Lucas had now used up all available equity and the debt had been called in. Lucas knew only too well that Reynolds was not a man to knock. Selling his house and most other belongings would just about cover the monies owed, but that was not a palatable option, especially as Lucas's wife was unaware of the financial mess her husband had got himself into. The Monastery proposal came just in the nick of time and bought Lucas an extra couple of months.

If The Monastery chose to take over YF&S rather than Club Wicked, then quite simply, Lucas would be ruined.

He had to win.

Kit sat at the outside bar of Pike's Hotel, enjoying the coolness of the shade after spending two hours in the sun, the first real opportunity he'd had to sunbathe since arriving in Ibiza.

The pool seemed smaller than he remembered it looking in Wham's 'Club Tropicana' video. The choice of Pike's as the setting for the Ibiza inspired hit helped put the hotel firmly on the map and in the succeeding years, it had become the venue of choice for the music and media industry. The legendary flamboyance of Australian owner Tony Pike was perfectly suited to the needs of DJs, pop stars and celebrities. The plethora of framed photos covering the walls in the reception only hinted at the two decades of hedonistic excess the venue had witnessed. Freddie Mercury, Grace Jones, Julio Iglesias a smiling testimony to the relaxed *joie de vivre* that was an extension of Tony's own personality. And all of this just a couple of kilometres from San Antonio.

Charles Moon walked along the poolside towards Kit with a mobile pressed against his ear, finishing the call as he reached the bar.

'That was IT Stan,' said Charles.

'A-ha,' replied Kit. 'Our very Information Technology whizzkid. A party animal of gigabyte proportions.'

'Liam Gallagher with a brain and a laptop,' added Charles fondly. 'And if it wasn't for him, I doubt that our little empire would be half the size it is.'

'True. When is he coming over?'

'Tomorrow night. He can't wait.'

'I bet. Is he planning to do any work?'

'Probably. You know what Stan's like, wherever he goes, his laptop goes too.'

Stan had been involved with The Monastery from the beginning after Charles befriended the party-loving, mildly eccentric loner at university. Charles was keen to have Stan as a member of his fledgling business partly because of his phenomenal IT skills and also because Stan had some money to invest through lucrative moonlighting along the M4 silicone valley, not too far removed from the shires and spires of their Oxford educational home.

'Oh well,' sighed Kit, 'Stan's picked a fine old time to come. I can almost understand a rep pointing a client in the right direction to score some gear, but I didn't think any of them would be stupid enough to set themselves up as a dealer. How reliable does Lucas say this source of his is?'

'One hundred per cent,' replied Charles.

'So what are we going to do if he's right? Are we going to call the police? Do you think it would be worthwhile issuing a press release? It could help reinforce our anti-drugs position.'

Charles shook his head. 'No, I thought about it but I think it's best we have no association with drugs at all, even if we're being seen to condemn them. The best course of action will be to sack the rep and dispose of the drugs. No police, no press, no fuss. As long as the reps all know how seriously we view it, that's the main point to get across.'

'I guess you're right. Why do you think Lucas has come to us with this?'

'Lucas knows how sensitive we are about being associated with drugs. If we found out for ourselves that one of his reps were dealing then it would have been worse for Club Wicked. I guess he sees it as damage limitation. At least this way he's trying to prove that his standpoint is similar to ours.'

'You think?'

Charles shrugged. 'Well, the quicker you get that cocktail down your neck, the quicker we'll find out.'

Rio had been trying to ring Greg all day. She was on a serious comedown. He had told her that he was working on the beach party but in her paranoid state, she wasn't convinced that he was telling the truth, especially as his phone had been switched off. Greg was clearly popular with girls, but now he had slept with her, Rio could not stand the thought of him being with anybody else. Why would he want to? She would do anything for him sexually and no girl could compete in that department, so as far as she was concerned, that should be more than enough.

However, as she marched into the Hotel Arena's reception and saw the posters advertising the beach party, she guessed that he had been telling the truth and felt chastened.

Still, she was there now and didn't fancy driving back to her apartment in Figueretes, especially as she wasn't working again until the following night. It was six o'clock and she knew that it was around that time that clients normally got back from excursions so he would have to be back soon. There was nobody at reception so on impulse, Rio grabbed the key to Greg's room. She took the lift to the third floor and let herself in. It would be a nice surprise when he got back.

chapter twenty-five

Greg couldn't believe his eyes. In fact, he couldn't believe his ears or any of the other senses that had stood him in good stead for the best part of three decades.

Vaz was a drug dealer.

It just didn't make sense. When Charles Moon had gathered all of the reps together while the clients were being entertained by a DJ on the beach, and told them that they had information a rep was dealing drugs, the last person Greg expected it to be was Vaz.

He was sure that Stig or one of the other Club Wicked reps would be the guilty party, especially as it was their bags that Charles Moon and Kit had searched first. Vaz's almost seemed to be an afterthought.

Greg thought that Vaz looked genuinely shocked when Kit held the pills aloft after removing them from Vaz's bag. Had he been looking to another part of the room then Greg would have also seen a faint smile exchanged between Mario and Alison, as well as Arabella staring at the floor.

Vaz had been marched out of the back of the beach café by Charles Moon, while the other reps sat in silence under the watchful gaze of Kit. After a few minutes, Charles returned and addressed them all.

'I cannot emphasise to you strongly enough how serious a matter this is, nor how strongly anti-drugs we are at The Monastery.' There were a few murmurs from the reps. Charles picked up on it. 'This might come as a surprise to some of you, given that we are at the very heart of dance culture, which clearly has an association with recreational narcotics. However, The Monastery is now an international, multi-million pound, high-profile business and we are under constant and close scrutiny from the press and politicians alike. Our personal views therefore become irrelevant. We have a duty to our investors and to our staff and I can assure you that there are many people who would derive great pleasure from our demise. We have been established for over a decade and despite legislation and licence changes, we are still here. There have been times in the past where we have nearly slipped up and underestimated how motivated certain quarters are to be rid of us and, it would seem, the whole clubbing scene. Let me assure all of you here today that when we take over we are going to be extremely vigilant in policing reps and making sure that the kind of thing we have discovered today is not going on.

'Vaz has been dismissed by H-B. A cab has just arrived to pick him up and he has an hour to be out of the hotel. What he does after that is up to him. He is extremely lucky that we have decided not to get the authorities involved but I promise each and every one of you here today that if we are put in this position again, the next person will not be so lucky. Do I make myself clear?'

The reps all mumbled yes. Greg guiltily fingered the small bag of six pills in his shorts pocket.

Charles Moon and Kit left.

The reps filtered back out to the clients, Mario a few steps behind Arabella.

'Who'd have thought it, eh?' he said in a voice loud enough for her to hear. 'Old Vaz a drug dealer. It just goes to prove that you can take the boy out of Peckham, but you can't take Peckham out of the boy.'

Arabella stopped. 'Mario.'

Mario waited until everyone had walked past. 'Well, it looks as though I didn't need you after all.'

'I couldn't go through with it. I thought he might get arrested and that didn't seem right.'

'You didn't have a problem switching his records over last Sunday.'

'That was different.'

'Yeah, whatever. Anyway, like I said, I don't need you.'

'Don't say it like that, Mario.' Arabella forced a smile. 'How about I make it up to you tonight? I could come round and cook you dinner this time . . . it might be a little less painful for me after your last effort.'

She gave a little laugh. Mario ignored it.

'I'm busy,' he replied curtly.

'Why, what are you doing?'

'I can't remember.'

'Oh Mario, please don't be like this with me. I said I was sorry. It shouldn't change things between us.'

'Us?' repeated Mario slowly. He started laughing.

'I'll come round tonight, about twelve,' added Arabella hurriedly.

Mario walked away, shaking his head. 'Yeah, right.'

Arabella stood there for a few moments, not knowing what to say, then ran off towards the toilets in tears. As she shot around the back of the small beach bar, she bumped into Greg.

'Whoah, what's up with you?'

Arabella started crying even more and sped off to the sanctuary of a cubicle.

Greg turned to Milly, a cute nineteen year-old client, who was looking at him questioningly.

'I don't always make girls cry, well,' he gave her a cheeky grin, 'only when I smack their bums a bit too hard.'

Milly giggled.

'What are you doing later?'

'Going to watch the video of the beach party with everyone else.'

'I mean after that.'

'I was going to have an early night.' She pointed to the top of her chest, which looked burned. 'I think I overdid it in the sun today.'

'Mmm, it's pretty bad. I know you'll think I'm winding you up, but they say that the old doo-dah's meant to be good for it.'

'The what?'

'Harry Monk.'

'What's that?'

'Spunk,' came a voice from over her shoulder. It was Ace. 'He's absolutely right. Something to do with the enzymes or collagen in it or something like that.'

'Collagen's the stuff that goes in your lips, isn't it?'

Ace just beat Greg to the punch line. 'Sounds good to me.'

'You're as bad as each other.'

'Cheers,' they chorused.

As she walked away, the two reps folded their arms and watched her. She turned and gave a little wave.

'Bonus point?' suggested Ace.

'Yeah. Or better still, whichever one of us doesn't nail her *loses* a point.'

'You're on. Mind you, I'm surprised you've got any energy left after what you were saying about Rio. Sounds great.'

Greg shook his head. 'To be honest, it got fucking boring after a while. I mean, she knows every trick in the book and then some. She'll do anything. She can put her legs in places they just shouldn't be able to go, gushes so much that the water content in her body must be close to zero by the time we finish and she screams like no other girl I've ever been with.'

'Sounds like heaven – what's the problem?'

'It's hard to put my finger on. What I do know is that Rio's got to be out of the way by next Thursday.'

'Why?'

'That girl Sandy – the one I took to Space – she's coming back over for the opening of Amnesia. I like her.'

'Nice one. But I still don't see why you can't carry on seeing Rio. Maybe you could get them to do a turn.'

'I don't think Sandy would be too keen.'

'You don't know if you don't ask.'

'True. Even so, I still want shot of Rio. She's a nutter.'

'Yeah, but if she's that good a shag . . .'

256

'That's the point though. I don't even really enjoy it. I guess there's something missing. It almost feels as though she's going through the motions, or that she's got another agenda. Like, she's trying to *prove* what a fantastic shag she is.'

Ace started laughing. 'Doesn't that ring any kind of bell?'

Greg looked confused. 'Not really. I don't think I've ever slept with anyone like her.'

Ace playfully slapped him round the back of the head. 'I meant us – you and me, most of the reps and props on this island. What's The Competition if it's not another agenda? How often do we just go through the motions or shag a girl just for the crack or the points or to prove how good we are?'

'Yeah, but we're not into those girls, whereas Rio seems to have gone all bunny boilery on me already.'

'Same difference – the sex part of it is meaningless on both counts. When we bone these gutter-sluts, all we worry about is the points and, like we've said on many occasions, we don't respect them or even think of them as proper people with mums and dads and feelings and shit. But most of the time, they're not bothered either, so no one really gets hurt or gives a toss.'

'But that's the whole point, Rio does.'

Ace waved his finger. 'No, she doesn't. You said it yourself earlier today, the sex thing with her is all about power. She's got a fucked up view of it. It's about her taking control. She's so used to guys eating out of her hand when she turns it on that if that fails, what else has she got?'

'Yeah, well following your logic, then what have we got? What have I got? What have you got?'

Ace put his arm round Greg's shoulder. 'What *I've* got Greg, is a degree in Philosophy and an old fella who wants me to train up to run the family plastic moulding company when I get back to the UK.'

'*Really?*'

'In fact, my dad thought I should see a bit of the world before I got bogged down in the real world. He was a bit of a fucking hippy in the sixties. I got stuck in Ibiza and Thailand, but fuck it, I've had a good time. No matter what happened out here this year I was always going back to the UK for good.'

Greg looked genuinely stunned. 'Shit, I didn't realise any of that: The degree, the family biz . . . I thought you were just one of us.'

Ace laughed. 'I still am, you plonker. We've all got something. There's a reason for us all being out here.'

'Is there?' Greg looked quite anxious. 'To be honest, I've never looked further than the following summer.'

Ace could see that he had struck a chord with Greg. He tried to lighten the tone. 'Well, maybe that's your purpose. To win The Competition, educate young men and bring pleasure to countless women.'

'Yeah, ha.'

Ace tried a different approach. 'Listen, mate. There's no saying that the way I'm going about things is right. I'm probably worse than you, the only difference is I've something set up for when I get back. I might hate it, then what would I do? I'd just have to take all the things I've learned out here and use them in the best way I can. I'm sure there's a reason you keep coming back – you just don't know what it is yet.'

'Well, it's not to listen to you, that's for sure. If your dad's business thing doesn't work out, don't get a job with the Samaritans – the suicide rate will double. Much more of you and I'll be trying to drown myself.'

Rio looked at her watch. It was almost eight o'clock and still no sign of Greg. She was bored. His apartment was pretty basic and there was no satellite although he did have a small TV with built-in video. She had spent the best part of an hour going through his bag of tapes but so far there had been three football and the rest were all pornos. The latter varied in quality, from beautiful Americans in exotic locations or period costume, through to dodgy Germans in someone's basement wearing gas masks and doing unthinkable things with household appliances.

She did stumble across a copy of *Life of Brian*, but having watched so many pornos had to keep reminding herself that it was a proper film and that John Cleese wasn't about to set upon a cross-dressing Eric Idle with a large candle.

Rio tried ringing Greg's number again but it went straight to voice mail. She vaguely remembered Greg telling her that they normally went to a bar after the beach party to watch a video of the day's proceedings. She couldn't remember which bar it was and even if she had, the thought of running the gauntlet of the West End in her economical clothing and with her ample bust held little appeal.

Rather than watch more pornos (which never really did it for her anyway), she decided to visit a friend who had a villa in nearby San Augustin. If Greg was going to a bar it was unlikely he would be back before midnight. But she intended returning to his apartment before then, and there seemed little point in putting the key back in reception.

As she left, she did briefly allow herself to consider the possibility that Greg would come back with another girl. She quickly dismissed the idea.

Of course he felt the same about her as she did him. He had to . . .

chapter twenty-six

The beach party video was being shown in a bar called Between the Posts round the back of the West End. With three large plasma screens it had been set up as a football bar but was off the main drag so attracted nowhere near the clientele it had anticipated. It also paid the tour companies almost double what any other bar was prepared to.

Stig was very drunk and had been bullying Sugar Ray more than usual. As ever though, he did it from the safety of a group because he knew he was no match for Sugar Ray's quick wit. As soon as Sugar Ray tried to say anything he was shouted down. Every time he went to go to the toilet, Stig would send in a couple of the group to bait him. It wasn't that any of the things said or done individually were particularly hurtful or distressing, but the sheer persistence and constant badgering without let-up was really beginning to get Sugar Ray down.

Arabella had been trying to talk to Mario all night, but he had done his best to ignore her. What made her feel particularly uncomfortable though was the manner in which he was ignoring her. She hoped it was just paranoia, but she felt that when ever he was amongst a group of people he would orchestrate for them to look over at her and laugh. This caused Arabella to keep away from him for the majority of the evening. Mario also spent a lot of time in Stig's group and, with Stig, took obvious delight in flirting with two equally drunk girls. Mario had told Arabella countless times that she shouldn't get jealous when he flirted with clients because he was only doing his job, but tonight he seemed to be deliberately winding her up.

The small bar normally only had one tour company in at a time, so having both YF&S and Club Wicked together meant that it was rammed. The reps were due to stay in the bar until eleven-thirty but fifteen minutes prior to that, Arabella couldn't see Mario, Stig or the two very drunk girls anywhere.

She bundled her way out of the bar, not caring that Greg or the other YF&S reps saw where she was going. Greg went after her, with Sugar Ray close behind. Arabella stopped near a building site about twenty metres from the bar.

'Bastard!' she screamed.

Mario and Stig were clearly involved in some kind of sexual liaison with the two drunk girls. Arabella was hysterical.

'Mario! How *could* you? After all I've done for you. Why are you treating me like this? I've given you everything. I've—'

Mario stepped forward and from a distance, it looked as though he had hit her. Greg dashed forward. 'You fucker! What do you think you're doing?'

Before Greg could get to him, Stig stuck an arm out and pushed Greg away, sending him flying. 'Piss off and take the posh slut with you.' Stig looked at Sugar Ray who had stepped forward. 'And if you're not out of my sight in five seconds, you fucking little faggot, I'll beat you to a pulp.'

Instead of walking away, Sugar Ray stood firm and started removing his watch and jewellery. Quite a few clients had spilled out of the bar. Even Arabella stopped sobbing for a few moments, as she wondered what on earth Sugar Ray was doing taking his shirt off. Some of Stig's cronies wolf-whistled and made camp comments at the sight of Sugar Ray's naked torso.

Stig stood there bemused. 'What you going to do, gay boy, undress and make me die of laughter when I see your dick?'

Sugar Ray said nothing, but rolled his shoulders and

stretched his arms. Stig soon realised that Sugar Ray was serious, though he could not quite believe it.

'You must be joking – I'm twice the size of you.'

Sugar Ray danced round. 'The only thing that's twice the size of me, you ugly, badly dressed, ignorant, homophobic puss-ball, is your mouth. So for once in your life shut it and get that lank, greasy mop on your head out of your face so I can see which part of you I'm going to hit.'

Even the clients who had been with Stig all night let out a small cheer, which was probably what sent Stig over the edge. He charged at Sugar Ray, arms flailing wildly. Sugar Ray stepped inside him and landed two jabs, connecting with Stig's nose. Stig yelped in pain and surprise. Sugar Ray went on to the balls of his feet, looking very confident.

Stig put his finger to his nose and wiped away some blood. 'You'll regret that, you little fuck. Now I'm not going to mess about.'

He came at Sugar Ray more deliberately and cautiously. Sugar Ray skipped round him, taking a couple of haymaker blows himself as he landed another jab. Stig aimed a wild swing at Sugar Ray and left his whole right side open. Sugar Ray measured him with a left jab then smashed into his jaw with a ferocious cross right that sent Stig tumbling to the floor, unconscious.

The amazing sight brought a huge cheer. Even Arabella smiled. Then, looking at Mario, who was agog at his prostrate colleague, she threw her own cross right. She hit him with every last ounce of dented pride in her body and although it didn't knock him out, the fact that he was so off guard sent him sprawling across Stig. This drew an even bigger cheer.

Greg went over to Sugar Ray, who was calmly putting back on his shirt and jewellery. 'Where did you learn that?'

'Didn't I tell you? I used to be ABA welterweight boxing champion. Why do you think I'm called Sugar Ray?'

'Er . . . because your name is Ray and you're gay?'

Sugar Ray smiled. 'It's funny,' he looked down at Stig who was just coming to, 'a lot of people make that mistake.'

Rio glanced at her watch. It was eleven forty-five and she knew that she should be leaving her friend Tanya's villa soon, especially as she had taken Greg's room key. But Tanya had at least another half a dozen lines left in her wrap and Rio always found it difficult to walk away from a line. She was sure that Greg could easily get a spare key or be let into his room. If she was a little late she would just crawl in beside him and wake him up with one of her speciality blow jobs.

Tanya chopped out two fat lines, not so much because she wanted any, more that she knew the quicker the cocaine went, the quicker her unwelcome visitor would leave. She wasn't all that keen on Rio either.

'. . . And oh my God, Tanya – the way he fingers me! He makes me come in seconds. Honestly, honey, I can't help myself.' Rio snorted the line and tossed her head back. 'I mean, I know he's a holiday rep,' she continued, wiping her upper lip with the back of her hand, 'but there's something about him. We've spent the last few days together and I just know he's mad about me.'

Tanya rubbed the remnants of her own line into her gums and smiled politely. She'd heard it all before.

Ace had admitted defeat with Milly and left Greg to it. His only hope of scoring any points that night seemed to be what Greg called the Last Chance Saloon, aka the hotel bar. There were nearly always a few girls who staggered back to the hotel totally obliterated, easily sweet-talked into a night of passion by their ever-caring rep.

As Greg approached the hotel with Milly, he began to wonder if he was actually capable of a night of passion. Although he'd taken it easy on the beach party he'd only managed to grab the minimum of sleep. Alcohol was his chosen poison at Between the Posts because the thought of taking another pill made him feel physically sick.

Milly had not been too difficult a nut to crack, especially as Hughie had disappeared an hour earlier with her fourteen-stone best friend. Greg was, however, a very tired boy.

Which was why he initially thought he was seeing things when he saw Imogen standing in reception, thankfully without her brother Lars.

Greg ushered Milly into the bar to wait for him, telling her he had a quick problem to deal with at reception. He still hadn't been out with Imogen and he'd been avoiding the Drunken Lizard like the plague. 'Hi, Imogen,' he said, trying to look and sound as tired as possible.

'Greg, you look dreadful.'

'Thanks. I'm bloody knackered. I've got to be up early too. I can't wait to get some shut-eye. Sorry I haven't been in touch but it's been manic. You know how it is.'

'Oh, that's all right,' replied Imogen, as breezily as possible. 'Actually, that's one of the reasons I came down here, I was hoping to catch up with you.' She took a deep breath. Greg steeled himself for a barrage of abuse and threats. 'I just wanted to tell you that I've met somebody this week I really like. He's not a rep so he's got time to see me. I know it's not your fault we couldn't spend more time together, it's just the job.'

Greg was completely taken aback. 'I . . . I don't know what to say.' This was largely true. 'I'm happy for you, it's just a shame we couldn't . . . you know. Like you said, the job and everything . . .'

'Exactly.' She looked at Greg. She still fancied him but she had suffered enough humiliation. Her lust for revenge had quickly subsided and meeting Lars's hunky friend Michael certainly helped matters. 'Just one thing though. Don't you ever tell anyone what happened. I know what you reps are like for telling stories. If I hear a whisper I swear I'll get Lars . . .'

Greg held his hands up. 'Say no more. You don't have to threaten me. I haven't told a soul.'

The little voice in his head said, 'Apart from Ace, Hughie, Vaz, Sugar Ray, Tamsin and my mate who's addicted to emailing stories back home and writes for a music magazine.'

'Good.' Imogen kissed him on both cheeks. As she turned to leave she held out a pair of shoes. 'Oh yeah. The other reason I came down. Arabella left these in the bar – said they were hurting her feet. Can you pass them on to her?'

Greg took them. 'No problem.'

'Thanks. See you around then.'

'For sure.'

As soon as Imogen was gone, Greg dashed back into the bar, but Milly was nowhere to be seen. Tamsin was sitting at a table on her own having a coffee and reading a newspaper.

'Tamsin, have you seen Milly?'

'Is that the pretty girl with short blonde hair, sunburnt chest?'

'Yeah, that's her.'

'She went upstairs with Ace a few minutes ago.'

'Shit!'

Ace had got one up on him. Still, had the tables been turned, he would have done the same. At least it meant he could get a good night's sleep. Shame about the points though.

An exhausted Greg trundled back to reception. 'Hola, Juan. Have you got my key, please?'

Juan went to the open-fronted box with Greg's room number above it. 'The key is no here,' he said. 'I have spare, but are you sure you no have?'

'Positive. Shit, where is it?'

'Be careful,' said Juan, 'because my friend in other hotel, he say the keys they sometimes go, and later bad boys use it to go into room.'

'Yeah, well if they come into my room they'll get a face full of CS Gas – I always sleep with a canister under my pillow.'

Juan smiled, clearly not understanding a word of what Greg had just said. Greg flopped against the desk. 'Come on then, Juan me old mate, let me into my room otherwise I'll be falling asleep right here in reception.'

Rio never worried too much about drink and driving. She had been stopped a few times but normally found the Spanish police receptive to a bit of flesh and flirting, especially when she gave them a Labiarinth business card and an invitation for a few free dances.

Making her way to Greg's hotel, she nearly ran over several drunk British holidaymakers, looking the wrong way and stepping out in front of her. Within seconds of realising they'd almost gone under the wheels of an old Renault 5, they would turn to swear at the driver, then seeing it was a fit female on her own, start jeering and making obscene comments and gestures. She promised herself that if any others stepped in front of her car she would run them over.

Thankfully she made it to Greg's hotel without adding to the Spanish RTA figures. It was just gone one o'clock in the morning.

She breezed past reception and into the lift. It was then that the cocaine paranoia hit her. By the time she had reached the third floor and walked along the corridor to Greg's room, she had convinced herself that he was going to be with someone else.

Gingerly she put the key into the lock, but the door was already open. She walked through his lounge and had almost got to his bedroom when she saw them – a pair of girls shoes casually tossed on the floor. Her momentary dizziness was soon replaced by a fast rising surge of anger. She looked round the room for something to hit Greg and his new squeeze with. The first thing she saw was a broom so she grabbed it and barged into his bedroom. It was dark and the way he was curled up looked as though he was snuggled up with a girl next to him. She brought the broom down with considerable force onto his torso.

'Bastard!' she screamed.

She had barely got the word out before Greg sprayed his CS gas in her face.

'Aaaaghhh!' she screamed at the top of her voice. 'I can't see, I can't breathe!'

She ran round in a blind panic. Greg ushered her to the kitchen. About to drop off, he had realised it was Rio and, had he been in total charge of his faculties, he probably wouldn't have gassed her, but he was so affronted by her cheek and so fed up with her persistence that in his drunken, tired state, he had not been able to help himself.

'Be quiet,' he urged, 'you'll wake everyone up.'

'Like I give a fuck!' she bawled. 'Who is she, who is the fucking slut bitch whore?'

'Who are you on about?'

'The girl you're with.' She rubbed her streaming eyes and gasped for breath.

The realisation annoyed Greg even more. How dare she invade his privacy?

'I'll fucking kill her and you too, you lousy no good sonofabitch. Get this shit out of my eyes.'

Greg was in no mood for Rio. He went to the fridge and took out a carton of milk that had been there for some time.

'Here, cup your hands and try this.' He poured it into her hands and she splashed it over her face. 'It's not working.'

'No? Then try this.' Greg aimed the whole carton in her face. This time the smell of rancid milk penetrated even the gas.

'Ooohh my Goood!' she screamed again. 'I'm going to be sick.' She rushed to the bathroom.

Greg called after her. 'I'm sure I read somewhere that off milk was the best thing for CS Gas.'

'CS Gas?' she yelled back, between being sick and splashing her face with water, the latter only making things worse. 'Why in the name of Jesus H. Christ did you fucking gas me?'

'Because you hit me with a stick and I thought you were a

burglar. My room key was missing. What was I supposed to think?'

'So whose shoes are they in your living room?'

'They belong to one of the other reps and she left them in a bar so the barmaid asked me to pass them on. I was asleep on my own – pleasantly asleep until you came barging in.'

Rio didn't give a coherent answer, just a mixture of gurgling and retching. At that moment, Ace came into the living room from his apartment down the corridor.

'What's going on?' he asked.

Greg ushered him onto the balcony. 'That fucking nutter Rio came round and thought I was in bed with someone and hit me with a stick, so I gassed her.'

Ace looked at him astonished. 'You cunt!' He started laughing. 'Brilliant.'

'And as for you, you bastard. Chain-sawing me on Milly like that.'

'Sorry, bud but it was too good an opportunity to miss. Anyway, when I saw Imogen, I figured I'd be doing you a favour.'

'Yeah, right.' Greg leaned on the balcony. 'What was she like?'

'OK. Worth the points. And don't forget – you lose one.'

chapter twenty-seven

Arabella needed somewhere quiet to drown her sorrows. As she guessed, Mikey's La Luna Café was practically empty. The music was down tempo, which reflected her mood.

She sat at the bar. 'A large gin and tonic please, Mikey.'

Mikey poured the drink and pulled up a stool in front of her. He had a half-empty glass of lager and toasted her. 'Salut.'

Arabella took a swig from her glass. 'Jesus, that's strong.'

'You look as though you need it.'

'Thanks, I do.'

Mikey took a sip from his own glass, saying nothing and waiting for Arabella to continue. She clearly needed to talk. He didn't have to wait long.

'I don't know what I'm doing here really. I didn't want to be on my own or at the hotel – and everyone says you're a good listener.'

'That all depends on what's being said and who's saying it.'

'Oh Mikey, I've been such a fool. You've got to promise not to repeat any of this.'

'Not a problem, but—'

'Because I'd die if anyone found out.'

'Fine, but—'

'I mean, I'll probably tell them in my own time, but I just need to work things out in my head first. Do you understand?'

'Of course I do, the thing is—'

'I don't know how to say this so I guess the best thing is to just blurt it out. I've been seeing Mario.'

'I wondered when you'd decide to tell us,' came a voice from behind her.

It was Vaz.

'Oh God, no,' she moaned. She looked at Mikey for help. He shrugged.

'Vaz,' said Arabella, 'what are you doing here?'

'The same as you by the look of things. Getting pissed and bending the consoling ear of Uncle Mikey.'

'I'm really sorry that you got the sack.'

'Yeah, well for what it's worth, I was framed.'

Arabella bit her lip. 'So what are you going to do now?'

'Until I spoke to Mikey I was probably going to go home. It's a bit late in the season to get a DJ job, which is the only thing I'd want to do. But good old Mikey has said I can DJ here and try to get some people in.'

'And do a bit of bar work,' added Mikey.

'Like I said, anything that allows me to stay here and DJ.'

'That's good. I'm glad you're not going,' said Arabella with genuine warmth.

'So what's happened between you and Mario then?' asked Mikey.

'Did you know too?' She turned to Vaz. 'And how long have you known for? How did you find out?'

'I'm not silly, Arabella. All I've had to do is watch the two of you. When I was practising my DJing down here I spoke to Mikey about it. He told me that you were a YF&S client over here last year. Then I remembered the training and how you were so determined to come to Ibiza. It wasn't exactly rocket science.'

'So what's Mario done?' asked Mikey.

'I thought he loved me,' she whispered, tears welling up. 'He could be so charming, so wonderful . . .'

'This is Mario we're talking about?' said Mikey.

'You don't know him like I do!' she wailed.

'Unfortunately, I probably do.'

Arabella started crying. 'He said some terrible things to me. He told me that he never even fancied me, that he hated sleeping with me and that he's got a stunning girlfriend who lives in America. And she's coming over here next week.'

Vaz put his arm round her. 'Come on, Arabella, you're not the first person to find out their partner's not the person they thought and I'm sure you won't be the last. It's not your fault. He's the bastard, you're the same person you were before you met him, just a little wiser perhaps.'

'Yes,' she cried, trying to gulp a breath between sobs, 'you're absolutely right. I *am* still the same person I was – a horrible, stuck-up, selfish bitch. I know that's what you all think of me and you're all right.' She pressed her face into Vaz's shoulder.

'That's it, let it all out,' said Vaz, not really sure what else to say.

A minute or so later Arabella sat up, had another swig of her drink and dabbed her face with some red napkins that Mikey passed to her. 'He was laughing at me. He was with that horrible Stig outside Between the Posts with two old slappers.'

'What happened?'

'When I saw him I lost my temper. He pushed me away. Greg thought he'd hit me so went for Mario but Stig knocked Greg over.'

'Looks like it might be time to pay Stig a little visit,' said Mikey.

'There's no need,' giggled Arabella in between sniffs. 'Sugar Ray sorted it.'

Mikey and Vaz looked at each other in disbelief.

'It was like David and Goliath, well, apart from the fact that David probably wasn't an ABA boxing champion.'

Mikey started laughing. 'So he's called Sugar Ray because of his boxing! Well I'll be . . .'

'After he did that, I don't know what came over me – I hit Mario.'

This time both Mikey and Vaz roared.

'Go on the Sloane massive,' teased Mikey. He went to get three more drinks.

Arabella giggled, glad of the emotional release. She

turned to Vaz. 'Look, I've made your shirt all wet where I've been crying. I'm sorry.'

'Don't worry about it. After today that's the least of my problems.'

Arabella said nothing, then thought about how horrible she had been to Vaz when he was being so nice to her. It set her off crying again. She really wanted to tell Vaz everything but she couldn't bring herself to, not just yet.

At that moment she hated herself so much that she didn't need anyone else to hate her too.

chapter twenty-eight

Brad knocking on Greg's door at ten in the morning gave him the perfect excuse to be rid of Rio. She had claimed to be too distressed to go home after the gassing incident, although not distressed enough to spend most of the night badgering Greg for sex. Eventually Greg became so irritated by her that he snapped and told her to leave him alone and insisted she sleep on the sofa.

Brad watched a clearly sulky and agitated Rio grab her things and leave the apartment, without so much as a hello or goodbye. As the door slammed, Greg emerged from the bedroom.

'Has she gone yet?'

'What did you do to rattle her cage?'

'Apart from gassing her?'

'*Gassing* her?'

'Mate, she's certifiable. She came to the hotel while we were at the beach party and took my room key, then let herself in after I'd gone to bed. She thought I was with another girl so started hitting me with a broomstick. At first I thought it was a burglar so I had my gas ready. Then when I realised it was her I was so wound up I thought fuck it, and gassed her anyway.'

'I bet that went down well.'

'Not as well as throwing a pint of milk in her face that had been in my fridge for ages,' laughed Greg.

'You bastard.'

'Hopefully she's got the message now.' Greg walked over to the small American kitchen and put the kettle on. 'Coffee?'

'Cheers.'

'So what brings you round here so early? I thought the meeting we were having with the powers-that-be was at eleven in the Bon Tiempo?'

'Yeah it is, but I needed to talk to you first.'

'What about?' asked Greg cautiously.

'A couple of things. You can ride a motorbike, can't you?'

'Yeah, I used to love 'em. Why?'

'The Monastery have got their IT whizz coming over. He's one of their shareholders but apparently he's a bit eccentric. He loves motorbikes so Charles Moon wants you to go to the airport and pick him up on a Harley he's hired, then take him wherever he wants to go.'

'Wicked! Although I'm not so keen on going out on the razz with a computer nerd.'

'Apparently he's anything but. They reckon he's a full-on party animal.'

'That's all right then. How will I recognise him?'

'He looks like Liam Gallagher and he'll be carrying a laptop.'

'What, no suitcase?'

Brad shook his head. 'From what they were saying that's all he ever takes with him.'

Greg laughed. 'He sounds quite a character.' Brad nodded. Then there was a long pause. Greg half knew what was coming next. 'So what was the other thing you wanted to talk about?'

'I've got the date through for my operation,' sighed Brad. 'I've got to leave next Wednesday morning.'

'Oh right. Well that's not so bad, is it? It means you'll only miss a couple of days before The Monastery make their decision on Friday.'

Brad pulled out one of the chairs round the small table in the lounge and sat down.

'It wouldn't be, except that the resort manager from each company has got to make a presentation on the Friday in front of Charles Moon and Kit, H-B and our Company Secretary and Lucas with theirs. A kind of summing up about our objectives and how we feel we'd like to move forward with The Monastery at the helm.'

'Shouldn't H-B and Lucas do it?'

'That's exactly what I said when H-B told me. He said that The Monastery wanted a rep's perspective.'

'Oh.' Greg started spooning some coffee into two cups. 'So what are you going to do?'

Brad sighed and leaned forward, resting his good arm on the table. 'Like I said, you're the only person who can do it, Greg. I know you don't want to be resort manager but if you don't, H-B is convinced that The Monastery will take over Club Wicked instead of us.' Brad allowed the comment to sink in.

'That's ludicrous,' replied Greg. 'What difference does it make who's resort manager for a couple of days?'

'All the difference in the world. The only person capable of doing it other than you is Mitch Clarke in Majorca, but he'd get eaten alive over here and he knows nothing about the island. Plus if we do get chosen, then we are going to need a resort manager for the rest of the season. It will look really bad if there's nobody competent enough to take over. Even The Monastery expect you to step in.'

'But that's the point – I'm not competent enough,' protested Greg. 'Anyway, surely you're not going to be in the UK for the whole summer? When are you coming back?'

'I don't know. The earliest will be a month but it could be longer. I was talking to H-B and he wants me to start working in the marketing department in head office. If it goes well then I won't be coming back at all because it's a good opportunity. It's a full-time all year round job.' Brad stood up and walked over to Greg. 'I don't want to be over melodramatic or to put pressure on you, but the whole future of YF&S could be down to you taking over as resort manager.'

'I'd hate to know what it would be like if you *were* putting pressure on.'

'But I'm serious. All of the people in head office, all of the reps on other resorts, most of the reps here, it could all come down to you.'

'No, no, I'm not having that.' Greg busied himself making the coffee. 'It's not just about me. There's got to be loads of other factors and surely the last three weeks are going to play a big part.'

'Of course they are. But from what H-B is saying he gets the impression that The Monastery are still undecided so it must be pretty close. In his opinion the presentation is going to be a very important factor. Also, it's not going to look very good on us if we haven't got anyone suitable to run things over here, is it? So that's what I'm actually saying – you refusing to take over as resort manager could be the thing that tips the balance one way or the other.'

Greg passed Brad his coffee, then sat on the arm of the sofa. 'I'm sorry, Brad, but I can't do it. I know myself. I'm too easily distracted, too irresponsible. Giving me the job would be handing it to Club Wicked on a plate.'

'I disagree. You'd be a brilliant resort manager if only you believed in yourself. Surely you don't want to be a rep all your life?'

Greg shrugged. 'I can think of worse jobs.'

'Oh come on. Let's not have this conversation again.' Brad was becoming exasperated. 'You're not telling me that when you first applied to work for YF&S you saw yourself still doing exactly the same job ten years later?'

Greg slumped into the armchair. After a moment or two he said, 'It seems so long ago now that I can hardly remember. I thought I'd have a laugh, do the job for a year – two at the most – meet someone then settle down in the UK. I used to have this picture in my head; married, steady job, kid, Old Trafford at weekends, car in the drive, me mum down the road ready to babysit. Now I've been out here for so long I'm fucked if I know what I want.'

Brad sat in the other armchair opposite Greg. 'I don't think that it's responsibility you're scared of. Maybe it's failure, maybe it's getting hurt. You say you can't trust girls but don't forget, we see them at their worst. There are thousands of girls who wouldn't dream of coming on a YF&S holiday so you can't tar them all with the same brush. That girl you met in your first week as a rep, the Dear John letter? Is that what fucked your head up? Greg, you have to move on. Taking over as resort manager is just what you need to achieve that.'

'So what, you're a career guidance counsellor as well as a resort manager now, are you?'

'No, but-'

'Brad, you're ambitious, you want to succeed, but we're not all like that. Some of us are happy to live day by day and to just enjoy each one as it comes.'

'And are you? Are you enjoying each day? I've known you for over a year now and it's fucking obvious there's something missing. Maybe it's that picture you had of yourself before you became a rep. What I do know is that trying to fill that gap by taking loads of pills and going out clubbing every night is a poor second best.'

'Well, that's ironic, seeing as it was you who gave me my first pill.'

'And if I'd known you then like I know you now I would never have given it to you. I even remember telling you last year to be careful and to control them rather than letting them control you.'

'I can handle them.'

Brad laughed. 'Fuck me, I wish I had a Euro for everyone I know who's said exactly that.' He finished his coffee. 'Look, we could go round in circles all day and get nowhere. This is what H-B has said we should do. He's telling Charles Moon that you're taking over as resort manager after I go.'

'He can't. I—'

'Hang on, hear me out. He's telling them that you're going to do the presentation on Friday. If you don't, then he'll just have to make an excuse. It won't look good but he'd rather do that than get Mitch or someone else over.'

'Why?'

'I guess H-B is supposing that you'll come good.'

'Well, he's supposing wrong,' snapped Greg.

'At least think about it. Even if you don't intend taking over, please consider doing the presentation.'

Greg stood up and paced around the room. Why did it all have to happen the following week? It was one of the busiest weeks for opening parties and there was no way he was going to miss going to the opening of Amnesia with Sandy on Thursday. If he went, though, he would be in no fit state to do a presentation the next day. But he couldn't tell Brad that. On the other hand, there was always the possibility he *could* do the presentation and bluff it. Maybe he'd put in a better performance buzzing anyway? On balance it was unlikely, but now wasn't the time to tell Brad.

'Brad, you should tell H-B he'd be better off getting someone else to do it.'

'Frankly, I told him that when he suggested you, but like I said, he was certain you'd come good.' Brad finished his coffee. 'Give it some serious thought though, Greg – a lot of people are counting on you. This time next week it'll be all over.'

After Brad had gone, Greg did think, something he did his best to avoid in Ibiza and it made him feel decidedly uncomfortable. He was therefore grateful to have his thoughts interrupted by his mobile ringing. It was Rich, one of the guys who worked in the West End. Greg had been clubbing with him a few times.

'Hi Greg. How's tricks?'

'Yeah cool. What's happening?'

'We're all going to get on it at Bora Bora tomorrow afternoon – fancy coming?'

'I've got a welcome meeting late morning and a bar crawl in the evening.'

'Well, that's all right then. Come over about two and stay for a few hours.'

'I should really try and get some sleep because I've got to pick up a VIP from the airport later then take him out, so I doubt if I'll get much tonight.'

'Come on, you wuss. There's plenty of time to sleep when you're dead. I've got some wicked new pills as well.'

Greg weighed things up. He could always catch up on sleep during the week. If he couldn't do the presentation then well . . . they shouldn't have asked him. He'd told them from day one he wasn't interested in being resort manager so it wasn't fair of them to try and put all of the responsibility on his shoulders. He wasn't ruling it out but in his list of priorities, it was not at the top.

'Fuck it,' said Greg, 'what time do you want to meet?'

chapter twenty-nine

Lucas had overheard Charles Moon instructing Greg to pick up IT Stan at the airport. He made a note of the time and was discussing how to make use of the information with Alison. 'If you get to the airport before Greg then you could collect Stan, take him out on the town and work your charm. I'll find a way to stall Greg for a while – the way he's been carrying on everybody will just assume he's been on one again.'

'Where should I take Stan?'

'A meal, a club, the casino. Just turn it on. Do what you do best.'

'What, you want me to give him a blow job?'

Lucas looked at her deadpan. 'If that's what it takes.'

Alison shrugged. 'No promises.'

Lucas smiled. 'That's my girl. And Alison . . .'

'What?'

'Please don't screw things up this time.'

Because of the conversation with Greg, Brad was the last one to turn up at the Bon Tiempo for the meeting. Trev was there again, teasing the hotel mongrel.

'Hi, Trev.'

'Brad! How you doing? Are you missing this place?'

'Yeah, a bit. I'm not missing you tormenting that dog though.'

'Oh, he loves it, don't you, boy?'

Brad walked into the Bon. It was the first time he had been in the apartments since working there the previous summer. The memories came flooding back and he felt a sense of warm nostalgia as he walked into the bar. He also felt a warm nose up his bum – the dog had followed him in.

'Oi, don't start,' he said, shooing the dog away.

'Not the first dog that's been near there, I bet,' laughed Ace as he came into the bar from the toilets.

'Hasn't the meeting started yet?' asked Brad.

'It's just about to. Ooh, look.' A girl with a nice body and plain face walked past the window. 'See that girl?'

'Yeah.'

'Candice. Apparently she gave two Club Wicked reps and eight clients blow jobs last night. This morning she says she's not feeling too well – reckons she swallowed too much Harry.'

'Ace, this job never ceases to amaze me.'

They started walking towards the small conference room – a large storeroom that had been given a lick of paint and been furnished with a large table and a dozen chairs.

'I hear you're going back to the UK on Wednesday.'

'Yep.'

'Who's taking over from you as resort manager.'

'Hopefully Greg, but it's not definite yet. There are a few things that need to be sorted out first.'

Ace nodded and opened the door.

'*Sorted* being the operative word where Greg's concerned, eh?'

Arabella had a night off from the airport so not long after Tamsin and Hughie had left to pick up the first flight of the evening, she made her way down to La Luna Café. She'd felt good there and Mikey had cheered her up.

When she walked in, she was surprised to see that there were actually some customers in the bar. Not many, only thirty or so, but by La Luna standards, it was busy.

Vaz was DJing and most of the people in there were dancing to the laidback funky house groove that he was laying down. He had a headphone pressed to his ear, but he gave Arabella a wave and a smile as soon as he saw her.

She sat at the bar and waited while Mikey served other customers. Patricia was out the back preparing some food.

Since the previous night Arabella had been doing a lot of thinking. Mario came round to see her in the morning and was beastly. He had said some awful things, about how he never loved her, how he barely even liked her and how he was only using her.

Worst of all, the previous summer she had foolishly let him take some Polaroids of her during their love-making. He had told her that if she said anything to the YF&S reps or managers about switching the records or in particular, planting the pills, then he would send the Polaroids to her father.

Mario had really hurt her and her blind love for him had made her a total bitch to those she worked with, in particular Vaz. She despised herself. She remembered Greg's comments and felt worthless, stranded and alone. She didn't belong and nobody liked her. What was the point in staying? No Mario, no friends . . . Without realising, her lip began to tremble and a tear forced itself over the brim of her eye and ran down her cheek.

'Hi, Ara—' Vaz had left a record to play and had come over to the bar. 'What's the matter?'

Arabella quickly pulled herself together and wiped her eyes. 'Oh nothing.'

'It doesn't look like nothing.'

'You don't understand. I've been such a bitch. I've done some terrible things.'

'They can't be that bad.'

'But they are.'

'Well, even so, it still doesn't matter. You wouldn't be the first person to do something because they believed they loved someone.'

'And everyone hates me. I'm crap at my job . . .'

Mikey came over. 'What's up?'

'Arabella thinks everyone hates her and that she's a crap rep.'

'Mmm.' Mikey paused. 'Well, we don't hate you, so that's

a start. And as for being crap at your job, well, I'm not really in a position to say. What I do know is that all the time you've had that dick-head Mario pulling your strings, you've not been able to give it a fair crack of the whip. Now you're shot of him, you might surprise yourself.'

Arabella smiled reluctantly. 'It's awfully nice of you to say those things, Mikey, but I'm afraid it's too late – I've decided to resign.'

'Arabella, you can't—' said Vaz.

'There's nothing for me to stay for, is there? My supposed ex-boyfriend hates me, all of the people I work with think I'm a stuck-up cow, and I'm an absolutely abysmal rep. It seems the most logical thing to do.'

'No, it isn't.' Vaz was thinking fast. 'I can think of one very good reason not to go.'

Arabella looked at Vaz, waiting for him to finish. For a split-second there was something in his eyes ... Further confirmation, she thought, that she was losing her grip.

'You can't go because I ... I ... because I got the sack!'

Both Arabella and Mikey looked confused.

'What's that got to do with it?' she asked.

'Don't you see?' asked Vaz, his line of reasoning quickly formulating. 'I've been sacked for drug dealing, Brad has got a broken arm so has got to go home, Greg is lost somewhere on planet ecstasy – if you go too, then YF&S haven't got a chance with The Monastery.'

Arabella considered this and had to concede that he did have a point. 'But if I stay, we'll probably still lose – I'm crap.'

'You're not crap. You're great. You're fantastic. You're ... oh shit!' Vaz realised that the record was about to run out. He dashed back to the DJ box. 'Talk some sense into her, Mikey.'

They watched Vaz scurry to the decks and despite everything, execute another perfect mix. He looked over and they both gave him a small round of applause.

'He's right you know, Arabella, you shouldn't jack it in just yet. At the very least give yourself a couple of weeks.

That way, you'll know what the job's like without Mario hovering in the background and it will give YF&S more of a chance of winning.'

'But that's the whole point – Mario is hovering in the background. He's going to be there all of the time, sneering at me, getting off with other girls . . . I don't think that I'll be able to stand it.'

'Listen to me, Arabella,' ordered Mikey, surprisingly sternly. 'There's no way of sugar-coating this but Mario has taken you for a ride. But you can't beat yourself up over it because you're not the first girl to fall for his charms and I'm sure you won't be the last. Most girls he does it to just toddle off with their tail between their legs, licking their wounds. You though, you're made of sterner stuff. You got through that twenty-four hour interview training course and you got through it on your terms. That takes some doing. Stand up to the toad. I'll even help you think of a way of getting back at the slime-ball if you want, although helping YF&S put Club Wicked out of business will be a good start.'

Arabella listened. He was right, but she still wasn't sure she had the strength to see it through. 'Oh Mikey, I don't know what to do.'

'Stay, woman! Prove to everyone that you're not what they think.'

'But I'm not even certain that I want to do the job.'

'So what! It's about more than that. It's about not letting your friends down. It's about getting back at Mario so he doesn't keep walking over girls. And there might be other reasons for staying too.'

'Like what?'

'Well, that's not really for me to say . . .'

week three

chapter thirty

It was only the beginning of their third week but Hughie and Tamsin already felt like old hands as they confidently counted up the arrivals making their way out of the airport into the warm night and towards the waiting coach.

They had just checked in the Bristol flight, every rep's favourite because its scheduled landing time was nine-fifty, so providing they weren't asked to go back to the airport again to do another unearthly hour arrival, it meant that they got an early night.

There were eighty-one arrivals and two coaches. Tamsin did the head count on one coach, Hughie the other. When they added their figures together they could only make them add up to eighty. They changed coaches, but still the count was the same. After a roll call they discovered that the missing client was one Ivan Pedriks.

A couple of girls remembered sitting next to him on the plane then standing by him at the baggage carousel, where he had picked up a distinctive luminous green backpack. They said he had a scraggy brown mop top and was scruffily dressed. Tamsin inspected the underbelly of the coach and it didn't take her long to locate Ivan's backpack. They checked the coach and the coach park again, looked around the airport and even put an announcement over the tannoy, but after fifteen minutes there was still no sign of him.

In the end, Hughie rang up Brad and asked what they should do. When Brad heard that the other clients had been waiting for so long he told them to head back for the hotel and that he'd get other reps coming up later to keep an eye out for him.

Brad suggested that perhaps he'd stuck his case onto the coach so he could get a taxi and head straight off to a club. It was a bit cheeky, but the odd client had done it the previous summer.

So, with yet another single-share proving to be off-centre on the normality scale, Hughie and Tamsin headed back to San An one passenger short.

It was the first time that Ivan had been to Ibiza. When he'd left his native New Zealand at the beginning of the year, Ibiza was very much at the top of his list of places to visit during his European tour.

He had been working in London as a chef and had entered the Farringdon travel agent with the simple request of the cheapest possible holiday to Ibiza. He had never heard of YF&S, but when they told him it was a holiday designed for 18–30 year olds it seemed ideal, even though he was just over the upper age limit. When they also told him it would be cheaper if he was prepared to share with a stranger, it seemed even more ideal. Touring round Bali, Thailand and Australia, he had been used to sleeping in dorms.

Ivan had turned up at the airport an unnecessary three hours prior to departure, so the logical thing to do was have a few drinks. When the plane was delayed for an hour, a few more drinks seemed in order. On the plane, to relieve the boredom, yet more. Then, once he'd put his backpack on the coach and the reps were taking forever, he didn't think it would do any harm to quickly nip back to the airport bar and round things off nicely by spending the last of his Euros on his first San Miguel on Spanish soil.

When he eventually tumbled back to the coach, he was more than a little confused to discover that it wasn't there.

There were several immediate problems:

He didn't know the name of his hotel.

Even if he did, he now didn't have any Euros on him to

get a taxi and there was nowhere open to cash his travellers' cheques.

His rucksack was on the coach with his travellers' cheques inside, so even if there was somewhere to cash them, it would have been of little use to him. It also contained all of the details as to where he was supposed to be staying.

He was still very, very drunk.

A possible solution struck him. He opened his hand luggage, a battered laptop case with various club promotion stickers plastered over it and hunted amongst the magazines and socks for a small bag of three pills that he had smuggled over. The questionable brainwave was to try to sell the pills to tourists arriving at the airport, then to use the money to get a taxi to San Antonio. From there he was sure that he would be able to track down a YF&S rep who would be able to steer him towards his hotel.

As he approached the younger tourists, most of them gave him a wide berth. Scruffy at the best of times, the alcohol made him look even more the worse for wear.

When his initial attempts proved unsuccessful, Ivan became more obvious in his sales technique. It wasn't until he saw two uniformed officers of the Guardia Civil walking towards him that he realised he might have been a little loud.

Not waiting to find out whether they were coming for him, Ivan popped all three pills in his mouth and swallowed. He calmly walked past the officers and out of the airport.

So that was that. No money, nothing to sell and no idea where he was going. There was only one thing to do.

Ivan saw a sign for San Antonio and started walking, sticking his thumb out every time a car went by.

Alison arrived at the airport in good time to pick up Stan. Typically, Lucas had forgotten to give her the flight number. His mobile was switched off and when he'd called fifteen minutes earlier to say that he'd managed to stall Greg, she hadn't thought to ask.

She wandered round the airport trying to find someone who matched Stan's description: Liam Gallagher carrying a laptop, early thirties. She'd looked everywhere for him without any luck, so decided to try outside. Apart from anything else, she fancied some fresh air and didn't want to hang around for too long inside the terminal itself in case her reps had any problems – she wasn't in the mood.

She lit a cigarette and walked up to the top road that led away from the airport. She tried Lucas again and left yet another message on his voice mail. As she looked towards the road that led to San Jose, she saw someone dancing next to a wall, trying to thumb a lift from passing cars. When the cars didn't stop, the hitchhiker carried on dancing. As there was no music and he wasn't wearing any headphones, it took Alison a while to realise that he was dancing along to the rhythm of a nearby road digger.

Alison looked a little closer. He had long straggly hair, a gangly physique, probably early thirties . . . then she saw the laptop case. Stan. She threw down her cigarette, squashing it into the tarmac with the sole of her high heels and walked over to him.

'Hi, Stan, is it? Are you waiting for Young Free & Single holidays?'

Ivan swung round. Wow, the girl who'd asked him the question was a babe. 'Yeah, sure am.'

Ivan was answering yes to the Young Free & Single part of the question. People got his name wrong so often that he seldom bothered correcting them. Besides, the last thing he needed at the moment was to get into a discussion about names. If she told him hers then he was buzzing so much that within a few minutes he would almost certainly be asking, 'What did you say your name was?'

'I've been looking for you everywhere,' said Alison.

'Yeah, sorry. I went for a drink in the bar.'

'Never mind, at least we've got you now. I'm Alison by the way. I'm the resort manager for Club Wicked.'

'Hi, Alison.'

'Somebody from Young Free & Single should have picked you up, but to be honest I think he's been out clubbing.'

'Cool,' said Ivan, nodding his head appreciatively. 'I can dig that.'

'Oh, of course, so can I,' replied Alison, hastily. 'It's just that there's a time and a place for it. If it interferes with collecting people from the airport, well . . .' Alison pointed her key at the car. 'Here we are.'

Ivan was surprised to see a car rather than a coach. 'Shit, you've brought a car just for me?'

'Of course,' laughed Alison, 'all part of the Club Wicked service.'

They got into the car.

'So, where to?' asked Alison. 'Do you fancy a bite to eat?'

Because it was dark she hadn't really noticed him gurning, or his eyes occasionally rolling round the back of his head. Ivan had got lost in his own world for a moment and didn't answer.

Alison drummed her fingers on the wheel waiting for a reply. 'Well?' she asked eventually.

'Huh?'

'Do you want to grab a bite to eat?'

'Where?'

'Anywhere you like. There are some nice restaurants in Ibiza Town.'

'Are there? Cool.'

There was another long pause. 'So what type of restaurant do you want to go to?'

'Yeah, what? When?'

'A restaurant. Now. To eat something.'

'Shit no,' said Ivan. 'I couldn't eat a thing.' He started going through the radio stations. 'Got any good music?'

Becoming a little short-tempered, Alison selected a Monastery mix CD. Ivan started nodding his head to the garage beat.

'Yeah, it's OK. But have you got anything a bit harder?'

'I thought you'd like it – it's one of your CDs.'

'Is it? I don't recognise it.' Ivan opened his laptop case, confused as to how a CD could have fallen out. As she was driving, Alison didn't see that there wasn't a computer in it. 'Here,' he said handing her another CD, 'try putting this on.'

It was banging hard techno. Ivan turned the volume on to full blast.

'Got to have this to the max to appreciate it,' Ivan shouted over the deafening music.

Alison smiled politely. 'So where do you want to go?' she yelled.

'You lead, I'm just a humble holidaymaker . . .'

The Harley swept into Pike's car park, sending a plume of dust up from the gravel as Stan expertly slid the bike to a halt. Tony Pike's dog stood in front of the throbbing two-wheeler, barking and wagging its tail, a little put out that the speed with which the bike entered the car park denied him his usual rather risky game of snapping at tyres.

Stan gave one final roar on the throttle and switched the engine off.

'Well, you certainly know how to handle her,' admired Greg, getting off the bike and removing his helmet.

'Harleys are a different class. I've got three at home. I love them. It was really thoughtful of Charles to hire this out for me. And thanks for picking me up. I hope the ride back wasn't too much of a white-knuckle one for you.'

'No, it was fantastic,' said Greg. 'Actually, I had to open her right out on the way to the airport. I was running late and I thought I might miss you, seeing as you only had hand luggage. I guessed you'd be coming straight through as soon as you landed.'

'In that case, it's just as well I bumped into my mate. They'd lost his bloody record box, so I ligged about while he tried to get things sorted. Anyway, it wouldn't have mattered if you were a bit late, especially seeing as you turned up on this beauty.'

'Just wish I could afford one.'

'Well, I'm going back on Wednesday. It probably doesn't cost much more to hire it for a week than it does four days. I'll have a word with the hire company and extend the rental so you can have it on Thursday and Friday if you want.'

'Oh no, I didn't mean . . . I couldn't . . . I mean, I'd love to but you can't—'

'Don't be silly, of course I can. I need to spend my money on something.'

'Are you sure?'

'Of course. Call it a thank you for picking me up.'

'Wow. I don't know what to say. Cheers, Stan.'

'No worries. Now, shall we go to the bar and get a drink? I'm gagging.'

'Yeah. Are you sure you don't want to go to a club or something, only Charles told me you were a bit of a party animal?'

'Is that what he said? Well, he's partly right, although I've calmed down a bit lately. To be honest, I had a bit of a mad one last night and there's not much going on over here on a Saturday night, is there?'

'Not really – it's changeover night.'

'Exactly. I'll be happy just to have a few drinks here.'

Greg and Stan walked up to the pool bar where Charles Moon quickly introduced Stan to Lucas, Hawthorne-Blythe and Brad, while Kit opened a bottle of champagne.

Once they had all toasted each other, Stan directed Greg's attention to a Scandinavian looking girl at the other end of the bar. She had a walnut tan, accentuated by a lacy white dress. She looked over and smiled.

'She's fit,' exclaimed Stan. 'Swedish or Danish?'

'Brummie.'

'No way! I wonder if she's got a boyfriend.'

'Yeah, I saw her with him earlier. Grey-haired bloke.'

'Typical. Still, I don't suppose you get many girls coming away with their other halves on a YF&S holiday, do you?'

'A few. A lot have boyfriends back home though. As soon

as they tell me that, I know I'm pretty much on for a definite shag.'

'How do you work that one out?'

'It's like that old Ultra Nate song, you know, the one they used on Ibiza Uncovered. They're free, to be who they want to be ... and when they come on holiday with us, the thing they seem to want more than anything else is to be shagged by a rep. They get away from all the responsibilities back home and suddenly they come to life and want to try something different. A lot are in boring relationships and just want some no-strings sex.'

'Mmm,' smiled Stan, 'an interesting perspective.' He reached across the bar and got the champagne bottle, then charged their glasses. 'No wonder you keep coming back year after year. I suppose the only problem with that is you get even more cynical with the passing of each season. If ever I've got a girlfriend I'll make sure she doesn't come away on a YF&S holiday – especially to Ibiza.'

'Well, if you do, let me know and I'll keep an eye on her.'

'That's about as likely as me letting Stevie Wonder take out one of my Harleys,' laughed Stan. Charles Moon beckoned him over. 'Nice talking to you, Greg. I think my Lord and Master is calling.'

As soon as Stan left, Lucas came over. 'How's things?'

'Fine.' Greg tried to hide his distaste for the man.

'Everything OK at the airport?'

'Yeah. Stan's a top bloke.'

'Good, good.' Lucas lit one of his small cigars. 'Um, Greg. I don't suppose you saw Alison up there, did you?'

'No, I was in and out pretty much straight away. Why, what's up?'

'Nothing.'

Lucas sat on a barstool apart from the group. What on earth was she doing?

Alison didn't know what to make of 'Stan'. He certainly didn't seem as though he was a major shareholder in a multi-million pound company and she couldn't imagine him as a computer whizz. But then again, she had been warned that he was a little eccentric.

The night had been a disaster. Not long after they left the airport Alison realised that Stan was buzzing his tits off. He spotted a bar where they did Flamenco dancing and insisted they have a look. Soon he was shouting and dancing like a raver to the Spanish folk music. At first the locals found him mildly amusing but they soon tired of his antics and virtually threw them both out.

The casino was even worse. When they wouldn't let him in because of his T-shirt and jeans he thought it would be really funny to buy a shirt and trousers from a total stranger. The only problem was he didn't have any money. Alison offered to pay and Stan had no qualms about offering random people three hundred Euros to swap clothes. After stopping about twenty people he found a middle-aged man from Huddersfield who had a T-shirt and shorts in the car, which he opted to put on rather than Stan's shabby apparel. The man was overjoyed with the transaction, which came as no surprise to Alison because looking at the clothes, she doubted that they cost more than fifty pounds new.

In the casino he had caned her credit card, as well as embarrassing the hell out of her, bad enough apart from the fact that a promoter she fancied was in there with some friends. Stan lost the chips as quickly as Alison passed them to him.

They ended up in El Divino, at a VIP table where she had to buy a bottle of vodka for almost two hundred Euros, which Stan barely touched. Alison drank quite a lot and took a few lines, so at least by the end of the night she was almost on his level. He was bordering on being entertaining company in a clubbing environment, although he certainly wasn't the best dancer she had come across.

Stan didn't want to leave the club and the only way Alison could get him out was to suggest he was on some kind of promise. Given his position, she didn't want to wind him up, but by the same token, she didn't want to have full sex with him.

Which was why she now found herself in Pike's car park giving him head.

'Shit, I can't come,' moaned Ivan, to a relieved Alison.

She pulled away. 'Oh well, never mind. Come on, we'd better go inside and meet the others.'

She stood outside the car while Ivan made the necessary adjustments. When he emerged and looked at Pike's he seemed surprised.

'Wow. I don't remember it being like this in the brochure.'

Alison laughed politely, assuming it was a joke. 'It was the setting for the old Wham video, Club Tropicana. Do you remember it?'

'Yeah sure, we had Wham in New Zealand,' replied Ivan, bursting into the chorus.

'I never knew you were from New Zealand. Nobody told me.'

'No?'

Personal details on every single client? What fantastic service UK travel agents provided, Ivan thought.

'How long have you been in London for?'

'This time about six months.'

'Really. I assumed you'd been there longer. I suppose you go back and forth quite a lot.'

'Yeah, I guess so.' It was Ivan's third ever trip, but compared to the way Brits travel, he figured that three times was 'a lot'. 'So do you look after all of your clients like this?' He was still hardly able to believe his luck.

'Oh no,' replied Alison, linking her arm through his, 'only the special ones.'

'Wicked.'

They were almost at the bar so Alison decided to quickly test the water. The night she'd just given him, he would surely put in a good word for Club Wicked and say how pissed off he was that Greg hadn't turned up.

'Stan, can I ask you something?'

Ivan almost corrected her on the name, but he thought he might as well leave it till later. 'Sure.'

'If I ask you to say something to Charles for me, would you do it?'

'Who's Charles?'

As the words left Ivan's mouth, they turned into the pool area and walked straight into Kit.

'Alison, we didn't think you were coming. The others are at the bar, if you want to get you and your . . . companion a drink.'

Alison felt a hollow feeling in the pit of her stomach, which got worse as she saw Lucas glaring at her, and worse still when she noticed an individual who bore a passing resemblance to Liam Gallagher deep in conversation with Charles Moon.

Lucas and everybody else's attention left Alison for a moment, turning instead towards the direction of a splash that Alison heard behind her.

Ivan had leaped backwards into the pool and was yelling a boisterous rendition of 'Club Tropicana'.

'Alison, I've someone for you to meet,' said Charles Moon as she drew closer. 'This is Stan, our IT expert, who's over for a few days.' Alison took Stan's hand, looking shell-shocked. Charles nodded towards Ivan, who was still singing and splashing around in the pool. 'Who's your new friend?'

chapter thirty-one

The third week's arrivals were almost thirty per cent up on the previous week. The YF&S welcome meeting had gone down fantastically, which was especially satisfying as Charles Moon, Kit and Stan had popped in to see how it went.

Clients were told that they had to come to the meeting to have their return tickets checked. The real reason was to give the reps an opportunity to persuade those who were wavering to book up for the excursions.

Surprisingly, Arabella had not sulked when she was told that she was doing part of the welcome meeting. In fact, she approached it with so much enthusiasm that Greg found her to be an absolute revelation. Initially he had thought she was going to be in for a hard time, as there were a few la-di-da comments when the clients heard her accent.

Every new arrival was given a cheap buck's fizz and told it was the first of many free drinks, to psyche them up to buy the excursions. When she proposed the toast, Arabella instructed the clients that they had to do it exactly as 'mater and pater' had taught her. With her tongue firmly in her cheek she got them to raise their little pinkies in the air, then told them to pronounce 'cheers' as 'chairs'. She finished it off by explaining that when they wanted to agree to something, rather than say yeah, or yes, they should try to say 'ears', which was, she assured them, the posh way of saying 'yes'.

It brought the house down and consequently, excursion and ticket sales were extremely good. Greg could see that

Arabella was pleasantly surprised by how the clients had all warmed to her. Charles Moon thought she was hilarious.

Greg sat at a desk before a long queue of clients waiting to sign up or show their tickets. Among the twenty-somethings, he occasionally caught sight of a little boy with white blonde hair running round the bar, which meant that there was at least one family booked with YF&S. Although the holidays were marketed for 18–30-year-olds, anybody could go on one. It was unusual, but by no means unheard of for families or elderly couples to arrive at the airport looking for their YF&S rep. More often than not the travel agent would have warned them what to expect. The reason they still booked was that the holidays were cheap, as YF&S relied on making more money out of their clients on excursions than did mainline tour operators catering for families and couples.

From a rep's point of view it could be annoying because it often affected sales figures. The reps received commission based upon the percentage of that week's clients they got to take up the excursion package, so if a couple of families came away together and didn't want to go on any of the trips – especially at the beginning or end of season when it was quieter – the reps' pay packet would be smaller than normal.

Greg made a mental note to find the little boy's parents and give them some extra attention. Perhaps the mother might be susceptible to a bit of good old-fashioned charm. He knew that if he could get the female of the partnership on his side then the battle was normally won. It wasn't always the mother though. The previous summer a middle-aged couple from Leeds came away with their teenage son and daughter. Greg turned his attentions on the daughter, subtly flirting with her, giving the mum some attention too and talking football with the father and son. As a result the whole family booked the excursion block.

It was the daughter though, that made the family particularly memorable to Greg. They had a problem with their rooms, in that they had booked three but only been given two. This meant that the son and daughter were having to share. The father made a big point of nudging and winking, saying that Ruth was cramping their Brian's style. Brian puffed his chest out whilst Ruth sat there, demure, sweet and innocent.

Except she wasn't.

Brian was a complete twat, who was roundly ridiculed by every single girl he tried it on with. Ruth, on the other hand, was an insatiable minx, who bedded Mario, Ace (when he was working as a prop), two other props and two holidaymakers – and that was only in her first week.

By the second week, Greg was top of her hit list, but by the second week he had also discovered something about young Ruth . . . she was fifteen years old. Admittedly, she could have easily passed for a girl three years older, but it didn't alter the fact that she was below the age of consent. In a surprising attack of morality, Greg steadfastly rejected her advances, which made her chase him all the more. He even swapped his flight transfer so he didn't have to take her back to the airport, in case she got any ideas in the terminal.

Greg part smiled and part shuddered at the memory. She'd be sixteen now. Maybe Ruth was planning to come back this year – now there was a thought.

He was pleased to note, however, that there was some excellent points potential amongst the week's new arrivals. The little boy kept coming in and talking to the female YF&S holidaymakers, his parents obviously outside. They all thought he was adorable.

'Hello, what's your name?' the boy asked a client standing in the queue.

'Helen. And what's yours?'

'Buzz Lightyear – to infinity and beyond!'

He zoomed off round the room, pulling the string on a bikini as he ran past. The girl in front of Greg laughed. 'You can see what he's going to be like when he gets older.'

Greg nodded. 'I dread to think what his old man is like.' He handed the girl her change and her excursion tickets.

'There you go, darling. The first trip is the cruise to Espalmador tomorrow, but don't forget the bar crawl tonight.'

After the last client finished booking excursions, Greg spent a few minutes at the table doing paperwork and checking the money he had correlated with the receipts.

The little boy came running back into the room and stood in front of him, not saying anything, but clearly demanding attention. In the end, Greg looked up.

'Where's your mummy?'

The little boy pointed behind Greg.

'Hello, Greg.'

Even after five years, Greg recognised the voice. His stomach somersaulted and his cheeks flushed. He had rehearsed this moment so many times after that first summer. But in the last couple of years, he had accepted that it would never occur and now he simply didn't have a clue what to say. Slowly he turned round.

'Dawn . . .'

Rio wasn't used to not getting her own way where men were concerned. It was quite beyond her range of comprehension as to why Greg hadn't called her.

Though her tactics when dealing with men could generously be described as two-dimensional, they were normally two very effective dimensions. With sex rendered an ineffective weapon, her arsenal was exhausted. She felt disempowered.

It was the first time she had ever been told to sleep on the sofa. The indignation, on top of the CS Gas and a faceful of sour milk was too much for her to bear. It was possible, of course, that he was just annoyed at her for taking his key and she did hit him first with the broom.

It wasn't long before she convinced herself that Greg's actions were understandable, all things considered, and that Greg could still be the soulmate she believed he was.

She needed to see him and knew that he normally did a welcome meeting every Sunday around lunch-time, so decided that just after the meeting would be the perfect time to catch him. She often went to the hotels and apartments on a Sunday morning anyway, because the reps always advised the departing clients not to risk taking drugs home with them. A quick rummage through bins or behind sofas often provided an unexpectedly fruitful bounty – Rio was surprised the reps hadn't thought of it themselves.

She did think about ringing Greg first but deep down was worried that he might tell her not to come over. If Rio knew one thing about herself it was that her powers of persuasion were far more effective face to face than over the phone. She had gone to great lengths to look as sexy as possible, with lots of flesh on show, high heels and full make-up.

This time, Greg wasn't going to be able to resist.

Greg and Dawn sat outside the hotel, watching her son kick a ball around. Most of the clients had dispersed so apart from a group of five lads inside playing pool, they were alone.

During the many times that Greg had thought of Dawn and imagined what it would be like to speak to her again, he had convinced himself of one thing: the feelings he had for her at the time were not genuine. How could they be? He had since slept with literally hundreds of women. Not one of them had the same effect on him. None came close. Dawn was practically the first girl he met as a rep, so he *couldn't* have really felt the way he did about her. It was a distortion. Selective memory. Ignorance. Naivety. It was about being new to repping, a new job and surroundings. It was about wanting to meet someone special, at that time of his life. There was no way that the cynical, hard-nosed, Shag Master General that he had become five years later would have fallen for her.

So why was it, Greg wondered, that he felt exactly the same? She looked a little older, but the barely noticeable laughter lines around her blue eyes served only to make them sparkle with added depth. Giving birth had changed her body shape slightly, yet she seemed more womanly and even sexier.

More than anything else, even talking to her for the short period he had, the same strength of character was there – only more so. Being a mother obviously agreed with her. The responsibility of being a parent, of living an existence that was not centred around oneself, had given her a perspective that seemed to transcend the pettiness of Greg's own world.

In short, she had grown up.

This made Greg a little uncomfortable, inadequate, almost as though she was privy to a great secret that he had yet to discover.

Despite this, he sensed there was still a warmth between them, even though the years had passed and she had given birth to another man's child.

'So,' said Greg as the waiter brought them both a drink, 'what football team does he support?'

'Man U of course,' smiled Dawn. 'Maidenhead just didn't have the right amount of glamour for him.'

Though the answer made Greg smile, the triviality of his question made him wince. For the past few minutes, seeking refuge in the banal had seemed the easiest thing to do. Questions jostled for position in Greg's mind but none made it to his mouth. A short awkward silence hung in the air. Dawn took control of the conversation.

'It's the first time I've been back, you know.'

Greg nodded. 'I've been here every year. I guessed that if you were on the island then the least you would have done was come to see me.' He winced again as he realised how reproachful his comment sounded. Thankfully, Dawn let it go.

'I would have thought you'd be a manager by now.'

'Well, you know me. Never really fancied it.' Greg gave himself another ten out of ten for a crap answer. 'They've just offered it to me again funnily enough. I'm chewing it over,' he added, doing his best to sound mature.

Again there was a silence, this one longer. Greg couldn't help himself.

'What happened, Dawn? One minute you were writing me letters, telling me how wonderful things were, how you couldn't wait to come back out here, planning to move up to me or for me to come down to you in the winter, then suddenly I get a letter saying you're back with your old boyfriend.'

'I'm sorry.'

'The least you could have done was speak to me. I started to think your mum was just a pre-recorded message. I didn't know what to do.'

'But you were out here, Greg – there was plenty to do. You'd just started as a holiday rep and it was obvious you loved it. I didn't want to get hurt.'

'But we discussed all of that. We spoke about it when you were here, in letters over the phone . . . what more could I do or say?'

'You could have said what you felt. It was as if I was doing all of the running.'

'Just because I didn't say something, it didn't mean I wasn't thinking it.' Greg immediately realised how lame this sounded.

'How was I supposed to know what you were thinking? I knew you cared about me otherwise we wouldn't have been talking about meeting up when you got back. But I didn't know how many other girls you'd said that to.'

'Oh come on, Dawn, what about all the calls and letters?'

'I was back home then. Things had changed. I didn't know if you were being genuine or just trying to line up another girl to visit for when you got back. I'd listened to the other reps bragging about having girls to stay with in every town when they were back in the UK during the winter.'

'You're not telling me that the only reason you got back with your old boyfriend was because of what you heard a few reps say?'

'I was nineteen years old, Greg, and you reps seemed so,

so . . .' Her voice trailed off. 'It was my first time abroad – it was all too perfect, it didn't seem real.'

'It was real enough to me.' Greg shook his head. 'I'm sorry, Dawn, but it still doesn't add up. Something isn't right.'

Dawn clasped and unclasped her hands. Then she took a deep breath and sat upright. 'There is something else.'

'What?'

She paused and bit her lip, looked skyward, then back at the floor, before meeting Greg's eye.

'I got pregnant.'

A wave of nausea swept over him. He wanted to Control Z what he had just heard, to wipe it from his memory, or better still, for the comment never to have existed at all. It had been bad enough imagining Dawn with someone else so soon after him, but for that someone else to get her pregnant?

Then an even worse thought struck him. 'Were you pregnant when you were over here, when you started seeing me?'

Dawn looked at him confused. 'No, of course not. I—'

'So how old is your son?'

'Five. He starts school in September.'

'Well, it was a close thing then. I mean, did you actually stop seeing this ex-boyfriend of yours?' Greg pushed his chair back and stood up. 'Jesus, Dawn. This might sound a bit of a cliché but I really thought what we had was special. Do you know how much time I've wasted thinking about you? Have you any idea of what the effect of what you did has had on me?'

'I . . . I guess I assumed you'd quickly forget about me.'

'Well, I didn't.'

'Oh.'

'The mad thing is that seeing you again, it even crossed my mind . . .' Greg shook his head as though trying to loosen the thought and fling it as far away as possible. 'But now you turn up here and confront me with this.' Greg snorted. 'It just confirms that I'm right about women. You're all the same.'

'Oh right,' replied Dawn, 'so that covers everyone from Mother Teresa to Moll Flanders, does it?'

'You know what I mean.'

'And what about you, Greg, can you be trusted?'

'I don't make false promises, that's for sure. I'm no angel but a girl always knows where she stands with me.'

'Stands? From what I've been hearing about you most of the girls you meet are horizontal.'

'What do you mean what you've been hearing about me? Who have you been talking to?'

'Things . . . people,' replied Dawn, caught slightly off-guard.

'Like what? From who? Why?'

'Pretty much everyone. Anyway,' Dawn quickly regained her composure, 'you don't exactly have to be a member of MI5 to hear about your reputation. I've only been here five minutes and I've already heard clients and other reps talking about you.'

'So why should it be any concern of yours?'

'It's not.' Dawn looked at the floor and bit her lip.

'Hang on a minute,' said Greg slowly. 'I think I get what this is all about.' He shook his head. 'Fucking hell, Dawn, I never thought you'd pull a stroke like this. You've come over here to see if I'm still interested, haven't you?'

'No, not really.'

Greg laughed. 'Yes, you have. Oh the irony of it! No – the fucking *cheek* of it!' He rested his hands on the table and leaned towards her. 'So, let me get this right. You dump me to get back with your ex-boyfriend without a word of explanation. I hear nothing from you for years. Then you turn up in Ibiza informing me that either just after or maybe even just before our little relationship, you got pregnant. And now, you're wondering if I still feel anything for you as if nothing has happened. What's up, did the kid's father see what a two-faced old slapper you were and dump you?'

Dawn's eyes filled with tears. 'You *bastard*!'

'Yeah, well, you turned me into one.'

Dawn stood up. 'Is that what you really think of me? Have you really become so arrogant and full of yourself that you honestly believe that if what you said was true, I would be so hard up that I'd travel all of this way just to find you? Do me a favour. If I was after a replacement father, you'd be way down the list.'

'Yeah, well by the sound of it, you'd have a pretty long list.'

'I knew this would be a waste of time.' Dawn snatched her bag from the table, pride and anger stopping the tears from flowing. 'If only you . . . oh, what the hell. You just don't get it, do you?' She called over to her son. 'Come on, Greg. Time to stop playing football – we're going to the beach.'

'Greg! Fucking hell. You've even given the boy my name! I bet his real dad loved—'

The realisation hit him like a kidney punch. His surroundings went into contra-zoom as he looked first at Dawn, then the boy.

Little Greg clumsily dribbled the brightly-coloured ball, laughing and looking over for recognition. 'Look, Mummy! I'm David Beckham.'

Dawn smiled, keeping her eyes fixed on her son rather than Greg.

'He's not . . . he can't be . . .'

'He's yours.'

'But, but . . . I thought . . .'

'That I was an "old slapper"? Sorry to ruin your theory about women, Greg, but there was no ex-boyfriend. In fact, other than the non-event of losing my virginity a year earlier, you were my first.'

'You made the ex-boyfriend up?'

'Yes.'

'Why, Dawn?' Little Greg was kicking the ball to another small boy a couple of years older. It was almost too much to comprehend. That was *his* son. 'I'm a father? I'm definitely the father?'

'Well, unless I was gestating for a year and you can get pregnant by an over-excited seventeen-year-old coming over your hand, yes, you are definitely the father. And the ex-boyfriend – because I thought it would stop you from calling.' A small tear ran down her cheek. 'When I found out I was pregnant, I didn't know what to do at first. In the end I told my mum and she was great. We spoke about having a termination but I knew I wouldn't be able to go through with it and Mum was dead against it too.' Dawn sat down and a still stunned Greg did the same. 'It wasn't like I just suddenly decided not to call you or not to tell you. I agonised and spoke about it for weeks . . . months. It was harder than you'll ever know, deciding to keep him. I didn't want to complicate things in my head. I assumed you'd want me to have an abortion.'

'Why?'

'I thought you'd run a mile.'

'You thought wrong.'

'Did I?' Dawn looked Greg in the eye and shook her head. 'No, I'm right. I knew you liked me a lot but you never exactly went overboard.'

'Yeah, but that's just me. I suppose I'm not very good at showing my feelings. I told you how much I liked you and how I wanted us to meet up in the letters I wrote.'

'Yes, but as I said, I didn't know what your real motives were. It wasn't as if you were declaring your undying love for me or saying that we should live together.'

'I know, but we'd only been together in the same place for just over a week.'

'Oh, Greg, I'm not blaming you. I wasn't expecting you to make a commitment. Sure, we got on great and there was a spark there, but this was a baby – a *lifelong* commitment. There didn't seem any point in involving you in that decision. It didn't seem fair.'

'You should have let me know.'

'Perhaps,' sighed Dawn. She shrugged. 'But I can't believe

that you would have wanted to give up the job you loved to start a family. You were only twenty-one yourself.'

Greg said nothing. He could barely remember what was going through his head in that first season. She was probably right. But he also knew that having a family, to be a father was a thought that was constantly lurking in the back of his mind, ready to tease and taunt him every time he allowed room for it. He put his head in his hands. 'This is all a bit much to take in.'

He watched Little Greg kick the ball to his new-found friend. His own flesh and blood. A son. A five-year-old who would be a teenager when Greg was still in his thirties. Able to play football together in the park on Sundays and watch it on Saturdays. But what about the other five days of the week? What about school? What about not being able to go out without a babysitter? Early mornings, no more going clubbing or getting twatted. No Competition, no YF&S reunions.

Positive and negative implications of parenthood, trivial and consequential, all hurtled into his consciousness quicker than he could assimilate. Then of course there was Dawn. It was obvious that something was still there, but she was right – despite all of the hours she had occupied his thoughts, they had still only ever spent less than a fortnight in each other's company.

It was as if Dawn could tell what he was thinking. 'I didn't know what to expect, or even quite why I came out here. It just seemed the right thing to do. He'll be starting school in September and I suppose I wanted him to know who his father was.' She picked at a beer-mat. 'Did you really mean what you said earlier – well, kind of said – about having feelings for me, Greg?'

Greg nodded. 'I thought about you loads. But . . . I figured that maybe I'd just got things messed up in my head. Perhaps it was because you stopped contacting me, you know, the old wanting what you can't have syndrome . . .' Greg noticed the momentary look of disappointment on Dawn's face. 'I'm sorry, Dawn. I'm just trying to be honest, with myself as much as anything else. I'm only saying that's one of the explanations that crossed my mind. On the other hand, seeing you again ... straight away, some of those old feelings were there. But were they caused by nostalgia, the shock of Little Greg?' Greg slumped back in his chair, rubbing his temples. 'I'm just thinking aloud.' He tried to pull himself together. 'So now what?'

'Well,' said Dawn slowly, 'I'm out here until next Friday morning. I thought we could spend a bit of time together. I was going to go to Espalmador on the ferry tomorrow. I know you've got the cruise excursion there so I thought we could come over on another ferry for a couple of hours once you'd done all of the stuff with your clients. Then, depending on how things go maybe you could take Greg, Little Greg, out to get to know him better – only if you want to of course,' she added hurriedly.

'I want to – I'd love to. Mind you, you could have picked a better week – and a better day to leave.'

'Why, what's up?'

'Don't worry – I'll explain another time. Leave the arranging side of it to me.'

'OK. I don't think it's a good idea to tell him who you are just yet – let's see how things go first of all.'

'But then what?'

'I don't know. If you get on all right, if we get on all right ... When you come home at the end of summer, maybe you can come down and see him, or I can bring him up to you. If I can afford it, maybe I'll come out again later in the season ... it's hard to plan really.'

'Lots of ifs and buts.'

'There are bound to be. The most important thing is Little Greg. I haven't let and I won't let, anyone into his life who isn't going to be around for a long time – and that includes you. I need to be sure that you're ready for that kind of commitment – I don't mean to me, but to him.'

At that moment, a Renault 5 pulled up on the kerb between the hotel patio and the wasteland where Little Greg was still playing football. Rio stepped from the car.

'Hi, honey,' she said to Greg, casting a dismissive glance at Dawn. She sauntered over to the table and picked up Greg's room key. 'Now if I let myself into your room again, you're not going to do the same as last time, are you, baby?' She didn't wait for a reply. 'I'll see you up there, honey. Don't be long now.'

'Rio, wait—'

Greg stood up but before he could say what he wanted she was in the hotel.

'That's not what it seems,' he protested, turning to Dawn. 'She's a nuisance. Stay there and I'll get shot of her.'

'She didn't look as though she was planning on leaving.'

'Trust me – she'll go. I made a mistake. She's mad.'

'I wasn't expecting you to have stayed celibate all of this time, Greg. She seems quite sexy – in a tarty kind of way.'

'She's not sexy. Well, she is but not to me. Well, she was. What I mean is . . . she stayed the other night. I made her sleep on the sofa.' Dawn raised her eyebrows. 'It's true. Dawn, I have changed, more in the last year than ever before. On my life, I swear.'

Greg felt comfortable swearing on his life for he had changed a lot in the last year. He was no longer the kind of bloke who would go out and get pissed, then chase after anything in a skirt. He was now the type of bloke who would go out clubbing all night, get loved-up on pills and then chase after anything in a skirt, particularly if its wearer was in a similar state and up for more drugs and a marathon sex session. But even that was beginning to lose its appeal.

He was confused. Dawn had got under his skin during that first season. Logic told him that it had all been a mistake. What he was now faced with was one week to get to know his son and to be sure that his feelings for Dawn had in fact been warped by the passage of time. One way or another, they needed exorcising.

There was of course, the unlikely chance that those feelings six years earlier had been genuine. Something still drew him to her, though he thought, it had to be the shock of seeing her after so long and discovering that the little boy who had been running round the bar undoing girls' bikinis was his child.

If he threw himself back into the 'real' world – went to a couple of clubs, scored a few points – then perhaps he'd get his true feelings for Dawn worked out? Briefly, he remembered the Thursday opening of Amnesia with Sandy. He'd deal with that later.

'I don't expect you to have changed totally, Greg. But I need to be sure you're reliable. That you take things more seriously than you did.'

'I have . . . I do. We'll spend a bit of time together on Espalmador tomorrow then on Tuesday, perhaps we could take Little Greg to the water park?'

'I'm not sure . . .'

'Please, Dawn.' Greg knew the comment he was about to make was near the mark, but he desperately wanted to spend some time with Little Greg, 'You've denied me seeing my son grow up all of this time. Is it fair to stop me now?'

Dawn looked as though she was about to give in. She walked over to Little Greg and picked him up. Ace came bounding out of the hotel. Noticing a mother and child he assumed that they had nothing to do with YF&S or Greg.

'Oi, Greg, I've just seen that fucking lap dancer you were shagging letting herself into your room again. There's no value in going there again surely, you've already got maximum points off her – unless you've got something particularly perverted lined up.' Ace was in full flow and didn't notice Greg trying to shut him up. 'I'm catching you up in The Competition, mate. I managed to bone that girl out of room one two four and got her to sing Bob the Builder while I was doing it. I reckon this could be it, mate – the first time in five years that you don't win. Watch out, Greg, there's a new kid on the block. Weh-hey! Right, can't stop. See you in the bar later.'

Greg stood there speechless and shame-faced. Dawn looked at him, shaking her head.

'You asked me why I denied letting you watch your little

312

boy grow up. Well, I think the reason's pretty obvious, don't you? There was another little boy that had to grow up first.' She came over to the table and picked up her things. 'And by the looks of things, he still has some way to go.'

chapter thirty-two

The atmosphere on the YF&S cruise to Espalmador was surprisingly relaxed, mainly because they were without Club Wicked and no Monastery observers were in attendance. The most senior member of YF&S staff there was Greg.

Before the cruise Brad had gathered the YF&S reps together to tell them that he was leaving on Wednesday for his operation and that Greg was taking over as resort manager. The latter piece of information surprised some, but what they did not know was that Brad had struck a deal with Greg once he had been made aware of Greg's new predicament.

Greg needed to spend some time with Dawn and Little Greg over the next few days, so Brad had agreed to work around this wherever possible providing that he was allowed to tell The Monastery that Greg was going to stand in as resort manager and do the presentation on Friday.

Despite the looming presentation and the shock of Dawn and Little Greg, Greg was still thinking about the opening of Amnesia and meeting Sandy again on Thursday night. He was torn. Various dishonourable options occurred to him. Dawn was leaving on Friday morning, so he could say his goodbyes on Thursday evening, using the presentation as an excuse. He could sleep as much as possible on Thursday then meet Sandy at Amnesia at about two in the morning. If he took his last pill about five and he could persuade Sandy to leave just before six, then they could have a couple of hours back at his apartment. If he resisted taking more pills and just settled for a few lines of Charlie then he would be just about in the right frame of mind to do the presentation . . .

He hadn't spoken to Dawn since the previous afternoon. Despite her withering final comment, she had mentioned coming to Espalmador and as such, Greg found himself periodically looking down the beach as each new ferry moored up, squinting as the searing sun reflected off the crystal clear sea, hoping that they would be amongst the new arrivals deposited on the small island for the afternoon.

Greg's vantage point was a small sand dune, away from the other reps and clients. As he watched the next ferry slowly manoeuvring its way between the private yachts anchored in the shallow bay, he ran his finger down a scratch mark on his right cheek.

After Dawn had left the hotel the day before, he had marched back up to his room, outraged at Rio's assumptive arrogance. He found her spread-eagled on his bed playing with herself. Quite why it repulsed him so much he wasn't sure, but after he yelled at her to leave she flew at him. Luckily Ace wasn't far behind and dragged her out, physically ejecting her kicking and screaming from the hotel, with Greg's flesh still under her fingernails.

It was another beautiful day on Espalmador and Vaz and Mikey had tagged along and were sitting with Arabella and some clients. Much to everyone's surprise Arabella had been the rep who led the clients to the mudbath where she had thrown herself into it whooping and hollering.

As Arabella was drying herself off, Mikey's mobile rang. He walked down the beach and over his shoulder thirty or so metres away, Arabella noticed Greg running towards a ferry where Dawn and Little Greg were walking down the gangplank onto the beach. Greg had told the reps about Dawn, but hadn't told them Little Greg's name or mentioned that he was the father.

'Greg's ex is here with her little boy,' said Arabella to Vaz, towel-drying the ends of her hair.

Vaz looked over. 'I haven't met her – what's she like?'

'I only chatted to her briefly yesterday. She seems really nice. Quite well-spoken. Doesn't seem as though she suffers fools.'

'That's Greg fucked then,' laughed Vaz. He reached into his bag and pulled out a bottle of Evian. 'Drink?'

Arabella nodded and took a small swig. Vaz laid down on the sand and closed his eyes. Arabella finished drying her hair, trying to pluck up the courage to say what she had been planning since persuading Vaz to come on the cruise earlier that morning.

Mario was by no means out of her thoughts, but she was now certain he was a total bastard. On the other hand, Vaz was a thoroughly decent person, who didn't deserve to have his name tarnished as a drug dealer.

She had therefore resolved to invite him along to the cruise and tell him that the drugs were planted by either Alison or Mario. She hoped that he wouldn't make a scene and prayed that he wouldn't do anything that would cause Mario to post the Polaroids to her father. If he did, she had steeled herself for it as best she could.

She looked over to Mikey who was still deeply engrossed in conversation on his mobile. It was the first time she had been alone with Vaz. She had to grab the opportunity. She took a deep breath.

'Vaz, there's something—'

'I know,' interrupted Vaz quickly, without even opening his eyes.

Arabella was momentarily dumbstruck. 'No, what it is—'

'I know,' he repeated, still not moving or opening his eyes.

'But you don't know what I'm going—'

'I know that it was you who switched my records and I know that you know it was Alison or Mario who planted the drugs on me.'

Vaz slowly sat up and looked Arabella in the eye, his face serious, though not stern. Arabella's jaw had dropped. 'It's not exactly hard to work out, Arabella. Motive, opportunity, history . . .'

'Oh my God. How long have you known for? How can you bear to be near me?'

'I knew pretty much straight away – and I know that you were besotted with Mario so I'm sure you weren't thinking straight.'

'How can you be so calm? Why haven't you done anything about it?'

'Like what? If the drugs thing had gone any further I might, but as it is, the police weren't involved and nobody else knows . . . without getting into taking fingerprints and shit.'

'You got the sack though!'

'I know. And at the time I was pretty devastated. But the truth is, I didn't come out here to be a rep.' He noticed the surprise on Arabella's face. 'In fact, I'm probably a bigger fraud than you. At least you came out here for someone else – even if it was a smarmy two-faced creep.' Vaz allowed himself a smile. 'I came out here for purely selfish reasons. I want to be a DJ. YF&S was just a means to that end. Now I guess all I'm doing is going about it in a different way. Switching the records probably did me more damage in that respect than the drugs.'

Arabella looked down at the sand. 'You must hate me.'

Vaz reached out and lifted her chin, so he could look into her eyes. 'Nothing could be further from the truth.'

Partly through the relief of sharing her burden of guilt, Arabella's eyes misted over and she flung her arms round Vaz's neck and buried her head into his shoulder. 'Oh Vaz, you're such a kind, special person.'

Vaz could feel her warm tears running down his chest. 'At least you're not soaking my shirt again this time,' he joked.

Arabella pulled away and smiled, wiping her eyes and sniffing. 'Oh God, what a relief. I've *so* been wanting to tell you. But I haven't been able to. Mario's been threatening me.'

Vaz's expression changed. 'I've had enough of him. When we get back I'm going to pay that wanker a visit.'

Arabella saw Vaz's muscles tense and had to admit that

his sturdy, well-toned physique looked more than capable of dealing with her former Latin lover. 'I'm half-tempted to say to hell with it, but I can't, Vaz. You see, he's been threatening me with some pictures.'

'What do you mean?'

Once again Arabella stared at the floor. 'He says he took some . . . compromising Polaroids of me last year. He told me that if I said anything to you or anyone about switching the records or them planting the drugs, then he'd send them to my father.'

Vaz digested this information for a few moments. 'Yet you still told me – why?'

Arabella looked up. 'Because it was the right thing to do.'

Vaz allowed himself a smile. He didn't say anything for a few moments, then took hold of her hands. 'It's funny how you can be so wrong about someone, isn't it?'

'Do you mean me or you?'

'Both of us.' He kissed her hand then jumped up. 'Don't you worry about Mario, I've got an idea forming. We'll get those photos back – if they even exist – *and* find a way of stitching him up.'

Mikey came over, having finished his call. 'What are you looking so pleased with yourself about?'

'Nothing at the moment, but watch this space,' replied Vaz, grinning at Arabella.

'Well, whatever it is or isn't, I think you're about to become even more pleased. That was Pablo, one of the managers at Es Paradis on the phone. The Monastery have decided not to have another joint YF&S and Club Wicked party on Wednesday night. Instead, they've hired out the club on Friday evening for their end of assessment party. After the resort managers have made their respective final presentations during the day Charles and the others are going to spend a few hours discussing things, then at ten-thirty they're going to have a little joint party in the upstairs funky room with all the clients. When the main club opens at midnight, all of the clients will go downstairs and they'll keep the reps in the funky room and announce their decision.'

'Are you trying to say they want me to play the set in the funky room?' said Vaz, thrilled.

Mikey smiled. 'Ah, but I've been saving the best bit until last. The resident DJ Reno has got a series of gigs back in Italy and he leaves tomorrow, so Pablo asked me if I knew a suitable DJ who could play the first set downstairs too, at short notice. Not only that, but if he likes the DJ, he might even offer him a residency. So who do you think I suggested?'

Vaz couldn't believe his ears. 'This had better not be a wind up.'

'What do you mean? I suggested Jimmy Saville.' Even Mikey's normally deadpan face couldn't stay straight. 'He's also going to let you play an hour set on Thursday night, just to see what you're like. So what have you got to say about that, Mr Romanov? Happy?'

Vaz grabbed hold of Mikey's shoulders. 'Happy? You beauty!' He planted a kiss on Mikey's forehead then did a series of backflips and twists down the beach, yelling with excitement. He dashed back over to Arabella, still barely able to contain his glee. 'How about that?' he said, winking at her. 'Just don't go changing my records over this time.'

Arabella smiled, but looked at Mikey and put a finger to her lips.

'What Mikey?' laughed Vaz. 'Oh don't worry about him. He helped me work out that it was you who switched them!'

'OK, I'm willing to accept I'm the father,' Greg smiled and passed the Solero he had just taken a bite of back to Dawn, 'but are you sure you're the mother?'

'What?' laughed Dawn, resting back on her elbows.

'I know this is going to sound as though I've been staring at your tits all afternoon, but I couldn't help noticing what fantastic shape you're in. There's no way that you could possibly have had a child.'

Dawn laughed and rolled over to lie on her front. 'Three nights a week down the gym and not eating these things.' She held the ice cream in the air. 'But thanks for noticing.'

The afternoon had gone better than Greg had dared hope. Rio's untimely arrival and Ace's inopportune comments of the previous day had been briefly discussed and, to Greg's relief, Dawn had not been as annoyed as he'd imagined. She accepted the story of Rio and repeated that she hadn't expected him to remain celibate. Greg did sense, however, that she had rather hoped he would have changed and decided to play down the more laddish side of his personality. It was hard to believe that he had not had any contact with Dawn for so long. The conversation flowed effortlessly and the surprising thing was that although they had so much to catch up on, most of the time they simply chatted.

Little Greg too had been an absolute joy. There was no shyness or tension and his acceptance of Greg was unconditional. Greg thoroughly enjoyed the child's company and was probably even more excited than Little Greg at the prospect of spending the next day at the water park together. He could hardly grasp the intensity of how proud his son made him feel.

However, Greg was still having trouble understanding his true feelings. He had never been a self-analytical person but trying to recognise little shifts in mood, especially when he was on pills and Charlie, had made him far more sensitive to what caused those changes in everyday life. One problem of course, was that a week had rarely gone by in the past year without Greg having at least one night of narcotic indulgence. Consequently, during that period his mood had hardly ever been totally free from the effects of drugs, if not under their influence, then often on some kind of comedown.

He kept remembering that this was to be the summer

of summers. It was supposed to be about meeting cool girls like Sandy, and a new future. Yet now, in Dawn and Little Greg, it was his past demanding his attention.

And for someone who had spent so long living in the present, it was all becoming very, very confusing.

chapter thirty-three

Giggling, Hughie leaned over from his balcony to Ace's and passed a snorkel.

When he heard Ace telling the girl what he was going to dress in next, Hughie almost laughed out loud, because the face mask that Ace had put on a few minutes earlier was making it sound as though someone was holding his nose.

He tried to picture what Ace must look like. So far he had passed a pair of flippers, a blond wig, a plastic gorilla's chest and stomach, a diving mask, a pair of inflatable arm bands, fancy dress angel's wings and a snorkel.

Ace had already overtaken him in The Competition, even though Hughie had been having a good run himself. It was a shame that the friend of the girl that Ace was currently shagging had got so drunk that she lost control of her bowels in a back street of San Antonio not far from the hotel. Her physique was well-suited to Hughie's penchant with rolls in all the right places and he had been making good progress. Still, even he had to draw the line somewhere.

The noise from the next room stopped and, a few minutes later, a grinning Ace came hurtling through Hughie's door, throwing a small camcorder on the bed.

'What a scream! And two bonus points as well. Have a look at it later. I've got it all on film. Thanks for letting me borrow your camera by the way.'

'No problem. You definitely didn't wipe over any of my efforts, did you?'

'They're all still there. I had a look at them earlier and I've got to say, Hughie, you are one sick man. How do you even get a boner with girls like that?'

'Each to his own, Ace. I tell you what though, even if I don't get bonus points for shagging the kind of girls I do, I should get bonus points for the ones I get on film. Or at least for collecting these.'

Hughie opened up a drawer and pulled out a handful of very large knickers. When Ace saw them he became hysterical.

'Fuck me, mate, some of those are so huge they should have Goodyear written down the side.' He patted him on the back. 'If it was down to me, I'd give you the bonus points, but Greg's the Shag Master General so you'll have to ask him.'

'I haven't seen him all day – where's he been? I heard a rumour he'd gone with his ex and her kid to the water park.'

'Yeah, that's what I heard too.'

'So when are you going to bring back my gear, the flippers and all that?'

Ace laughed. 'Shit, I forgot the best bit. I told Amy that seeing as I dressed up for her, then she should dress up for me. She's gone up to her room and she's probably putting on the snorkel and face mask as we speak!'

'You bastard. What are you going to do when you go up there?'

'Fuck that. I'm going down Eden.'

'You're not going to leave her sitting in her room wearing all that?'

'Fucking right I am! It's almost worth going up there to take a picture. That Amy's such a divvy that I reckon she'll probably be sitting there like that for at least an hour before she realises I'm not coming back.'

'You're worse than Greg. Which room is she in?'

'Two one three, I think. No, it might be three one two. Why, are you thinking of having a go?'

'Of course not – she's too skinny for me. I was going to

tell her you'd been called away. You can't leave the poor
cow sitting there all night. Anyway, I want my stuff back.'

'Haven't you got enough pervey stuff in that drawer of
yours.'

'A little bit of bondage gear isn't pervey, it's healthy.'

'Yeah, well, whatever it is, at the moment it's not getting
you any points. I tell you what, there aren't that many fat
girls here this week, so you should try . . .' Ace searched for
the right word, '. . . *narrowing* your sights. You never know,
you might actually like it. One thing's for sure, if you don't,
you're going to lose The Competition to me.' Ace went to
the fridge and took a swig of water. 'I'm off. What time's
Brad leaving in the morning?'

'About midday I think. Will you be around?'

'Probably.'

'OK. I'll see you tomorrow then.'

Just after Ace had left, Hughie made his way up to room
two one three to reclaim his snorkelling gear. He was
therefore surprised when Candice – the blow job queen, he
remembered when he saw her – answered the door. Her
face lit up.

'Hiya, what are you doing here?'

'Oh, sorry, I thought this was Amy's room.'

'Amy? I think she's in three one two.' She looked Hughie
up and down seductively. 'Won't I do?'

Under normal circumstances Hughie would have said no
– Candice simply didn't do it for him. However, Ace was
right – he was falling behind in The Competition.

He walked in and Candice started kissing him. It was as
simple as that. She ran her hand up his leg and started
squeezing him through his trousers, but even after a minute
or so of fondling, Hughie remained in a flaccid state.

'I know what will sort that out,' said Candice confidently,
as she sank to her knees and undid his belt.

She took Hughie in her mouth, but despite her best
efforts, there was still no reaction. Eventually she gave in.

'What's up?' she asked.

'I guess I'm not turned on,' replied Hughie, shrugging.

'You'd be the first,' she retorted. She was clearly unimpressed.

'How many blokes have you shagged this week, Candice?'

'Only one so far this week. Last week it was three, plus that night when I gave ten blow jobs on the trot,' she added proudly.

'Oh well,' he said doing his trousers up, 'having one bloke who doesn't fancy you isn't going to dent your confidence that much, is it?'

'But I saw you with that horrible fat girl the other night. How can you fancy her more than me?'

'I just do. Sorry.'

'Is it because I've been with other blokes?'

'Not really, although I must admit, hearing that you felt sick because you'd swallowed too much spunk doesn't exactly put you the top of my must-shag list.'

'You blokes all screw around and it's all right – why can't I?' She was angry.

Hughie ignored it. 'Candice, darling, I'm the last person to judge you. You can do *what*ever you like and with *who*ever you like – just not with me. Now,' he moved her out of the way, 'I've got to go. Goodnight.'

As he walked down the corridor, she screamed, '*Weirdo!*'

Brad entered the Hotel Arena bar the next morning. Juan had brought down his two suitcases filled to bursting. He had just been round all of the rooms to say goodbye to the reps and was finding it hard to actually leave. He loved being on resort, but circumstance had taken a hand and Brad was a great believer in recognising when fate seemed to be telling him to do something.

The job he was going to start in head office after his operation was a good career move. Of course, if The Monastery chose to take over Club Wicked instead of YF&S then there would probably be no company to have a career within, but there was now little he could do about that.

Hawthorne-Blythe was standing just outside the bar and was on his mobile. Greg was sitting at one of the tables.

'I just went up to your room. I was worried I was going to miss you.'

'I wouldn't let you go without seeing you off,' said Greg. 'I had a few things to sort out.'

'So, are you all set to take over as resort manager then?'

'Of course.'

'Are you sure?' asked Brad, who had known Greg long enough to recognise the lack of conviction in his voice. 'You seem as though you've got a lot on your mind.'

Brad was absolutely right. The day at the water park with Little Greg had been fantastic. Greg had almost forgotten that it was possible to have fun without drugs. Dawn was clearly pleased that father and son had bonded so well and she suggested rounding off the evening with them all having a meal together. Greg took them to a fabulous restaurant on the old town called El Olivo. That too, had been immensely enjoyable and at the end of the evening a moment passed between Dawn and Greg where, had Little Greg not been there, they would almost certainly have kissed.

Greg wanted to kiss her – and more – and he had to keep reminding himself that he didn't like revisits. But Little Greg had changed everything. They were only in Ibiza until Friday. He wanted to see as much of them as possible, but he still didn't know what to do about the opening of Amnesia on Thursday night with Sandy. He also had to get the guts of a presentation together and at least appear to be running things for a couple of days.

So Greg did indeed have a lot on his mind, though he could see little point in burdening Brad with it.

'No, everything's fine,' insisted Greg, smiling as reassuringly as possible. 'I won't let you down, don't worry.'

'Good.' Hawthorne-Blythe walked back into the bar looking unusually perplexed. 'Everything OK, H-B?'

'Kind of.'

'What's wrong?'

'Not so much wrong. It's just . . . oh, never mind.'

'Go on,' urged Brad, 'what's up?'

'I've just been speaking to Kit and I've now got some serious reservations about The Monastery's plans if we do win and they take us over.'

'Like what?'

'Generally speaking, I'm just not convinced that The Monastery are right in their assumptions about the travel market. They do not seem to have grasped the core of what youth holidays are all about.'

'In what way?'

'Well, they seem to be convinced that kids no longer want our kind of package holiday. The emphasis is *totally* on clubbing.'

'Clubbing is what most of them come for, H-B,' said Greg, 'especially in Ibiza.'

'I know. But I still believe that the reason they *really* come away is to be part of something and to meet a member or members of the opposite sex. These type of holidays are an institution, a rite-of-passage. Of course we need to change with the times, but I believe that means trying to incorporate the facets of club culture that are relevant to our type of holiday. It seems that The Monastery are trying to incorporate the most basic of our ideals into *their* culture. It's like they want to simply transfer their club into a sunny environment with a captive audience, and I'm not at all sure that it will work. It seems to me that we are in a lose-lose situation. If Club Wicked are chosen then we go out of business; if The Monastery take us over, then the business will probably change so much that I doubt I'll enjoy it any more.'

'I'm sure it will be fine, H-B,' said Brad, surprised that H-B had opened up so readily and concerned that a defeatist attitude was the last thing Greg needed.

'I'm sure it will too,' agreed Hawthorne-Blythe, also realising that he'd gone into more depth than he normally would. 'I'll just have to educate them to our way of thinking as best I can I suppose. Right then, enough of this.' He clapped his hands together. 'Let's get you to the airport.'

Juan hauled Brad's cases out to Hawthorne-Blythe's car. As they were loading them, a Guardia Civil police car pulled up. Two policemen got out with the client Greg recognised as Candice.

'I wonder what they want?' asked Brad. 'What do you think she's done?

'Knowing Candice, she's probably given them a blow job as well,' said Greg.

Brad walked up to one of the policemen; the other marched into the hotel with Candice.

Greg and Hawthorne-Blythe stood watching. Brad came back. 'He doesn't speak any English and my Spanish is crap. Do you want to talk to him, H-B? It's something to do with Hughie.'

As an increasingly grave looking Hawthorne-Blythe spoke to the policeman, the other emerged from the hotel with Hughie . . . in handcuffs.

'What the—?' Brad strode over. 'What's going on? Hughie?'

The policeman became very angry and shoved Hughie into the back of the car. Hawthorne-Blythe came over and said something in Spanish, which seemed to calm the policeman down slightly.

'What's going on, H-B?'

'This client is claiming that Hughie raped her.'

'What?' Brad and Greg were utterly shocked.

'The officer I was just talking to wants to search Hughie's room. I think it might be an idea if we go up there with him.'

'I'll give the airport a call and tell them I've been held up,' said Brad. 'I've got about ten minutes. If the worst comes to the worst, I'll get a cab.'

Hawthorne-Blythe, Brad and Greg followed the policeman upstairs and into Hughie's room. While the policeman started going through Hughie's things, Greg noticed the camcorder on the breakfast bar in the adjoining room.

Carefully, he sidled out of the bedroom and slipped it into his pocket. He didn't know what had been recorded but he had a fair idea its contents probably would not help Hughie's cause.

As he tiptoed back into the bedroom, the policeman had obviously found something. He was pulling out knickers from Hughie's conquests drawer, then got even more excited when he found some leather straps and handcuffs at the bottom. It was clear the policeman thought he had his man. As he marched out of the apartment with his evidence, Hawthorne-Blythe chased after him, protesting in Spanish. Brad walked a few paces behind with Greg.

When they emerged from the hotel, Hawthorne-Blythe turned to Greg and Brad. 'This isn't looking good,' he said. 'You both know Hughie a lot better than me. Is there any possibility at all that you think he could have done it?'

'No way,' said Brad.

'Candice is a nutty single-share,' added Greg. 'She's slept with half the island.'

'And from what I know of Hughie,' added Brad, 'she definitely isn't his type.'

Hawthorne-Blythe shook his head. 'What a mess. That little treasure trove they've just found isn't exactly going to help his case.' He looked at his watch. 'There's not much more I can do for now. I'll quickly run you to the airport, Brad, then I'll pop into the police station on the way back.' He turned to Greg. 'I'm afraid you're going to have to deal with this for now.' Greg looked horrified. 'The policeman said you can have a quick word with Hughie. Find out what you can. If you need me, you've got my mobile number, haven't you?'

Greg nodded. He walked over to the police car and poked his head through the back window. Hughie looked ashen-faced.

'What happened, Hugh?'

'You tell me. That policeman came crashing into my room with Candice. She pointed at me and said, That's him, then the next thing he's shouting at me, roughing me up and manacling me with these handcuffs.'

'She's claiming you raped her.'

'*She's what?*' Hughie was panicked. 'Greg, I swear I didn't.'

'It's all right, mate, you don't have to convince me. Why would she say you had though?'

'I went to her room last night – it was a mistake.'

'So you *did* shag her then?'

'No, no. She wanted me to, she tried to get me to, but I wouldn't . . . I couldn't. She wasn't . . . you know . . .'

'What?'

'Fat,' whispered Hughie. 'I genuinely only fancy big girls, it's not an act. Candice didn't do it for me. I couldn't get a stiffy, so I left. I knew she had the hump but I didn't think she'd pull a stroke like this. What the fuck am I going to do? Can't you tell the police that I only like fat girls?'

'That would make a great defence,' said Greg. 'Maybe we could get all the fat girls you've shagged as character witnesses.' Hughie looked hopeful. 'I'm joking, Hughie. Apart from anything else, we probably wouldn't be able to fit any of them in the witness box.'

Hughie was too worried to find that amusing. 'Shit, Greg, I'm fucked.'

'No, you're not. Leave it with me.'

'What are you going to do?

Before Greg could answer, his phone rang. Sandy.

'Hang on Hughie, won't be a minute.' He walked away from the car.

'Greg!' Hughie called after him.

Greg held his hand up and took the call. 'Hi, Sandy. How's tricks?'

'Not so good. I don't have to come over to Ibiza for work now. The promoter I was meant to be meeting has had to go to Israel for a week.'

'I see.' Greg paused, not sure how to react. 'So aren't you coming to Amnesia?'

'That's what I was ringing about.' There was a pause. 'The

thing is, Greg, I've been thinking about you since I got back. I . . . like you, y'know?'

'Oh, that's . . . good,' said Greg. At this point, his brain was fried.

'The hotel and flight are still booked, but if I come back to Ibiza I'd really only be coming over to see you . . . and to go to the opening of Amnesia, of course. So, I wanted to check that you'd still like to meet up.'

This was not a good time for any decision-making, or for Greg to run through the million things that were going through his mind. All he could think at that particular moment was that Dawn was the past; *Sandy* was the future.

'Of course I want you to come,' he said.

There was a little squeal of delight at the other end of the phone. 'Excellent! We'll have a wicked time, Greg. I know one of the DJs so—'

'Sorry, Sandy, I'm not being rude, but I'm in the middle of a bit of an incident at the hotel. Can we have this conversation a bit later?'

'Of course. Give me a call.'

Greg returned to Hughie.

'Important, was it?'

'Eh?'

'The phone call. I'm just about to be carted off to the nick and all you seem worried about is your points tally.'

'Sorry, it was a call from the UK and I had to take it.' The policeman came up to Greg and indicated it was time to go. 'Look, I promise you I'll come up with something.'

'Yeah, well make sure you come up *with* something and not come up *on* something for once . . . I need you straight for this, Greg.'

Lucas, Alison and Mario were sitting outside the Bon Tiempo when she received the call.

'I don't believe it,' she said grinning. 'Hughie's just been arrested for raping one of his clients.'

'What!' exclaimed Lucas, almost leaping from his seat with joy.

'Who?' asked Mario.

'Oh what was her name . . .?' Alison drummed her fingers on the table. 'Sounds like a fungal infection . . . um . . . Chlam . . . Can . . . Candice. That's it.'

'Candice – shit! I shagged her,' said Mario. 'She's a right old slapper.'

'Yeah, well, best you keep that to yourself,' advised Alison. 'At least until after The Monastery have made their decision. If he's still banged up on Friday, I reckon we've got this in the bag.'

'No thanks to you,' said Lucas. 'After what you did to that client you thought was Stan, you're lucky he didn't accuse *you* of rape.'

Mario tittered. He'd heard all about Alison's case of mistaken identity.

'There's no need to have a go at me,' snapped Alison. 'I gave him head – to help *our* cause, I might add – and it was my money he ended up spending in the casino, seeing as you won't reimburse me.'

'Bloody right too!' replied Lucas. 'The way you've performed this last couple of weeks, there have been times when I think you've actually wanted us to lose. I'm going to the bar.' As he stood up he almost stumbled over the apartment's dog. 'Get out of the bloody way, you manky mutt – Trev's not here to play with you so piss off.'

When Lucas was out of earshot Mario said quietly, 'Suppose we do lose – not that we will, of course – what will you do then?'

'The same as last winter.'

'Is that the sunglasses thing?'

'It's not a "thing", it's a bloody successful little business, especially as I only really need to do it for six months of the year.'

'How come?'

'During the winter I set up all of the accounts, show the shops the new lines and get the orders in. Then in the summer I've got someone who delivers the stock for me and takes the re-orders. I could do that bit myself but I normally earn more over here than I pay the girl I employ, so it works out well. I get the best of both worlds. But if Club Wicked lose I can easily go back and do that.'

'So what, you travel all over the country?'

'Pretty much. That's why I need my car. I'd be lost without my little pride and joy.'

Alison had shown Mario the pictures of her 'pride and joy' enough times for him not to want to pursue that line of conversation. 'I doubt if I'll be back here next year.'

'Why's that?'

'Coral. She's flying over on Friday. Her dad's in the UK at the moment looking at a few scripts. When I go back in September he's going to line up some castings for me. He reckons I've got the look.'

Alison had also heard more than enough of Mario going on about his Hollywood film prospects. 'Yes, you've told me.'

'Coral's great. I mean, I've been out with better looking girls but she's the complete package. And she gets into all the top clubs without queuing or paying.'

'Marvellous.'

Lucas walked back out of the bar talking on his mobile, trying to get a better reception. When he finished the conversation he looked agitated.

'What's up – one of your horses not come in?' asked Alison, who knew all about Lucas's gambling habit.

'Not just one I'm afraid.'

'Trouble?' asked Alison.

'No, not if I go and live somewhere in South America it isn't.'

'It's not that bad, is it?'

'Worse. Let's put it this way, if Club Wicked doesn't get bought out by The Monastery then I'm going to have to sell my houses, cars, the lot.'

'Surely you've got something stashed away,' suggested Mario.

'If I had something stashed away, don't you think I'd be using that before I started selling everything, you moron?'

'It was only a suggestion.'

'Yes, well, I've got a suggestion for you two. If you pair of little darlings could pull out all of the fucking stops so I can carry on with my existing lifestyle, which I actually rather enjoy, I would be *awfully* grateful. Or at the very least, stop cocking things up every time my back's turned. And to think I employed you two to give me an edge.'

'Don't worry, Lucas,' said Alison. 'Now this thing with Hughie has happened, we can't lose.'

'Please don't say that,' said Lucas, holding up a hand, 'because every time you do, something goes horribly wrong . . .'

chapter thirty-four

Arabella hadn't smoked a cigarette for years and even then, she had only ever been the most occasional of smokers. Now though, she needed something to calm her nerves.

It only really struck her after the cruise just how dishy Vaz actually was. It was perfect. Not only was he one of the nicest people she had ever met, but she actually fancied him too – *really* fancied him.

That was the thing about beaches, they were a great leveller. All you had was the person and their body and in Vaz's case, she had never properly noticed what an incredible body it was. A deep, rounded, well-defined chest, muscular legs, strong arms and a six-pack to die for.

One problem of course, was that she had never gone out of her way to be nice to him or to simply be nice full stop – quite the opposite in fact. Vaz had seen her at her absolute worst.

Yet, in the last few days in particular, she sensed that he was actually quite fond of her. What had encouraged her still further was talking to Sugar Ray about it. Sugar was fairly certain that Vaz was interested.

Which was why Arabella now found herself in a petrol station near the hotel, on a hot Wednesday afternoon on the second day in July, about to buy some cigarettes to steady her nerves as she worked out the best way to approach him.

As well as a packet of condoms, just in case her hunch was right.

Vaz had arranged to meet her the next afternoon – he said he had a plan to get back at Mario. Meeting today was out because he had to do a short set at Es Paradis and had gone to Ibiza Town to buy some records.

Arabella had therefore decided to tell Vaz how she felt about him when they were together the next day. She had a gut feeling that something was going to happen between them and it made her both excited and nervous.

As she looked through the condoms, she was dismayed to hear that the young Spanish male cashier spoke perfect English, probably someone who had British parents but was raised in Ibiza, she thought. Arabella didn't embarrass easy, but she was already on tenterhooks over how she was going to say what she wanted to Vaz.

She was also dismayed to see that the only condoms on sale were novelty shapes and flavours.

She waited until the shop was empty and approached the cashier. 'Hello. Could I have a packet of cigarettes and a packet of condoms,' she asked as breezily as possible.

'Sure, what type?'

'Um,' Arabella glanced over at the condoms and gave an embarrassed smile. 'Perhaps the lager-flavoured ones.'

'OK,' replied the cashier deadpan, 'but actually I meant what type of cigarettes . . .'

'Oh right. Marlboro Lights.'

She fumbled in her purse for the money, stuffed the cigarettes and condoms into her handbag, and fled. As she turned the corner a couple of blocks away from the hotel she heard her name being called.

'Arabella!'

It was Greg, running.

'Hi, Greg.'

'Thank God I've found you. Listen, I need your help.'

'Sure, what's wrong?'

'Have you heard about Hughie?'

'What's he done this time?' she laughed, raising her eyebrows in mock despair.

'He's been arrested. Candice has accused him of raping her.'

'Oh my God,' exclaimed Arabella, clasping her hand to her mouth.

'He swears he didn't do it.'

'From what I've heard about her, he wouldn't have to – isn't she the one who performed oral sex on all of those Club Wicked clients?'

'That's her.' They started walking to the hotel. 'The problem is, they've all gone home and I can't exactly see Club Wicked falling over themselves to help us. I've got an idea though and I need your help.'

'What do you want me to do?'

'I'm going to talk to Candice.'

'Is that wise?'

'On my own, probably not. That's why I want you there. I don't really need you to say anything, just nod in the right places and agree with me.'

'What are you planning?'

'I'm not totally sure yet – I'm going to have to improvise.'

'Come in.'

Candice could tell by the look on Greg's face as he walked through the door and the fact he was with Arabella, that it wasn't a social call.

'What do you want?' she snapped.

'I think we need to talk.'

Greg and Arabella both sat on the unoccupied other single bed. The girl who had originally been sharing with Candice had moved after the first night, preferring to pay a single room supplement than put up with her.

'So?' asked Candice, belligerently lighting a cigarette.

'Why, Candice?'

'Why what?'

Greg stared at her. 'You're a liar. I know Hughie didn't rape you.'

'You wasn't here.'

'Hughie didn't even have sex with you,' continued Greg calmly. 'And I know why.' Candice drew a deep lungful of smoke, saying nothing. 'He couldn't get it up because he didn't fancy you. And because he didn't fancy you, you decided to accuse him of rape.'

'Rubbish,' contradicted Candice. 'He forced me to have sex with him.'

'No, Candice,' Greg continued in a calm and deliberate voice, 'you know he didn't and I know he didn't.'

Candice stubbed out the barely smoked cigarette and walked over to the window. 'He's a bastard.'

'Mmm. That he may be. He may also have strange taste in women, but one thing he most definitely isn't, is a rapist.'

'You're all the same, you reps. You think you're God's gift.'

'Candice, come over here and sit down.' Greg pointed to the other bed. 'Please.'

Candice sat down. She hadn't expected Greg to be so calm. She thought he would be yelling and screaming. It had thrown her and now she found it difficult to look him in the eye.

'Let's forget about Hughie for a moment,' said Greg. 'Let's talk about you. Why do you sleep with so many blokes?'

Candice shrugged. 'Why not?'

'But what do you get out of it?'

'I enjoy it of course.'

'But it's just meaningless sex.'

'So?'

'So you don't *have* to do it.'

'I know I don't have to. I do it because I want to. And when I don't want to do it – like with Hughie last night – then no means no.'

This tactic wasn't going as Greg had planned. He felt sure that Candice was mixed up, another Rio, someone who confused sex with love. He thought he would be able to talk her round, to get into her head, for her to have a cathartic moment where she burst into tears on his shoulder, then, as he was telling her everything would be all right, she would agree to drop the charges against Hughie. At the moment, that was not looking a very likely outcome.

'But come on, Candice, it's not normal to give ten blokes a blow job in the same night.'

'Isn't it? So is it normal to have a competition where you get an extra point for shagging a girl up the backside, or getting her to say something stupid while you're doing it.' She noticed the look of surprise on Greg's face. 'What, surely you didn't think this competition of yours is a big secret? Why should it be different for you lot, eh? How many points would you get if you went down on ten girls in a night? It's the age-old story, isn't it? You're Jack-the-lads and we're old slags. Well, fuck you. Fuck the lot of you!'

Greg was a little taken aback by Candice's outburst.

Arabella stepped in. 'You're absolutely right, Candice, but that's not a good enough reason to potentially ruin someone's career and life by saying that they raped you. Hughie could face an awfully long time in prison. In a Spanish prison. Have you any idea what that could be like for him? A sex offender in a foreign jail? Does he really deserve that if he is innocent?' Candice sat stony-faced. 'Candice?'

'It's too late now.'

'No, it's not,' said Greg.

'If I went back on what I said, it would be *me* who gets in trouble.'

'Well, you're in trouble anyway.' Greg reached into his case. Arabella was confused. Candice looked worried. He pulled out an A4 sheet of paper. 'I've been to see the boss of Club Wicked and I have here a list of the names and addresses of those ten guys you gave a blow job to. I've rung them up and while most of them weren't interested, two have said that they'll come back and testify if needs be. Now the last thing I want to do is a character assassination on you, but we all know Hughie is innocent. If needs be, I'll dig even more dirt, and you can guarantee that the British press would love it.' Greg put the piece of paper back into his case. 'So what's it to be, Candice?'

For the first time, Candice looked genuinely concerned. 'But I *can't* say I was lying. I'll get into trouble.'

'I can help,' said Greg. 'But first you've got to be honest with us. Hughie didn't rape you, did he? He didn't even shag you.'

Struggling to hold back the tears, Candice finally broke down. 'I was . . . annoyed. After what happened earlier in the week I felt everyone was laughing at me – I felt used.'

'OK,' said Greg, springing into action. 'What's done is done. Let's concentrate on putting things right. This is what we'll do. If you go back to the police, you're right, you probably will get into trouble. It might not be too serious but why risk it? You're meant to be going home on Saturday, but I can get you on a flight tonight. Also,' Greg reached into his pocket and pulled out three fifty pound notes, 'here's a hundred and fifty quid. Let's just call it compensation for missing the last three days of your holiday. Does that sound acceptable?'

Candice nodded. 'I guess I should say I'm sorry.'

'You can say whatever you like, Candice. I'd rather you left a note though, explaining that you made a mistake and that you want to drop charges. I'll give you this money at the airport tonight. Do we have a deal?'

'Yes.'

'Good. I'll come round personally and take you to the airport later. Be ready to be picked up at just gone nine. I'll see you then.'

Greg picked up his case and strode out of the room, with Arabella tucked in behind him. Once outside he leaned against the wall in the corridor.

'Phew, I thought I'd blown it for a moment there.'

'You did brilliantly. Cometh the hour, cometh the man. I didn't know you'd been to see Club Wicked and got the list of those boys' names and addresses.'

'I hadn't. That sheet of paper was a flight manifest for tonight.'

'Well, it worked. Hughie will be over the moon.'

'I'll give H-B a call and get him to sort things out with the police. We'll probably have to leave Hughie there overnight until Candice has gone.'

'I'm sure he'll think that's a small price to pay for getting the charges dropped.'

They made their way to the lift.

'So, yet another single-share who's turned out to be weird,' remarked Greg.

'Mmm – I'm not sure. I thought she made a very good point. When was the last time you had anything other than meaningless sex? How many times do you have sex when you don't really feel like it, just to score points? All right, maybe Candice hasn't got a race track and a little car with her name on it, and admittedly, it's not the lifestyle that I would pursue, but then again, I doubt if all blokes would want to be in your position either.'

'No? I think most blokes would give their eye teeth to be doing this job. If you ask all the male reps why they applied, then I guarantee that if they're being truthful, most will say it's to meet women. And why do you think so many blokes book to come on a YF&S holiday after programmes like Ibiza Uncovered? It's because they want to get laid. Face it – men and women are different.'

'Or maybe we're just judged differently.' Arabella pressed the call button on the lift. 'I tell you one thing though.'

'What?'

'You might be right about guys being envious of your lifestyle, but I doubt if many would want to be doing it for as long as you have.'

'Fucking hell,' laughed Greg, 'were you speaking to Brad this morning before he left? Is this some kind of conspiracy?'

'No, of course not. It's just Candice may be weird, but then a lot of people might say the same thing about you.' She noticed that Greg had gone unusually quiet. 'Sorry, I didn't mean to cause offence.' They got into the lift 'You're not all that weird.' Arabella tried to lighten the tone. 'Just a bit of a perve.'

Greg's normal reaction to such a comment would have been to grin and say, 'Cheers.'

But now it was just one more thing to think about.

chapter thirty-five

'Be careful!'

Vaz edged himself along the narrow ledge, fifteen metres above the quiet street below. The white walls of the Bon Tiempo apartments were still cool under his palm, despite it being three o'clock in the afternoon of another sweltering hot day.

Arabella nervously peered through the stairwell window that Vaz had just climbed out of. She still couldn't believe that he was risking life and limb to break into Mario's room and retrieve the Polaroids.

Club Wicked were on their Thursday beach party excursion and as it was the final trip of the assessment period, Charles Moon and Kit had decided to go along. Because of this, the reps had pulled out all of the stops to get maximum attendance. The apartments were therefore virtually deserted.

Vaz stretched out to grab hold of the guard rail that ran along the top of Mario's balcony. 'Shit, I can't reach it.'

'Vaz, leave it. Come back. It's not worth it you'll be . . . Vaz!'

Arabella screamed as Vaz leapt to the balcony, grabbing the rail with both hands then deftly hauling himself up.

'There you go. I said it'd be easy,' he said, dusting himself off. 'Come round the front and I'll let you in.'

Moments later, Arabella was in Mario's apartment with Vaz. She thought that she might feel a little strange, but she felt nothing.

'Right,' said Vaz, 'I'll check the living room, you take the bedroom. If they're in here, we'll find them.'

It wasn't long before Arabella found all sorts of evidence that Mario had been anything but faithful during their time together. Letters from other girls, photos, even a little booklet listing his conquests. Surely, she thought, I should be upset or angry, given how little time has passed? Yet she didn't and the reason, she suspected, was banging around in the room next door.

She had met up briefly with Vaz for a bite to eat the previous evening prior to his DJ spot at Es Paradis. She smiled to herself. Vaz had still been very careful not to overstep the mark but it was now obvious he fancied her. The most amazing part of it was the respect he offered her. She felt a warm glow as she recalled his words at Espalmador a couple of weeks earlier, when he said he'd treat any girl he was with like a princess.

After the meal Vaz walked her to her room and they kissed . . . properly. It had been wonderful and the fact that he made no attempt to take things further made her want him all the more. Even better was that there had been no awkwardness when they met up again. They both felt the anticipation and the excitement and it was as though neither wanted to risk breaking its spell.

Underneath Mario's bed, Arabella found a small sports bag. There were various videos and a ridiculous red leather posing pouch, which, thankfully, Mario had spared her. At the bottom of the bag she found what she was looking for. She was relieved that the Polaroids were all relatively tame, although still far too explicit for her to even contemplate her father seeing.

'Vaz, I've got them.'

Vaz came into the room. She waved them at him.

'Excellent, though I'd rather not see them if it's all the same to you.'

'Don't worry. I'm going to rip them up into little shreds.'

Vaz took in Mario's bedroom. On a little table by the entrance to the en-suite bathroom, he spotted the Polaroid camera. Suddenly, he had an idea, part designed to stitch up Mario and part to heighten the growing expectation between him and Arabella.

'Arabella – do you fancy giving Mario a taste of his own medicine?'

'How?'

'I've just remembered something Brad told me about how they got their own back on Alison last year. Apparently Mario videoed himself shagging her and Brad got hold of the tape, then switched it during the showing of the beach party video so all the clients saw it. I think Alison's mum and dad were over at the time too.'

'I heard about that.'

'Well, it's given me an idea. You know he's been seeing some American girl who's dad's a film director, don't you?'

'Her name's Coral. He took great pleasure in telling me. She's coming over tomorrow.'

'Exactly. What if she thinks he's still seeing you?'

'He'd deny it. You know what a convincing liar he is.'

'But what if there was proof.'

'These pictures are no good. He'll just say they're from last year. In fact, he's even written the date on them.'

'So what about if there was a more current picture? One taken of you being naughty, in this room. We can write today's date on the bottom – it'd be difficult to deny.'

'Are you suggesting what I think you are?'

Vaz picked up the camera. 'It doesn't have to be too explicit. Just topless on his bed will do. Nothing I haven't seen before.'

'But he could send it to my father.'

'Like I said, it doesn't have to be too explicit. Besides, I'm sure he's bluffing. You told me he didn't have your parents' address.'

Arabella's mouth went slightly dry, as she found herself getting quite turned on by the idea. 'OK,' she said, a coy smile forming. 'Give me a moment to go into the bathroom.'

Vaz thought that she was taking longer than needed to get undressed. He assumed she was feeling shy. In fact, Arabella was applying full make-up.

She emerged from the bathroom with a towel around her and her hair tumbling over her shoulders.

'Now then, where do you want me?'

Vaz felt a stirring. 'On the bed, of course.'

Vaz was only wearing tracksuit bottoms and Arabella was pleased to notice the effect she was having on him. It encouraged her to play up even more.

She dropped the towel and knelt on the bed, her back arched. There was now no doubting the fact that Vaz was attracted to her.

'Jesus,' moaned Vaz, 'how could Mario not fancy someone as sexy as you?'

Arabella giggled, then turned towards him, cupping her left breast with her hand. 'Was something like this what you had in mind?'

Vaz could contain himself no longer. He moved towards the bed, bent down, placed his hand behind Arabella's neck and kissed her. She pulled him towards her, then rolled onto her back as he laid on top of her. She could feel him hard against her leg. Urgently, she tugged at his tracksuit bottoms and Vaz quickly slipped out of them.

Once Vaz was naked on the bed, Arabella jumped up and got the packet of condoms from her bag.

Vaz looked at her. 'I thought this was all my idea.'

Laughing, Arabella took out the condom packet. 'These were all they had, I'm afraid.'

'Lager flavoured?' Vaz smiled. 'I always had you marked down as a Pimm's or champagne girl.'

Arabella pushed him back onto the bed, and tore open the condom packet with her teeth.

'Well, now I'm with a Peckham boy, I suppose I'll just have to re-educate my palate . . .'

'I can't believe it's my last night,' sighed Dawn, slipping her arm through Greg's, as they walked down the cobbled streets of Ibiza's old town, Dalt Vila. Little Greg was proudly sat upon his father's shoulders, pretending he had an imaginary bow and arrow, which he was firing at everyone they passed.

'We've had a fantastic time, Greg . . . thanks to you. I was so nervous about bringing Little Greg over to see you. I didn't know how you'd react, whether you'd be able to forgive me for not telling you straight away.'

Greg lifted his son from his shoulders and they watched him run down the hill. 'How can I be angry when you've got such a fantastic kid?'

Dawn stopped and looked Greg in the eye. 'We, Greg, we've got a fantastic kid.'

Greg fell into silence for a few moments. 'You're his mum, Dawn. You've brought him up, done all of the hard work. I'm just a man he's played football and slid down some water chutes with.' Little Greg had stopped by an ice cream shop and was impatiently waiting for them to catch up.

'I haven't told him that you're his father yet, but I had to be sure that you were . . . well, able to cope, get on with him, all that kind of stuff.'

'It's all right, Dawn, I understand.'

'The thing is, you've been better with him than I could ever have imagined.'

'That's probably because I'm still just a big kid myself.'

Dawn shook her head. 'You're not, Greg. You don't realise it but you've grown up a lot.'

'I was only joking.'

'Yes, I know you were but I'm serious. I don't know what's going through that head of yours and I don't know if you're ready for the responsibility, but I do know you make a great dad.'

'Thanks.'

'Which is why I'm about to do this. I hope I'm not wrong about you.'

They had just about caught up with Little Greg.

'Can I have an ice cream, Mummy?'

'Yes, in a minute.' She picked him up and sat him on a wall. 'Now then, Greg, there's something important I have to tell you. You know how some of the other boys and girls at nursery have mummies *and* daddies, and sometimes you ask me where your daddy is?'

'Dawn, you don't have to—' Greg began then lapsed into silence.

Little Greg nodded, his innocent eyes staring out intently from beneath his foppish fringe.

'Well, one of the reasons that we came out here is that I wanted you to meet your daddy. But I wanted to be sure that you liked him first. Do you like Greg?' Little Greg nodded. 'So would you be pleased if I told you that Greg is your daddy?'

Greg looked helplessly at the little boy, praying that he didn't burst into tears, or run off in a temper tantrum.

Little Greg's face slowly broke into a smile. 'That's silly. He's got the same name as me.'

'I know,' said Dawn. 'Big Greg and Little Greg.'

Little Greg found this highly amusing and started giggling infectiously. Greg breathed a huge sigh of relief.

'If he's my daddy,' said Little Greg when he'd stopped laughing, 'does that mean he can buy me an ice cream?'

'We'd better be going, it's nearly eight o'clock. Mario will be back soon.'

Gently, Vaz kissed the end of her nose. 'You're a sexy little thing, aren't you?'

Arabella giggled. 'You must bring out the best in me.'

'Arabella, I mean it. I'd love us to have a proper relationship but even if we don't, trust me when I tell you that you are absolutely fantastic. Forget about what anybody else has said, or how anyone else has made you feel, you are the dog's bollocks.'

Arabella brushed his cheek with the outside of her hand, kissed him then snuggled into his chest. 'Just a couple more minutes.'

She was blissfully happy. Their love-making had been the

most incredible she had ever experienced. He was tender and passionate, strong and quietly confident. He spoke to her throughout, telling her what he was going to do, telling her how much she turned him on. He was incredibly supple and after three hours had proven that there was nothing wrong with his level of fitness either.

The second time they made love was less intense but relaxed and just as enjoyable, and as Vaz came, he aimed for Mario's pillow, which although she pretended to be shocked, Arabella found highly amusing.

Arabella kissed him on the chest and nestled in still further. 'What happened to the you-can't-screw-the-crew rule?'

'I always thought the rule was that you didn't get caught. Anyway,' Vaz jumped out of bed, 'I'm not crew any more, am I?'

'Mmm,' Arabella sat up, 'maybe I should go out and buy Alison a little present.'

'Why would you do that?'

'Because,' Arabella slid across to the edge of the bed, put her arms round his waist and rested her head on his tummy, 'if she hadn't put those pills in your bag then you wouldn't be here now.'

Arabella reached across to the bedside cabinet for the Polaroid Vaz had taken of her earlier.

Vaz sat next to her and looked at it. 'Wow. It seems a shame to waste such a sexy picture on Mario.'

'We can take some more risky ones another time if you like,' giggled Arabella, picking up her bag and opening it.

'Now you're talking.' He noticed her searching through her bag. 'What are you looking for?'

Arabella held aloft a felt pen. 'This.' On the bottom of the photograph she wrote the date and added:

This room is better than last year's! Got to get a photo of your birthmark! A xxx

'What's that all about?' asked Vaz.

'Well, hopefully Coral will think I'm a long-term fling.'

'And the birthmark?'

Arabella giggled again. 'Mario's got a little birthmark on his willy.'

'No!' laughed Vaz.

'I thought mentioning it would add more cred.'

'Genius,' said Vaz. He took the picture from her. 'It's a really nasty thing to do though, isn't it? And you look so bloody sexy in this photo it seems a shame not to keep it.'

'Are you serious?'

'Yeah. I mean, suppose he somehow gets to it before her? If we just leave it here there's every chance that could happen.'

'Mmm, you may be right.

'Plus, I know he's a nasty piece of work, but why sink to his level?'

Arabella took the photo. 'I tell you what. Why don't we keep it as security? If he does anything else, then maybe we'll use it then, agreed?'

'Agreed.'

She took his face in her hands and kissed him. 'I can't believe that after all he's done, you can still be so forgiving.'

'It's got nothing to do with being forgiving,' said Vaz, rolling on top of her, 'I just don't want him having any pictures of my girlfriend.'

'A-ha,' teased Arabella, wiping a droplet of sweat from his brow. 'So I'm your girlfriend, am I?'

'Do you want to be?'

She started kissing him. Things very quickly became extremely passionate again and within moments, Vaz was using the last condom, stopping only to say, 'I'll take that as a yes then, shall I?'

Dawn opened the door to her apartment as Greg carried in Little Greg, who was fast asleep, took him straight into the bedroom, got him undressed and tucked him up in bed.

When he came back into the living room, Dawn was sitting on the balcony. The sun had just set and the scattering of dappled clouds looked as though their bottoms had been dipped into a reddish-ochre paint pot.

Dawn let out a contented sigh – things couldn't have been more perfect. The truth was that she had never stopped thinking about Greg, though she was too practical to go so far as to say that she had never stopped loving him. She knew that theirs had been a holiday romance that promised much but realised little.

He was by no means perfect. She hadn't expected him to have become such a big clubber and he still seemed to have a problem looking too far into the future. The signs were good though. Despite Greg's initial fears, Dawn got the impression that he was getting quite a lot of satisfaction out of being resort manager, and was particularly pleased to have helped Hughie, who had been released that afternoon.

And the way he had been around Little Greg had been amazing. In a way, that was what was troubling her.

Dawn was almost certain that she still had very strong feelings for Greg. She tried not to allow it, but a little daydream of them all being together as a happy family kept pushing its way into her head. It scared her. It made her question whether her feelings for Greg were as genuine as she felt them to be, or whether the appeal was as much the logic of having her son's father as her partner.

The one thing she was sure of was that it was her last night and something had to be said or done.

Greg came out and leaned on the balcony next to her. 'He's fast asleep – totally exhausted.'

'I know how he feels.' Dawn stretched and yawned, her short dress riding over her hips and pulling tight across her underwear free bust. She noticed Greg quickly take in her form. She ran her fingers through her hair, then leaned against the wall. Perhaps nothing would need to be said after all? She looked Greg in the eye, nervously biting her lip as her breathing quickened.

Greg reached out and took her hand. He stepped towards her until he was so close she could feel his warm breath on her cheek. He brushed his lips against hers then kissed her forehead. He pulled back slightly to look deep into her eyes, as if he wasn't entirely sure that this was what she wanted.

Dawn stood on tiptoe, cupped Greg's face in her hands and kissed him. As their kissing became more passionate, Greg pinned her against the wall, stretching her arms out and gently running his tongue from the inside of her wrist to the nape of her neck. Dawn let out a little moan and pushed against him. He pulled her dress up and she quickly wriggled out of it, her large breasts bouncing free to Greg's obvious approval.

Greg took the cushions from the plastic chairs on the balcony and put them on the floor. Dawn lay on them, raising her hips and slipping off her tiny thong. Greg threw off his trainers and his trousers, ducking behind the balcony as his erection sprang free. He knelt between her legs, then leaned forward and kissed her. All Dawn wanted was to feel him inside her and as Greg gently fulfilled her wish, it was blissfully clear that he felt exactly the same.

And for once, points were the last thing on his mind.

Trev was pleasantly surprised when Alison knocked on his door. She had not responded to any of his recent invitations to pay him a visit.

'Come in! How's tricks?'

'Busy. I can't stop.'

'That's a shame,' replied Trev, realising that she probably hadn't come round for a session. Still, he had to try. 'Do you want a drink?'

'No thanks.'

Trev shooed the hotel mongrel from the armchair so Alison could sit down.

'Trev, people are going to start talking about you and that dog if you're not careful.'

'He just wants a bit of affection. The bastards at the hotel who own him don't give him any – I don't think they even feed him.'

Alison sat down. 'So, big day tomorrow.'

'Of course, you've got to do the presentation to The Monastery bigwigs, haven't you?'

'Yes, at midday.'

'So you won't be going to the opening of Amnesia tonight then?'

'No. A quick bit of revision then beddy-byes for me I'm afraid. What about you?'

'I'll put my head round the door for a couple of hours. I'm not planning a late one.'

'That's good.' Alison twirled her hair round her finger. 'Trev,' she said in a sing-song, child-like voice, 'you know how after we have sex you always fall asleep.'

'Not always.'

'No, but most of the time.'

'Well, occasionally maybe.'

'Yes, well, whatever. Anyway, you know how I'm always the total opposite. Like I could run a marathon, conquer the world . . . on a total high.'

Trev knew only too well – it drove him mad. 'Yes,' he replied slowly, not sure where this was leading.

'Well, I want to feel like that tomorrow. I want to go into that meeting to do my presentation feeling like a million dollars, ready to knock 'em dead.'

Trev thought he got the gist of where this was leading. 'OK.'

'So I was thinking that maybe I could come round here about eleven tomorrow morning and we could have a mad, no-holds-barred session. I'll even dress up for you if you like,' she added seductively.

Trev could feel himself getting an erection just at the thought. 'Sounds great. But why don't you just stay tonight?'

Alison shook her head. 'I can't. I need to get things prepared for tomorrow and get a good night's sleep. I think your snoring would put pay to that. No, I'll come round just before eleven, if that's all right with you?'

'Of course it's all right,' replied Trev, unable to believe his luck.

'Good,' replied Alison, standing up and heading for the

door. She pecked him on the cheek. 'And Trev,' she added, as she stepped into the corridor, 'promise me there'll be no delay spray this time.'

chapter thirty-six

Greg gently pulled his arm from under Dawn. She'd fallen asleep. It was twenty minutes to midnight.

Sleeping with Dawn again had been very special. It was the first time for as long as he could remember that he actually cared about the person he was making love to, rather than trying to think of something different to do so that he could tell the rest of the lads about it afterwards.

He went to the kitchen to get some water. His mobile was on the breakfast bar and he noticed the message received light was flashing. It was from Sandy.

Landed OK. Sorted guest list. Meet you in VIP at 12.45 as arranged.

Shit! The special intimacy of the last few hours, the rekindling of his feelings for Dawn, the enormity of the decision he had to make regarding what role to play in Little Greg's life, the commitment they represented, the Big C, had caused him to completely forget the night that had been dominating his thoughts for over a week.

Part of him still wanted to go to Amnesia. He now had absolutely no intention of sleeping with Sandy, but perhaps, he thought, if he went, it would confirm that the decision he felt inclined to make about Dawn was the right one. Yet once he was in that environment, once he had taken a pill ... Greg knew himself well enough to know that rational thought would not be his primary attribute. But he couldn't stand her up. Sandy had come all the way out from the UK just for this night.

He took the phone into the corridor and dialled. He didn't have a clue what he was going to say. As it turned out, it didn't matter. The phone went straight to her UK voice mail. There was no point in leaving a message because Sandy had previously told him that she could not pick them up in Ibiza. For a moment, he considered sending a text, but dismissed the idea almost immediately. The more he thought about it, the more he realised that, uncharacteristically, he'd led Sandy to believe that there was more to their fling than there was and he felt he should at least tell her to her face. Clearly, it wouldn't be fair to mention Dawn. He would say that he had to do a very important presentation the next day and couldn't stay at Amnesia – she would be bound to know people there. He'd tell Dawn the same thing – it was the easiest way.

He deleted the text, put the phone back on the breakfast bar and went back into the bedroom.

Dawn stirred. 'Hey you,' she purred.

'Sorry, I didn't mean to wake you.'

'That's OK. What are you doing?'

'I've got to go.'

Dawn rubbed her eyes. 'Why?'

'I've got to do that presentation tomorrow.'

'What presentation?'

'The presentation to The Monastery.' Greg cursed himself for not priming Dawn. 'I'm sure I told you about it.'

Dawn sat up. 'If you did, I can't remember.'

'It's really important. I've got to do a summary in front of all the bigwigs, highlighting why YF&S are the company that should be taken over. Alison's got to do one too. Brad was supposed to do ours but now I've taken over as resort manager . . .'

'Oh,' replied Dawn, obviously disappointed. 'What time do you have to do it?'

'Noon, but I've got to do some preparation first. I don't want to go to sleep with any uncertainty on my mind, I want to wake up confident that I know exactly how I'm going to play it. I really need to run through it a couple of times before I go to sleep tonight, then again in the morning.'

'So when will I see you? I've got to be at the airport for no later than eleven-thirty.'

'I'll come down and see you just before you go.'

Dawn looked concerned. 'I hope you weren't just thinking of popping in and saying "see ya" . . . we've got things to talk about.'

'I know, of course we have, we'll have plenty of time . . . I promise.'

Dawn seemed to relax. 'OK.' She stood up and gave him a lingering kiss. 'We'll see you tomorrow morning.'

Greg scurried from the room as quickly as possible, hating himself for having to lie to Dawn. Yet he'd hate himself almost as much if he left a girl who had travelled the best part of two thousand miles to see him, standing alone in a club. It was a lose-lose situation.

After he showered and got changed, he made sure that everything was ready for the next morning's presentation. Thankfully, Brad had had the foresight to prepare overhead projection transparencies as well as a comprehensive point by point synopsis of how he thought YF&S would be best represented. Greg had no reason (or time) to change any of Brad's ideas, so all he'd had to do was learn its content then use his natural presentation skills to convey it as effectively as possible. He had been through it all several times and he was confident that a quick read-through in the morning before the presentation would be enough.

He looked at his watch – it was just gone twelve-thirty. Even on the Harley that Stan had let him keep on hire for a few days, he was probably going to be a little late, so he decided to try to call Sandy again.

It was then that he realised he'd been in such a hurry to get out of Dawn's room, he'd left his mobile there.

For a moment, he had a sick feeling, as he quickly tried to remember if his phone contained any incriminating messages. He had been with Dawn for most of the week so had been careful to screen his calls and to wipe off texts from Rio and the two he had received from Sandy. No, he convinced himself, leaving his phone with Dawn was not going to present him with a problem. He wasn't going to need to call anybody, nor was he expecting anybody to call him. Greg relaxed and grabbed the keys to the Harley.

The opening of Amnesia, one of the nights he had been looking forward to all winter – he'd never expected it to turn out anything like this.

At first, Dawn thought it was an alarm clock.

It took her a few moments to realise where she was. As soon as Greg had left she had immediately fallen into a deep sleep on the sofa.

The noise stopped before she could find its source. She sat up, smiling to herself, reminded of how wonderful the day and evening had been.

There were another two short beeps, which she recognised as a text message. The tone was different to hers and she quickly deduced that Greg must have left his in the room.

She went over to the breakfast bar and picked up Greg's phone. The small Samsung indicated that there had been one missed call and an incoming message. She put the phone down and went to the fridge to get some water.

The mobile sat there, growing with every second, dominating the room and drawing Dawn back to it. She was not a naturally suspicious person, but her hopes and expectations for Greg were high. In the end curiosity got the better of her.

She pressed the 'Missed Call' button. The name that came up was 'Sandy UK'. Her first thought, more optimistic that realistic, was that Sandy could be male. The incoming message quickly confirmed this not to be the case.

Got to Amnesia a bit early. It's wicked. Can't wait 2 c u. In VIP. Sandy xxx.

She read it again. Sandy could be male. After all, she thought, I put kisses on the end of messages to some of my girlfriends. But do guys do that? More to the point, would any of Greg's friends do that? What about the gay rep?

Wasn't his name something like Sandy? But if it was, why would he put 'can't wait 2 c u'?

It didn't take much time for the obvious to become apparent. Greg had clearly lied about staying in to do his paperwork and had gone to Amnesia to meet a girl called Sandy.

Dawn felt numb. She walked into Little Greg, fast asleep, a four-year-old unaware that he too had been betrayed by the man who had been introduced as his father just hours before. She walked back on to the balcony, the cushions on the floor now making her feel almost physically sick.

She checked on Little Greg again then slipped on a sweatshirt and tracksuit bottoms, took Greg's phone and quietly left the room. She wasn't expecting to find Greg in, but went to his room and knocked on his door anyway. Sure enough, there was no answer.

She went down to reception then looked outside the hotel and the Harley was gone. The night porter was asleep in the back room, so Dawn left Greg a note and put the mobile in his pigeon-hole.

The numbness started to fade and as Dawn stepped into the lift, she felt a pain that she had not felt for many years. She looked at herself in the lift mirror, tears now rolling down her face.

'You idiot.'

chapter thirty-seven

Whenever Greg went out on a special club night, he always had the same set of feelings.

Prior to leaving home or just after he left, his stomach tightened and he would feel slightly nauseous. It was almost like an internal salivation, an intestinal Pavlov's dog anticipating yet another influx of MDMA. Then, as he approached the club, he would find his pace quickening, anxious to be past the queue and in the thick of it. As soon as he was in, he would take a pill and find some friends to start buzzing off to make the pill kick in as quickly and as effectively as possible.

This time though, there had been none of that. Once he had negotiated San Antonio and started the relatively short journey along the Ibiza Town road on which the club was situated, the nagging guilt of leaving Dawn began to dominate his thoughts.

The walk from the car park to the club was made at near funereal pace rather than his usual urgent trot. Once in the club itself, he felt absolutely no compulsion to take a pill, nor in any great hurry to get to see Sandy in the VIP. Instead, he took a slow walk around the club, trying to work out what to say to her.

Something was different, other than the fact he wasn't buzzing. The music was as good as ever, if not better, and the club already had the kind of atmosphere that would normally have had Greg bouncing off the walls. But now, it all seemed so unimportant. It was as if he had been transported there as a visitor from another planet, trying to make sense of the bizarre ritual before him.

And for the first time, he couldn't.

For the best part of the last year, he had lived for the weekend. As summer approached, all he had been able to think about and look forward to were nights like tonight. Nothing else was remotely as important. To be accepted as a fully-fledged member of the Chemical Generation was all that mattered. It was his chosen playing field and he wanted to be recognised as a player within it. Which, he now realised, was one of the reasons Sandy had seemed so attractive.

He made his way upstairs, bumping into Trev on the way. Trev told him that he was seeing Alison the next morning and asked Greg if he could get hold of any more Viagras. Greg told him he couldn't and as soon as a disappointed Trev disappeared downstairs, mumbling he'd need an early night to keep his strength up, Greg found a spot by a pillar where he could see the VIP section but could not be seen by those in it. It wasn't long before he caught sight of Sandy. He watched her for a while. She was clearly already buzzing, expertly working the room, flirting with guys Greg half-recognised as DJs, chatting to island and industry movers and shakers.

Greg didn't resent her, he didn't feel in awe of her. He didn't feel jealous, superior, inferior . . . he didn't feel anything. And that was the problem. Sandy's appeal had been within the clubbing context. Consequently, distancing himself from that environment also removed most of her appeal. She was undoubtedly sexy, attractive and still had that special enigmatic quality that drew men to her but watching her now, all Greg could see was points, a way of moving his toy E-Type further round the race-track.

And after the events of the last few days, Greg needed, at the very least, a long pit stop.

He made his way out of the main room onto the terrace. He was walking towards the exit when he was spotted by Ace, standing at a bar with Mikey and Patricia.

'Oi, Greg,' he yelled, 'over here.'

Greg made his way over.

'I didn't expect to see you here,' said Mikey shaking his hand, 'I thought you'd be having an early night ready for the big presentation.'

'He's come to meet up with that bird Sandy, the one he went to the opening of Space with,' said Ace. 'I think there was a bonus point up for grabs if you nailed her, wasn't there?'

Greg nodded. 'I'm going to blow her out though.'

'You're what? Why?'

'Oh you know . . .' Greg tried to change the conversation. He reached out for Ace's drink. 'Let's have a drop of your beer, mate.'

'Um, I wouldn't do that if I were you,' suggested Ace, pulling the glass away from him.

'What have you laced it with?'

'Actually, I've pissed in it.'

'You what?'

'I get so fed up with sad ponces in clubs coming up to me all the time and gurning, "Can I have a swig of your beer mate?" that I thought I'd have a spare drink just for them.'

'That's disgusting.'

'Yeah, I know. Here,' he said, passing him a different glass, 'this one's all right.'

'Cheers.'

'So anyway, why aren't you bothering with Sandy?' persisted Ace.

Greg took a deep breath. 'You know that I've been seeing quite a lot of Dawn since she got here?'

'What, the girl with the kid who *dumped* you in your first season.'

'Yeah. Well the reason she *dumped* me,' replied Greg, 'was that when she finished her holiday and went back to the UK she discovered she was pregnant – with my child.'

Ace spluttered into his beer, Patricia's bottom jaw dropped and a smile slowly spread across Mikey's face.

'That explains a lot,' said Mikey nodding.

'You're a fucking dad!' exclaimed Ace.

Greg nodded. 'I've been getting to know Little Greg –

that's his name.' He gave a sheepish smile, part proud and part embarrassed. 'He's a fantastic little kid. Really smart.'

'Smart? Have you done a paternity test?' joked Ace.

Greg ignored him.'Then today, she told him I was his dad.'

'Aaah,' cooed Patricia.

'How did he take it?' asked Mikey.

'Great. He just asked if I'd buy him an ice cream.' Greg laughed.

'So how have you and Dawn been getting on?' asked Patricia.

He took another swig of Ace's beer and ran his hand through his hair. 'It's been a bit weird. We've got on brilliantly but it's like, I don't know . . . I've been keeping her at arm's length. I didn't want to give her the wrong impression, make promises I couldn't keep. But then tonight, we'd had such a special day, it seemed so right . . .'

'What, you boned her?' asked Ace excitedly. 'Nice one, I think you should award yourself a bonus point for that.'

Greg shot Ace a furious look.

'What?' protested Ace, holding his arms out innocently.

'You can be so insensitive,' said Patricia.

'Yeah, well, I'm not the prick who's just shagged the mother of his kid for the first time in God knows how many years, then left her to come to the opening of Amnesia to meet some other girl.'

'Thanks, Ace,' said Greg. He paused. 'You're right – I am a prick. All I wanted during the winter was this.' He looked around the club. 'I've been in Ibiza for over five years and this has been going on without me. I wanted to be part of it, in the thick of it. I had it all planned, it was meant to be so easy. Then all of a sudden, I'm getting responsibility thrust at me from all directions. First of all I'm asked to be resort manager, then I'm told I'm a dad . . . it's all too much. I came out here to be *irresponsible*.'

'And where's Dawn now?' asked Patricia.

'I left her in her room and told her I had to prepare for the presentation tomorrow,' said Greg, shame-faced. 'Like

Ace said, I was supposed to be meeting this girl Sandy. She's a clubbing babe, knows everyone, seems really cool. I thought she was just what I wanted. But after what happened today, with Little Greg, Dawn . . .'

'You should have asked me,' said Ace. 'That Sandy isn't cool – she's a donut and a Jockey Slut.'

'A what?'

'A DJ groupie. To be honest I'm surprised you got a look in. She's probably using you more than you were going to use her.'

Rather than feel disappointed, Greg actually felt relieved by Ace's revelation. 'How do you know?'

'Unlike you, mate, I've been clubbing for years. I've seen her around, you get to hear things.'

'Now you tell me.' Greg pulled up a stool. 'Well, seeing as you're such a clubbing veteran, explain to me why suddenly it doesn't seem the same any more.'

'A-ha,' answered Ace, 'now that's the thing with clubbing. When you first start you have a few really special nights that you measure all subsequent ones against. It might be the music, a brilliant pill or just getting off with someone you really fancy. Instead of an E you feel like you've taken a pill that makes you the wittiest, most popular man on the planet, the best dancer in the universe and the greatest lover in the history of mankind. Who wouldn't want to experience that again? So what do you do? You chase the buzz. Suddenly, you don't want to miss a night in case you're missing out on *that* night, the night where you feel like you did at the beginning. But it never happens, or if you're lucky, it *sometimes* happens. What's for sure is it doesn't happen often enough to justify all those nights out, all those pills and God knows what else chucked down your neck, all that sleep lost, all those comedowns . . .'

'So what's the answer?' asked Greg, with a hint of despair in his voice. 'I'd hate never to go clubbing again.'

'You still can but the only way to recapture that initial buzz is to take a step back from it all. Stop chasing it. Only go out when there's something worth going out for. Pick and choose your nights.'

Greg nodded. 'You're probably right.'

'There's no probably about it. So why don't you do yourself a favour and fuck off back to your apartment, get a good night's sleep, then get up in the morning and do what you've got to do with Dawn? She doesn't know you've come here and what she doesn't know won't hurt her.'

'Fucking hell, Ace,' said Greg. 'You're the last person I expected to be telling me I should be sensible. But what should I do about Sandy? Should I go and explain things to her?'

'Fuck that,' said Ace. 'She'll be fine. I don't want to piss on your fireworks, mate, but she probably only wanted to have you here as a bit of a safety net in the slim chance that she didn't know anyone else in Amnesia. Just leave her. She'll have a slightly bruised ego, nothing more.'

'Are you sure?'

'Trust me.'

'OK. In that case I'd better be heading back to the hotel – big day ahead. Thanks Ace.'

'Don't mention it. Right then,' he finished off his drink, 'good luck tomorrow. I'm off.'

'Where are you going?'

Ace looked at Greg as though he had forgotten his name. 'Up to the VIP of course. If you're not going to get the points with Sandy then one of us should. See you later . . .'

chapter thirty-eight

Friday, 4 July. D-Day.

Rio was surprised not to see Greg at Amnesia.

She finished dancing at the Labiarinth Strip Club at five in the morning and went straight to Amnesia. It was very busy but had Greg been there, she was certain she would have seen him, or at the very least, heard he was somewhere around. She could not get him out of her head: She had never been dumped before. When she saw him again it was going to be a toss up between wanting to fuck him, kill him or marry him.

Amnesia was still busy when she left at eight in the morning. Tanya had invited a few people back to her villa. She hadn't invited Rio directly, but Rio knew there would be quite a lot of cocaine on offer, so had invited herself regardless.

Tanya's villa in San Augustin wasn't too far from San Antonio. After a couple of hours and a good couple of grams of cocaine, the idea of going to Greg's apartment one last time seemed increasingly appealing.

The antique grandfather clock in Tanya's hallway struck eleven. Rio did one last line, said her goodbyes and within ten minutes had left, much to Tanya and everyone else's relief. None of them thought it was a good idea for her to go to Greg's, but all told her exactly the opposite just to be rid of her.

'Thank God she's gone,' said one of Tanya's other guests. 'Who's the poor guy she's going to see?'

'Some holiday rep who dumped her,' replied Tanya. 'She's going to find out why.'

'I wouldn't like to be in his shoes,' said the guest. 'She's a fucking psycho.'

'I know,' agreed Tanya, nodding, 'believe me, I know . . .'

Trev was almost bursting with excitement. Quarter past eleven couldn't come quickly enough. He was dying to have sex with Alison. It had got to the stage where he didn't care if it was all over quickly. After the last effort, all he wanted to do was to be inside her. If she didn't come then, tough, he could finish her off with his fingers. Sometimes he felt that was the only reason she came to see him anyway.

He had tidied his flat, poured some wine, chopped out some coke, even trimmed his pubes to make his knob look bigger. He'd closed his Venetian blinds to stop the bright sunlight flooding his flat and a Chilled Ibiza CD drifted from his speakers to set the mood.

He had decided to hold off the actual act for as long as possible, because he knew it would be over within minutes – probably seconds if she'd dressed up in stockings and suspenders as she had threatened. It was abundantly clear however, that by allowing just over half an hour her expectations were not too great.

Just before eleven-fifteen there was a knock on the door. He leapt up and opened it before she'd reached the third knock. Alison was carrying a bag and wearing a raincoat and high heels, despite it being in the mid-twenties outside.

'Room service,' she said, licking bright red lips, and flashed open her coat to reveal a basque complete with stockings and suspenders.

Trevor gulped.

If he were a betting man he would have had a good few quid on him not making it beyond eleven-thirty.

Despite being tired when he returned from Amnesia, Greg had spent a couple of hours preparing for the presentation before going to bed. He had intended to pop back down to reception when he remembered that he didn't have his mobile and therefore no alarm call, but he had forgotten and fallen asleep.

He was therefore horrified when he woke up and discovered it was ten to eleven. Dawn was due to leave at eleven, quarter past at the absolute latest. Plus he wanted to have another quick read-through of his presentation before he was due to deliver it at twelve in the Hotel Arena's boardroom.

He leaped out of bed, quickly slipped on some shorts and dashed to Dawn's room. En route, it crossed his mind that he was surprised she hadn't come round to his apartment to wake him up. Unless she had of course and he'd been so comatose that he'd slept through it.

He knocked on her door full of anticipation. After leaving Amnesia, the more he thought about it, the more he realised that making a go of it with Dawn was what he wanted to do. He wasn't sure if what he felt for her was love, but it was certainly different to how he'd felt about any other girl and he wanted to spend as much time with her as possible. And as for Little Greg . . . again he didn't want to jump the gun, but if things with Dawn did work out, then his son was everything he could possibly want.

When there was no answer, he knocked again and called out her name, worried that she may have slept in. But then he remembered Little Greg and how unlikely that would be with a boisterous four-year-old who was, by all accounts, full of life before eight o'clock every morning.

Assuming they were in the bar waiting for him, he bounded down the stairs. He skipped into the bar with a smile on his face, which soon disappeared when he saw they were not there either. Confused he went to the reception.

'Juan, have you seen Dawn and Little Greg?'

'Your friend? Yes she go to airport, maybe fifteen minutes. I call for her a taxi.'

Greg could not understand what had happened. Then he looked at his pigeon-hole and saw a sheet of paper with his phone.

Greg

I trusted you and let you into my son's life. I really believed that there was something special between us and that Little Greg meant something to you. I was wrong – you haven't grown up at all.

I could carry on writing about how I feel and what you've done to me for pages, but I have wasted enough of my life with you in my head.

I hope Sandy was worth it. Do you get any bonus points for breaking someone's heart?

Dawn

More than anything else it was the sadness and bitterness contained within the short letter that upset him. He had lost her again and, this time, he was responsible . . . or should that be irresponsible?

He looked at the mobile phone and saw the message from Sandy, telling him she'd see him in the VIP. There were three other Unread Messages, all sent later in the evening, all also from Sandy. He was so disgusted with himself that he couldn't be bothered to read them. He tried ringing Dawn's mobile but, as he guessed, it was switched off.

It was almost ten past eleven. There was no way he could get to the airport, talk to Dawn – assuming he was even able to catch her before she went through passport control – and get back for the presentation.

The choice was simple – Dawn or YF&S.

Greg dashed upstairs, got the bike keys and headed for the airport.

Rio just missed Greg. She staggered into the hotel, wired on cocaine and still half-drunk. She banged on his door screaming until a holidaymaker in a nearby room came out and told her to piss off.

Rather than have a wasted journey, she did her usual round of toilets and down the back of seats, in search of drugs discarded by departing holidaymakers. Her tally was a little disappointing, two pills and three microdot acid tabs.

She was walking along the corridor to leave the apartments when she noticed a door ajar. Previously a small games room, she saw it was set up as a board room. Nobody was about. A thought occurred to her and she tiptoed in. Around the table were nameplate cards and at the very top of the table was Greg's name. As well as the nameplates, each chair had a glass of orange already poured in front of it. Laughing to herself, Rio got the three microdots and one by one, put them into Greg's drink, although she was so wasted that the third one missed the glass. She started looking for it when the apartments receptionist came into the room.

'Hey, what you do?'

'Sorry, honey, I took the wrong door.'

Smiling, Rio left. She would have loved to have waited around to see the outcome. If the microdots were the same ones that were doing the rounds on the island then just two would be enough to convince a horse it was a Pegasus. With that much acid she was sure an interesting story would eventually reach her ears.

And with any luck, the story would be that Greg had either got the sack, been admitted to hospital, or left the island. Of course, it wasn't that she felt bitter about being dumped . . .

The speed with which Greg's Harley took the road to Ibiza Airport, he was lucky that he didn't end up in hospital anyway, or the crematorium.

He could have kissed IT Stan for leaving him the Harley for the extra day, because without it there was no way he would have had any chance of catching Dawn before she checked-in and went through passport control. As it was he knew that it would be touch and go.

What he didn't know was exactly what he was going to say if he managed to stop her. All he could do was be honest. There was no point telling her what he thought she might want to hear, nor was there any point in making promises he did not feel able to keep.

Quite simply, the time for bullshit was over. He was prepared to give up repping to make a go of things with Dawn and Little Greg.

Greg parked up the bike and hurtled into the airport, frantically looking at the departures board to see what desk Dawn's Gatwick flight was checking in at. He quickly saw that is was fourteen to sixteen, directly in front of him. The queues were empty apart from a few latecomers.

The flight was due to leave at 12.20, less than forty minutes. Greg knew that assuming it was on time, the boarding message would be up soon. The chances were that they'd already gone through passport control and if that was the case then without his uniform on there was no way he would be allowed airside.

He bound up the stairs to the restaurant and shops area, hoping that Dawn would have decided to have a cup of coffee before going through to the gates. At the top of the stairs he glanced to his right where there was a short queue waiting to put their hand luggage through the X-ray machine. They were not in it. Greg paced round the restaurant, gift shop and newsagent, but there was no sign of them. Finally as a last resort, he jogged back over to passport control and tried to see if he could see them through the glass but that too proved fruitless.

Greg turned away, putting his head in his hands and rubbing his face. He only had himself to blame. He could ring her or write to her when she was back in the UK, but he was certain that his chances of being taken with any kind of credibility by then would be slim. Dawn would just assume he'd been blown out by Sandy or had some other agenda. And who could blame her? She hadn't made any demands on him other than asking him to be part of Little Greg's life. When they had made love the previous night Greg had known then that Dawn was special, that she was worth making sacrifices for.

And in a strange way, although Dawn might not believe

it, going to Amnesia had perhaps played a part in making him re-evaluate his attitude to clubbing and repping.

He looked at his watch. If he really hammered it, he could just about get back in time for the presentation. But at the moment, his mind was completely elsewhere. YF&S would be better served if he didn't turn up. He would do something to the bike and pretend it had broken down on the way back from the airport. If they insisted he did the presentation later, then hopefully he would be in a better mood, though he doubted it.

Greg trundled to the exit. Coming towards him, out of the toilets were Dawn and Little Greg. 'Dawn!'

Little Greg's face lit up he ran towards his father. Greg instinctively picked him up.

Dawn didn't meet his eye. 'Our plane's boarding. We've got to go.' She took Little Greg back. 'Come on, treasure.'

'Dawn, wait, please.'

'There's no point. It was a mistake coming to Ibiza.'

'It wasn't. The only mistakes that have been made in the last few days are by me.'

'Yes, well, excuses, apologies . . . what's the point? You're you and that's it.' She went to step by him. 'Excuse me, we've got a plane to catch – back to normality.'

Greg stepped in front of her. 'Please, Dawn. I don't want to make excuses. I *do* want to apologise, but most of all I want to explain.' Dawn hesitated for a moment. 'Please. This could be one of the most important things I ever say in my life, so at least let me say it, even if you laugh in my face afterwards.'

Dawn looked at her watch and put Little Greg down. 'Baby, do you want to go over to that window and watch the planes taking off and landing? Mummy wants to talk to Greg alone for a few minutes. We'll be sitting here watching you. Call us when you see one.' An excited Little Greg ran off. 'I haven't got long.'

'OK, OK.' They both sat down. Greg had so many things to say he didn't know where to start. 'Right. First things first – I'm sorry. Last night was a mistake.'

'I gathered that,' replied Dawn curtly.

'No, shit, I didn't mean ...' Not the best of starts, thought Greg. 'Not us – that was the only bit that wasn't a mistake. That was perfect.'

'So perfect that you sneaked off to Amnesia to meet another girl.'

Greg looked at the floor, gathering his thoughts. 'It might seem silly saying this to you, but that girl is the most insignificant part of all this.'

'I can assure you that it doesn't seem so when the man you've thought about constantly for six years, who you've just introduced to your son as his father, who you've just made love to and want to spend the night with, *lies* in order to go and see this other woman. Trust me, Greg, she seems anything but insignificant then.'

'What I mean is, it wasn't her that I was going to see. Look, just try to get inside this crap head of mine for a moment. When I started as a rep I thought I'd meet someone in my first year and live happily ever after and to be honest, I still believe that someone was you. But you were right, I probably wasn't ready for that kind of relationship and as much as I might kid myself, I certainly wasn't ready to be a father. After you didn't get in touch I went a bit off the rails and ever since then I've used you as an excuse, as a justification for the way I treat women. But I know that's bollocks. The reason I've been like I have is because I've been allowed to get away with it and if I haven't, it hasn't mattered. I've not been looking for anything more. I've been living day by day but that's only because I wasn't too keen on what might be round the corner.'

'Greg,' said Dawn, her tone softening, 'don't you think I already *know* all of this? Everyone seems to know it apart from you. All you're talking about is growing up.'

'You're right – everyone else does seem to know it. When I got into clubbing last year it was like a whole new world and I wanted to be in the middle of it. It seems so shallow now, but that was my challenge. But this last week, with you and Little Greg, it's opened my eyes. I know now that I can't carry on doing this.'

'That's one of the truest things you've said so far. But it still doesn't explain you leaving me last night, Greg.'

'I know. I shouldn't have gone. But it had nothing to do with that girl – I don't even want to say her name because it makes her seem more important than she is.'

'Sandy,' offered Dawn, with a hint of bitterness.

'I went up there to blow her out. I'd tried phoning and it didn't seem right just to leave her there on her own. I only stayed there for half an hour. I saw Mikey and Ace and told them that I wanted to be with you.'

'And what about Sandy?'

'I met her a few weeks ago. I really wanted to go to the opening of Amnesia and she was coming back out for it and we arranged to meet up – that's all. Yeah, we might have got off with each other if things had been different, but after the time you and I spent together I completely forgot about her and Amnesia, which has got to say something. In the end, I didn't even bother finding her.' Dawn eyed him suspiciously. Greg remembered the Unread Messages. 'Look, she sent me texts. That's how much she means to me – I haven't even read them.'

Greg pressed the first one.

Taken wicked pill. Need to see you. We have unfinished bizniz!

'OK,' conceded Greg, 'maybe not the best start. But at least it proves we never finished the business in the first place.'

The time on the second message was 02.58.

Where r u? Am in VIP. Any probs getting in? Pls txt me.

Greg scrolled to the third message. 04.23

Fuk u! Met Ace. Said u left & u hve a kid. Bastard.

'So you left early?' Dawn was quieter now.

'After half an hour there, I came back to prepare for the presentation then fell asleep and because you had my phone, I didn't have an alarm to wake me up this morning.'

'So what time's the presentation?'

Greg looked at his watch. 'About now. But that's not important. You and Little Greg are.'

Dawn looked horrified. 'But from what you said, the future of YF&S could be down to you doing this presentation! Oh Greg, you still don't get it, do you?'

'Get what?'

'This isn't just about me and Little Greg. This is about you facing up to your responsibilities – all of them. Yes, you've a responsibility to me, to Little Greg, but you also have a duty to everyone you work with, and most of all to yourself. All the while you keep running away from things, you're no good to me, and you're certainly no good to Little Greg. Yes, maybe you have decided clubbing isn't for you and perhaps you can see now that there's more to life than Ibiza and repping. But it's the bigger picture, Greg. This is about you becoming *responsible*.'

It was a home truth that hit Greg like a thunderbolt.

'I'm a fucking twat. I wish I had a bigger brain – mine gets full too quickly. I'm a selfish, small-brained fucking twat.'

'Misguided rather than selfish maybe.' Dawn allowed herself a little smile. 'Small-brained is about right though.'

'I've got to go, haven't I?'

'It's for you to decide, Greg. I can't tell you what to do.'

He looked at his watch. 'Maybe I can salvage things. What a screw-up.'

'You've had better days,' said Dawn lightly.

'Listen, Dawn, before I go there's something I've got to tell you. I know I'm not going to change overnight. YF&S might go out of business and if they do then I'll have to do some serious thinking about the future. And even if we win, then it's time for me to change. I've got a reason to now. I don't want to get slushy because it's not me, but what I said about you being special and all that . . .'

Dawn smiled, knowing that this was about as close to the 'L' word as Greg was likely to get. 'You can be a nightmare but you're special to me too.'

'I wish I hadn't fucked up so badly, I wish we had more time.' Greg suddenly had an idea. 'Dawn, why don't you both stay until Sunday? I can get you another flight for nothing and you'll be back Sunday night so you won't miss work – you can both move into my apartment.'

'I . . . I don't know.'

'Please Dawn. It's only another two days. If The Monastery take over Club Wicked rather than us then I'll probably come back to the UK. If that happens then I know that I'd want to see you both. If you stay, you'll see how serious I am about you.'

'What – in a couple of days?'

'Yes. One thing I have learned in this last week is that you probably know me better than anyone – better than I know myself. It's got to be worth a try.'

'And what about if YF&S win?'

'The truth?' Dawn nodded. 'I'd probably stay out here as resort manager until things got back on track. The only reason I didn't accept the position before was because I didn't want it to interfere with clubbing, but now? To be honest, I'm quite looking forward to the challenge. If I stay out here, then I'm sure we could work it so that you and Little Greg could come out for a few weekends or another week or two. It'll whizz by – we'll be in September before we know it.'

Dawn could tell it was an honest answer and she had to admit, not the kind of answer she would have previously expected from him. 'I'm still not sure, Greg.'

'OK.' Greg gave her a resigned smile. 'Well, at least I've said what I wanted to and that's why I came here. I didn't want you leaving thinking that you hadn't had any effect on me or that I was blasé about what happened between us.' He looked at his watch again. 'Shit. I've really got to go.'

He ran over to Little Greg, picked him up. Dawn couldn't hear what he was saying but Little Greg started chuckling. He kissed him then ran back and hugged Dawn.

'Thanks, Dawn.' She was sure she saw the trace of a tear in his eye and that *was* a first. He coughed and put on a smile. 'If you do get this flight, at least send me a text to let me know you've got back safely.'

'I'll call you,' she said, then added with a smile, 'although I gather you don't always read your texts.'

Greg laughed. 'I would yours. Wish me luck.'

Greg sprinted out of the airport. He had been genuine about doing his best with the presentation and now he'd spoken to Dawn, felt in the perfect mood to do it. The only problem was that it was five to twelve and it would take at best, fifteen minutes to get back to the hotel then another five to prepare himself.

He could ring H-B to get him to tell The Monastery people that he'd had a problem with the bike and would be fifteen minutes late. What he also needed to do was to stall Alison too, because he knew that she would make maximum gain from his tardy arrival.

'Trev!' he suddenly said to himself, as he remembered Trev asking him for Viagras in Amnesia the previous night because he was seeing Alison in the morning. Was it possible that Alison was still there? It was worth a go.

He took his mobile from his pocket and dialled Trev's number.

Trev was relieved when his mobile rang.

He had managed to put off actually having proper sex with Alison until nearly quarter to twelve. It hadn't proved difficult because for most of the time she had been talking about herself, in between making snide comments regarding his prowess. For the first time it dawned on him that he didn't actually *like* her. She was self-centred, arrogant and actually, none too bright.

Unfortunately though, he still found her as horny as hell.

Even so, he had managed to stop himself from coming. Admittedly, he hadn't really got a proper rhythm going and needed to get his magic fingers working to stop her moaning, or rather, to *start* her moaning. So when the mobile rang at five to twelve, it gave him the perfect excuse to halt proceedings and let his sap subside.

'Hi, Trev, don't let Alison know who it is on the phone,' said Greg quickly. 'Is she still with you?'

'Um, yes,' he said, looking over at her lying on the bed, playing with herself in his absence.

'Excellent. Trev, I need you to do me a big favour. She's meant to be going to the Hotel Arena down the road in a few minutes for this presentation.'

'Yes, I know.'

'I need you to keep her there for me as long as possible.'

'How?'

'You know what she's like. Give her a good seeing to and she'll lose track of time.'

'I know, but—'

'Trev, I've got to go, mate. I'm about to get on a motorbike and I haven't got a headset.'

'Yes but you don't understand, I—'

'Trev, there's an eight-ball of nose in this for you if you can keep her there for another ten minutes. That's all I ask. Ten minutes. I'm sure a man of your experience can manage that.'

'But—'

Greg was gone.

Ten minutes. That was just over the same amount of time that he'd already managed. He'd never do it.

'Come on, Trev,' said Alison, fingering herself close to a climax, 'come over here and fuck me. Hard.'

Trev felt his balls ache just looking at her. Even as she grabbed him to pull him into her he thought he was going to come. She was soon bucking underneath, letting out little screams that made it even harder for Trev to stop himself. He screwed his face up in a mask of concentration, occasionally breaking Alison's rhythm to her obvious annoyance.

It was no good – he was going to have to let Greg down. He opened his eyes to prepare for the inevitable and then he saw it. An old football magazine with Peter Beardsley on the front cover on his bedside table. Why hadn't he noticed it before? Good old Pete. He studied every contour of Beardsley's asymmetric features, the lank hair, the crooked teeth.

Trev was so engrossed in his new found and effective diversion, that he did not notice the hotel mongrel, who had been consigned to the balcony for the duration of Alison's session. Trev had not shut the balcony door properly, so the dog had nudged it open and found its way into the bedroom. Perhaps, given how Trev had spent so much time teasing the dog and tickling its balls, the opportunity for such appropriate revenge was too much to resist. Or perhaps, the dog remembered catching Brad in a similar position the previous summer. Whatever the reason, the dog sneaked up behind Trev and before he knew what was happening, had jumped onto the bed, stuck its cold nose up Trev's backside and licked his balls.

'What the . . .. oh shit!'

Trev pulled out and shot all over Alison.

'You stupid fucking dog . . . you've made me come!'

The dog scurried back out to the balcony.

'What did you call me?' said Alison, resting on her elbows and grabbing a towel to wipe herself down.

'Not you,' said Trev, 'the . . .'

He realised that explaining what had actually happened would probably eventually end up causing him to be the object of considerable ridicule. Far better, he therefore decided, for Alison to think he was being derogatory towards her.

'Um, sorry, I thought you liked me talking dirty.'

'I do. But I don't like you calling me a dog. You're no fucking oil painting yourself. What's the time?' she reached for the bedside clock. 'Fuck, it's five past twelve. I'm late.' She dashed into the bathroom. 'That wasn't too bad, Trev. In fact, I feel fucking great now – ready to take on the world.' She poked her head round the bathroom door. 'And you didn't even need the delay spray.'

Trev smiled. Who needs delay spray, he thought, when you've got Peter Beardsley?

chapter thirty-nine

Charles Moon sat at one end of the table in the makeshift boardroom. To his left was Kit, to his right Irene Withers, The Monastery Company Secretary.

Lucas and his wife Vanessa – the Club Wicked Company Secretary – were sitting on the same side of the table as Kit; Hawthorne-Blythe and the recently arrived Jane Hunter from YF&S were facing them.

Greg's name plate was at the opposite head of the table to Charles Moon, Alison's was alongside, next to Lucas.

Alison strode confidently into the room at quarter past twelve, just as a dishevelled Greg pulled up on the Harley. He had put some oil over his hands and arms to make it look as though the bike had broken down. He dashed into the room behind Alison.

'Sorry, I'm late. I know it was good of Stan to let me use the bike but the bloody thing broke down. Did you get the message, H-B?'

'Yes, no problem, Greg.'

'Alison's only just turned up anyway,' added Jane Hunter.

It was the first time that Jane had seen Alison since the court case for the massive fraud during the winter, where Alison had testified against Felipe Gomez to save her own skin. Jane found it almost impossible to believe that she was now sitting in the same room as this woman, who now potentially would have a large part to play in putting YF&S out of business.

'Good old Greg,' sighed Alison, determined to have the last word, 'reliable as ever.'

When she saw Greg's name at the top of the table, she

gave a little snort of disgust and changed it with her own, then occupied what she clearly perceived as the prime seat.

In a professional manner, she took out all of her overhead transparencies and notes and neatly laid them on the table in front of her. When she was happy, she leaned forward and took the glass of orange, putting some ice in it from the nearby ice bucket.

'Phew, it's hot in here,' she remarked, then downed the orange in one.

Mario walked into the main club of Es Paradis with the boxes of champagne he had been asked to take there for the after presentation party, where The Monastery were going to make their announcement. His just arrived Anglo-American girlfriend Coral was with him.

'Hello?' he yelled. 'Anyone about?'

His voice echoed around the large club. It was as beautiful during the day as it was at night, with its huge, glass pyramid roof and all-white décor.

'Wow,' said Coral appreciatively, 'this is one helluva place.'

'Yeah, I guess it is,' said Mario, trying to appear nonchalant.

He noticed that a small stage had been built near the DJ stand in the main room and assumed that this was going to be used as an alternative to the normal DJ booth. He went and stood on it. It felt impressive and he couldn't help feeling a twinge of envy, knowing that Vaz would be playing there later.

'Have you ever DJed here?' asked Coral

'Yeah, loads of times,' lied Mario.

'It must be great. Y'know, it'd really turn me on to see you up there working a crowd of this size.'

This instantly made Mario even more resentful of Vaz. 'Yeah, it's pretty cool. Shall we go?'

'Sure, honey, let me just use the wash-aaghh!' Coral slipped and ended on her Anglo-American backside-butt.

'What happened?'

Next to Coral was a tub of industrial grease, presumably for putting the podium together, and a dollop of it was on the marble floor.

'Jeez, some fool's not cleaned up this grease properly – it's as slippery as hell.'

'Are you all right?' he asked, helping her to her feet.

She brushed herself down. 'Yeah, nothing broken. I'm just going to the washroom. Back soon.'

As she disappeared into the ladies' Mario had an idea. He picked up the tub of grease and smeared it on the lower level of the new DJ stage.

With any luck, thought Mario, Vaz would 'go down' later that night far better than he planned.

Due to Greg running late, Alison had given her presentation first and loathe though Greg was to admit it, she had done extremely well. Towards the very end though, Greg noticed that she was beginning to look slightly confused.

Greg was glad that he had spent the time reading through Brad's notes before going to bed the previous night. Despite this and being a natural performer and salesman, he still got off to a slightly shaky start. However, his performance improved tenfold when he looked through the window and saw Dawn and Little Greg emerging from a taxi with their cases.

Greg was just coming to the end of his presentation, when inappropriately, Alison burst out laughing and pointed at him. Greg tried to ignore her and continue, but Alison laughed even more.

'Are you all right, Alison?' asked Charles Moon.

Alison swung round and stared at Charles. Then her eyes opened wide and her jaw dropped. 'Look at the size and colour of your nose,' she gasped.

Charles looked stunned. Five seconds later she was laughing manically again. Lucas sunk his head in his hands. Kit, Jane and H-B looked even more startled. Greg wrapped up his presentation.

'So, as I was saying. We feel that the experience of Young

Free & Single, positioned as we are as the market leader in youth travel, combined with the strong branding of The Monastery, undoubtedly the leading brand in the clubbing environment, is the perfect marriage. As a consequence—'

'Love and marriage, love and marriage . . .' Alison sang. Just as suddenly, she clasped her hand to her mouth as she realised everyone was looking at her, her eyes darting round the table like a paranoid child. 'What? Why are you all looking at me? *Fuck off*!' She started laughing again. 'God, it's hot in here.' She started undoing her blouse. 'Got to get them out.'

'Alison!' yelled Lucas.

'What?' She seemed to forget that she was in the process of getting undressed and stopped. 'Lucas!' she exclaimed, as though she had just seen him. She climbed onto the table and crawled over to him. Charles Moon stood, then sat down again. Alison stopped and looked at Vanessa. 'Is this your wife?' She rolled onto the table, laughing so much that she had to hold her sides. She started making mooing noises. 'Oh, Tyrone Lucas. Do it to me, baby. Shall I stick my finger up your bum? You know you like it. Wow. What a mad ceiling.' She started singing again. 'Pink and orange and yellow and blue . . .'

'Um, I'm pretty much done, Charles, shall I sit down?' asked Greg.

Transfixed by Alison's antics, Charles Moon could only nod.

'Come on Lucas, we haven't done it for ages. Now, on this table, whaddya reckon?'

Alison screwed her eyes up and made shapes with her hands, in between giggling fits and singing.

Lucas's wife Vanessa got up from the table and left the room. Lucas got up to follow her. As he did so, he noticed the third microdot acid tab next to the ice bucket near where Alison was sitting.

'Look,' he exclaimed picking it up, 'an acid tab. No wonder she's behaving like this. Her drink has been spiked.'

He turned to Charles Moon. 'Charles, this is sick. I want to lodge a formal protest.'

'This isn't the Olympic Games, Lucas,' said Kit.

'Well, I want to protest nevertheless. I thought this was supposed to be a fair contest.'

'You're a fine one to talk,' said Hawthorne-Blythe. 'You've been up to no good since day one.'

'Nonsense. I've got proof here that you've tried to stitch us up.'

'Stitch-ups? Let's not even go there, Lucas.'

'So what are you accusing me of? Where's *your* proof?'

'Um, can I say something?' asked Greg, trying to keep a straight face. Alison was still singing to herself and clearly away with the fairies.

'Go on, Greg,' said Charles.

'I came in here earlier on . . .'

'See, he admits it!' yelled Lucas.

'Shut up, Lucas,' snapped Hawthorne-Blythe uncharacteristically, 'and let Greg finish.'

'Thanks, H-B. What I was going to say was that I put my head round the door earlier and noticed that my name was at the other end of the table. When I came back, Alison had swapped places with me, which wasn't a problem seeing as I was a little late. My point is though, that if her drink was spiked, then it was actually *my* drink that was spiked, so if anything, *someone*,' the implication in the word was obvious, 'has tried to stitch *me* up.'

'Why would we do that?' asked Lucas.

'I didn't say you did,' replied Greg calmly, 'and equally, you shouldn't be accusing us.'

'Crap. You must have done it somehow.'

After that, everybody started talking at once, throwing accusations back and forth. In the end, Charles Moon stood up.

'Gentlemen. Ladies and Gentleman, please . . .' He couldn't be heard over the racket. 'If we could all calm down . . .' Still he was roundly ignored. '*Will you all shut the fuck up!*' That got everyone's attention. 'Thank you. Now then. There is no point in having this argument, it's getting us nowhere. We've had both of your presentations and we've had three very long weeks on resort. What we need is to spend a couple of hours on our own to confirm our eventual decision. Given the circumstances I think it best we all disperse, freshen up then re-convene at Es Paradis at ten-thirty tonight as previously arranged.'

Everyone mumbled their agreement. Charles Moon could not get out of the room quickly enough. Lucas chased after him.

'Charles, Charles . . .' He caught up with him just as he was getting into his car. 'Look, I'm really sorry about earlier. Obviously we're all a little on edge. And as for Alison, I trust you can tell it wasn't her fault.'

'It doesn't matter, Lucas.'

'So, aren't you going to tell myself and Hawthorne-Blythe your decision first, surely that would be the right way to do things?'

'Sorry, no. I want all of the reps to find out at the same time from me. It's their futures too.'

'OK, whatever you say. But Alison being spiked, it didn't—'

'No.'

'Good, good. So it won't make any difference to your decision then?'

'No,' replied Charles winding up his window, 'no difference at all. I promise.'

chapter forty

The funky room in Es Paradis was packed and with Vaz playing a blistering set, the atmosphere was electric, as midnight and the time for the announcement approached.

Most of the reps were letting their hair down, glad that the assessment was finished and excited by the prospect of change. Only the management showed any sign of tension.

Lucas was outside, talking to his wife, trying to persuade her that nothing had gone on between him and Alison. He was fairly confident of convincing her – the lifestyle his money allowed her to enjoy ensured that she tolerated some of his less attractive qualities. If Club Wicked lost and he had to sell up and pay off his gambling debt though . . . he shuddered. It didn't bear thinking about.

Alison had only just arrived at the club looking shame-faced and bedraggled. After the presentation, Trev had talked her down from her trip until it was more or less out of her system. She was still feeling fragile though and hovered outside of the funky room away from the flashing lights.

Mario was strutting round with his glamorous girlfriend like the cat that had got the cream. Coral had confirmed that she could twirl her director father round her little finger. As such Mario didn't really care what The Monastery's decision was – he was Hollywood bound regardless.

The other cat with the cream was Greg. Dawn and Little Greg were staying for the weekend. He had found a babysitter for Little Greg and had not left Dawn's side all evening.

Hughie, Ace and Mikey were all standing at the bar together, watching Greg with Dawn.

'Looks like it's between me and you then, Hughie,' said Ace.

'Aye, I reckon we're going to have to stop calling The Golden Dick The Greg after this.'

'The way I'm going you'll be calling it The Ace. Another four points last night.'

'What, up the balloon knot? Who?'

'No, just a normal three-pointer, but there was a bonus point up for grabs – it was that Sandy that Greg was supposed to meet.'

'You wee fucker,' said Hughie. 'Did you tell Greg?'

'Are you joking?' exclaimed Ace. 'Of course I did. I couldn't wait, especially as I did her in the bogs at Amnesia. Just a dirty old bog-bird.'

'Just as well Greg's out of the game – he was obviously losing his touch.'

'She was a crap shag too. When I finished she made me promise not to tell anyone. I think she'd been flirting with that DJ – I can't remember his name – the one with the spiky blond hair. She wanted me to walk out a few minutes after her.'

'And did you?'

'Did I fuck! I walked out straight behind her and straight into the DJ. "Where have you two been?" he asks. I still had the full condom in my hand so I slapped him round the face with it and said, "Here's a clue". I don't know who wanted to kill me the most. I just fucked off and left 'em to it.'

'So have you ever seen Greg like this, Mikey?' asked Hughie.

Mikey shook his head. 'Never. It had to happen though. You could tell he was looking for something – most people who come over here are. He just didn't know what it was. I reckon that this is the last time you'll see Peter Pan in Never-Never Land.'

'And what about if we win?' said Ace. 'Do you reckon he'll stay as resort manager?'

'Yes, I think so. He's always known he'd be good at it, he's just had other things to distract him. Now he's got something to aim for.'

'Well, I think it's lovely,' said Patricia, slipping her arm through Mikey's. She noticed Charles Moon signalling over to the reps. She looked at her watch. It was almost midnight.

'I think it's time for us to go. It looks like Charles is about to make the announcement. Good luck, everyone. We'll be downstairs with the champagne on ice.'

Vaz stopped the music, got his record box and headed downstairs, shaking hands with a few of the reps on the way.

Charles Moon stepped behind the DJ stand with Kit, waiting until all of the clients and non-YF&S and Club Wicked personnel had left the room. He switched the microphone on and gestured to one of the barmaids to turn the lights on.

'Hello, can you all hear me OK?' There was a chorus of yes. 'Excellent. Right, well as you all know we have been over here watching you, um ... perform,' his deliberate choice of word drew a few cat-calls, 'over the last three weeks. In many ways, it has felt more like three months. I must say, I never realised how much was involved or quite how hard you all had to work. It has been a total eye-opener. So before we go any further I think you should all give yourselves a round of applause for a job well done.'

There was a brief burst of applause and a few whistles.

'Now to the serious stuff. As you know, the reason for this assessment has been to choose either Young Free & Single or Club Wicked as The Monastery's partner, the aim being to form the leading provider of holidays aimed at the specialist youth market.'

There was silence, the air now heavy with anticipation.

'So,' continued Charles, 'I would imagine that you would all like to know what we have decided.'

For Lucas in particular, the tension was almost unbearable. He wanted to yell, 'Get on with it' but he didn't dare.

'It has been very close,' said Charles. 'The two resort managers both gave excellent presentations today arguing the case for their respective companies. Alison, a very professional job for Club Wicked,' there was a cheer from all of the Club Wicked reps, 'and at short notice, Greg proved he is every bit a resort manager for Young Free & Single.'

As the YF&S reps cheered, Lucas smiled in relief. No mention of Alison's behaviour – that had to be a good sign.

'To tell the truth though, we had pretty much made up our minds prior to those presentations.' Charles coughed, clearly enjoying the theatrical element of his announcement. 'So, I'm afraid to say that we are not going to be taking over Young Free & Single . . .'

It had all been too much for Lucas and he was unable to contain his excitement. 'Yes, yes, yes!' he yelled. 'In your face,' he laughed, turning to H-B.

'. . . *or*,' continued Charles, 'Club Wicked.'

The words stopped Lucas in mid-celebratory dance. 'You what?' he said.

'I will be explaining the whys and wherefores to your respective chairmen privately after this, but suffice to say that we made a misjudgement about what is a very specialist market place and we do not yet feel ready or able to commit the full resources of The Monastery to it. I would however, like to thank you all for the tremendous effort that you have put in and wish you every success for the future. And now, if you'd like to all make your way downstairs, I believe the main part of the club is filling up for one of Es Paradis's legendary Fiestas del Agua. Have a good night and if you go to the top bar, I've put a few crates of champagne behind it for you all.'

There was a small cheer and the reps filed out. Lucas virtually sprinted over to Charles Moon.

'What do you mean, you're not taking over either of us. You can't! You must!'

'I'm sorry, Lucas,' said Charles. 'The whole point of the assessment was to see which of your two companies was the most viable option. The conclusion we came to is that neither would be suitable for The Monastery branding.'

'But how can you say that?' argued Lucas. 'Club Wicked is all about clubbing. We're on totally the same wavelength.'

'We disagree,' said Kit, who had long since lost patience with Lucas and had had a good idea that Lucas hadn't been playing by the rules. 'Charles is far too professional to get personal, whereas I am not. I think you are a devious manipulator and even if we had decided to take over Club Wicked, we would have paid you off so you had no involvement.'

'Great!' said Lucas, his eyes lighting up, the insult like water off a duck's back. 'Pay me off. I'll go. Happily. I bet H-B wouldn't do that.'

'We wouldn't want him to,' said Kit.

'It makes no difference, Lucas,' said Moon. 'Personal issues aside, it simply isn't a viable proposition for us at the moment. H-B was right – there still is a market for his kind of holiday. We wouldn't have believed it if we hadn't seen it ourselves, but a lot of these kids do come away and have all the thinking laid on for them. They don't want to have to decide which club to go to or what to do during the day. And I'm afraid that's not what we're about.'

'Neither are we!' pleaded Lucas. 'We must be able to work something out. There's got to be a way.'

'There isn't,' replied Kit flatly.

'Please!'

It was becoming too much for his wife Vanessa. 'Come on, Tyrone, you're making a fool of yourself,' she said, tugging at his sleeve.

'*Fuck off, you silly cow*,' he spat. 'You don't get it, do you? I'm ruined. I'm up to my neck in it and the type of people I owe I can't run away from.'

Vanessa's eyes narrowed. 'Gambling?'

'No, I've given it all to charity,' sang Lucas sarcastically. 'Of course it's fucking gambling.'

Charles and Kit moved towards Hawthorne-Blythe. Vanessa stormed from the room.

Lucas suddenly had a reality check. 'Oh shit.' He chased her out of the club calling her name.

'I hope you're not about to behave like that, H-B,' said Kit.

'No,' smiled H-B. 'I don't normally wish ill on anyone, but in Lucas's case I'm prepared to make an exception. Do you know that I found out today he planted those pills in Vaz's bag?'

Kit looked at Charles. 'What did I tell you?'

'You knew?' asked Hawthorne-Blythe, with surprise in his voice.

'Let's say I had a hunch,' replied Kit. 'I take it you've offered him his job back?'

'I did, but he seems to be doing rather well for himself as a DJ. He's playing downstairs now. Very talented if what I hear is correct.'

'Well, if he's that good, the least we can do is get him a spot at The Monastery,' said Charles. 'We'll have to check him out in a minute, what do you think, Kit?'

'Sounds only fair to me,' he smiled. 'And what about you, H-B? What's the future hold for YF&S?'

'Well, it's going to be tough. We've got a few cash flow problems, but if Club Wicked fold as it seems they will, then I'm sure we'll pick up their business. We'll be all right.'

'I hope you are, H-B,' said Charles. 'Like I said before, you're an institution.'

Hawthorne-Blythe laughed. 'Nice of you to say so. And for what it's worth, I think you made the right decision.'

They all shook hands.

'Right then,' said Charles, 'shall we go downstairs and get a drink then check out this Vaz?'

Alison and Mario stood at the downstairs bar. Vaz was DJing and, as usual, the place was going off. Mario was appreciatively watching Coral dancing, along with most other red-blooded males in Es Paradis.

'Look at her, fucking gorgeous, isn't she?'

Alison could only grunt a reply. She was leaning on the bar with her head in her hands.

'Shame about old Lucas. I never knew he was such a heavy gambler. By the sounds of it he's ruined. Oh well, we did our best, didn't we? At least you and me are all right.'

'I can't claim to feel particularly "all right" at the moment.'

'I'm not surprised. I just wonder how many of those microdots were in the drink and more to the point, who put them there?'

'God knows. Don't remind me.'

'When do you think Lucas will have the plug pulled on Club Wicked then?'

'I don't know and I don't care.'

'I suppose you'll go back to your sunglasses business, won't you?'

'Mario, at the moment I can't think any further ahead than the next few seconds.' She drank some of her water. 'I spoke to the girl who's working for me and it's going really well, so yes, that's exactly what I'll be doing. I doubt if I'll stay here longer than absolutely necessary. In fact, I think I might see if I can get a flight tomorrow.'

Mario laughed. 'I'd do the same but seeing as Coral's over I might as well make the most of it. She's mad about me – jealous as fuck. She goes loopy if I even look at another woman.'

'Oh well, that's Americans for you.'

'I think it's more to do with the fact that her last boyfriend just used her to get a leg-up into films then fucked off with the leading actress of his first movie.'

'And that thought would never cross your mind, would it?' said Alison.

'Fuck no!' Mario turned round and leaned on the bar. 'I'd wait until at least my second film before I did that. Do you want another drink?'

'Just a water, please.'

Mario ordered the drinks then reached into Coral's bag, which he was looking after while she was dancing.

'We had some wicked professional pictures taken together. Do you want to see them?'

'Not right now, thanks. The way I feel they'd probably look like a Dali painting.'

'Oh, all right then,' said Mario, putting them back in the bag a little disappointed. 'She's a wicked dancer though, isn't she?'

'For fuck's sake, Mario, yes! She's beautiful, she's a wicked dancer and her dad's worth a fortune and is going to make you a movie star. And for all I know or care, her shit doesn't stink. So will you please just stop going on about her and give my fucking head a rest?'

'Ooh,' replied Mario sarcastically.

He didn't see Sugar Ray come up behind him to get a drink.

'Anyway,' said Alison, 'I thought you'd done something to stitch up Vaz.'

Sugar Ray edged behind a pillar.

'I did. I thought that podium over there was the new DJ stand, so I greased one of the steps. If it had been, then Vaz would have gone flying. At the very least he would have looked a twat but he would have probably fucked himself pretty bad – I doubt if he would have been able to play.'

'You're actually quite a nasty piece of work, aren't you?'

Mario smiled and chinked glasses with her. 'I had a good teacher, didn't I?'

Sugar Ray ducked away from the bar and quickly found Arabella. 'Vaz isn't due to go up on that podium at any point tonight, is he?'

'No,' replied Arabella, 'why?'

'I just heard that scumbag Mario. He greased the steps because he thought it was the DJ stand. He wanted Vaz to slip on it and by the sounds of it, he was hoping he'd break a leg or something equally bad. I don't mind a practical joke, but that just isn't funny.'

'Right, that's it,' said Arabella, her face fixing in a determined scowl. 'Where is he?'

'Over there.' He pointed to the bar, where Alison had just left Mario's side to be replaced by Stig and a group of clients.

Arabella started to march over, but stopped halfway when she saw Coral reach into her bag next to Mario to get a cigarette, before returning to the dance floor. She turned round to Sugar Ray who had been following close behind.

'Can I ask you to do me a favour, Sugar Ray? Do you think you could attract Mario's attention for a few moments?'

'Sure, shouldn't be a problem.'

Sugar Ray strode in front of the group while Arabella edged along the bar to creep up behind Mario.

'All right, boys,' said Sugar Ray. 'Hi Stig,' he added, in an outrageously camp voice. 'I'd watch these two reps if I were you, lads. They might give it loads about shagging girls, but they're a pair of old queens. I've had them both. And that Stig,' he crooked his little finger, 'the smallest one I've ever seen.'

The clients all started laughing. Sugar Ray was enjoying this.

'Fuck off, Sugar Ray,' said Mario, 'you were lucky last time.'

'Ooh, and I hope I'm lucky again with you, handsome.' Arabella gave him the thumbs up. 'Love to chat but I'm off.'

Sugar Ray caught up with Arabella a few moments later on the other side of the club, next to Hawthorne-Blythe, Jane Hunter, Charles and Kit.

'What was all that about?'

'If all goes according to plan, sweet revenge.'

Quite suddenly, the lights went out. Vaz stopped his set and a pre-recorded tape began. A gap had been made in the crowd through which two fire jugglers ran. They stopped just below the DJ stand and started throwing the blazing batons to each other.

'A little something we arranged as special entertainment,'

explained Charles. 'We've used them at the club in London and they happened to be over here. They're fantastic.'

The crowd seemed equally appreciative. After a couple of minutes, one of the jugglers stepped up on to the podium.

Arabella and Sugar Ray both realised what was probably about to happen at the same time, but it was too late. The juggler slipped on the step and he went crashing to the floor, his fire-sticks just missing him. There was a small gasp from the crowd, who let out a collective sigh of relief when he hobbled to his feet.

Then, explosively, Vaz somersaulted out of the DJ box, landing next to the fire-sticks, still alight on the floor. He picked them up and began juggling.

'What the . . .' Like the rest of the crowd, Charles Moon did not have a clue what was going on.

'Oh, he used to work in a circus,' said Arabella, by way of explanation. 'Apparently this was one of his specialities.'

Once Vaz had clearly demonstrated to the other juggler that he knew what he was doing, they did an impromptu act, throwing the fire-sticks to each other. The crowd went wild and even the injured juggler, now leaning against a wall, cheered his appreciation.

As the music came to an end, Vaz jumped back up to his booth and put another pumping record on. The whole club, including Charles and Kit, went absolutely wild.

'Well, I tell you what,' said Charles, 'I was going to give him a spot after listening to his DJing, but after that he deserves a bloody residency!'

A proud and excited Arabella went running over to the DJ stand. Vaz beckoned her up.

'That was wicked!' squealed Arabella.

'Yeah, I must admit I enjoyed it,' said Vaz. 'I was a bit rusty though.'

'I thought you were afraid of fire?'

Vaz shrugged. 'I thought I was too. I've never really confronted it before. I guess that the natural show-off in me just took over.'

'Well, I've got something to tell you that will give you reason to show off even more.'

'What?'

'Charles is going to give you a DJ spot at The Monastery.'

'*What?* Not because of my juggling, surely?'

'Don't be silly, although I don't think you exactly did yourself any harm stepping in like that – he loved it. No, it's because he found out you were stitched up with the pills but mainly because he thinks you're a bloody good DJ.'

'Really?'

'Really.'

'That's wicked.'

Then, at the bar nearest the DJ stand, they became aware of a commotion. Through the crowd, they saw Coral snatch her bag, pour a drink over Mario's head, slap him round the face and storm off. Vaz looked at Arabella.

'You didn't.'

She nodded. 'Afraid so.'

'But I thought you said you'd only show it to her if he did something else.'

'He did.'

'What?'

'I'll tell you later. Anyway, I didn't show it to her – I put it in her bag. I didn't expect her to find it in the club.'

'Oh right, so that was just a bonus, was it?'

'What are you two laughing at?' It was Greg, holding hands with Dawn, as he had for most of the night.

'Did you see what just happened to Mario?' asked Vaz.

'Yeah. Why did she do that to him?'

'Oh, I'll tell you another time,' said Vaz. 'How many points do you think he should have deducted for having a drink poured over his head, his face slapped and his girlfriend storm out of a club on him?'

'I don't know,' replied Greg. Smiling he turned to Dawn and kissed her. 'And to be honest, I couldn't care less.'

the following december . . .

chapter forty-one

Greg scooped Little Greg from the back seat of the car and helped him zip up the front of his small quilted coat.

'That's better, mate . . . we don't want you catching cold, do we? It's Christmas next week and we can't have you in bed with a runny nose. You'll want to be watching telly, or be in the park playing football.'

'Is Santa really going to bring me a Man U football kit?'

'Did you write him a letter?'

'Yes.'

'Did you write "please"?'

'I wrote six of them.'

'Good boy. Well, when you wake up in the morning on Christmas Day, we'll have to see if he's come down the chimney and put it at the end of the bed.'

Little Greg looked concerned. 'But we haven't got a chimney. They've got one at Nana's house. We've got Economy 7 here.'

Greg smiled. 'And how do you know that?'

'I heard Mum talking to Nana the other day. She said that Economy 7 is a load of shit and too expensive.'

'Greg!' scalded Dawn, as she was getting the shopping out of the boot. 'I've told you before you mustn't say words like that. They're naughty.'

'But you said it!'

'I know and I shouldn't have. I'm a naughty mummy.'

'You're a naughty mummy,' repeated Little Greg.

'That's right,' added Greg. 'She's a naughty mummy.' He playfully smacked Dawn's bottom. Dawn giggled. Greg lifted Little Greg on to his shoulders. 'Come on then, let's get you inside. Footie starts in half hour.'

Dawn watched the two of them disappear into the house. She could not believe that this was the same Greg who had a ten-inch gold-plated dick named after him (awarded to Ace at the Young Free & Single reunion a month earlier – the first reunion that Greg had not bothered to attend).

She still marvelled at the change in him. Most incredibly of all, he had not taken a single pill or sniffed a single line since leaving Ibiza. It was as if being a father was all he ever wanted. The only people who seemed to be happier than Greg were his parents. They had virtually resigned themselves to the family name (if not the blood line) ending with their itinerant son. They loved Little Greg instantly and couldn't help but warm to Dawn. After all, as they saw it, it would more than likely have only been a matter of time before their son was all over the tabloids as a result of some kind of excessive behaviour in Ibiza, so Dawn's taming of him spared them that particular embarrassment with the neighbours.

Unsurprisingly, Dawn's mum was more cautious when she met Greg. In fact, she was quite frosty. However, Greg's charm was one that transcended age, so the 'He's not as bad as I imagined' after their first meeting had turned into 'Oh Dawn, he's so lovely' by the third. Her dad just wanted his daughter to be happy. And on Greg's part, it wasn't an act. Quite simply, he had willingly, eagerly turned into the near-perfect partner and father.

The signs were good that this transformation was to be a permanent one, although there were a couple of things that were still troubling her. The first was the worry that he would go back to Ibiza.

Greg had stayed on as resort manager to the end of the season. It had been a successful year, made even more successful when Club Wicked folded before the end of July. Greg had enjoyed the experience and thrived on the responsibility, the team of reps growing to the biggest it had ever been when YF&S took on half of the Ibiza Club

Wicked reps once they started picking up some of their bookings in August. Dawn and Little Greg managed to come out for another couple of long weekends as well as a fortnight's holiday.

At the end of the season YF&S asked him to return as resort manager again the following summer, and he had initially said yes, as much as anything else to prove that he was now willing to accept responsibility.

As soon Greg got back to the UK, he moved down south to live with Dawn and Little Greg, for the first two weeks with her parents in Maidenhead, then subsequently renting a small semi a few miles away. He started working for an ex-YF&S rep who had a fairly successful corporate entertainment business based in Bracknell. The job was meant to be for the winter, but things were going really well and there was talk of him becoming a partner.

Greg was now dismissive whenever a return to Ibiza was mentioned. Dawn hoped he would stay in the UK because although she had initially said she would go back with him, she knew it would not be practical. Little Greg had started school and this meant she would only be able to visit Ibiza during the school holidays. As much as Greg had changed, she seriously doubted that the relationship would survive either the time apart or the temptations that the job placed before him.

The way things were going, however, she was fairly confident that his repping days were over – they were even looking at houses to buy together. Occasionally though, Greg would tease her and get out his precious rep's badge that he had worn since his first season, and wave it under her nose, pretending he was considering going back. He still hadn't given YF&S a definite 'no'.

The other thing that was troubling her was of far greater concern.

During the last few weeks, she felt that something was going on. It was as if there was another woman, yet her instinct told her this was not the case. She could not put her finger on it, but he was definitely hiding something from her. There were certain phone calls he would not take in front of her. If he did and she asked who it was, she just knew he was lying when he mumbled that it was someone from work. Once, he had even switched off his mobile pretending that the call had dropped.

Greg had undoubtedly been the biggest of Lotharios and as such, there were two schools of thought. The first was simply that a leopard does not change its spots and that no matter how blissful domestic life was, the roving eye never goes away. The other was that he had sown enough oats to sate a rugby team and had nothing to prove.

Dawn was sure that Greg fell into the second category but there was still a niggling doubt in the back of her mind. The seed of a fear had planted itself and within the last few days it had taken on a life of its own.

It was sown when Dawn remembered that Greg had told her about a party held by promoters Rich 'n' Famous not far from where they were now living, just before the start of the season. It had been highly successful and the promoters were therefore planning another at the same venue. Greg had raved about the first. He said it was far grander than he had expected and that if you turned up in a car worth less than twenty grand, everyone thought you a pauper. When Dawn asked him who he had gone to the party with, Greg had told her quite truthfully and matter-of-factly that he went with an ex-client called Bex. Dawn knew that Bex lived close by. She also knew that, during the start of summer at least, she had kept in touch with Greg.

And tonight Rich 'n' Famous were having their second party at the same venue. It was tortuous. Dawn had worked herself up into a state, convinced that Greg had been secretly seeing Bex and that he was going to meet her at the party. It felt like Sandy all over again.

Of course, she had considered confronting him about it. However, it was still early in their relationship and one thing she had promised herself was that she would not let Greg's history ruin things. What was done was done. Theirs was the present and future, not the past. If Greg proved not to be the man she believed he was, then as upsetting as it would be, she would push him out of her life again. There was another Greg to look after now.

When she had woken up earlier in the morning, she fully expected Greg to be making secret phone calls, perhaps buying clothes or visiting the hairdressers. She had braced herself for him to prime her with an excuse for going out that night.

But the day was perfectly normal.

After they got back from shopping, she started to relax. Greg was happily watching football with his son. Seeing them together put Dawn's mind at ease even more.

Then, just after four-thirty, the phone rang. Greg jumped out of the seat and was in the hallway within seconds. He pushed the hallway door to, so all Dawn could hear was a low mumble. Moments later he poked his head round the door.

'I've just got to go out for a few hours.'

Dawn felt a sick feeling in the pit of her stomach. 'Where are you going?'

'Oh, er, just something to do with work. I shouldn't be late but don't wait up.'

Before she had a chance to protest, the door slammed. She watched him walk down the drive. He was wearing jogging bottoms and trainers, but that proved nothing – he could quite easily have a change of clothes. She might have even bought them for him. Maybe he was going round her house to get changed.

Dawn tried to stop her inner voice from tormenting her, but it was telling her to see who had just called. She dialled 1471. It was a local number. Oh God, she prayed it wasn't going to be Bex who answered the phone.

She dialled 141, then tentatively pressed the rest of the numbers. The phone started ringing.

'Hello. Kingston Sports Car Hire.'

Dawn replaced the phone immediately.

So that was it. He was going to hire a flash car and go to

Rich 'n' Famous, just as he'd always wanted to. Probably with Bex.

She ran upstairs and fell on to the bed sobbing.

How could she have been so wrong?

Greg pulled up outside Kingston Sports Car Hire just after five o'clock and dashed inside.

Ten minutes later, he had the keys to a convertible Topaz Blue Z3 BMW. He took out his mobile and dialled a number.

'I've got the car ... Yeah, it's perfect ... Have you got them? Excellent, I'll see you there in twenty ... Make sure you're on time.'

Twenty minutes later he was parked outside a bar in Putney, when a taxi pulled up.

Vaz paid the driver, then jumped into the car next to Greg. 'Nice wheels, mate. How you doing?'

'Yeah, brilliant.' They shook hands. 'Great to see you again. All set?'

'Raring to go.'

'Have you got them?'

'In my bag with my clothes for tonight.' Vaz smiled conspiratorially. 'And the tickets?'

Greg tapped his pocket. 'Safe and sound.' He started the car. 'Right then, first things first. Let's find a quiet road somewhere.'

They headed north out of Kingston along Kingston Vale.

'I didn't tell you,' said Vaz, once they were under way, 'that I was down the King's Road the other day and guess who I bumped into?'

'Go on.'

'Mario. He was working in a clothes shop.'

'That's right, his brother owns it. So much for Hollywood, eh?'

'I think the closest he'll ever get is Hollywoods Club in Romford.'

Greg laughed. 'And I think that's closed. So, are you looking forward to your first Rich 'n' Famous party?'

'Can't wait. I hope they're as good as you say they are. I was supposed to be DJing in Birmingham tonight.'

'What, and you blew it out to go to Rich 'n' Famous?' Greg whistled. 'Fuck me, you're keen.'

'Only because you kept going on during the summer about the last one you went to, you tosser! Anyway, I've been playing every weekend – one night won't hurt.'

'Any more news on the residency at The Monastery?'

'Nothing definite, but I'm playing there virtually every other week so I'm more or less a resident anyway. What they did promise me is that I'll be doing their club night every other week in Ibiza next summer.'

'That's brilliant. Looks like it's all taking off for you then?'

'Early days, but fingers crossed. Doing that residency at Es Paradis and helping to turn Mikey's bar into a success really got me off to a flyer. Have you spoken to Brad lately?'

'Yeah, last week – he's back with Carmen, the love of his life from last summer. The job's going well too. One thing he did tell me was that Lucas's trying to start up a double glazing company.'

'I hope I don't need any bloody windows then,' laughed Vaz. 'How the mighty have fallen.'

'Apparently he's not totally broke but he's not far off – plus his missus left him.'

'What goes round comes around.' Vaz sat back and took in the surroundings. 'Isn't Richmond Park up here on the left?'

'Yeah. How have you and Arabella been getting on?'

'Yeah, fantastic. It's early days, but she's cool. Once you scratch below the surface she's a really caring, sweet girl. It's all a front with her, just a way to stop herself from getting hurt. I met her parents the other day. Fuck me, what a house they've got. Massive. Yeah, all in all things are fine. We'll just see how it goes.'

'Cool.'

'And what about you? How are you enjoying domestic bliss?'

'It's fucking great. I love it. I tell you what, Little Greg'll end up playing for United one day – you should see him kick a ball.'

'And what about Dawn . . . how's she?'

'Brilliant. More than brilliant. I've not taken a pill, snorted a line or even looked at another girl since I got back. What's the point? I've got everything I want.'

'I bet you wished you'd done it earlier, don't you?'

Greg thought for a moment. 'I wish I'd been there to watch Little Greg grow up, that's true. And from the first day I met Dawn, I just had a feeling about her. But you know what? She's one smart cookie and she probably knew me better than I knew myself, even then. I wasn't ready for it. I was too young and I would have resented her whereas now it's just perfect.'

'Who would ever have believed it?'

'Not me, that's for sure.' Greg turned right into a quiet road next to a petrol station. 'This looks like as good a place as any.' He stopped the car. 'Come on then, Vaz. Let's see them.'

Vaz pulled out a pair of number-plates from inside his jacket. The number on them was A15 BMW, with a screw cap stuck between the '1' and the '5', so that the plate appeared to read 'AL'S BMW.

'Are you sure that the screw cap is in exactly the same place as hers?'

'Positive,' replied Greg. 'Brad went round to her house and took a picture of the car in the drive, then scanned it in and emailed it to me. It took me ages to find a car exactly the same colour though.'

'Fucking hell. This seems more like a military operation every day.'

'You don't know the half of it. I've hated not being able to tell Dawn.'

'Why couldn't you tell her? She must detest Alison almost as much as the rest of us. She would have loved the idea of getting a car the same as hers, copying her plates then getting flashed for speeding.'

'Yeah, she would have loved the idea but she would have just worried I'd get into trouble and tried to talk me out if it.'

'You really are totally in love with her, aren't you?'

Greg smiled and nodded.

'I'm really pleased for you. So have you told YF&S you're not going back yet?'

'No. They sent me a contract ready to sign earlier in the week. I'm going to post it to them with my official resignation on Monday – providing tonight goes according to plan.'

'Why, what's happening tonight?'

For a moment Greg looked unusually sheepish. 'Well, while you and Arabella are enjoying yourselves at Rich 'n' Famous with these free tickets I was sent,' Greg took them from his pocket like a magician pulling a rabbit from a hat, and handed them to Vaz, 'I shall be taking the biggest decision of my life.'

Vaz grinned. 'Go on.'

'Well, it seemed such a shame to only use this car to stitch Alison up. As soon as we've finished doing this and I've dropped you off at Rich 'n' Famous, I'm going to pick up Dawn and whisk her off to a flash restaurant I've booked. Then, I'm going to give her a little pressie . . .'

He opened a small box to reveal a ring.

'Fucking hell, Greg, congratulations.'

Greg was beaming.

'You bloody old romantic.' Vaz opened the car door. 'What a difference a summer makes, eh?'

'You can say that again.' Greg opened the car door. 'Right then, shall we do this? The quicker we finish then the quicker I can get back and see if Dawn wants to be made into an honest woman.'

They got out the car and both took a number plate with some double-sided sticky pads.

'We'll get these on, then head down the A3 – there's loads of speed cameras there,' said Greg. 'Then we'll go round the M25 and along the M4. I'll drop you off at the hotel then head back. Simple.' He stood back from the car to look at the plate he had just stuck on. 'Perfect. Are you ready?'

Vaz stood up and made his way to the passenger door. 'Let's do it.'

Moments later they were on the A3. Greg put his foot down and was soon nudging a ton. It took less than a minute before the first speed camera got them. When it did, they let out a cheer and started laughing.

Another minute and they had been caught again. The speedo was touching 120mph.

'That one's for Sugar Ray,' yelled Vaz.

'I reckon we should aim to get a picture for every single person that bitch has upset or had over,' laughed Greg, the adrenaline pumping.

'Fuck that,' replied a giggling Vaz. 'We'll be driving until next Christmas before we get even close to it.'

'All right then, let's just settle for a dozen or so. That should be more than enough to get the old trollop banned. No licence, no car . . . no car, no sunglasses business.'

'And it couldn't happen to a nicer girl!'

chapter forty-two

The trust had gone and without that, thought Dawn, what's the point?

She had never felt the inclination to go through his things before. Why should she? Everything had been so perfect. Maybe that was the sign she missed – it was too perfect.

After she realised that Greg had gone to Rich 'n' Famous she went through his personal things. Admittedly there were no letters from other girls, or photographs – after all, even Greg wouldn't be that stupid – but she did find the letter from the head of Rich 'n' Famous telling him that there were two free invites and a hotel room booked.

He had obviously gone there and she was steeling herself for the inevitable phone call from him with some intricate excuse as to why he couldn't get home that night.

Next she had found the contract from YF&S offering Greg the job as resort manager for the coming summer. After all he had said, all he had promised, how could he lie so blatantly?

Dawn could not stand to be in the house where there were so many reminders of his treachery. She took Little Greg from his bed and drove up to her parents' house. She spent the whole journey on her mobile, crying down the phone to her mother and to various friends. The battery ran out before Dawn's need to be comforted.

Once at her mother's she was restless. She could not stand the thought of Greg at the party, enjoying himself without a care in the world, while her world seemed to have fallen apart. He had to be with Bex. There was only one thing for it. Luckily, she still had some decent clothes at her mum's. She put on her war paint and set off.

For her own peace of mind, she had to confront him, and what Coral had done to Mario in Es Paradis during the summer was going to be tame compared to what she felt capable of doing to Greg.

It was weird, but Greg felt nervous driving up to his own home. He reconciled that it was perhaps understandable, after all, it wasn't every day he proposed to someone.

He was therefore more than a little perturbed when he found the house empty. There was no note, but when he saw his things angrily tipped over the bed, with the invitation letter from Rich 'n' Famous and the YF&S resort manager's job contract in prime position, he had a rough idea as to what might have happened.

It was obviously only a misunderstanding, so he tried not to be too concerned. Things had been going so well with Dawn since he got back, that he was sure she now trusted him . . . well, almost.

He tried to ring her mobile, but it was switched off. He was fairly certain she would be at her mum's so he tried ringing there, but the phone was engaged. Over the next fifteen minutes he kept trying, but he still couldn't get through. That was pretty much all the proof he needed that Dawn was on her way round there. The only person that her mum ever spoke to on the phone for any length of time was her daughter.

He figured that the chances were he'd get round there before she was off the phone. It was a little disappointing that the night wasn't going as planned, but proposing to her at her mum's would actually be pretty cool, he decided.

But when he got there, Dawn's car wasn't outside. The small street of semi-detached maisonettes was not busy, so her car would have been easy to see.

He knocked on the door. Her mother looked surprised to see him.

'Hi, Margaret. You don't know where Dawn is, do you?'

'What are you doing here?'

'Nice to see you too,' he replied. 'What's going on?'

It wasn't until Greg was almost at Rich 'n' Famous that he realised he still had Alison's plate on the car. It was probably just as well – the speed at which he'd driven he would have been flashed at least half a dozen times.

Margaret explained exactly how Dawn had grabbed hold of the wrong end of the stick. Greg was beside himself – he had wanted the night to be so perfect. It was by no means certain that Dawn would have accepted his proposal, even if everything had gone as planned. Now, Greg was worried that she would think he had decided not to go to the Rich 'n' Famous party as a result of her finding the invites.

The trust in their relationship had grown so much that it was never called into question or raised as an issue. Greg did sometimes wonder though if Dawn thought she had clipped his wings or that he was yearning for his old ways. Nothing could have been further from the truth, but Greg never brought it up or laboured the point about how happy he was, because he was too busy actually *being* happy.

He was lucky enough to find a parking spot near the entrance. He couldn't see Dawn's car.

It took Greg a while to blag his way in, largely because of his scruffy attire (and of course, lack of ticket). Luckily one of the promoters he knew from Ibiza came out to the door and escorted Greg through to the party, and even gave him some drinks vouchers. The party was in three sections – a large marquee attached to the manor house, a smaller tent in the garden and the ballroom of the main house.

As he looked frantically around he felt a tap on the shoulder.

'Hi, Greg.'

He turned round. It was Bex. Probably the last person he needed to see. He had spoken to her a few times during the summer and at one point she had been planning to come out. But after getting back with Dawn he had ignored her texts and by August, she had given up.

'Bex. How are you doing?'

'I wondered where you were. When I checked into the hotel I saw your name on one of the rooms. You're on the same floor as me, I think.'

'Oh right.' Greg had neither the time nor the inclination to explain his predicament. 'Listen, Bex, I've got a few people to catch up with. I'll see you a bit later, yeah?'

Greg hurried off. The main marquee was busy, but he was fairly sure that he would have seen Dawn had she been there. Almost as soon as he walked into the ballroom he was spotted by Vaz and Arabella.

'Greg,' yelled Vaz. 'Thank fuck you're here.'

'Have you seen Dawn?'

'No, but Arabella saw her earlier.'

'What did she say?'

'She asked where you were,' said Arabella. 'I told her that I hadn't seen you and that I didn't know you were coming. She was a bit off to be honest. I got the impression that she didn't believe me. I even told her you'd got us the hotel reservation and tickets. I'm sorry, Greg, but Vaz has only just told me what you were planning for Dawn tonight – you old romantic.'

'Where did she go?'

'She didn't say.'

'Shit.' He paced round running his fingers through his hair. 'Shit, Vaz, what am I going to do? Her phone's turned off.'

'You could always stay here and see if she turns up again.'

'I'm not exactly in the party mood. Besides, it's bad enough that she thinks I was planning to come here all along. She'd never believe me if I told her I was here by default.'

'You can stay at the hotel if you want,' said Vaz. 'We were only using the room to get changed in. Arabella's folks are away so we're going there straight from the party. The room's still in your name.'

Greg considered the option. He didn't want to go back home. Dawn wouldn't be there anyway. The night was a wash-out. At least if he stayed in the hotel, he could drown his sorrows without worrying about driving home. Then it was only tomorrow and the rest of his life he had to worry about. He could leave a message on their home answerphone and with her mum, saying where he was.

'Yeah, all right. Cheers, Vaz. Thanks, Arabella.'

'Good luck,' they said in unison.

Greg drove back to the hotel, clutching his mobile. There was no call from Dawn.

He checked into his room dispiritedly. He'd had it all planned so perfectly. Now, through being so set on getting revenge on Alison, everything had gone horribly wrong. The irony of it.

For the next couple of hours, he steadily got more and more drunk at the hotel bar. A few people started drifting in from the party, mainly couples, which made Greg even more depressed. He was just about to go to bed when he heard a girl's voice.

'I wondered where you'd got to.'

It was Bex again.

'Sorry, Bex. I wanted to get away.'

At first she said nothing, but just looked him up and down. 'I've missed you.'

Greg just nodded, more of a drunken nod to confirm he was still conscious than a reply.

Bex smiled. 'Shall we go upstairs?'

chapter forty-three

Dawn had looked round Rich 'n' Famous but had only stayed there for a few minutes. She had seen Arabella but was convinced that she was covering for Greg.

When she left the party, she popped round to her friend Suzy's house in nearby Weybridge. She didn't want to go back to the house she shared with Greg, plus she felt sure that he would end up in the hotel – probably with this girl, Bex. The next day she would not want to believe the worst so felt she might be vulnerable to lies and excuses. Therefore, the only way of removing any doubt would be to catch him in the act.

By two-thirty Suzy wanted to go to bed, so Dawn headed for the hotel Arabella had mentioned. He had to be there. She guessed that she would have to wait for at least a couple of hours before he got back from the party, so she was surprised and apprehensive when she arrived at the hotel and the receptionist told her that Greg was already in his room. It could mean only one thing.

Deep down, she was hoping that there would be a logical explanation, that he would be there on his own, but as hard as she tried, no reason or justification would come to mind.

Dawn counted down the room numbers, becoming increasingly nervous and shaky as his room came in sight. She had not planned what to say or how to react, especially if her worst fears were realised.

She stood outside his room for a few moments wondering what to do. There was no noise. Perhaps there was an explanation after all? But her heart sank when she heard his familiar, if slightly drunk voice.

'Oh, Bex. No, not there . . . Come on Bex, you can do it. It's been long enough. Ooh, those curls . . .'

It was real. She had not been imagining it. It was almost more than Dawn could bear and her instinct was to turn and flee. But this was about more than just her. It was about Little Greg too. And that made her angry. Angry enough to kick the door down if she had to.

Surprisingly though, when she turned the handle, the door wasn't locked. She took a deep breath and burst in.

'You bastard, how could you, after all—' She froze.

Greg was sitting up in bed in his boxer shorts, with a jumbo size packet of peanuts on his chest and a beer on his hand. She looked round the room. He was on his own.

'Dawn!' yelled Greg, leaping up and sending peanuts all over the floor. 'Thank God. I've been looking everywhere for you.'

'But I thought—'

'I know you did,' replied Greg excitedly, not realising that she was about to say I thought you were with Bex. 'But I never planned to come here. I got sent the tickets and gave them to Vaz. I met up with him earlier – we've done something really bad to Alison, but I'll tell you about it later,' he laughed, before continuing at a hundred miles an hour. 'Anyway, I left Vaz and went back to ours, but you'd gone. Then I saw the letter from Rich 'n' Famous and the contract from YF&S and I guessed you'd got the wrong end of the stick. I tried your mobile and it was off and your mum's phone was engaged, so I drove up there and she told me what you thought had happened. I zoomed down to Rich 'n' Famous but couldn't find you and I really didn't want to go home with you not being there, so Vaz and Arabella said I could stay here.'

'So you didn't come here to meet Bex?'

'What? What on earth gave you that idea? Have you just seen her? Oh no, of course, you've never met her, have you?'

'So you have seen her?'

'I saw her in the bar. I even walked upstairs with her, said goodnight, then came in here and left about ten more bloody messages on our answerphone.'

Dawn looked at him suspiciously. He had to be lying. She'd heard him with her own ears. She jumped up and flung open the door to the wardrobe.

'Dawn, what are you doing?

'Where is she?' Dawn looked in the bathroom then under the bed.

'Dawn what are you on about?'

'Greg, I was standing outside the door just now. Bex – I heard you calling out her name!'

Greg looked bewildered. 'Huh?'

'You were saying, "Ooh Bex," and I love your hair or your curls or something.'

For a moment Greg looked blank. Then, aiming the remote control at the TV, he started laughing. Football highlights.

'Becks, not Bex – David Beckham. I was watching the football, you donut!'

Dawn slumped into a chair. 'Oh.'

'Oh,' repeated Greg, smiling.

'But what about hiring the sports car?'

'How did you know about that?'

'After you left,' Dawn looked a little shame-faced, 'I dialled 1471. I'd never normally do something like that, it's just that I got it in my head . . .' Her voice trailed off.

Greg leaned forward and took her hands. 'Vaz and I hired a BMW Z3 like Alison's and had some plates made up the same as hers then went and collected about thirty speeding tickets.'

'You never!'

'Afraid so. Then I dropped Vaz off at Rich 'n' Famous. It all went a bit wrong after that. It was meant to be a very special night. I had the car until tomorrow and I'd booked us a table at a restaurant in Windsor.'

'Oh God,' sighed Dawn, putting her head in her hands, 'what a screw-up. We'll have to do it next weekend. I'll get Mum to babysit.'

Greg stood up, wiping peanut crumbs from his chest hair. His trousers were on the floor where he'd stepped out of them. He bent down and picked them up.

'It won't be the same next weekend. I won't have the car, plus,' he took something from his trouser pocket, 'I don't think I could wait another week wondering how you'd react to this.'

He passed her a small box. She opened it.

'Um, is this what I think it is?'

'What do you think it is?' asked Greg.

'An engagement ring?' Greg nodded. Dawn's face almost broke into a smile. 'And . . .?'

'What do you mean "and"?'

'Aren't you supposed to ask me something?'

Greg shrugged. 'I thought that's what I was doing.'

'Go on then, ask me.' Dawn couldn't stop a smile spreading across her face.

'Do you like it?' Greg started smiling too.

'No, not that.'

'I don't know what you mean then.'

'You don't have to get on one knee,' she teased. 'Just ask me.'

'The room might be bugged. You could have a camera and show it to all my mates. I'd never live it down.'

'Greg . . .'

'Suppose you say no?'

Dawn raised her eyebrows.

'All right then,' said Greg, taking a deep breath. 'Willyou-marryme?'

'That wasn't so bad, was it?'

'I don't know – you haven't answered yet.'

She looked at the ring again. It was beautiful. A classic, enormous diamond solitaire. It was impossible to keep up any kind of pretence or the smile from her face. She nodded and whispered, 'Yes.'

It had not gone exactly as Greg planned, but he had got there in the end. He took her face in his hands and they shared a slow tender kiss. When they stopped, Dawn broke free and looked at the TV screen. David Beckham was doing a post match interview. She picked up the remote, switched the TV off and pulled Greg towards her.

'Who needs Golden Balls when I've got my very own Golden Dick?'

Things quickly became passionate – then Greg stopped.

'What's up?' panted Dawn.

'Your ring . . .'

'Greg, let's just have normal sex.'

'I mean your engagement—yes, very funny.'

Grinning, Dawn reached over and slipped the ring on, holding her hand out to admire it. 'It's lovely.'

'So are you.'

'You old romantic.' She kissed him on the forehead.

'Anyway,' continued Greg with a glint in his eye, 'as I was saying. Your ring.'

Dawn looked shocked. 'But I'm a respectable engaged woman now and we don't do that sort of thing.' Then she whispered in his ear, 'Apart from with our fiancés of course . . .'